CW00519975

FORBIDDL.. KNOWLEDGE

VOLUME 1: DEATH OF A DEMON

© STEVE HEWITT

FIRST PUBLISHED 2018
SECOND EDITION PUBLISHED 2022
ISBN NO.: 9781980999843

CONTENTS

AUTHOR'S NOTE AND DISCLAIMER

Most of the characters and events portrayed in this novel are fictitious and any similarity to any person living or dead is purely coincidental. However, there are a small number of important exceptions.

To begin with, the Cathar heresy was a Gnostic revival movement that flourished in 12th and 13th century southern France and northern Italy. It provoked a violent suppression from the Catholic Church which did not accept it as a true Christian belief.

There really was a Pope Innocent III (c1160-1216) and a Raymond VI, Count of Toulouse, (1156-1222). Raymond was involved in a lengthy and at times bitter battle with the Church because he refused to take active measures to suppress the Cathars on his own estates.

Raymond was (briefly) excommunicated after the assassination of the Papal legate, Pierre de Castelnau, on 15 January 1208 (although it is not known for certain what role, if any, Raymond actually played in de Castelnau's murder).

The Battle of Muret (between forces led by Simon de Montfort and King Peter of Aragon) really did take place on 12 September 1213. However, my version of what happened there and on that day is fictitious.

Apart from these basic facts, any other actions and comments in this book took place only in my own imagination and should not be taken as genuine historical facts.

ACKNOWLEDGEMENTS AND DEDICATION

My grateful thanks go to my fellow novelists for their advice, support, and constructive feedback. Take a bow, Rosie Gilligan (who suggested the title), Sue Pacey, Celia Renshaw, Gaynor Roberts, and Claire Walker. Thank you, ladies. Of course, any remaining errors and typographical mistakes remain my sole responsibility.

The artwork for the cover was created by the talented Colyn Broom.

This one is for Anne, the love of my life.

PROLOGUE

The dream came again that night. It was always the same. An irascible old man sought to lure him into a bargain. A bargain that was too good to resist. And yet, deep down, he suspected things could soon turn sour. The sleeping figure muttered something incoherent and turned on its side. The old man beckoned to him, urging him to accept his fate …

… and the warrior awoke from a terrible dream. He'd been drowning in blood yet unable to die, trapped in a world shrouded in mist and teeming with malevolence. Drenched in sweat, he rose from his sleeping pallet and went in search of water.

At the edge of the stream, a sentry spoke softly. 'Tomorrow, we do God's work and kill the blasphemers, brother.'

'I'm not your brother! I kill for coin, not for a God I can't see.'

'Of what use is coin when you stand awaiting judgement?'

'What use is faith when you're drenched in blood?

'Take care, brother. God sees and hears everything.'

The warrior shook his head and walked away.

Later that same night, the sentry whispered in the ear of his leader. Both turned to look towards where the dreaming warrior lay sleeping once more. Molitor shook his head and gestured for the sentry to resume his lonely vigil. He watched the departing soldier for a few moments before making his way to the tent of his friend Dubois.

Meanwhile, in his dream, the warrior was searching for an old man who had offered him a bargain. Without warning, his world turned the colour of blood …

6

1 : THE HERETIC

Early September 1213, southern France.

The flimsy door exploded inwards in a shower of dust and sharp splinters. As if he were oblivious to the stinging pain in his lacerated cheek, the old man continued to stand with arms folded across his scrawny chest and a look of cold defiance on his face. He barely flinched when a huge warrior burst through the opening, sword already rising in anticipation of the killing down-stroke. The new arrival wore a plain chain-mail hauberk but no helmet. Mismatched greaves protected his legs, and a simple piece of cloth cord kept the long black hair from his eyes. The older man's face bore a look of intense concentration as they locked eyes. With a shock of recognition, the warrior started to arrest his action.

Nearby, in the small hearth, a battered cauldron hung from an iron pot-hanger, its gruesome contents still bubbling as they were warmed by the dying fire. Now and again it released a nauseating, sweet and putrid smell that carried a hint of pork and yet was somehow not quite right. The old man considered himself fortunate when the new arrival displayed no interest in investigating the contents of the cauldron. To the other side of the hearth, a small and ancient oak table supported the remains of a meagre breakfast. Crumbs of millet bread formed an untidy halo around a large clay bowl; whilst the remains of its contents were congealing into an unhealthy–looking stain around the rim. An upturned jug lay on the crude bench. A small trickle of viscous red liquid dripped from its lip to join the puddle on the floor below.

'You're the old man who has been haunting my dreams!' exclaimed the warrior. A look of fear crept into his face as he struggled to tear his gaze away from the man he had been about to kill, moments before. 'How do you enter my dreams? Are you a sorcerer?'

Screams and shouts pursued the intruder through the shattered doorway, almost drowning out the last few pleas for mercy. The old man knew that such requests were doomed to fall on deaf ears, for the attackers were consumed by bloodlust and would not stop until they had completed their grisly task. Acrid smoke drifted into the room and swirled around at the prompting of a lazy breeze. It stung his eyes, while the stench of burning flesh assailed his nostrils. Even so, he watched the warrior and the approaching sword with a calm detachment.

'No, I'm not a sorcerer. But it is good that you recognise me. I had to find a way to bring you here, for you have been... chosen.' He emphasised the last word. The speaker wore a grubby cloth blouse with a broad and battered leather belt cinched around his waist. His woollen trousers were patched on both knees and his large boots were covered in dust. The belt had an unusual ornate clasp, fashioned after some strange sort of symbol. A small wallet hung from it but there was no sign of any sheath or the knife that most peasants carried.

The blood-stained blade halted its descent, inches from his neck. A look of confusion had crept into the warrior's large green eyes, and he appeared to be genuinely perplexed by the fact that this victim had attempted neither to escape, nor to beg for his life. 'What do you mean, I have been chosen?'

Now the old man spoke softly - aware that his next words might well be his last. 'A wise decision my friend. Slay me, and you throw away a priceless opportunity to gain both wealth and power.' He swallowed, rehearsing the improvised strategy in his mind. It was vital not to push the other man too hard or too far. A mistake now might well prove fatal.

'What are you saying, heretic? You didn't answer my question.' The words were spat out as though they were poison. 'What do you mean? Do you have hidden treasure?' he demanded, as his eyes lit up in eager anticipation.

The other man tapped the side of his head with gnarled fingers. 'In here lies forbidden knowledge and in knowledge lies power. With power comes wealth.'

The warrior contemplated this for a few moments then began to lift the sword once more. 'And if I separate your

8

ugly head from your shoulders, will I be able to pour out this knowledge into my hand?'

Alarmed, the old man shook his head and took a step back. 'No, I'm offering you instruction and learning. I know and have seen things you can't imagine. Don't throw away this rare and valuable chance.'

Outside, an eerie silence fell on the village; its burning remains and numerous scattered corpses bearing mute testimony to the savagery of the attackers. Before the warrior could respond, one of his comrades paused outside the gaping hole, where once the door had been. 'Wallace, finish the old fool and make haste. We ride west to the next nest of these foul, God-cursed, snivelling heretics!'

Wallace held up his right hand, 'Leave us for a moment. This one may have treasure to yield. I won't need long to find out and I'll catch up with you.'

His comrade hesitated for the briefest moment before grinning. 'Cut off his fingers; they usually start talking after the first two,' he called over his shoulder as he strode away.

Wallace sheathed his sword and plucked a curved dagger from his belt. 'Florimond Dubois offers good advice,' he said, bending towards his prisoner.

'Not in this instance,' said the old man. 'What I offer requires you to leave me unharmed.'

The warrior burst out laughing. 'You're very brave for one in such a difficult position. I could kill you here and now. Talk, old man, and explain what you meant when you said I had been chosen. Then convince me as to why I should spare your worthless life.' As he spoke, he stepped nearer to the old man before pushing the dagger back inside his belt. His cold eyes never left the other man's face.

'My name is Clovis Muller, and I am a disciple of the ... Elder Gods. They ruled mankind long before the Jesu of the Roman Church had even been born. Has it never occurred to you to wonder why the Roman faith is so worried about those who open their eyes and see through the illusion it strives so hard to maintain?'

Wallace grunted. 'Take care, Muller, lest you condemn yourself anew with such blasphemous words,' he warned. Pointing to the cross on his chest, he asked, 'Is it possible that you don't know what this symbol means?'

It was Muller's turn to laugh. 'Perhaps more so than you, my brave warrior, if you refer to what it *really* stands for! *I* can set you on the path to limitless wealth and immortality, for you are yet young enough to reap that harvest. My own eyes were opened a little too late. Now it seems I have allowed myself to be caught up in this Albigensian mess.'

Wallace shrugged, as if the offer held little interest for him. 'You prattle to buy time, old man. The Holy Father has promised me remission for my sins in return for 40 days of God's work. I'm guaranteed a place in Heaven. What could you offer me to compete with that prize?'

Muller risked a wry grin. 'Perhaps you should read this. If I may?' He began to reach inside his blouse, holding his other hand, palm upwards, out in front of him to reassure the warrior that he held no weapon.

Even so, the other man took a precautionary step backwards and his own left hand fell towards the hilt of his sword as he said, 'No tricks or I won't hesitate to kill you.'

Pulling out a scroll, Muller said, in a low voice, 'Your eyes suggest a sharp mind, so I doubt you have unquestioning faith in the Church's promise. If ever a Pope chose the wrong name, it would be Lothar of Segni. He calls himself Innocent. Ha! He's anything but an innocent! Your Holy Father is a duplicitous, avaricious monster who presides over a powerful but corrupt empire. Have you never thought to ask yourself how the Church could bear such false witness to the very dogma it commands everyone else to accept as gospel?'

Outside, a woman's scream rent the air. It rose in pitch, before cutting off abruptly, to be replaced a few moments later by the sound of cruel male laughter.

Muller swallowed, trying to act as if nothing had happened. Yet, despite his best efforts, his voice quavered a little as he said, 'The clergy care nothing for the spiritual welfare of their fellows. When was the last time you heard a

10

priest preach a proper sermon? All they care about is material wealth and power – hence the ferocity with which they respond to any who dare to question whether their religion has lost its way.' He paused, trying to gauge the impact of his words upon the other man. As if unable to stop himself, he glanced towards a pile of straw-filled sacks stacked on the bare, dirt floor in a corner of the hut.

Wallace's face betrayed little emotion, but there was a brief flicker of interest in his eyes. Trusting that his instinct had been right and that he now had the man's full attention, Muller continued, 'Do you truly believe the Christian God would forgive all of their sins and welcome into Heaven some of the brutes who have accepted Innocent's promise of redemption? Is your faith so strong … or so blind?' He held out the scroll, inviting Wallace to read it.

When no immediate response was forthcoming, the old man began to sweat, fearing that his gamble had failed. His breathing became shallow and more rapid as he struggled to control his anxiety. Then the warrior spoke, in a quiet voice. 'I admit there is some merit in your words old man, and I sense you are not like the other heretics we have cleansed from this pathetic village. And I still want to know how you can enter my dreams. *If* I choose to spare your life, what will you give me as a token of goodwill?' He held out his left hand for the scroll.

Muller handed over the document and watched the other man's furled brow and moving lips as the warrior struggled to read the document. On reaching the end he looked up and said, 'This is a writ of safe conduct, signed by Raymond, the Count of Toulouse. What makes *you* so important? And if you are not one of the heretics, why are you on such good terms with that God-forsaken prince?'

Muller nodded towards the pile of straw-filled sacks that served as a bed. 'Under there lies a valuable gold statue. I'm supposed to take it to my master. It has great value to him – not as gold, but in terms of what it represents. Help me to deliver it to him and he will reward you handsomely in coin.' He studied Wallace for a few moments before adding words of caution, 'Steal it from me and you will have made yourself a terrifying enemy. My master has tremendous power and even your undoubted skills as a warrior will avail you little in the way of protection from his wrath. But given time, he can set you on the path to enlightenment. You too could acquire such power, but only *if* you are willing to work for it.'

Wallace looked uncertain. He pulled his sword from its scabbard, using it to point towards the side of the hut furthest from the sacks as he said, 'Move back over there old man, where I can keep an eye on you.' Muller did as he had been instructed and backed away. His old eyes narrowed as he watched the warrior use the tip of his blade to poke among the sacks. It soon encountered the statue and, with a quick glance at his prisoner, Wallace stepped forward and bent to retrieve his prize.

Now I learn whether or not he is interested in my offer, Muller told himself. *May the Gods protect me!* Wallace straightened up and held out the small statue for a closer inspection. As he turned it around, puzzled by the strange figure it depicted, the statue gleamed in the early morning light. Muller could almost hear the warrior's thoughts as he struggled to keep a smile from his lips.

'What sort of devilish figure is this?' demanded the warrior, holding it out towards the other man. The winged figure had a horned goat's head, a stubby tail, and cloven feet.

Muller held out his hand for the statue. 'It represents one of the Elder Gods. A being known by many names but, for now, 'Lu'Ki'Fer' will serve as well as any. In my faith, he is the Lord of Death. All must appear before him for his final judgement. But those who acquire full enlightenment can postpone this meeting – almost indefinitely.' He paused, waiting to see what Wallace would make of this claim.

The warrior stared at the statue for long moments, shrugged and then growled, 'This little misshapen statue can make me immortal? Do you take me for a fool?'

Muller shook his head. 'It's not the statue itself that has this power. Its function is to furnish a means of communicating with Lu'Ki'Fer; but this requires a great deal of knowledge and skill. To you or me it is nothing more than a lifeless statue. The gift of near immortality is not an easy thing to win. But my master has that knowledge and skill, which is why he wants this statue. Trust in me, he *will* reward you in a gracious manner for its safe delivery. All you have - '

Wallace held up his hand, interrupting Muller. 'Wait! Let me make sure I understand you. This little statue can serve to make its owner almost immortal if they know how to use it?

The old man nodded his head in agreement. 'Given its weight in gold, I'd say it might be worth, say, 20 silver marks to anyone willing to buy it for what it is. Help me to deliver it to my master and I can guarantee he'll give you 50 silver marks. Do we have an agreement?'

The warrior stared at Muller. 'And how long will it take us to reach your master?'

'About three days if we're not on foot. Although, I would imagine that your friends have made off with my horse, so we'll need to find another one - unless yours can carry two men without attracting attention from those we meet along the way.' Muller raised an eyebrow as he finished speaking, picked up a woollen mantle from the bed and began to move towards where the door had been. Realising that he was not being followed, the old man stopped on the threshold and turned to look back.

Wallace still made no answer, seeming instead to be intent on studying the statue from a variety of angles. He appeared to be lost in his own thoughts and startled Muller when he suddenly asked, 'Is this thing alive?' Muller looked into his eyes and was frightened by what he saw there for the briefest of moments. The chilling promise of menace disappeared when Wallace cocked his head to one side, waiting for a response.

Sensing that he should tread with care, Muller said, 'What makes you ask that?'

Wallace pondered this for a short while and then said, 'If your master can use this object to converse with ... Lu'Ki'Fer? ... then I presume the statue is either alive or can become so.'

Muller was still considering the implications of this deduction as he replied, 'A reasonable assumption. Though the truth is, I don't know the answer to your question. I haven't given the matter much thought, although now you have raised the subject, I suppose your suggestion would make sense. As I told you, the exact details are beyond my limited knowledge and powers.' He paused, hoping the warrior would not press this delicate issue any further. Hoping to distract him, Muller began to put on the mantle. It reached almost to his ankles, but the other man didn't appear to notice this, sparing the old man from having to explain why he was wearing someone else's clothing.

Relief flooded through him when Wallace shrugged, threw the statue in his direction, and said, 'Well, I suppose we should go and find you a horse. I can promise you that mine isn't going to carry both of us. But mark my words well, old man, for if I suspect you of playing me false, I *will* take off your head.'

As the unlikely companions emerged from the hut, a lone figure watched from a nearby copse. Sheltered from prying eyes by the thick foliage, Florimond Dubois' face creased into an evil grin. It seemed that the leader of their company, Jambres Molitor, had been correct in his suspicions about Wallace. Their orders had been clear enough and yet the heretic still lived. Either the old man had bargained sufficient treasure in return for his life, or he had somehow converted the Crusader. Whatever the explanation, it was clear that Wallace had failed to carry out his instructions.

As expected, Dubois would now have to keep an eye on the mismatched pair. His grin widened as a new thought struck him. *Play this right, and I may gain both the gratitude of Molitor and the old man's treasure for myself.* Of course, that outcome was almost bound to require two more deaths to be added to the long and still growing list of recent casualties in the Occitanian region. Dubois felt confident this would present no real problem, since the list was already so long that no-one would take much notice of two more bodies. He glanced backwards, to where his horse was tethered to a sturdy tree and contentedly munching on some stolen hay. Signalling his companions to remain quiet, he turned back to watch as the two conspirators began to search for something.

Once outside the hut Wallace took the lead and set off for where he had left his horse, on the outskirts of the village. The huge animal gave a soft whinny as he approached and tried to nuzzle his hand as he stroked its long neck. With surprising agility for one so large, the warrior mounted the horse and cast carefully around. Muller assumed he was checking for stragglers or survivors.

'It seems we are alone,' announced Wallace. I can see a few horses over there – he pointed behind the old man – so let's go and find out if any of them are suitable for you.' As an after-thought he added, 'I take it you *can* ride a horse and don't expect me to find a cart as well?'

Muller nodded his assurance before turning round and heading back into the ruined and smouldering village. The hut where he had met with his new companion was now the only one still standing and bodies lay strewn around. Almost all of them had been local peasants, trying to scratch a living from the soil. A single one had arrived with their attackers – a slim and inexperienced youth who had been impaled on the end of a pitchfork. As Muller passed by some of the bodies, clouds of angry birds took to wing, hoarse cries registering their protest at being interrupted in their feeding. The old man put a hand over his nose, trying to block out the smell of charred flesh, the iron tang of blood and the swirl of choking smoke. Human faeces and urine, baking in the morning sun, did nothing to improve the aroma that threatened to overwhelm his stomach. As they reached the middle of the doomed settlement, where the concentration of death had been sharpest, his stomach at last gave way and he stopped suddenly, retching on the ground, and splattering his own feet in gobbets of vomit and bile.

When he'd emptied his stomach and felt strong enough to straighten up again, he glanced towards Wallace. The warrior sat waiting, a wry smile curling the corner of his lips. 'Finished?' he asked, making no effort to hide his amusement.

Muller glared at him. 'Doesn't this affect you at all? What sort of person are you to be unmoved by this carnage?' he spat out, wiping his mouth with a grubby sleeve.

'I'm a warrior, old man. I've seen worse than this. After a while you become used to the horrors of warfare. For men like me, this is just another part of our work.' He spurred his horse forward, leaning to one side to add, 'You get used to it after a while.'

Muller heard the warrior laugh, as he urged his horse forward again, and then hurried to catch up. Glad as he was to still be alive, he was beginning to wonder about the strange man in front of him. *There's more to him than we expected.*

With the stench of death fading in his nostrils, Muller glanced back towards the village, noting that the flock of carrion birds had already returned to their gruesome feast. The old mare beneath him continued to plod on, happy to follow the stallion carrying Wallace. They had been lucky to find this horse, the best of the three left behind by the Papal soldiers. With the practised eye of an expert in horseflesh, Wallace had taken little time to select it as the best of a poor bunch. 'She'll be slow and steady, but she looks healthy enough to have some endurance,' he'd explained. 'That one over there,' he'd pointed towards the largest of the three horses in the field, 'is going lame in its left foreleg. And that one,' pointing to the smallest, 'is bow-backed. She was broken too soon and will never be able to carry you far.'

Muller knew little of horses and was happy to be guided by the Crusader. 'There's no saddle, though.'

'You'll have to ride bareback then,' was the unsympathetic answer. My former allies won't have left anything serviceable behind. I can lend you some crude reins and a spare bit, so at least you'll be able to steer her. Besides, she's broad across the back. If you're any sort of horseman, you'll be able to stay on her. Although you might get some pain in your bony arse come night-time!' Wallace had guffawed at his own joke, doubtless enjoying the look of distaste that etched Muller's features. 'Come on, mount up. Or maybe you are considering walking all the way to the meeting with your master?'

Wallace watched with amusement as his companion struggled to seat himself on the mare and then wasted several minutes sorting out the reins. At last, Muller signalled his readiness to get going. Wallace made no effort to move. 'What are we waiting for?' asked the old man, allowing a little irritation to creep into his voice whilst being careful not to sound too challenging. He suspected that Wallace might well prove unpredictable, and, in his experience, such men could sometimes be angered over the most trivial of perceived slights.

'You forgot to mention where we are headed,' suggested Wallace.

'Indeed. Forgive an old man his lack of forethought. We need to head for Muret.'

Wallace gave a start. 'Isn't that close to Toulouse?' he asked.

'Yes, it's a little to the south-west of the city. Is that a problem?'

'You must know that Toulouse is the centre of the heresy I was sent here to destroy! We will not receive a warm welcome if I arrive wearing this garb.'

'Then perhaps you need to find some different attire?' suggested Muller. 'We're bound to meet someone along the way. If the worst happens, you can remain under cover once we get close and I will bring your reward back to you.'

Wallace snorted and his piercing green eyes flashed. 'Do you think me a total fool?' he shouted. 'Stay under cover and either never see you again or find myself ambushed by a party of Raymond's men!'

Alarmed by this display of temper, Muller rushed to calm the other man. 'No, no, that's not the plan at all. You can stay under cover with the statue whilst I meet my master and return with your reward.' He pulled the statue from its nestling place inside his blouse and held it out for Wallace to take. There, I'll fetch the coins and you may either exchange the statue for them and ride away, or, if you choose to trust me, you can keep them and, I'll take you to the master if you are interested in receiving the further instruction I spoke of. And of course, if you see armed men heading towards your hiding place, you can always slip away – then I lose the statue and incur my master's anger. As I told you before, that is not something any sensible person would wish to do,'

Wallace turned this over in his mind and then grinned, his anger disappearing in a flash of white teeth. 'You have a deal then, Muller. But don't forget my earlier warning if you think to trick me.' He paused, as if remembering something, then spoke again, 'Dubois said we were supposed to be heading west. I'm assuming you have little desire to run into them again and I might struggle to persuade their leader to let me re-join his merry band - unless I kill you first! We'll have to go a round-about route. I suggest we head north for a while and then swing west. It might be a good idea to rest somewhere for a few days, so as to put some distance between my former friends and ourselves.'

Muller started to argue, 'But my master … '

'Would doubtless prefer to see you a few days late rather than not at all,' interrupted Wallace. 'You asked me to escort you, so that's what I'm going to do. But let me decide how we get there in one piece. I have no desire to risk meeting my maker for the sake of 50 silver marks.'

'As you wish,' agreed Muller. *But if I know my master, I fully expect you'll be meeting Lu'Ki'Fer very soon!*

2: A PLEA FOR HELP

Early September 1872, Islington, London, England.

He decided to read the covering letter one more time. It had been placed alongside a tidy pile of papers. These were stacked face-down on the middle of a small, woodwormriddled desk. Underneath the papers sat a large envelope. It already bore the name of its intended recipient in a neat gothic script.

His hands shook as he picked up the first page. Still worried about the need to venture out, he glanced towards the door, where his thick black coat hung from a small brass hook. With a shrug, he settled into the battered chair positioned alongside the desk.

The room was poorly furnished with little else to make it comfortable. An old iron-framed bed stood in the corner. It was dressed in a moth-eaten blanket of indeterminate colour. Nearby a small table supported a worn enamelled washbowl and a plain and chipped jug. A sparse heap of rumpled clothing occupied a corner opposite the bed. He'd been quietly removing his personal possessions for the last two weeks. Now there was little left in the room to indicate that he had ever occupied it. In his profession, a man didn't need many possessions.

A lot of thought had been committed to the wording of this letter. It was vital that the recipient take it seriously enough to read the accompanying material. He had no doubt that they would then recognise the full implications. Arthur Fulbright was not much given to imagination. He was also famously impatient with anything he deemed to be a 'flight of fancy'. On the other hand, Fulbright possessed a formidable intelligence and an incisive analytical mind. Once he chose to believe something, it would be impossible for him not to act upon that belief.

Thinking about his old friend, a small smile pursed his thin lips. It had just struck him that those very qualities were somehow ideal in a priest. After all, wasn't acceptance of God nothing more than a conscious decision to believe in something? Even if that 'something' was beyond the known realms of proof? Lemuel offered a small prayer of apology to The Lord, grateful that no-one else could see the slight flush on his cheeks or read his thoughts.

He pondered the twists and turns of fate that had brought him to this moment. To all appearances he was nothing more than a humble parish priest. Few knew that he led a second and hidden life as a member of a small but determined group of Church warriors. Things had not gone well in recent months. He feared they were engaged in a losing battle against a fearsome enemy. The brotherhood of The White Shield had almost certainly lost two of their best assassins. Lemuel had seen the mangled remains of Zachary Coxe with his own eyes. It had fallen to him to arrange a secret burial for what was left of the younger man. He still had nightmares about what sort of opponent could, in the most literal sense, turn a human being inside out.

The High Council, even now, clung to the hope that Thomas Farral was still alive. They wanted to believe that he had somehow survived and was hiding whilst his wounds healed. Lemuel did not share this hope. His own investigation had uncovered a witness to Farral's last battle. It had taken Lemuel a month to persuade her to reveal what she had seen in the fertiliser factory that night. In return he'd been made to promise that he would arrange for her to be spirited away to Italy. As agreed, she'd been furnished with a new identity and means for supporting herself and her young child. Her description of his comrade, falling 30 feet or more into a vat of oil of vitriol, made it almost certain that the quiet young monk had gone to meet his maker.

Lemuel had received news that this witness had died in a tragic drowning accident, just two days after arriving in Venice. Perhaps it had been an unfortunate coincidence, yet he feared that it pointed to a traitor within their own ranks. For this, and other reasons of his own, he had not dared to share his information with The High Council. Hence, this package for Brother Arthur, who was one of the few men yet alive that he was still willing to trust. He started to read his own very stylised script.

My dearest Brother Artie,

I send you these documents in the hope that you will make good use of them. I fear I might fail to return from my next mission. I know that we have long had our differences as to how best to deal with the foul threat posed by The Black Blades. But, even now, I beg you to reconsider your position. I hope such a change of heart need not be motivated by a desire to avenge my death.

Make no mistake my Brother, for it is not just my life but my very soul which I am about to risk in the service of The White Shield. Our enemies are well-organised, powerful, and ruthless. They delight in inflicting pain and suffering on the innocent. Their pleasure is heightened still further when they are able to torment those of us resolute enough to oppose them. They regard us as heretics and vermin!

I have tried to arrange the material into some sort of order. Should you choose to read it – and I beg of you to accede to this request – you will find the detail incomplete. I have done my best, but the scope of what we face is far greater than any of The High Council has ever acknowledged. Even so, I trust you will agree that my research more than hints at a dreadful plot. If we cannot find a way to frustrate their plans, our enemy will be free to embark upon the corruption and destruction of all that we hold dear in our hearts.

Reading that last paragraph, I can picture your face, screwed up in mild amusement. I fear you will be tempted to dismiss this latest missive as little more than the ravings of a disturbed mind. How to convince you otherwise? Perhaps I should begin by asking if you have given further thought to the meaning of the dream you mentioned in your last letter. You have made known your opposition to my own theories in the strongest of terms. Yet I discern that something is still troubling you about this subject. I also note that you have offered no alternative explanation as to how Brother Gervaise could have died.

A noise outside his bedroom window made him look up. Anxious pale brown eyes scanned the dimly lit alley that ran the length of the rear of the building. In the fading evening light, he thought he could discern the outline of a feline predator; but, maybe, that was just his imagination. Rising from his chair, he pulled the thin curtains closed, resumed his seat, and read on.

Even you must acknowledge that the look of terror on his face was, at the very least, somewhat unusual. Nor is it normal for a healthy and active young man, in his mid-20s, to die from a sudden failure of the heart. Yes, I know that is what it says on his death certificate. But consider this – there is no trace of the mysterious Dr Forsythe. The man who provided that worthless certificate cannot be found! Nor does that convenient diagnosis explain the curious marks on his chest. I implore you, Brother, to reconsider your stubborn opposition to my explanation. As the minimum one feels entitled to expect from a clever and learned man, I ask you to re-examine the evidence. Are you, in all honesty, still prepared to swear before your maker that Brother Gervaise died of natural causes?

But this debate is beside the point I must remain focused on the most important issue. As the most senior remaining assassin, I have concluded that I must ignore the instructions of the High Council. I must attempt to eliminate he who cannot be named once and for all. By allowing him to continue his nefarious schemes, I fear for the future of humanity. I cannot ignore my conscience. If I am wrong, then may a merciful God forgive me for what I am about to do.

Of course, my decision means that I am forced to act alone and against almost insurmountable odds. The one of whom I speak is well schooled in the dark arts and has many servants under his command. He will not hesitate to use any weapon or to sacrifice any servant in order to protect his own life. I cannot best him if I am in any way distracted. My best hope is to trust to my own knowledge and my years of training. I have to believe that what I plan to do will enjoy God's favour.

The noise came again, a little louder this time. It reminded him of the scratching of mice or rats. He checked the loaded pistol by his side and took a large swig of amber liquid from the glass stood next to the pile of papers. The sound, common enough in this part of London, unnerved him. There was no knowing what agents *they* might choose to employ against him. *And rodents would be ideal for destroying written evidence*, he told himself with a growing sense of dread. With his ears now straining for any sound, he forced himself to read further.

The enclosed materials are, in the main, unofficial, and drawn from my own extensive research. One or two items have been procured in a somewhat unorthodox manner. They are best kept under lock and key and for your eyes only. To reveal them to a wider audience would risk exposing my sources to danger. In the event of my death or disappearance, I am convinced that someone has to continue my work. There is no-one else that I can turn to and in whom I can trust.

Do not fail me my Brother for the end is nigh, and together we may now be the last hope for humanity. Dark forces gather about us, and we must provide and protect the light of salvation. Go forward in peace and be forever vigilant in the certain knowledge that our enemies grow in strength and power.

Yours affectionately,
Lemuel
6th September 1872.

With a sigh, he leant back in his chair and thought of the task ahead. His plan was bold – there was no doubt about that – but there were so many unpredictable things that could go wrong. It was no simple thing to confront and defeat a member of The Seven. The price of failure would be not just physical death but an eternity of excruciating spiritual torture. Writing this letter had been the last thing on his list of preparations. He'd lodged his will with a reputable legal firm, several days earlier. Now all that remained was to deliver this package of papers. The die had been cast ... there would be no turning back.

Outside, and hidden in shadow, a large tabby cat sat motionless beneath a bedroom window. It was far from home and in an unfamiliar alley. Faint light spilled out from a gap between the drawn curtains. Left to its own devices, it would have raced back to its own territory. It wanted to be there, where it could follow its usual habit and sate its appetite with a few mice or rats.

Tonight was different. The stranger in its head had forced it to come hither and watch this window. The cat had soon tired of this unnatural occupation, yet it dared not move. Dull as it was to sit watching a window, the alternative was even less appealing. It still remembered the last time it had disobeyed the stranger and the dreadful pain in its head which had almost killed it.

At last, the glow of light went out. Soon after, the cat sensed that the unwelcome stranger had noted this uninteresting development. Then, to its surprise, the stranger was no longer there. The cat waited for a few moments. It was unwilling to risk the wrath of this mysterious being if the task was not yet complete. But, when the presence failed to return, the cat purred for a few moments, licked its front paws, and then set off in search of food. It was annoyed at being forced to wait until now to begin its usual nocturnal search for sustenance. Now it was eager to exact some measure of vengeance on the next rodent unfortunate enough to attract its attention. It's sharp ears soon caught the patter of small feet and it forgot the stranger and the light.

3: BEYOND THE VEIL OF NIGHT

Summer, 1203. Location unknown.

Unnatural darkness slowed his progress to a crawl. Above, an inky black sky was almost bereft of stars. A few faint pinpricks of light offered little relief from the relentless gloom of deepest night. The only light source was the weak illumination provided by the blood red full moon hanging low to his left. It cast eerie shadows across the path. The hot still air carried a cloying sweet scent that failed to mask the rank odour of rotting vegetation and decay. Flickers of movement betrayed the presence of other life as a shrill cry rent the silence. Nearby, a ghost was hunting. He felt a brief moment of pity for its hapless prey and said a silent prayer of thanks that he was not destined to be its next meal.

He froze, straining his eyes in an effort to discern any clue as to what else might lie ahead. *Stay on the path and you will be safe. Easier said than done!* Penetrating The Veil required but little effort and for a brief while it appeared as if the path towards his goal would be an easy one to follow. Yet the light had faded rapidly, and any remaining optimism died with the next bone-chilling cry of the much-feared night-hunter. He jumped as a despairing scream faded into a deafening silence and his resolve began to weaken. This was his first journey to this strange dream-like world, and he was aware that there were things here that could and would try to harm him. Other Seekers had suffered physical damage, madness or even worse and death was no stranger in this realm. And yet the potential prize was undeniably worth these risks.

The blackness played tricks with his mind, and he began to imagine all sorts of horrors waiting to catch him with his guard down. It didn't help that he could barely see his own feet, let alone make out the path ahead. He could feel the heat rising from the ancient stone slabs through the soles of his knee-length boots. His greatest fear was that he would become lost in the eternal night. A distant sucking sound hinted that the ghost had begun to feed on its luckless victim.

The only way forward was to edge with caution towards the marker that awaited him at the crossroad.

A paler patch of darkness detached itself from the deep shadows ahead. It resolved itself into something impossible to gaze at for more than a few seconds. The creature was composed of many different body parts, which flickered in and out of this continuum at a bewildering speed. He began to feel dizzy and tried to force his gaze away, worried that he would become disoriented if he watched the creature for much longer.

Shock threatened to steal his very breath away when he heard the demand inside his head, *'Who dares to walk the path of enlightenment? Give me your name, creature!'* There was no sound for his ears other than the pounding of his own heart and the message was unpleasant as it reverberated inside his skull. He was vaguely aware that the creature was probing his mental defences, looking for an opening through which it could exploit any weakness. Fighting down an emerging panic, he replied with just a hint of forced defiance, *'You* have no need of my name!'

The Keeper didn't respond at once but continued to block his way. He had the distinct impression that it was weighing up its options and he felt his stomach constrict in revulsion. Then a new message echoed inside his head, *'It was worth a try. Some fall at the first test and ... I can be patient.'*

He sensed the amusement beneath the disappointment. 'You will have no choice other than to be patient with me, Keeper. I intend to find what I came for.' His words were spoken with more force this time, in the hope of convincing the other of his determination. Cursing, he looked down towards his feet, no longer able to maintain eye contact with the nauseating images still flickering in front of him.

'We will see. Many have boasted of their intentions and failed here. I welcome them all into my embrace ... eventually.'

He couldn't decide which was worse – the chilling confidence behind the thought or the knowing chuckle which followed it. Daring to look up again, he was surprised to find nothing but darkness once more in front of him. Deep in thought, he resumed his slow progress.

It is difficult to measure time beyond the Veil. Periods may take a few minutes, hours or even days. It is as if the normal rules of time and space have no meaning there and perhaps this is what makes it such a dangerous place. The words of his mentor came back to him as he inched forward. He thought he might be feeling hungry, but the unceasing tension in his stomach was a constant reminder of his anxiety. Tiredness was creeping up on him and the effort of making certain he stuck to the path was beginning to wear him down. Of course, this meant that he was more prone towards making a mistake, but he dismissed the alluring temptation to sleep as an invitation to disaster. There were things here that would use the cover of sleep to crawl inside his mind. Such creatures would delight in controlling his body and forcing him to do unspeakable things. Once tired of their game, they would lead him off the path and to his doom.

As he neared the crossroads, the darkness began to fade a little. Looking up, he now noticed a second and larger moon had risen a little above the horizon. Its pale blue colour was less harsh than that of its sister. As his eyes adjusted themselves to the emerging gloom, he became aware of furtive rustling among the undergrowth that bordered the path. It took a while for him to realise that something was keeping pace with him, just out of view and careful not to encroach upon the smooth stone. He paused and then turned from side to side, as he struggled to discern what was tracking his progress. Although he could see nothing, he now discovered that the rustling sounds were coming from both sides. His mouth felt dry, and he struggled to increase his pace. He had no wish to meet any more denizens of this accursed place and a growing suspicion made him check the hilt of the gold dagger riding in the sheath at his belt.

By tiny degrees, the light level continued to increase, and he added concern about why this should be to his other worries. The accompanying sounds were also growing more frequent, and, in his imagination, he worried that they were growing louder. Pausing once more, his effort to scan the undergrowth now revealed multiple glimpses of tiny, amber, and malevolent eyes on both sides of the path. A low bark sounded to his left and he sensed movement from his right. Out of the undergrowth swarmed dozens of small hairless creatures, each about the size of a large rodent on his home planet. Eyes glittered in anticipation and spittle dripped from venomous incisors as the creatures closed in.

27

At the back of his mind he thought he heard a chuckle. There was no time to dwell on this distraction. His memory supplied a name for the advancing swarm. *K'liggen!* He drew the dagger from its sheath and whirled around. In desperation, he sought the k'liggen leader. He almost missed it, as the nearest of them began to race for his legs. Then, with calm deliberation, his right arm was throwing the dagger. At the same time, the first of the creatures sank fangs into the thick leather protecting his lower legs. Frustrated, it began to scrabble for purchase as it tried to climb up his shin. Others of its kind followed suit. Once one of them found exposed flesh, he was as good as dead.

Then the dagger buried itself in the head of a pure white k'liggen. The creature responded with a howl of pain. Staggering, it took two steps towards the undergrowth, before collapsing in agony. The flesh around the dagger entry point was already turning black. Charred flesh was peeling away from the skull. As swift as their attack had been, the rest of the pack whirled and raced towards their stricken leader.

He watched the k'liggen tear their former leader to pieces for just a few seconds, before setting off once more towards his goal. According to his teacher, the rodent pack would take a little while to choose their new leader and, in turn, this particular k'liggen would have to assert its authority over any number of challengers. He didn't intend to wait around to find out whether this explanation was right or not. One encounter with the pack was more than enough and he'd lost the dagger! *Sagana would be furious with him.*

His breathing slowed once more, and his pulse dropped back towards a more normal level. *That was close. Too damned close!* He was still pondering the implications of the attack when his peripheral awareness made him stop. Ahead lay the crossroads. As he took his next step towards it, a shape resolved itself in front of him.

The irritating itch inside his skull appeared just a few moments sooner than the Keeper's new message. *'We meet* again, Seeker. By making it this far, you have passed the first test and may now consider yourself a Neophyte. Your journey here is done for this night, and you will return to your home.'

He glared at the Keeper and almost spat out his response, 'Wait! I was told the path was safe and yet I was attacked. What sort of game are you playing here?'

The Keeper seemed to grow larger, and its flickering grew in intensity. 'Silence! Do you dare to question the Lord Lu'Ki'Fer? This is no game, foolish mortal. You chose this path of your own free will and have no say in what happens. Now go, before I lose my temper and make you wish we had never met. Go!'

The final word of command exploded in his head, and he fell to his knees, so intense was the pressure inside his skull. Waves of pain lashed inside his head and every nerve of his body began to burn. He screwed his eyes tight shut, afraid to see what stood before him; afraid to find out what power the Keeper possessed. Then, as abruptly as it had begun, the pressure was gone. As faint as an echo, he imagined he could hear a malicious chuckle.

He opened tear-stained eyes the merest fraction to find he was once more alone. With cautious deliberation, he rose to his feet, conscious that every part of him ached as if he had been whipped. Deep in his mind, he thought bitter thoughts and vowed that one day there would be a reckoning with the Keeper. He soiled himself when a distant voice intruded upon those thoughts, advising him that the Keeper looked forward to that day. With a sudden chill, he recalled the earlier boast; I welcome them all into my embrace … eventually.

Weariness threatened to overwhelm him as he trudged back along the path. His nerves were strung taught as he tried to keep alert to any further threat. At the same time, he worried about his rash promise and the implications for his future safety on this side of The Veil. One moment of stupid pride might have made a formidable enemy of one whose help would be needed during future excursions into this dangerous place.

His musing almost made him miss the dagger. It lay discarded at the side of the path, where its nearest companion was a pile of small bones, nestled underneath some sort of thick bush. His first instinct was to pick it up, but caution made him hesitate. The dagger had struck the K'liggen leader in open space, so it seemed a little suspicious that it now lay under a bush. And now he looked more carefully, even the poor light could not hide the vicious looking thorns that protruded from the diseased-looking branches of the foliage. *Another trap?*

With deliberate care, he unbuckled the belt around his waist and coiled its length into a small ball around the buckle. Then, taking care to stand as far back as he could, he jerked the belt towards the dagger. As the belt unravelled, he realised that the buckle would fall somewhat short of its target. He counted to five and, when nothing happened, slowly pulled the belt back and then re-coiled it. Taking one step closer towards the edge of the path, he made a second attempt to snag the precious object. This time, the buckle landed on top of the dagger hilt. He tried to pull it towards him and started to smile when the weapon moved a fraction nearer.

The smile died, stillborn, as the nearest branches whipped towards the belt and dagger. His eyes opened wide as the branches, displaying unexpected suppleness, wrapped themselves around the belt and then began to tighten their grip, pulling the other end out of his hand. In his imagination, he could almost feel the sharp thorns penetrating his skin, had he been foolish enough to attempt to pick up the dagger.

He watched, both fascinated and appalled, as the branches held on to the belt for several seconds, before releasing their grip. Even as he continued to watch, the bush resumed its previous appearance, no doubt waiting for more appetising prey. With great deliberation and without drawing breath, he reached for the nearest end of the belt and pulled it back towards the path. He froze with concern when the bush seemed to ripple, as if it were aware of him. Exhaling through pursed lips, he risked taking in a deep breath before resuming the effort to retrieve the belt. Sweat dripped from his forehead as he eased it away from the bush until, judging that the belt was out of reach of the dangerous branches, he jerked it back. Relief washed over him when the branches appeared to have lost interest in his actions.

As he secured the belt once more around his waist, he looked thoughtfully at the strange bush. He would have loved to have retrieved the dagger but could see no way to do so without putting himself at risk. Shrugging, he concluded that he had best forget about the weapon and continued on his way back to The Rent.

As he approached the passage through The Veil, he could not be sure whether or not he imagined a whisper; *'Now you are learning, Seeker.'* His skin crawled at the thought of meeting the Keeper again and he hurried through the unresisting Veil, back towards the safety of his familiar surroundings. *The wrath of Sagana would be nothing compared to that of the Keeper.*

4: An unexpected welcome

The sky began to cloud over as they left the village behind. Dark storm clouds raced in from the north-west and the air temperature began to fall. As the wind freshened, Clovis Muller found himself struggling to retain his seat. He needed more time to think about his new companion; at the back of his mind a growing sense of unease nibbled away at his earlier confidence. Back in the hut, he'd assumed that the warrior would be like all of the others bribed into doing the Pope's dirty work. He certainly looked like a typical warrior, with his long hair, padded gambeson and chainmail plus a variety of weapons. They were all dangerous men. Muller didn't doubt that some of them might even believe that they were doing righteous work on behalf of their God. Yet, from personal observation and rumour alike, Muller knew that most were driven by stronger motives. The craving for violence, the chance to rape and an insatiable lust for wealth were sufficient reason for most men.

Wallace seemed to be an odd exception to this rule. True, he had burst into the hut prepared to kill anyone inside. But something had stopped him from blindly carrying out that task. *What was it he had said when I was trying to convince him that the Pope's motives were questionable? Ah yes, that was it. He'd said, 'I admit there is some merit in your words old man, and I sense that you are not like the other heretics.' An interesting choice of word that. Not I see or I suspect, but I sense. Was it possible that this man possessed some latent talent for enlightenment?*

His musing was interrupted when Wallace reined to a halt, waiting for Muller to catch up alongside him. 'Old man, I think this storm could be heavy. We'd best find shelter somewhere,' he said, turning away as if he was about to ride on. Muller was on the verge of responding when the other man turned back towards him and added, 'Do you think those black clouds are a sign that we've upset either the Pope or your Gods?'

Muller couldn't tell whether or not the comment was made in jest, so he settled for a non-committal shrug and then said, 'You'll hear no quarrel from me if you wish to find shelter. Or from my bony backside either.' He smiled, recalling the earlier comment from Wallace which had so amused the warrior.

Wallace also smiled as he said, 'So you do have a sense of humour!' Then he pointed ahead and slightly to their left. 'I see smoke rising from behind that small wood. With any luck, it'll be another village. Maybe we can find a place to wait out the worst of the weather.'

Muller squinted in the indicated direction, but all his old eyes could make out was an indistinct blur. 'Well, your eyes are much better than mine and I've no desire to be soaked. Perhaps the settlement will be large enough to boast a tavern. I could use a drink right now!'

'Let's make haste then,' said Wallace, spurring his horse forward. A few moments later, the first clap of thunder was followed by ominously fat drops of rain. Muller's horse shied as the sound died away, but then calmed and resumed its steady plodding course towards the approaching treeline.

As they neared the edge of the wood, smoke continued to rise above the treetops. The rain was coming down in sheets now, driven into their backs by the increasing ferocity of the wind. Wallace calmly surveyed the tight stand of trees and the thick undergrowth. 'I doubt it would be worth trying to push our way through if it's all like that,' he said, pointing ahead. 'It's not a large wood, so we can save time by going round it to find what lies on the other side.' Muller pulled his cloak tighter around his thin frame as he nodded his agreement to this proposal. Already tired and wet, he had no desire to attempt forcing a passage through the wood.

Wallace turned his horse to the right. He figured it would be better to skirt the eastern side of the obstacle rather than risk running into any stragglers from Molitor's small army. The latter ought to be to the south-west, but he saw little advantage in taking an unnecessary risk. Another clap of thunder was soon followed by a burst of forked lightening, which grounded itself through one of the trees on the edge of the wood. The sound unnerved Muller's mount and he struggled to retain his seat. A cracking sound announced that the unfortunate tree had taken damage. Moments later a large branch slewed sideways. It was prevented from tumbling to the ground by its neighbours' thick network of criss-crossing branches.

'It seems your decision was wiser than I thought,' called Muller.

The two riders pressed on. Each was lost in his own thoughts, while the rain showed no sign of easing up until they had almost rounded the wood and started to head north-west. With the thunder moving away and reduced to periodic rumbles, the rain began to ease a little. Ahead, they could make out a larger village than the one they had left behind. Turning in his saddle, Wallace said, 'Let's hope yonder settlement is indeed large enough to boast a tavern. Better still, one where we can find warmth, food, and drink.'

'I'd settle for a roaring fire right now,' was the weary response from the older man. His companion snorted and then pointed towards their destination. 'There's still smoke coming out of that larger building, so there must be a fire somewhere. There doesn't seem to be much activity though.' He slowed his mount, waiting for Muller to draw alongside. 'Keep those old eyes wide open and shout if you see anything untoward. I've got an uneasy feeling about this place. It's a little too quiet. Something isn't quite right here.'

Muller sighed. 'Are you always this suspicious? It's been pouring with rain and yet you expect to see people out and about. I'll wager that the villagers have more sense than us and decided to take shelter. Come on, I'm cold, wet, and hungry. And I could still use a good drink.' So saying, he urged his horse forward, heading for a large building with a sign hung outside its door. Wallace shrugged and then put spur to horseflesh, doubtless unwilling to lose sight of the old man and the potential profit he offered.

They dismounted outside the dilapidated looking tavern. Wallace secured both horses to a railing that had seen years of use. Overhead, the faded picture of a crown creaked as it swung in the breeze. The rain had further increased in its intensity. It was being driven towards the tavern door by the frequent strong gusts of wind. An eerie silence lay across the village. Muller suddenly had the unsettling thought that it was holding its breath, as if awaiting some dramatic event.

Wallace paused at the door, where he turned to look back. His eyes swept around the cluster of humble dwellings, huddled together in the damp conditions. Seeming satisfied, he turned back, without a word, and pushed the door open. Muller followed him into the tavern, glad to escape from the elements and already unfastening the clasp to his cloak.

No sooner had the pair crossed the threshold than they were seized from behind by rough hands. With their arms forced behind their backs', rough cord was used to secure their wrists. One of their assailants took Wallace's sword from its scabbard. Wallace paid him no heed, his attention already focused on the back of the man stood at the crude counter, whilst Muller began looking around the room in confusion and panic. The older man started to protest, drawing a stinging slap across his mouth from one of their captors.

Wallace said nothing, allowing his eyes to grow accustomed to the gloomy interior of the building. The feeble light from sputtering candles failed to penetrate into the furthest recesses of the room. To the left, a fire in the large hearth did little to add detail to the scene. Instead it poured forth copious clouds of smoke from the damp and sputtering logs it was struggling to consume. As his eyes adjusted to the gloom, he turned his head a little and noted the rough trestle-tables and benches. The floor was strewn with filthy straw and three smirking men now stood behind him and his companion.

Dubois turned slowly from the counter, leant back against it, and began making a show of pulling on his gauntlet. Trickles of blood seeped from the three long scratches gouged out of his right cheek, but he ignored them, pretending instead to pay great attention to his right hand as he fiddled with the gauntlet. Appearing to be satisfied at last, he looked up at the prisoners. His lips parted and his tongue crept out to lick the top one. 'Well, well. What a surprise. My old friend Wallace *and* the old heretic,' he said, before fixing his gaze on Muller. 'I thought you'd have gone to meet the devil by now, old man. I was certain Wallace here would have ended your miserable existence.' He paused for effect and then added, 'But I suppose you must have persuaded him to spare your miserable worthless life. What did you offer in return, I wonder? Was it gold, silver, or precious stones? Perhaps it was a mixture of all three? Well, no matter, I expect I'll find out soon enough.' He pushed himself away from the counter and took a single step forward. Nodding as he spoke, he commanded, 'You three, take the old man outside and keep a close eye on him. When I'm finished here, we'll have a good roasting fire to warm us up. But first, I'll have a little chat with my old friend Wallace. I'm sure I can persuade him to share his recent good fortune with us, before he dies in the service of our Lord.'

Moans from the right-hand side back corner of the room attracted his attention. All eyes in the room turned in the same direction. A shapeless form struggled to right itself from a bench pushed up against the outer wall. It tottered into the dim light. A pale slim hand groped for the counter as the shape resolved itself into the form of a young woman. She struggled to remain upright whilst also attempting to pull the remnants of her torn shift together. To her evident distress, she failed to hide her ample breasts. Wallace tensed as he took in the bite marks around both nipples, the bruising around her right eye and her split lips. Between her legs, the shift was stained with fresh bright red blood.

Dubois spoke again, 'I'd almost forgotten you, harlot. Get out of here before I have you arrested for sorcery!' He turned back towards Wallace and Muller before continuing, 'The strumpet must have bewitched me and my men. But God, she was a fair ride, I must confess.' Laughing at his own joke, he waved a hand in dismissal to his three men and then urged the woman to make haste.

He watched as she struggled to stay on her feet and then hobbled out of the room. His cruel eyes never left the woman, except for a brief moment when she stumbled and almost fell against Wallace on her way to the door. 'She must have cast her spell on me first,' said Dubois. 'I suppose a virgin would want her first time to be something to remember.' He shrugged, and then added in a more menacing tone, 'Now my friend, we can get down to business. But first I think I'll have a little sport. A feisty wench always makes me feel like hurting someone.' He looked around the now empty room and then feigned surprise as he added, 'Oh dear, it seems you are the only other person here. Ah well, no hard feelings, eh? I'm sure you'd do the same in my position.'

He stepped closer to Wallace and then frowned. 'But your hands are tied my dear friend, so you are defenceless. Oh well, that won't stop us from having a little fun before we discuss old times. Have you ever wondered how you would look without your ears, my friend? No? Although they do tend to bleed a lot when removed, so perhaps I'll take a few fingers instead.' As he spoke, he was watching Wallace's face for signs of a reaction and, seeing none, he began to grow angry, his emotion betrayed by the raising of his voice. 'Did you think that Molitor wasn't watching you, traitor? He asked *me* to keep an eye on you and it seems he was right, as usual. So, now I'm going to make you beg for mercy, give up whatever the old man offered you and then I will do the Lord's work and send you to hell!' As he delivered this threat, he moved closer to Wallace, drawing a long dagger from his belt and holding it point down by his side.

Dubois stopped, about a foot away from Wallace and leered into the taller man's face. 'I'm going to enjoy this,' he snarled, adding, 'I think I'll begin by cleaving your nose. It seems somehow appropriate for a treacherous pig.' Without warning, Wallace spat a large globule of phlegm into his tormentor's face. The other man merely laughed and started to raise his dagger … and then screamed. In a blur of motion, Wallace's left hand erupted from behind his back and surged in an upward sweep. It ended when he planted his own dagger through the other man's right eye. He then used his height, weight, and forward momentum to drive the blade into the brain. Dubois slumped to his knees, a look of shock etched on a face now masked by rivulets of fresh blood. Wallace grabbed for the sword, still in its scabbard, at the dying man's hip.

The anguished cry from within the tavern prompted consternation outside. Muller was roughly pushed to one side, falling face down into a large and muddy puddle. He rolled over spluttering, fearing that he would drown in the foul slop, just as the first of Dubois' men made it to the tavern door … which opened even as he stretched out a hand towards it, revealing a grim-faced Wallace. A massive downward sweep of the sword in the crusader's hand cut clean through the thin leather jacket of the soldier, opening him up from his right shoulder and almost down to his left hip. The reverse stroke sliced open his stomach and the doomed man staggered back, trying to cup steaming entrails as they spilled out into his hands. The rain helped to wash away the copious amount of blood streaming from the wound, but the soldier was already too close to death to either notice or care. Wallace smashed the hilt of his sword into the dying man's face, knocking him backwards and into his two startled companions, who had followed close behind. One fell onto his rump, but the other managed to stay on his feet, struggling to unsheathe his own weapon.

Muller, meanwhile, knelt frozen in near disbelief as Wallace, bellowing a triumphant battle cry, charged out of the door, leaping the two downed men as he swung his sword in a long arc. Steel met bone and gristle moments before blood spurted in a crimson spray, as the second soldier was almost decapitated by the force of Wallace's blow. Kicking at the man's stomach, Wallace struggled to pull his weapon free from where it had buried itself in its second victim's neck.

Hands still tied behind his back, Muller had managed to regain his feet and now snapped out of his amazement, registering that the third soldier was preparing to stab Wallace in the back. With a cry of his own, he dropped his right shoulder and charged into this last remaining captor. The soldier half turned to meet him, so that Muller could do no more than deliver a glancing blow. In despair, he tried to retain his footing, conscious that the man was now free to strike the defenceless Wallace, even as the latter continued his desperate efforts to free his own sword.

The third soldier stepped towards Wallace with a smirk on his face. 'You'll pay for ...,' he managed to sneer; before the muscles in his face went slack and he too sank, in slow motion, to his knees. The shaft of a crossbow bolt protruded from his neck and a bloody froth oozed from his lips, mingling with the rain as it ran down his chin, before dripping to the ground. His eyes glazed over, and the body toppled sideways. Both Muller and Wallace looked down the street towards the young woman standing there. Her torn shift fluttered in the wind and a small crossbow slipped from her fingers to crash to the hard-packed earth.

Wallace recovered first and stepped cautiously towards her, holding out his now empty hands as he approached. She looked up into his face as he closed the gap between them, tears streaming down her cheeks, mingling with the relentless rain. 'I thank you for your well-timed assistance,' he said, half turning to gesture towards the soldier she had killed. 'That was quite some shot,' he added, pausing for her reply.

Long moments dragged by, during which Muller joined the small group. He coughed, twice, and then asked, 'Could one of you untie my wrists? Or at least cut me free!'

Wallace laughed as he produced a small dagger and began to hack at the cords binding the older man. As the strands parted, he nodded towards the young woman, 'She saved us. My damned sword was jammed in that idiot's neck.'

The woman was still struggling to speak, but then surprised them both by saying, 'My father was a soldier. He had no son, so he taught me to shoot. And I didn't do it to save your life. I did it because those animals laughed as they took it in turns to force themselves upon me.'

Wallace looked from her to Muller and back. When neither said anything more he spoke, 'Well, whatever the reason, we three are now free. I can promise you that neither of us offers you any threat, young woman. Indeed, I'm curious to know why you would appear to be the only one left in this place and what you plan to do next.'

Muller tugged at Wallace's sleeve. 'How did you manage to get free of your own bonds?'

Ignoring him, Wallace shook off the old man's hand before turning back towards the woman. 'We are headed for Muret if you wish to accompany us. It would be safer than travelling alone.'

The young woman stared at him for a few moments and then said, 'I'm Madeleine de LeDrede and this is … was … my home. Some days ago, we received word of what the soldiers have been doing in the south and most of the villagers fled for Toulouse. My father rode out a week ago, hoping to find other men willing to fight and defend our homes, but we'd heard nothing from him since.' She paused, choking back an anguished gulp. 'So I came back to the village to see if he was here or had perhaps left me a message. I had just found his body when I was taken prisoner by those men. They used me ill and I'd given up all hope of escape when you arrived.'

'Where is your father's body?' asked Wallace, watching the young woman with studied concern.

Madeleine turned away and began to walk towards the fire-damaged building. She said nothing as they approached, seemingly lost in her own thoughts and memories. The warrior followed a step behind, whilst wondering how her father had died.

Battle-hardened as he was, even Wallace flinched when they stopped outside the building, and he saw what awaited them inside. What remained of her father's body was a fire-blackened corpse, still pinned to the back wall of the building in a familiar position. Wallace surmised that the poor man had been run through the chest with a spear before having his hands nailed to the wall in a mockery of the crucifixion position. He turned towards the dead man's daughter and saw her wipe fresh tears from her eyes, as she stared at the gruesome sight.

'You see what they did to him?'

Wallace cleared his throat and said, 'I'm guessing they ran him through with a spear and then nailed his dead body there. But why would they do that?'

Her head snapped towards him, and her eyes flashed. 'He wasn't dead when they did that! He was still alive when I found him, although it was already much too late to save him. They'd drained too much of his blood.'

It was Wallace's turn to be shocked. 'What do you mean, they'd drained too much of his blood?' he sputtered. 'Why would Dubois and his men do that?

Madeleine answered him a withering snort of derision. 'It wasn't Dubois who did that to him. That bastard simply set fire to the building, laughing as he declared my father a heretic and thanking *them* for saving him and his men from the trouble of erecting a stake and building a pyre. This is the work of the Blood Cult.'

Wallace was confused. 'I don't understand. Who or what is this Blood Cult you speak of. And why would they do this to your father?'

Madeleine sighed in exasperation. 'Are you so ignorant that you've never heard of the Disciples of Lu'Ki'Fer?'

Her words made Wallace take a pace backwards. 'Lu'Ki'Fer! The old man has spoken of him as some sort of old god. He has a gold statue and offers to pay me to make sure it reaches his master.' He was about to add the revelation that Muller's master knew how to use the statue to unlock the secret of gaining near immortality, but caution gained the upper hand among his reeling thoughts.

The young woman gave him a horrified look. 'You're helping him? But they worship devils and perform blood sacrifice.' She put a hand to her mouth and started to back away, her face pale and her eyes wide with fear. It was then that Muller called to them from the other end of the street.

5: HUNTED

Lemuel Unwin took a last look around the room he'd called home for the last four months. His landlady had been careful not to intrude upon his privacy and happy to have a priest for a lodger. She'd boasted of her good fortune in the company of friends. After all, if you couldn't trust a man of God to pay his rent on time then who could you trust? Even better, he'd paid six months in advance!

The priest did not begrudge the woman her imminent windfall of two months' rental. Whatever happened, he would not be returning to this room. Yet he couldn't ask for the money back without arousing unwanted suspicion. As a senior member of The Shield, he wasn't short of funds in any event. Pausing to adjust the thumb of his left glove, he picked up the package and his walking stick. Then he quietly opened the door leading out onto the corridor. With a sigh, he set off for the stairs, avoiding the creaking floorboard immediately outside on the landing. The room on his left had been vacant for the last few weeks. A deaf and aged widow, who seldom set foot outside, occupied the room on the other side. The lodgings had been an almost perfect base, offering little risk of being observed as he went about his business.

He was almost at the foot of the stairs, and thanking the saints for his good fortune, when the landlady emerged from the front parlour. 'Good evening, Father,' she said, bestowing her usual beaming smile upon the startled man. He couldn't help but notice how her generous bosom moved up and down. He'd already formed the impression that her breasts might escape the confines of her dress at any moment.

Silently reproaching himself for such thoughts, he responded to her greeting, adding, 'I'm going out to return this most interesting book to a dear friend. He's offered to entertain me tonight, so I'll be out for most of the evening. You needn't wait up, Mrs Crawford, I have my key. Good night to you.' So saying, he squeezed past the simpering woman, opened the front door, and beat a hasty retreat.

Outside, the sweat on his forehead chilled in the cool night air. He briefly pondered, the thought that he would rather face one of The Black Blades than be trapped in a room with his landlady. It brought a brief smile to his face. The woman reeked of animal sex. Worse, she'd made it very clear that she had no objection to becoming more 'intimate' with a man of the cloth. The irony was that it was his secret life which prevented him from taking advantage of her undoubted charms and not his public life as a priest. *After all,* he thought, in an effort to console himself, *I wouldn't be the first priest to taste forbidden fruit!*

Agnes returned to her parlour. She closed the door behind her and composed her face into a professional smile, waiting for the tall man standing near to the window to turn round. He was looking out at the street. Agnes couldn't see the intensity with which he watched the departing figure, laden with a large package and walking stick, as it hurried away. On hearing her gentle cough, he turned and smiled back at the woman, revealing large and curiously shaped teeth. Her own smile faltered a little before she rallied and asked, 'Can I get you any refreshment, sir?'

The visitor walked over to the large settle, carefully positioned by the roaring log fire, and swept back his coat tails before seating himself. He looked up and patted his hand on the cushion at his side. 'Why don't you take a seat, and we can get to know each other a ... little better?'

The landlady's face lit up with a wide smile as she shook her head in agreement. 'I was supposing you'd be eager to view the room itself. It's been empty for a few weeks, but everything is clean and tidy. Still, I do prefer to indulge in a little social intercourse with my gentlemen tenants. I like to feel that they view me as something more than just their landlady.' She cocked her head to one side, in what she considered to be a coquettish manner, before adding, 'Make yourself comfortable and we'll see how things develop over a glass of good wine.' She turned on her heel and swept out of the room, in search of a bottle and two clean glasses.

On her return she noted that the heavy curtains at the window had been closed. If she found that a little presumptuous, she gave no sign. Instead, she busied herself with transferring the contents of a battered tin tray onto a small table located next to the settle. Her prospective new tenant sat upright, a small fob watch dangling from his fingers. 'I don't often drink, Mr Black, but I'll take a glass with you,' she said in a husky voice, as she approached the fireplace. At the back of her mind she wondered what his Christian name might be. It was unusual to omit this from a calling card but, if things worked out as she was beginning to hope, that particular mystery would be resolved very soon.

As she prepared to take the seat next to him, she noticed with some fascination how the firelight reflected off the surface of his slowly revolving watch. It hung, suspended, from a thick silver chain. She was conscious that her visitor was saying something to her. Spellbound by the smooth rich baritone tones, she half-turned towards him. The glass of wine in her right hand remained untouched by her full and slightly parted lips. At the back of her mind, a vague sense of unease began to grow as the room started to spin around her. To her surprise, the corners of the room seemed to recede into a strange fog. The spinning sensation was becoming worse, and she realised that she was staring into Mr Black's face. She tried to break the eye contact but found this simple act beyond her. It was almost as if she was drowning in liquid pools of green, flecked with specks of amber and gold. The glass slipped, unnoticed, from her grasp, and shattered itself on the hard wooden floor. Her last conscious thought was to wonder what it would be like to relax into Mr Black's arms as his lover.

Pulling his coat tighter against the chill wind, Father Unwin walked briskly towards Saint Augustine's Church, clutching the package under his left arm tight to his body. His eyes swept the street from side to side and every few yards he paused to glance behind him. Although he could discern nothing untoward, some instinct warned him that he was in danger. *Oh God, did I stay too long? Have their agents found me?*

Training and experience had long since taught him the wisdom of paying heed to his instincts, even when the available evidence seemed to render them wrong or foolish. Although he couldn't explain how, he was convinced that someone or something was observing him. He flinched when a dog howled its forlorn cry from a neighbouring street. *Calm down. You're letting your nerves get the better of you*, he told himself.

Ahead, he could see the outline of his destination. He glanced up towards the top of the church spire. As he did so, he caught the merest flicker of movement out of the corner of his left eye. A shadow ducked back into an alleyway. Unwin's mind suggested the shape matched that of a large dog or perhaps even a wolf. He paused, uncertain as to what this observation might signify. From the same alleyway a new howl was met by an immediate answer. Unwin's thoughts flashed back to an incident that had taken place several years earlier in northern Germany. He was in no hurry to relive that evening and the terror of being hunted by those vicious four-legged predators.

He patted the reassuring lump of metal in his pocket and took another step forwards. A large creature emerged from the alleyway, openly tracking his progress with feral eyes. Unwin felt his blood run cold even as his skin became clammy. His German comrade had been accurate in his description of the devil-dogs. Known as chyvol, they were relentless and vicious hunters. Unwin was also aware that they always hunted in packs, but this was not his greatest cause for concern. Their presence here suggested that a being of great power was controlling them from somewhere nearby. It was no easy task to persuade these creatures to leave their home-world and cross the dark barrier into T'Erran space.

The worried priest quickened his pace, transferring his walking stick to his left hand whilst straining for any sound of pursuit. A strange call to his left – a cross between a grunt and a bark – was answered by others from all around. There were at least four of them and possibly more. Fighting the urge to run, Unwin groped inside his coat pocket. His fingers closed around the barrel of a revolver.

He could sense one of the dogs closing behind him as he turned and fired at close range. As the echo of his shot rolled around the street, the large brute dropped to its knees. What was left of its face wore a look of stunned fury as its life ebbed away. The priest barely had time to carefully place his precious package on the ground before a second creature appeared. As it leapt out of the shadow to his right, he somehow managed to turn the gun towards it in time before pulling back on the trigger. This second attacker met a similar fate to the first. Unfortunately for Unwin, its falling body crashed into his arm, knocking the gun from his despairing grip. The fading echo of the second gunshot was accompanied by the sound of several windows being opened. Questioning voices were full of both anger and alarm.

Struggling to retain his feet, Unwin pressed a small button on his walking stick. He heard a reassuring but brief snickering sound. The six-inch blade of toughened and sharpened steel had slid smoothly from its housing and now extended beyond the end of the stick. Almost as if this action were a signal, two more of the brutes charged towards their prey, seeking to take him from both sides. Covered in coarse black hair and heavily muscled, the creatures were surprisingly fast and agile. In desperation, Unwin looked around for a more defensible position. Racing across the street, he prepared to meet them with a high garden wall at his back. As they closed in, the priest suddenly ducked down whilst swinging his swordstick in a long arc above his head. The first dog had leapt for the priest's throat but found its jaws closing on thin air as the sharp blade sliced its stomach open. It collapsed in a heap, blood pouring from its wounds. Yet it still struggled to regain its feet, all the time howling in pain. Unwin became conscious of the human figures spilling out of doorways and into the street. More voices now demanded to know what was happening.

He paid them no heed, his attention focused on the fourth devil-dog. A little larger than its companions, this one seemed possessed of more cunning. Its blood-red eyes watched him with a cold intensity as it circled. It seemed intent on staying out of range of the swordstick, which had been used with such devastating effect against its dying brother. Then it paused in its movements and cocked its head to one side as if listening to something. Expecting a sudden attack, Unwin tensed, preparing to defend himself once more. The two antagonists stood locked in a frozen tableau for several seconds. Then the dog abruptly turned tail and sped away towards the end of the street, racing past several startled inhabitants.

A shout broke the almost palpable tension. 'Look out; it's got hold of something. Bloody 'ell, give it room!'

Someone fired a pistol at the retreating form and a howl of pain confirmed that they had hit their target. Unwin watched as the animal staggered, fell on its side and then tried to rise back to its feet. A second shot delivered from close range finished it off.

'Good Lord will you look at the size of this thing! What sort of dog is it?'

'That's not a dog. It's a bleedin' 'orse!'

With adrenaline pumping through his body and his heart racing, Lemuel Unwin said a silent prayer of thanks to his Maker. He wasted a few seconds pondering the implications of this attack before grasping the significance of the shouted comment. His eyes travelled away from the small crowd gathering around the dead chyvol and towards the place where he'd laid down his package for Brother Fulbright. There was nothing there save the empty street. To his horror, he realised that there had been a fifth devil-dog and that it had taken his notes. *The Blades have my materials and will soon be aware of my intentions,* he realised. The attack had been little more than a distraction; the real objective had been to rob him.

He was well aware that whoever or whatever had been controlling the creatures would have suffered a small portion of their pain and suffering. This would render them vulnerable for a short while until they could recover their full life-force. *Should I try to find them? Were they up on the church tower? Whoever it was might turn out to be my intended target and this would be a golden opportunity to improve the chance of completing my mission*, he told himself. Then common sense reasserted itself. *Such a convenient circumstance only ever happens in children's stories. Your first priority is still to alert Brother Fulbright.* With grim determination, he stepped towards the gathering crowd and prepared to answer their questions and hoping to allay their confusion.

As Agnes Crawford sank into an induced sleep, Mr Black smiled to himself and gently ran his tongue across teeth filed to razor-sharp points. The unexpected departure of Unwin had thwarted its original intention. A contingency plan was already in place to deal with such a disappointing turn of events. *The communication stones were so useful in a situation like this!* Nor was this visit a total waste of time and energy. An unexpected development had presented Mr Black with a new and delicious opportunity. He intended to take full advantage as compensation for the loss of his chance to repay an old grudge. After rising from the settle he went and stood motionless at the room door. It took a few moments to satisfy himself that he could detect no indication of activity elsewhere in the building. Mr Black turned back towards the sleeping landlady, confident that the two of them were unlikely to be disturbed. He began to contemplate the delightful morsels awaiting his imminent pleasure. His first move was to moisten his lips with a flickering tongue.

The church stood in darkness. Its outline was just discernible against the night sky. Unwin had been here many times before and knew the general layout well enough to find his way around despite the gloom. The new moon was one of the reasons he'd chosen this night to make his delivery. As he opened the main door he patted his pocket, reassuring himself that his pistol still nestled there. A faint smell caused him to pause, as did the unexpected lack of any internal light. Not a single candle burned inside. Unable to identify the smell, he shook his head, drew out the pistol, and set off towards the back of the church. His mind recalled the figure he'd glimpsed near the church spire. Someone or something might be waiting for him in the dark interior. He had inched almost halfway down the aisle, making frequent stops to listen for any sound. Then he resolved the mystery of the unexpected fragrance. He stopped once more, shocked by the recognition of the unexpected stench of death.

Thinking rapidly, he quietly retraced his steps to the entrance. After some groping around, his hand found a candle on the table by the door. Resting his stick against his leg and his pistol on the small table, he fumbled around inside one of his coat pockets. After locating a flint, he was able to produce some light. He quickly lit several more candles before jamming the largest into a holder.

Unwin retrieved his pistol but left the walking stick leant up against the table. Sweeping up the candle holder, he turned and began to walk back towards the altar. He hadn't taken more than a few steps when he let out an involuntary cry. In the gloomy light, he could just make out a pair of boots hanging in front of his face. He extended his arm and thus raised the flickering candle as high as he could reach. As his gaze travelled up from the boots, he found himself looking at a body. It was hanging from one of the rafters supporting the church roof.

Father Arthur Fulbright stared through glassy eyes at the next life.

Below him, Lemuel Unwin fought to avoid vomiting up the bile that rose in his throat. As his oldest friend swayed in some unfelt breeze, it was clear that he had been horribly mutilated. His genitalia had been hacked off and then stuffed into his mouth. Both arms had been bent at an unnatural angle and outwards from the elbow. *It's a warning for me. Poor Artie! If I'd come sooner, I might have saved you!*

Hot tears slid down his face as Father Unwin tried to decide what he should do next. But first, he made a silent vow to avenge his friend.

The next morning, Augustin Greene rose early. This had become his normal habit since taking an enforced retirement on a modest annual income. Worried about a potential scandal, his last employer had also agreed not to notify the authorities. It suited both parties not to draw their attention to Augustin's innovative book-keeping practices. Mr Greene liked to consume an enormous breakfast prior to taking the air during a short morning stroll.

On this particular day, he was somewhat surprised and disappointed not to find Mrs Crawford bustling about in the kitchen. They often shared a morning cup of tea together. Augustin also enjoyed the rare opportunity to converse with such a charming and well-endowed woman. It occurred to him that the good lady of the dwelling might be in the front parlour. He soon found himself knocking on the door, although this elicited no response. Observing that the door had swung slightly ajar in response to his efforts, he threw caution to the wind. Pushing the door further back, he shuffled into the room. What confronted him there put an immediate end to both his appetite and any thoughts of a pleasant conversation.

Despite being possessed of a strong aversion to the police, Greene realised that he would have to raise the alarm. He staggered out into the hallway, pressing a handkerchief to his mouth. With a shaking hand, he wiped his face and struggled to return the soiled cloth to a coat pocket, before shouting as loud as he could to arouse his fellow tenants. 'Murder! Help! Murder!' he sang out.

Upstairs, a door opened and the sound of heavy boots on the bare wooden floorboards carried down the stairs. A young man with a foppish dress sense followed the owner of the booted feet down into the hallway. 'What the devil do you mean by shouting like that?' demanded Angus Grey, panting from the novelty of having run to investigate what was causing all the fuss. Grey was a big man, a dockworker by trade and his coarse jacket reeked of spices. Behind him, the young aspiring poet, known as Simon Strutt, wore his usual perplexed expression on a clean-shaven face.

Augustin said nothing in response to Grey but pointed towards the parlour door. Neither of the two newcomers made any effort to move. 'In there. It's horrible. We need to fetch the local bobby.'

Grey and Strutt looked at each other before Grey pushed the old man to one side. 'What are you babbling about?' he said, striding into the parlour. Strutt remained outside in the hallway, looking closely at Greene. 'Oh God!' came the cry from within the room. Strutt started towards the door and almost collided with Grey. 'Don't go in there young 'un,' advised the bigger man. His face was ashen, and he grabbed Greene by the shoulders. 'You might have warned me, stupid old fool!' he shouted, spittle erupting from his lips to land on the older man's chin. He turned his attention to

50

Strutt, 'Go and find a bobby.' 'Now!' he shouted, as Simon hesitated in confusion.

An hour later and several policemen were busy trying to establish who had found what and when. The senior of the two was writing in a notebook. As he wrote, he checked that he had the correct details from Greene, who sat at one end of the kitchen table. All heads turned towards the kitchen door, as the hastily summoned doctor entered the room. Dr Dugald Samson was a small wiry man of middle years, but still the proud owner of a fine head of thick ginger hair. His long sideburns, drooping moustache and neatly trimmed beard gave him an almost comical appearance. On more than one occasion he had been mistaken for an actor. Now though, his face was grim. He walked over to the sink and rinsed his hands in a bucket of cold water. Casting round for a towel, he espied one over a drying rack at the back of the room and proceeded to make use of it.

No-one spoke until he had finished these oblations and then several other people started to speak at once. 'Silence!' ordered the police sergeant. 'Let the doctor speak. Now then Dr Samson, if you would be so good as to tell us 'ow the poor lady died?'

The doctor let out a breath with an audible sigh and seemed to gather his thoughts with some difficulty. 'It's difficult to say for certain how she died. From the state of the body, it is my opinion that she died late last night. I've never seen anything like it.' He swallowed and then asked for a glass of water.

'Would you prefer a swig of brandy, sir?' asked the police sergeant, holding out a small hip flask.

The doctor nodded and took the flask with a look of gratitude on his pale face. After a long swig, he handed the flask back and resumed his report. 'The poor woman died from loss of blood. There were some very odd wounds. Her eyes have been gouged out of the sockets and her tongue has been ripped out. Something very sharp, long, and thin punctured her neck. Whoever did this was either very lucky or, and this seems the more probable explanation, is in possession of medical training. The injury to her neck ruptured the carotid artery and this would have bled profusely.' He paused and looked around the room, making eye contact with each of its occupants in turn. 'Her arms and shoulders appear to have been nibbled by something with very sharp teeth. But the worst thing is that I can't find her eyeballs or her tongue.'

A buzz of disbelief burst forth from his audience. It subsided with surprising rapidity when Samson held up his hand. 'I know that sounds incredible, but other bits of her appear to have been consumed by her attacker. The bite marks show definite signs of chewing. I can't be sure, but I suspect the poor woman was still alive when her killer began to feed upon her body. God alone knows what sort of person could do such terrible things to another human being.'

A stunned silence greeted this last revelation. The junior policeman was the first to react. 'Is there anyone missing who ought to be here?' he asked the assembled tenants.

His sergeant shot him a dark glance and, before anyone else could speak he growled, 'Leave the thinking to me Whiston. Now, is there any of you tenants missing?'

Several people mentioned the quiet priest, Father Unwin. The sergeant wrote the priest's name in his little book before he said, 'Whiston, you lead the way upstairs. I want to take a look in Unwin's room.'

6: CHYVOL

He pushed his way through The Veil and then stopped dead in his tracks. Without thinking about it, he'd expected to encounter the same stone path, the hot foul-smelling air, and the blood-red moon. Instead, he was standing alone on a vast plain and already shivering in the strong and biting cold wind. To his right, a large gibbous moon cast a baleful yellow light.

Although it was lighter than on his previous visit, there was little or nothing to see. All around him lay an unrelenting flat landscape, unrelieved by any feature or even a single tree. He pulled his cloak tight around his shoulders and tried to work out what he was supposed to be doing here. Far away and ahead, he caught the eerie howl of some creature, but was unsure whether to head towards it or to try to give it a wide berth. He hefted the wooden club in his right hand and decided to make for the source of the sound. As he walked, his ears strained to pick up anything above the whistle and roar of the wind.

When he'd asked what he was supposed to do with this crude weapon, Sagana had laughed before becoming deadly serious. 'Use it when needed. And this time, try to bring it back!'

He took a few steps and then paused again. How would he find his way back across this deserted plain? Looking back, he could see the outline of his boots in the dirt but, even as he watched, the unrelenting wind was scouring them away. It was as if the elements were determined to make the landscape as uniform as possible. Raising his gaze, he could make out a shimmering wedge at the end of his footprints and realised that this was The Rent. His spirits rose for a few instants before subsiding again when he realised that he would need to be this close to the exit in order to see it.

'It's a test of faith!' he said out loud, wincing as the wind took his words away.

'*Yes*', came a familiar voice inside his head. '*Welcome back, Seeker. I salute your courage … if not your wisdom. But then, the search for wisdom is why you are here, isn't it? Or have you come to carry out your vow?*'

'Forget the vow. It was made in anger and ignorance. I … apologise for my error.' He paused, awaiting the response.

None was forthcoming.

Sensing that he was alone again, he set off once more. He had no idea where he was going or what he might face, but there was no point in standing around. At the back of his mind, he felt certain that whatever he was meant to meet would either find him or at least provide a clue as to where it hid. He still wasn't comfortable with the idea of defending himself with a club though.

He had lost all track of time and was starting to feel numb. The chill wind had been relentless in working its way into his bones and his fingers were turning numb. The howling sound had been repeated at irregular intervals, but its source still appeared to be far ahead. In fact, now that he thought about it, it always came from directly ahead. Almost as if it were leading him on towards his fate! *Not a reassuring thought.*

Stopping to rest, he dropped the club to the ground, crouched down and tried to warm his hands under his armpits. The howling resumed immediately and in earnest. He allowed himself a wry smile. 'You may be impatient, but you'll just have to wait. I'll find you when *I'm* ready,' he said out loud.

'*Take care that your fate doesn't creep up on you before you're ready,*' hammered inside his skull.

Standing, he turned in a slow circle as he scanned the horizon. The view was one of unrelenting monotony. And then, from the corner of his right eye, he caught a flash of movement. Intrigued, he turned towards it, but could see nothing. Behind him, a howl sounded. It was closer now and he whirled towards it in panic, just as an answering yelp spoke to his right. Whatever was out there, there were at least three of them and they were either well-camouflaged or, worse, invisible.

He half expected to hear a chuckle as he whirled back towards the origin of the first howl. This time, he saw definite movement, closing in and slightly to his left. His mind raced, as he tried to work out what he was facing and whether to run or to stand and find out.

Behind, a deep-pitched growl set his heart racing. A new smell suddenly assailed his senses and he realised, with a shock, that it reminded him of a wet dog. *Are dogs hunting me? Why are they wet?*

He bent down to retrieve the club and made sure of his grip as he straightened. Shadows were circling him now. He could make out three creatures. They reminded him of large and powerful dogs. They were slowly closing the circle. His mind raced, considering his few options. Although the creatures seemed wary of the club, he knew they would attack soon. It would be wise to attempt to seize the initiative. He began to turn slowly, in the opposite direction to his attackers. Waiting for the right moment…

He almost missed the opportunity. One of the chyvol came a little closer and he exploded towards it. The swinging club smashed into the creatures' shoulder. He smiled at the sharp sound of snapping bone but had no time to savour his triumph. All three dogs charged towards him.

Later, he reasoned that he had acted on pure instinct. As the dogs converged on his position, he leapt high in the air, bringing the club down on the head of the largest of the three. The creature went down on its knees, blood pouring from the shattered skull. Its killer didn't wait to see the results of his blow, but leapt again, this time missing with another ferocious downswing of the club but managing to kick the first dog in its already wounded shoulder. This second strike forced a pained squeal from the animal, which cut short as he smashed in its head with a vicious backhanded blow from the heavy club.

Half turning towards the remaining creature, he noticed that it was the only one now moving. It was too close for him to jump out of its way and there was no time to use the club. Massive jaws tried to snap shut on his right arm and he lashed out with his left foot. Pain raced through his right arm as the powerful teeth bit through flesh, a few fractions of a second before his foot connected with the fleshy part of the dog's throat. Taken by surprise, the creature released the grip on his arm and staggered back, making a strange hacking sound. It wasn't until after he'd beaten it to a bloody pulp with the trusty club, that he realised his kick had crushed the dog's windpipe. The hacking sound had been its desperate effort to breathe.

Uttering a cry of triumph, he'd slumped to the floor. The shakes soon followed as his body reacted to the effort involved in the fight. He was still shaking when foul-tasting bile erupted from his mouth.

With an empty stomach and steady nerves, he got to his feet and began to consider what his next action should be. It was a while before he noticed the dancing light far off ahead and slightly to his left. With no other objective in sight, he set off towards it.

It felt as if he had walked for hours, although with no way to measure the passage of time he couldn't be sure of his assessment. However long it had been since the chyvol attack, he was now becoming very hungry as well as thirsty. Checking his bearings again, he stopped and frowned. The dancing light seemed no closer now than when he'd first spotted it. *Is it moving away from me?*

He considered discarding the club, which seemed to be gaining weight as he went along, but then thought back to the earlier fight and decided against such a rash course of action. Without it, he would be defenceless and there was no way of knowing what other creatures might be roaming this land. He sat down for a rest, promising himself that he would stop for just a short while.

He came too with a jerk and experienced a moment of panic as he realised that he'd fallen asleep. Looking about, he discovered that he was still alone and relaxed as the thudding in his ears eased off. Having lost his bearings, he looked for the dancing light and let out an involuntary gasp. It had moved closer while he was sleeping! Bewildered, he tried to rationalise this odd phenomenon.

It made no sense at all. Then again, he was beyond The Veil, so it was safe to assume that the normal 'rules' of everyday life didn't hold here. Then it hit him. He cursed at the amount of effort he'd wasted, before laughing out loud at the simplicity of ending this task. On his feet once more, he began to walk away from the light source. After counting off 100 paces, he turned to look over his shoulder. Sure enough, the distance between him and the light had narrowed once more. He ran the next 100 paces then checked again. The light was even closer now and he thought he could see the vague outline of a shape inside it. His elation started to evaporate as the light continued to edge towards him and the shape began to coalesce into something more familiar.

Starting to panic, he took a step towards his pursuer and then realised the futility of this approach. Sooner or later he'd fall asleep again – if he didn't die of hunger first! Fighting to regain control, he sat down, cross-legged and with the club resting in his lap. He concentrated on slowing his breathing and waited.

With painful slowness, the light edged closer, allowing him to study the flickering shape at its heart. It was a curious mixture of relief and anxiety that swept over him when he recognised the Keeper.

Struggling to his feet, he bowed the merest fraction towards the other as the shape began to solidify. The Keeper looked at him with studied amusement. *'You will need to learn faster if you plan to survive the later tests,'* was his eventual comment. As before, the words echoed around his mind. Despite listening carefully, he was almost certain that no sound had broken the gentle sighing of the ever-present wind.

The Keeper laughed, drawing his concentration back towards the strange creature. The pressure increased inside his head, moments before the next words formed in his mind. *'There is no sound, fool! At least, not within the limited range available to your puny brain. Pay attention with your mind. I do not give the same advice twice.'*

He waited, but nothing else was forthcoming. 'I have a question if I may?' The strange creature before him rippled from silver-white to a threatening shade of dark red and he took a step backwards in alarm. The colour faded back towards its usual hue as the Keeper chuckled. *'I like you, mortal. You have courage. Ask then.'*

'I was wondering how many of these tests have been created and what proportion of Seekers is successful in completing all of them?'

To his surprise, the other seemed to ponder this question before the pressure, which he now recognised as signalling the imminent arrival of a new communication, began to build once more inside his head.

'That is for me to know and you to discover,' was the Keeper's blunt response. The creature began to flicker as a final comment arrived in his mind. *'Go now, Acolyte, before my mood changes. I hunger.'* The words continued to echo inside his head as the fading figure lifted its left arm to point towards the horizon.

He licked dry lips as he trudged in the indicated direction. It was some time before his weary legs brought him within visual range of The Rent. Exhausted, he forced his way through and sank into a deep sleep. His dreams were not pleasant. Death played a leading role in all of them that night. He cried out more than once.

7: SUSPICION

Wallace acknowledged the older man with a wave of his left arm, as he spoke rapidly out of the side of his mouth, 'Say nothing to Muller about our conversation. If what you say is true, I need to think about my arrangement with him. The Lord knows, I've done some bad things in my life, but I would never take a part in something so evil. At least when I kill it's as quick and clean as I can make it. I don't feel the need to bleed people to death in order to satisfy some crazy religious fervour. Don't worry - I won't let him harm you.' He started to walk towards Muller.

Madeleine said little in response, except to observe, 'You don't consider the murder of heretics to be driven by a crazy religious fervour?'

58

Wallace paused in mid-step, glancing her way, 'That's the sort of talk that could land you in serious trouble with the Church, young woman. Have a care!' He grinned so as to take the hard edge off his comment.

The pair walked the rest of the way in silence, neither commenting on the slackening force of the rain. Overhead, dirty grey clouds began to part, revealing small patches of pale blue sky. A weak shaft of sunlight fell from a sun still partly obscured by the clouds. It struck the front of the tavern.

Muller glanced at Wallace before addressing himself to Madeleine, 'I've found where they tethered their horses – it's in a small copse behind the tavern, but there's not much inside in the way of food or drink. I suppose we could always take some small weapons from the bodies, and you already have the crossbow…'

'And did you think to look for clothing?' asked Wallace. 'But why are we discussing this out here in the open? Let's retire to the tavern and see if we can't dry out a little whilst we make our plans. Mind, but I'm still keen to move on in case we should be visited by any more unwelcome surprises. Don't worry about the bodies – I'll drag them inside the tavern. We can leave them there to rot. The rain will soon wash away the blood.' He strode off to begin the gruesome task, as if dismissing his two companions as too weak to offer any useful assistance.'

As they headed for the tavern, Muller placed a hand on Madeleine's arm. She turned towards him and caught an unsettling look of appraisal in his eyes. Pulling the now sodden as well as tattered remnants of her shift together, she noticed how his eyes had dropped downwards before he looked back up and allowed them to settle on her face. 'Don't look so worried,' he said, trying to reassure her by patting her arm. 'I mean you no harm, my dear. After all, I'm an old man and probably too feeble to even entertain such desires as you appear to suspect me of harbouring. In truth, I was wondering if one of the soldiers might furnish you with a jerkin that would serve to both protect your modesty and offer some shelter from the elements.' He grinned, revealing misshapen and grey teeth. Madeleine said nothing in response, but hurried on towards the tavern door, which still stood open to the swirling gusts of rain. Muller frowned as he hurried to catch up, his thumb gently rubbing the smooth polished stone hidden in the palm of his right hand, as he muttered something in a strange tongue.

Inside the tavern, Madeleine stopped abruptly and put a hand to her mouth as her eyes, adjusting to the gloom, settled on the body of the late Florimond Dubois. A blade stood rigid in the remains of his left eye with just the hilt protruding from the sightless socket. Water pooled around her feet as the shift shed its excessive load of rainwater. Muller followed her into the room and paused to let his own eyes adjust. Dull light spilling in from the still open door helped to alleviate the gloom.

While she stood there staring, he calmly walked behind the crude bar and pulled out several jugs. He sniffed at each of them in turn, before selecting the first one and holding it up to his lips. Madeleine could hear him swallowing, as he slaked his thirst with deep gulps.

She jumped when he threw the now empty jug against the wall and belched twice. The old man wiped a sleeve across his mouth before saying, 'Do you want some? I'm afraid I've taken the best this poor establishment has to offer, but this one – he indicated a small jug sat in front of him – should be palatable.' He laughed, and then continued, 'I suppose we ought to save some for our brave warrior though?'

Madeleine heard a grunt from outside and turned back towards the door, just as Wallace dragged one of the dead men inside. He was pulling the body by the feet and the partially severed head of the corpse bounced up and down against the muddy earth. He saw her watching him and said, 'Best to keep these away from prying eyes. If I take them round the back, they might spook the horses. Although, I'm a little concerned that leaving them inside, near the fire, runs the risk that they'll soon start to smell,' he added as an afterthought.

She gave him a weak grin and said, 'Muller was helping himself to the wine. I'd take a drink now, if I were you, before he decides to finish it.'

The old man chortled as he eased her to one side and held out a large jug. The warrior shook his head, 'Not before I finish moving the other two. But make sure there's some left. And a bite of food wouldn't go amiss. Fighting always gives me an appetite!' He turned as if to return to the task outside but then stopped and turned back. 'Oh and Muller, leave the young woman alone. She's suffered enough for one day.'

A strained silence filled the room after he had left, until Muller found his voice; 'It's not me you need to worry about girl. *He's* taken the Pope's indulgence and is sworn to kill heretics. I've seen the mark on your neck that you're so desperate to hide and I know what it means. No, don't look at me like that. I have my own secrets, so I'll make you a deal. You act right towards me, and I'll hold my tongue. Let yours flap and there's every chance that we'll both end up dead.'

Madeleine could feel the heat rising on her cheeks. 'I thought he'd agreed to help you with your task. *If* he's so set on killing heretics, why do *you* still live?'

Muller held up a hand. 'I've persuaded him that I am not a heretic, or at least not in the sense that he is familiar with. And I've offered to make it worth his while to help me. What do you have to offer him, apart from your despoiled body?'

She struggled to hold her temper, aware that the old man was trying to rile her. Taking a deep breath, she replied, 'You forget that I saved his life. Whatever else he might be, Wallace has enough honour to feel he owes me something in return. So, don't threaten me old man. You hold your peace and I'll hold mine but, should you try to betray me, I won't hesitate to tell him what you *really* are!'

Muller's eyes narrowed and his complexion turned a nasty-looking shade of dark red as he spat out, 'Very well, but don't presume to mess with me young woman; you have no idea what you are getting yourself involved in. Now, perhaps you should look for some food, while I make sure there's something for our companion to drink?'

As he finished speaking, they could hear Wallace dragging away the second body from the front of the building. The bolt had snapped as it was scraped across the ground, and little more than a broken stump now protruded from the neck. Wallace heaved the corpse half on top of its comrade and then straightened up, panting from the exertion. 'Are you ... two still ...standing idle and ...talking?' he asked. 'I told you ... I'm hungry. Have some ... food ready ... when I bring in ... the last one.' He turned and stomped out once more into the light drizzle.

Muller shrugged before starting to hunt for more wine. 'There might be some food through there,' he suggested, pointing to a curtain that hung across an opening in the back wall and to the left of the bar.

Madeleine glared at the old man, before walking slowly towards the curtain. 'Who decided I would be the servant?' she muttered. Warming to her theme, she complained, 'Just because I'm a woman doesn't mean I have to do all the work!' Her shoulders tensed as she caught the sound of the old man's mocking snort of amusement. In frustration, she pushed the curtain out of her way and disappeared from Muller's sight.

Muller stared at the curtain for a few seconds, before he began to rub the strange stone that now nestled once more in his hand. His body became rigid and his eyes unfocused as he communed with his master, lips moving the merest fraction as he repeated his new instructions. Sensing the return of Wallace, he broke the link and resumed his search for more wine.

Wallace dragged in the third soldier, making a new greasy mess on the floor as visceral fluids, blood and rainwater mixed together. The Crusader kicked the tavern door shut before struggling to pull the corpse behind the bar, nudging the older man out of his way with a sharp elbow. Muller grunted, spilling wine from the upturned jug at his lips, then barked out a sharp laugh. 'Is there any point in hiding the body, when you've left a rather obvious trail?' he asked.

He stepped back as Wallace spun round, snatching the jug from his hand, and upending it over his mouth. The warrior took several huge gulps of the dark red liquid before slamming the empty vessel down onto the bar. 'I don't recall you offering to help!' he said. 'But there's still Dubois to take care of. I'll stand around and watch while you find somewhere to put him.'

Muller was about to respond when Madeleine reappeared from the back room with a platter of bread and cheese. 'It's not much,' she apologised, adding 'and the bread is a bit stale. But it's either this or nothing,' she finished, revealing almost perfectly aligned teeth as she grinned uncertainly at the two men.

Wallace nodded towards her and took the platter over to a table, near the hearth. Righting an upturned stool, he tore a large chunk from the loaf as he sat, then used the dagger from his belt to slice the cheese in half. He took a bite from the bread and followed with another from the cheese. The room was silent while he chewed noisily for a few moments. The peace ended in a spray of crumbs, as he demanded, 'Are you two going to stand there all day?'

Madeleine shook her head, explaining in a flat and tired voice that she had no appetite. Muller said nothing as he picked up another stool and joined Wallace at the table. He helped himself to some of the food and then turned towards Madeleine. 'Could you find us something to drink?'

The young woman glared at him and was about to express her obvious indignation when Wallace stood up and said, 'She's not our servant. *I'll* find us something.' With his back to the older man, he winked at Madeleine as he strode towards the counter, before continuing, 'Perhaps you'd prefer to search for some more suitable clothing?

It didn't take the two men long to finish their sparse meal or to wash it down with the contents of a small jug that Wallace managed to unearth from under a bench pushed up against the rear wall. The warrior smacked his lips, before wiping his mouth with the back of his hand. He sighed and then announced, 'It's time to leave. Molitor will send men here, to find out what Dubois is doing. We can't assume our luck will continue to hold, so we need to put some distance between this place and ourselves. Besides,' he turned to look straight at Muller, 'I have a delivery to make.'

Muller took the hint and stood up, saying, 'The sooner you complete your side of the bargain the sooner you will receive your reward.' Wallace chuckled as though he was unaware of the frown that slid across Madeleine's face as she emerged once more from the back room. She was wearing a pair of dirty breeches and a grubby shirt that was several sizes too big for her. A frayed piece of rope held it tied around her middle.

'Perhaps some rewards aren't worth the effort involved in earning them,' she suggested, hands planted firmly on her hips.

'Hold your tongue woman,' said Muller in a sharp tone. 'The warrior and I have an understanding and it's not your place to interfere!'

Wallace held up his left hand as he interrupted the rebuke. 'She's right to be cautious after what she's been through. But, as you say, we have an agreement and I think I'll make my own choices. However, she did help in the fight, and that earns her the right to speak her mind, even if I choose to ignore her advice.'

The old man looked stunned, and his face turned puce. He muttered something under his breath before saying, 'You're a fool to pay *any* attention to a mere woman!'

In a whirlwind of fury, Madeleine was upon the old man, her fingers clawing at his face. Her nails raked bloody lines down both of his cheeks and Wallace had to almost throw her sideways before he could prise her away from the object of her ire. Her temper subsided almost as quickly as it had

64

erupted, and all three stood panting, watching each other to see who would make the next move.

Wallace glared at both of them and said, 'Right. Let's stop this bickering. In case you didn't understand what I was saying just now, we need to leave here before we receive some unwelcome visitors. Now we can travel and hope that we can find safety by working together, or we can go our separate ways and take our chances. *But*, if we stay together, this squabbling has to stop! Now what is it to be because I'm about ready to set off for Muret?'

The other two said nothing at first. Muller appeared to be debating something with himself and Madeleine shuffled her feet whilst staring at the floor as though it held some sudden fascination. Wallace sighed, shrugged, gathered up his things and set off for the door leading out of the tavern. This simple act triggered a response from the young woman, who looked around for her crossbow and a small quiver of bolts. Locating them, she hurried to follow the warrior. Muller took a little longer to arrive at his decision. A careful observer might have noticed that he was juggling a small object in his right hand and, just before moving towards the door, that he gave a small affirmative nod of his head.

Wallace pulled at the door and then leapt back with a yelp. An arrowhead buried itself in the frame, mere inches from his left ear. He slammed the door shut and spoke rapidly, 'We've tarried too long. It must be more of Molitor's men! We're trapped in here.' He glanced towards Madeleine and said, 'I don't suppose there's a back way out?'

Before she could respond to Wallace's question, a voice from outside demanded, 'In the tavern. If you have Madeleine de LeDrede in there, and if you value your life, then let her come out.' Wallace shot a look at the young woman, his raised eyebrow asking for an explanation.

'It's alright,' she said. 'I recognise that voice. It's Gilles Picart, my father's best friend.' She raised her voice and shouted, 'Gilles, I'm safe. The two men in here rescued me from the soldiers. There's no need for more fighting.' She stepped towards the door and threw it open. 'Come in, all of you.'

Half a dozen men came into the tavern, led by a short fat man with a shock of red hair. Wallace noted that this was the archer who had just missed his head moments earlier, for the man carried a quiver on his shoulder. It was full of arrows with distinctive blood red shafts, identical to the one now protruding from the doorframe.

Picart looked slowly around the room. A frown creased his pudgy face as his eyes fell on Madeleine. 'Why do you wear those ridiculous clothes?' he asked.

Madeleine glanced towards Wallace, before taking a step closer to the new arrival. 'It's a long story, Gilles,' she said in a soft voice. 'I was having a hard time when these two blundered in here. There was a fight and, well, to keep it simple, my captors died, and we live.' She gestured towards the body of Dubois, which still lay where it had fallen. It was now stiff and surrounded by dark congealed blood. An unpleasant odour was beginning to spread out from the recently released body fluids.

Picart's eyes swept across the bodies of the two dead soldiers, and he took a step back, wrinkling his nose in disgust. He stared at the dagger hilt protruding from Dubois' left eye for a few seconds then tipped his head back a little as he addressed himself to Wallace. 'Your work?' he asked.

'Yes.'

Arriving at a decision, he turned towards his men and instructed them to post a look-out at each end of the village. 'Is there anything here to eat or drink?' he enquired. 'We've been riding since the dawn.'

Muller shook his head. 'I'm afraid we've just consumed what little there was. And now we must be on our way, for we have urgent business elsewhere.'

'Not yet you don't,' said Picart. I need to talk with the woman first. 'You might look like a traveller, but the tall warrior wears the garb of our oppressors. I would know what his intentions are before anyone leaves here.'

Madeleine coughed to attract his attention. 'The rude old man is Muller and the other one is called Wallace. It's true that he was once with the Papal forces, but he has come to some sort of arrangement with Muller and has just killed that one – she spat towards the corpse of Dubois – plus the others. So, I doubt he'll be re-joining our enemies any time soon. I'll vouch for him.'

Picart considered this but then surprised her by asking, 'And where is your father? He was supposed to be scouting ahead of us, yet I don't see him here.'

This time it was Wallace who spoke first. 'Madeleine's father is no longer with us. He was killed before Muller, and I arrived. You'll find his body in the building that has been fired at the end of the village. For her sake, we ought to give him a decent burial.'

Madeleine seemed to be on the point of adding to this explanation, but Muller beat her to it by saying, 'He died trying to protect this village. What's left of him is not pretty to look at, but the Crusader is right. It's the least we can do for him now.' As he finished speaking, his gaze fell on the dead man's daughter and the pair locked eyes for the briefest of moments.

Picart, meanwhile, continued to stare at Wallace, as if he couldn't quite believe what he'd been told. His lips began to move, but no sound came out of his mouth until, his words little more than a whisper, he asked, 'Did he die alone?'

Wallace sighed and let his shoulders slump. 'Yes, he died alone. We've told you, it's not a pretty sight. But why do you ask if he was alone?'

The other man went and sat on one of the benches before answering, 'LeDrede was supposed to be riding with another villager. I'm wondering what happened to him, that's all.'

'Well we haven't made a search of every hut or the surrounding area,' said Wallace. 'Perhaps his companion was killed and left nearby. Or maybe he was wounded but managed to escape. Perhaps Madeleine's father came here alone. Who knows? Does it matter now?'

'I suppose not.' Gilles Picart stood and began to issue orders to his remaining men. 'And I want him buried with all due respect,' he finished. One of his men cast him an odd look and seemed to be on the point of saying something. 'Now!' snapped Picart.

8: RETRIBUTION

In his agile mind, Unwin raced through a number of options. It was clear that his plan now lay in tatters. There was no-one else to whom he could deliver the all-important package. That, of course, was assuming that he could recover it before it fell into the hands of a senior member of The Black Blades. At the same time an almost overwhelming desire threatened to distort his judgement. He yearned to inflict vengeance on those responsible for the death of Father Fulbright. His main mission was supposed to be all that mattered in the grand scheme of things. Yet, in his heart, he knew that he could not put his personal feelings to one side.

Outside, a cat mewled at something unseen; its cry was met by an outburst of barking from several nearby dogs. Lemuel's head snapped up as the sound reached a crescendo of noise. A man's angry voice carried a promise of uncertain violence until it was cut off by the slamming of a window. Unwin was already moving towards the back of the church. At a point beyond the altar he stopped and knelt down. He paused to check for any indication of unwelcome company. Then, satisfied that he was alone in the building, he pressed on certain flagstones in a specific sequence. There was a short-lived grinding noise as some sort of mechanism triggered into life. Its efforts moved one particular flagstone downwards and then slid it under its neighbour. This small opening revealed the entrance to a tunnel. Unwin knew it came out towards the back of the graveyard. He ran back to the front of the church, retrieved his walking stick, and then returned to the tunnel entrance. After lowering himself down through the opening, it was a simple matter to push the flagstone back into its former position. Unwin used the candle to check the dark tunnel that stretched ahead into total darkness.

Taking great care to walk softly on the earth floor he set off for the other exit. He clutched his walking stick in his right hand. A few minutes later he paused beneath a small wooden trapdoor hidden behind a thick holly bush. He used wet fingers to snuff out his candle before placing it on the ground. Mounting a small flight of stone steps, he opened the trapdoor a fraction. The sound of its hinges, squealing in protest at being disturbed after several years of disuse, made him wince. He waited for his eyes to adjust to the gloom outside and his heart to return to a more normal rhythm.

As he wrestled his emotions under control, a new plan began to form in his mind. Although it was a gamble, he felt sure that his friend's killer would have remained somewhere close. They might be hoping to feed on the negative emotions released by whoever was the first to stumble across their night's gruesome work. Lemuel was pinning his own hopes on the idea that the killer would not have been expecting him to arrive at the church quite so soon. If they were resting somewhere nearby, then he might be able to surprise them!

At last, satisfied that the outside world offered no immediate threat, he pulled himself up out of the tunnel. After surveying his surroundings, he gently lowered the door back into its normal position. The bush obscured much of his view, but it couldn't prevent him from spotting the outline of two creatures. Both were crouched against the back wall of the church. One was dog-like. The other, although humanoid, appeared to ripple, as if it were fading in and out of sight.

Unwin grimaced. The larger of the two was almost certainly the being which had co-ordinated the earlier attack by the devil-dogs. That it was struggling to maintain a humanoid shape suggested two possibilities. The first was that it was about to cross the boundary between this and another reality. The second was that it was still weakened by the exertions of the fight. Unwin knew the two were not mutually exclusive. He dared to hope that the creature was struggling, and tiredness was the cause of its difficulties. It would be even better if *this* were the creature responsible for the death of his friend. If all went well, it was going to pay for that atrocity very soon.

Moving with great care, so as not to make any noise, he drew the pistol from his pocket. He paused to offer up a brief prayer to God, then started to work his way towards the church. As he crept closer, he took full advantage of the cover offered by the well-stocked graveyard. It was packed with gravestones, mature bushes and trees which crowded against each other. Sweat began to stand out on his forehead. Conflicting emotions urged him both to hurry and make sure of his revenge and to remain cautious and avoid alerting his intended prey.

Inching his way closer, Unwin could make out more detail of the humanoid creature. Its outline continued to flicker, although less so than when he'd first discovered its location. Several brief glimpses were enough for him to identify it as a sig'areth. He knew these hideous life-forms were native to a very different reality. On their home world they lived in a bizarre forest of flesh-eating semi-sentient trees and in an almost perpetual fog. In its natural form, a sig'areth resembled a glutinous mass. Unwin recalled being told that this would burn human skin on contact. These creatures would crawl from one tree to another, and the two species helped each other to survive. The sig'areth ambushed other creatures wandering about the forest floor. It would smother the life from them and then drag the carcass among the roots of its host. The tree would send out multiple whip-like 'shooters'. These were equipped with vicious thorns which it sank into the flesh of the dead creature. The tree used the thorns to inject the corpse with fluids which sped up the rotting process. Later, the tree roots would suck out nutrients from the decaying flesh. Meanwhile, the sig'areth gorged itself on the fruit of the tree. It would also shelter from larger predators by resting among its higher branches. Once the crop of fruit had been exhausted, it would move on to another tree. This would be the signal for its previous host to produce a fresh crop of fruit.

Unwin smiled to himself, savouring the image of what he was about to do. He rummaged in one of the inner pockets of his coat. Moment slater, his hands began to shake as he loaded the pistol with six unusual and very special bullets. Eager to exact his vengeance, he started to creep forward once more. As his concentration relaxed, he inadvertently stepped onto a dry twig. It cracked with a sound like a cannon-shot.

Two heads swung in his direction. The dog's ears shot erect as it sought the exact location of the sound. Realising that he'd lost the element of surprise; Unwin knelt on one knee and steadied the pistol as he lined it up on the chyvol. The devil-dog had located Unwin and was already charging straight at him. No doubt hoping to escape in the time its pet would buy for it, the sig'areth struggled to turn away. The chyvol's master clutched a package to its chest. It hugged its prize with the vicious claws that protruded from the end of many tiny arms. Unwin knew that he must deal with the dog first.

The priest squeezed the trigger and watched with satisfaction as the dog's chest exploded in a spray of red mist. It continued to race towards him for a few more seconds, too stupid to realise that it was already dead. At the same time, Unwin began to close in on his real target. The sig'areth was still struggling to move away towards the side of the church. As he moved close enough to see more detail, Unwin was surprised to note that its left shoulder was an ugly mass of raw tissue. A dark liquid was oozing from this fresh wound. Realisation brought a smile to his lips. 'The priest in the church threw holy water on you!' he said out loud.

The creature stopped and glared at him, its ugly and alien face twisted in pain. 'It didn't save that sanctimonious old fool - we still took his miserable life.' Its voice was soft and sibilant. Even as it spoke, its shape began to flicker faster, and Unwin knew that it was preparing for a shift to some other reality. He would have preferred to have sufficient time to interrogate the damned thing, but he wasn't prepared to let it escape.

When he pointed his pistol towards it, the creature started to whine. Unwin placed the first bullet into the chest of the revolting creature. For a second or two, nothing happened, and the whining changed to a grating laugh, until a sudden increase in pitch changed it into an agonised scream. Unwin watched in fascination as the wound site began to writhe. Acrid smoke started to pour from the expanding wound. The creature's face now wore a look of horror as it realised what was happening. 'The bullet contains sodium?' it asked.

'Yes,' replied Unwin. 'It contained pure sodium. As it spreads through your system, you'll burn first and then dissolve. Have another shot,' he added, firing a second bullet into the creature's stomach and a third into its head. As the creature slumped to the floor, its outline began to fade, and Unwin caught a brief glimpse of its true form. He edged around the steaming mess of the dying creature and stooped to retrieve his precious package from the floor. He shuddered in distaste as his fingers closed on the saliva-covered envelope. 'Damned dog!' he muttered to himself, wiping his fingers on the side of his coat. Then he pocketed his pistol and ran for the holly bush, retrieved his walking stick, and set off for the rear gate of the graveyard. Behind him, he could hear a growing chorus of voices as local residents, worried by the gunfire, dared each other to investigate. Lemuel Unwin had no desire to answer their questions. Nor was he willing to explain the recent events that had taken place in and outside of the church.

Once clear of the graveyard, he turned up his collar and walked slowly away. He paused to bid 'good evening' to a man running towards the church. Then, as the moon disappeared behind a cloud, Father Unwin also vanished from sight.

Sergeant Mindelen was an impatient man by nature. He fidgeted and swore under his breath when Whiston suggested that there must be a key to the room somewhere. Mindelen would have preferred to break the door down.

Grey suggested that someone search the corpse for a key. Mindelen began to mutter something under his breath but stopped when the doctor offered to carry out the grisly task. Dr Samson was soon back from the lounge. In his left hand he now held a large bunch of keys.

The whole party stood on the landing, watching as the sergeant tried one key after another. He became more flustered with each failure. There were just two remaining when he found the right one and eased open the door to the priest's room. If he'd expected to find the man hiding there, perhaps covered in blood, he was disappointed. The room looked clean and tidy, the curtains were drawn and there was no sign of occupation save a small bundle of untidy clothes on the floor in one corner.

'It looks like he's gone and done a runner, then,' said Greene. 'Unwin is obviously the killer!'

'Not so,' said Whiston. He ignored the glare this observation drew from his irritated colleague. 'It could be just a coincidence.'

Dr Samson cleared his throat, attracting everyone's attention. 'Whoever the killer is, we are looking for a deranged and dangerous person.' This prompted some muttering. Raising his voice, the doctor continued, 'Sergeant, I suggest that you report back to your commander and request more help. Before this murderer strikes again.'

'Now sir, there's no call for you to be telling me 'ow to do my work. I didn't get these stripes for nothing, you know. I was just about to send young Whiston 'ere back to the station to ask for help. Don't you worry, sir, we'll soon catch the priest and get the truth out of 'im.' He turned towards the younger policeman and barked, 'You still 'ere Whiston? What're you waiting for, lad? Didn't you 'ear what I just told the good doctor?'

Whiston gave the doctor a thoughtful look, then turned and headed for the front door. 'On my way, sergeant,' he called over his shoulder, as he reached for the handle. As he left the building and set off on his task, he failed to notice a tall figure standing motionless in the shadows of a nearby alleyway.

Unwin followed a leisurely route towards Paddington railway station. He was anxious to leave London and head west. Yet caution forced him to act in an inconspicuous manner. *It wouldn't do for someone to remark upon my appearance and remember me later if questioned,* he reminded himself. It wasn't so much the police that he was concerned about. There had been witnesses to the desperate fight with the dogs in the street near to the church. However, he doubted anyone had seen him actually enter or leave that particular building. No, he was more concerned about possible Blade agents trying to relocate him. If they thought anyone had seen him, they would be none too gentle with the witness. As he made his way, he scanned his surroundings for any sign of recognition or of potential trouble.

Closing in on his objective, he began to plan his next move in his head. The sig'areth had inadvertently told him that there had been more than one of them involved in the murder of Artie. Apart from this he had no other clue as to the identity of its accomplice or accomplices. That left him with no option other than to return to his original plan, the assassination of one of *The Seven*. His face was grim as he strode into the railway station. Several other passengers decided to make haste in removing themselves from his path.

Edward Whiston liked his job as a policeman, although he wasn't too keen on his sergeant. Joseph Mindelen was a decent enough sort of fellow but altogether too pompous. And, if the truth were to be told, he didn't appear to be all that clever. The sergeant loved to pull rank on his young partner. He never missed an opportunity to try to impress others with his detection skills. *But we both know that I'm the clever one, don't we sergeant?* the young man told himself. He'd joined the police full of good intentions and with high hopes of rapid progress through the ranks. Yet he found himself working with a man of limited intellect. Worse, the pair of them were at the beck and call of an incompetent old man.

He was still pondering on how much longer he could bear to play the junior role when he arrived at his station. Once inside, he asked to see the Inspector but was told to wait for a few minutes. Sat outside the Inspector's cramped office, Whiston tried to arrange his thoughts. The old man was a stickler for brevity and well known for instructing his men in the virtue of 'keeping to the facts'.

Whiston rose to his feet as the office door began to open and barely paused to look at the young woman who came out. She was busy pulling a shawl tighter around her slender shoulders and seemed surprised to see the young policeman. Wiping the back of her hand across tear-spattered cheeks, she hurried on her way. As she disappeared around a corner, Whiston took a deep breath and walked into the Inspector's lair. He closed the door behind him and then began to make his report.

9: INITIATION

Blinding sunlight hurt his eyes as he threw up a shielding arm. Blistering heat threatened to suck the air from his lungs and sweat soaked his armpits. *I'm in Hell*, he thought. A dry, rasping laugh slipped between his lips as he considered the possibility that Hell might be a more welcome prospect.

Sagana had warned him that this time his task would be much harder. 'The time for games is finished,' he'd said, before refusing to elaborate on what this meant. Then, just before he drank the travel potion, Sagana had said, 'This third test will demonstrate whether or not you are truly committed to this path. Do not let me down, for failure will have consequences beyond the worst your imagination can conjure.' His mentor had then turned away and left him alone in the Great Chamber.

Struggling to orient himself, he steeled his resolve and began to search for the Tree of Life. Somewhere, out in that vast desert, the tree held its precious fruit. One bite of the golden flesh would equip him with tremendous power, albeit for a brief period. He would need this power to complete the test and advance to the rank of an apprentice in the old faith. The strange pebble in his left hand would grow colder as his heading came closer to the direction leading to the tree. His only other equipment was a short length of leather.

He turned towards his right and felt the pebble grow hotter. *Wrong way!* Turning the other way, he completed almost a half-circle before the direction finder ceased to cool and began to heat up again. He had his heading.

As he walked, the blazing sun crept with agonising slowness away to his right, although it didn't appear to be any lower in the sky. He stopped to rest and pondered this strange observation. It felt as though he had been walking for several hours, in which case this realm must be much larger than his native home. *Or maybe the heat had rendered his sense of time defective, and he'd been walking for just a few minutes.* This latter explanation sent a shiver of alarm down his damp and clammy back. If it were true, then he was tiring much too quick, for the tree was still beyond the horizon. Or maybe the sun here didn't behave like the one back home? Whatever the explanation, he knew he had to resume his journey before the exhausting heat overcame his determination.

Walking once more, he realised that he had come across no other sign of life. There had been no sound save for his own footsteps, not even the cry of a bird. The air was dead calm without any hint of a breeze and the landscape was a uniform sheet of sand, unbroken by even a single small hill or blade of grass. There was nothing at all to see or to use as a reference point.

He was cursing his lack of a water-skin when he found himself falling forwards. As the ground rushed up to meet him, he instinctively put out his arms, palms down. Although this broke his fall and saved his face from smashing into the hard ground, he cried out as searing heat began to burn the skin from his palms. Scrambling to his feet, he looked down at the root which had snagged his unwary feet. It took a few moments to realise the significance of what he was looking at.

He lifted his gaze towards the horizon, half afraid of what he might see. A sigh marked the point at which he first caught sight of a tiny tree in the distance. He wasn't sure if it was his imagination or if the sunlight really was reflecting sparks of iridescence from something in the branches.

Brushing dust from his clothing, he inspected his hands. The palms were scorched a bright shade of red and blood trickled from a few minor cuts. He shrugged and resumed his trek. The injuries weren't serious, and the tree fruit would help to make them irrelevant.

It took longer than he'd expected to reach the tree. Now, as he stood under the shade of its leafy and fruit-laden branches, he could see that it was huge. He estimated that four men couldn't link hands around its trunk. Worse, the lowest branches bearing fruit were the height of three men and more above his head.

He looked for a way to climb the tree but soon dismissed this as an option. The bottom branches were above his head height, and he didn't trust them to support his weight, even if he could have pulled himself up onto one of them. The smooth bark that covered the tree offered no grip to a would-be climber. In frustration, he sat down to contemplate how he was going to gain access to the inviting golden fruit.

The answer came to him almost immediately. Grinning, he fashioned a crude sling from the leather and fished the direction pebble from his belt purse. Stepping back to the edge of the shaded area, he took careful aim and fired the pebble towards a clump of the fruit.

It soared upwards, hit a small branch, and plummeted back. He repeated this exercise several times, growing more uncertain with each failure. The pebble had an almost uncanny ability to either bounce off a small branch or lose impetus among a clump of the large dark blue leaves. After yet another failure, he decided to change tactic and stepped out into the blazing sunshine. With his left hand shading his eyes, he made another attempt to dislodge some of the fruit.

Excitement gripped him when this latest effort succeeded in smashing a small branch from one of the main boughs. As it fell, he noted a thick cluster of leaves wrapped around several specimens of the golden fruit. He gathered up the pebble, returned both it and the thong to his purse, and then bent to retrieve his prize.

He stripped away the leaves, discarding them at random and then held up two of the fruit. Each was the size of a large apple and covered with a tough golden skin that sprouted a multitude of small and very fine short hairs. The smaller of the two was oozing a viscous liquid from a bruise where it had impacted the ground. He sat down with his back against the tree trunk and gently placed the damaged fruit to one side. Then he turned his attention to the other fruit. A cursory inspection revealed no blemish, so he raised it to his mouth and bit into the pulpy flesh.

The bitter tang reminded him of sour beer and the skin was quite tough to chew. Nevertheless, he forced himself to eat the whole of the fruit, save for the nut at its core, and then licked the last of the sticky juice from his lips.

A few moments later a terrible cramp seized his stomach, and he groaned in pain. His brow felt as if it had been encased in a shrinking steel band and vision started to blur. Numbness spread from the tips of his fingers and toes. Alarmed, he tried to stand, but found himself sinking into a forbidding darkness.

There was no way of working out how much time had passed when he regained an awareness of his surroundings. He lay slumped against the trunk of the same tree and was still in its cool shade. A sharp line marked the boundary of this sanctuary; beyond the sun beat down with the same ferocity as before he'd fallen asleep.

He rose gingerly and was surprised to find that he felt refreshed. There was something unpleasant about the dreams fading from his memory, but the more he tried to recall them the quicker they evaporated. *'Now what?'* he said to the empty landscape.

'Now we come to the difficult part,' said a familiar voice inside his head.

He spun round, seeking the Keeper, but could see no evidence of the other's presence. Without understanding how, he sensed amusement from that being. Stiffening his resolve, he asked the obvious question.

The answer sent shock racing through his system. 'But that's unfair!' he protested, the ill-judged words exploding from him.

'This is not about what is or isn't fair in your opinion. When you chose to follow this path, you also agreed to do as we instruct. Of course, if you no longer seek enlightenment, I can arrange a different ending for you.' The Keeper seemed to be growing more solid, larger, and angry red flashes streaked along its outline.

Fighting down panic, he struggled to order his thoughts. 'No. I mean yes. I still choose to follow the sacred path. But I don't understand why this is necessary.'

'Enlightenment will come though action. You might also consider that night is approaching in this realm, and you cannot find the Rent in the darkness, or before you have completed your task. You don't want to be here at night. That's when the denizens of this world feed.'

He was too busy considering the implications of this stark message to note the Keeper's departure. With a heavy heart, he set off into the sunlight, heading for a small cloud on the distant horizon. As he walked, his mind tried to gauge how long it would be before the light began to fade. Shielding his eyes, he found that the glowing orb had already gone past the high point of the sky and had begun its descent towards evening. He cursed and then quickened his pace, relieved to feel the pebble becoming colder in his hand. The small cloud was beginning to resolve itself into more detail. Ahead lay a clump of trees.

He stopped to wipe sweat from his face with the back of a hand. The tall trees grew in a thick clump, the sole vegetation in a bleak land. The long and thin leaves were an odd shade of dull green. They undulated gently in an unfelt breeze. Some sort of instinct made him nervous, and his right hand gripped the thong even tighter. Keeping one eye on the trees, he tried to fasten one end of the thong around the direction pebble, hoping to fashion some sort of weapon.

A rasping call, overhead, made him look up. A large bird was gliding towards the trees, its four wings stretched out as it slowed its descent. It was the first creature he'd seen in this realm, and he wondered where it had come from and if it was alone. It alighted on a thick branch, half-hidden by the mass of leaves and ceased its cries. The peace which followed lasted no more than a few seconds.

In an explosion of movement, the bird tried to take flight, flapping its wings and cawing for all it was worth. It struggled to rise, held back by the leaves and he watched in fascination as feathers and bits of flesh began to fall from the branch. The cries became more frantic as the leaves wrapped their deadly embrace around the luckless creature. The piteous cries gave way to an eerie silence.

He struggled to make sense of what he'd witnessed and stepped back when a small shower of bones and feathers fell from the tree. There was no sign of the bird. *How am I supposed to find the clearing?*

Walking with care around the edge of the clump, he spotted a small gap between two large trees. It looked wide enough to provide him with a safe passage. Mindful of the fate of the strange bird, he inched forward, taking care not to touch any of the low-hanging branches or leaves. A few minutes later, he heaved a sigh and stood on the edge of a small clearing.

A small pond occupied the exact centre of this clearing. His attention, however, was drawn to the woman who sat by the pond, trailing her left hand through the inviting water. Small ripples crawled across the surface of the water as she looked up and smiled at him. Long blonde hair fell to her naked shoulders and a surprisingly low-cut blue dress revealed heaving and well-shaped breasts. She was stunning to look at, with perfect white teeth and striking blue eyes. A small tongue wet her lips before she said, 'A saviour at last. Please come and rest awhile before you free me from this accursed place.' Her voice was warm and husky, and he felt the first stirrings of lust in his groin as he walked towards her.

His tongue felt too big, and his breathing had become shallow. Here was a woman of rare beauty and she was smiling again. As he closed the gap between them, on unsteady legs, the woman patted the ground at her side. 'Please, sit beside me. Tell me your name and then you may kiss me.'

He found himself sinking down beside this extraordinary woman, even as a small alarm bell began to ring at the back of his mind. The woman dipped her fingers deeper in the water and trailed them across his forehead. Her touch was cool, and the droplets soothed his fevered brow. He felt himself relaxing, eager to obey her every command.

'Your name?' she prompted, leaning forward so that he found himself staring at her magnificent cleavage. Lust threatened to overwhelm him. With a mighty effort of will, he cleared his thoughts and forced himself to concentrate on her words. 'I knew you would come. I've been so lonely here. I dare not leave the safety of the trees, for here there is water, and the night predators fear to come close. I waited for...'

He was no longer listening but thinking of his last conversation with the Keeper. Clutching the sling, he leant forward to kiss the most alluring woman he'd ever met. As the gap between their lips narrowed, he pulled her towards him, his arms circling hers as both hands met behind her back.

A flicker of triumph lit up her eyes.

10: A NARROW ESCAPE

Wallace led with Muller bringing up the rear. Picart stood in the tavern doorway and watched them depart. 'The old man's no horseman!' he called over his shoulder and faint laughter drifted out from behind him. 'But the other one ...' His voice tailed off as his thoughts turned inwards and he wondered why Wallace believed that changing his clothes would disguise his obvious status as a warrior. The give-away clothing was stuffed into a bag hanging from the saddle of his destrier - and that horse alone marked him out as an accomplished fighter. He bit his lower lip as his thoughts returned to Madeleine. Despite his protests, she had insisted on travelling with Wallace. Picart sensed that the tall warrior bore no ill will towards her, but he harboured grave misgivings about the older man. His sharp eyes hadn't missed the furtive glances Muller had cast her way when he thought she wasn't watching him. His ruminations were interrupted by a question from one of his men.

Wallace set a good pace as the trio of unlikely allies headed away from the village and westwards towards Murat. There was little conversation as each rider surrendered to their own thoughts. After an hour or so, Wallace brought them to a stop in a wooded hollow. 'We'll rest here for a few moments whilst I consider Picart's map,' he said, sliding from the back of his mount as he spoke. Madeleine accepted his offer to help her down and the corners of her mouth turned up a little when he ignored the old man, leaving the latter to half dismount and half fall from his own horse.

Muller glared at the woman before shrugging and then loosening the ties on the saddlebag which dangled from his

82

saddle. He pulled out a large lump of cheese and a few small apples, wandered over to sit with his back to a large oak tree and began to eat. Wallace looked up from the crudely drawn map in his left hand in time to catch Madeleine's frown and pursed lips, and he swung in the direction of her stare. 'Perhaps your companions are also feeling a little hungry?' he asked, walking towards Muller with his left hand on the pommel of the sword sitting in the scabbard on his right hip.

The old man looked up and grinned. 'Nobody said anything about having to share our meagre provisions,' he replied. His eyes narrowed as his gaze took in the location of Wallace's left hand. Lowering his voice to a whisper, he added, 'You need me to lead you to my master. We don't need the woman.'

Wallace stopped a few paces in front of the tree. 'I don't know what the problem is between you two, and I don't much care. But you will accept her as a companion until I say otherwise. She helped both of us back in the village and we owe her a debt of honour,' he said.

Muller raised an eyebrow and started to speak, but Wallace cut him off. 'You may well be surprised, but I can assure you that I am familiar with the concept of honour. The least we can do is see her safely to Murat. After that, it depends on what I find there!' The warrior turned about on his heel and started to walk back toward his horse. 'Are you hungry?' he asked Madeleine.

'No,' she said, and then inclined her head a fraction towards the old man before continuing in a lower voice, 'but I don't trust him. He could be leading you into a trap.' Wallace stared at her, saying nothing for so long that she began to wonder if he'd heard her warning.

She was about to repeat her words when he gave a sad smile and shook his head. 'I share your suspicion,' he said, 'but I need to play this game out to its conclusion. After what happened back in the tavern, I can't return to my former masters!' He paused, as if he wanted to say more, before raising his voice so that Muller could hear him. 'Mount up, we ride again. The light will fade soon, and we don't want to be caught out in the open.'

They spent the evening hidden in a small wood and tried their best to shelter from the incessant drizzle that began not long after sunset. Strong gusts of rain from were still making life unpleasant when the sun broke through the morning cloud cover. Hungry and tired, the small group remounted and set off once more towards Murat.

By mid-morning, the strong sunshine had dried their clothes and they were making good progress. Wallace insisted they skirt the first few hamlets and a solitary farm but, as noon approached, he gave in to Madeleine's pleas and agreed that they would seek food at the next dwelling they encountered.

This turned out to be a small village, nestled in a small dry valley. Leaving his two companions to hide in a clearing inside a thicket of large bushes, Wallace rode on ahead and entered the village from its eastern end. There were a few people about and all of them openly stared at the lone rider. He couldn't read their faces and looked about him before dismounting, keeping the reins in his right hand.

From out of the shadows stepped a thick-set man with huge upper arm muscles, large hands, and a straggling moustache. He wiped dirty hands on a tattered apron and stopped beyond sword reach of Wallace. Sweat had traced little paths through the dirt on his face. 'What do you want?' he asked before spitting on the ground between them.

Wallace stared back at the man for a few moments, noting how several more men were inching towards him from all sides. 'I seek nothing more than food and drink for myself, a few companions, and our horses. They have money to pay. And I have some advice for you. Troops loyal to the Holy Church are heading this way. They're killing and burning anyone they suspect of heresy, and they're not too bothered about finding proof. If I were you,' and he turned to glare at a man, armed with a scythe, who had closed almost to within striking distance of his back, 'I'd think about hiding your women and children.' As he spoke, he let go of the reins and placed his left hand on the hilt of his sword.

The muscular man held up a hand and his fellow villagers stepped back, giving Wallace more room. 'How do we know you're not one of them?'

Wallace shrugged and let his sword hand fall down by his side. 'Would I ride in here alone to warn you if I were?' The question hung in the air until the other man arrived at his decision.

'I'm Brinvilliers, the blacksmith. We don't like strangers around here, but we've heard about the purge of the Cathars. There's water and some bread for coin but you're not welcome to stay. If the Pope's men come, we'll be ready for them.'

Wallace nodded his agreement to the proposal whilst wondering what this handful of villagers thought they could achieve against Molitor and his men. He refrained from voicing these thoughts but produced several small coins from his wallet. Holding them out in the palm of his right hand, he said, 'Will this be enough?'

Brinvilliers glanced at the coins and looked up at Wallace. 'They'll suffice. We can give you a couple of water skins and two loaves of bread. Your horses can use the trough at the other end of the village.' He paused before adding, 'On your way through.'

'Agreed.' It was Wallace's turn to pause. 'There are more than thirty men coming your way. Some are mercenaries and they'll give no quarter. It's your choice, of course, but you might want to consider hiding yourselves with your loved ones. Trust me, you can't bargain with these men.'

Brinvilliers gave nothing away in his face. 'Thanks for the advice but it's not your village. This is all we have and we're not going to be forced into hiding, like little children afraid of the dark.' Wallace shrugged and turned to re-mount his horse.

He entered the thicket to find his two companions sat as far apart as they could be without leaving the clearing. Muller's face bore an angry welt across the right cheek, and he was muttering to himself. Without alighting, Wallace said, 'I've negotiated water for the horses and purchased some basic provisions for the three of us. But the villagers are suspicious of outsiders, and we can't rest there. You must do as I say, or I fear they may attack us.' He paused to look at Muller, then continued, 'I tried to warn them about Molitor, but they seem determined to stand and fight if he chooses to attack their village. That may buy us some more time, although it's also possible that they'll tell him about us and hope to divert his attention.'

He unslung one of the water skins from his horse and threw it towards Madeleine. 'Drink sparingly and share it with the old man.' He urged his horse nearer to Muller and leant forwards in his saddle. 'What happened to your face?'

'Muller glanced towards the woman, who was pretending not to be listening, and looked up at the warrior. 'I was restless and wanted to take a look around. I walked into a low-hanging branch.' He locked eyes with Wallace, daring him to push the matter further. The horseman returned the stare without blinking until Muller gave up and looked down at the ground.

Madeleine chose that moment to throw the water-skin towards the old man and he used the distraction to avoid looking at Wallace for a few more moments. The warrior said nothing more about the old man's face, choosing to ignore the hand-shaped impression that was still outlined on his cheek. He took one of the loaves from his saddlebag and broke it into three more or less equal parts. 'Here, take one of these,' he said, holding out a portion in each hand.

'Why does she get an equal share?' complained Muller in a sullen tone.

'Because *I* say so,' said Wallace. 'Or would you like another bruise to match the one on your cheek?' he added, with a malicious gleam in his eyes.

'It's just that she's smaller than either of us and I'm used to better fare,' said Muller. 'How can I be expected to survive on this pittance?'

Wallace shook his head. 'Without her crossbow, hunger would be the least of your worries right now. That's assuming you were still alive to have any.' He raised his voice and said, 'Mount up. We can eat as we ride. The longer we delay here the more likely we are to meet up with Molitor and his men.' Without bothering to check if they had complied with his instruction, he turned his horse towards the clearing's exit.

Madeleine glared at Muller and then climbed up onto her horse. The old man was still chewing on a mouthful of bread as she hissed, 'touch me again and you're a dead man!'

The old man spluttered, spraying out a mouthful of crumbs as he struggled to swallow the bread. Following her out of the clearing he whispered, 'He won't always be around to protect you.' Madeleine kicked her heels into her horse's ribs and cantered forward to catch up with Wallace. Behind her, the old man chuckled, contemplating the fate he had planned for both of his erstwhile companions. There would be blood. A lot of blood!

The three rode towards the village in silence. As they made their way to a large stone trough, at the western end of the village, a few men favoured them with surly looks and Wallace quietly told Muller and Madeleine that they would water their horses one at a time. 'Keep your eyes and ears open, ready for any sudden attack,' he said in a low voice.

Nothing untoward happened though and when Wallace, the last to finish, took one final look back at the small settlement he was surprised to find the street was deserted. Then his sharp eyes detected movement on the valley slope, back towards the thicket where their small group had recently sheltered. His experience and instinct warned him that a sizeable group of riders was coming their way. 'Ride,' he shouted, 'Horsemen heading this way.' His two companions needed no further encouragement.

It wasn't long before Muller's horse began to drop behind the other two. As the gap widened, the old man called out for the others to wait. Wallace reined his horse to one side and turned to look back. 'I don't suppose we can out-run them. Of course, it may not be Molitor and his men. Even so, we can't take that risk.'

'Either way, they might stop in the village,' suggested Madeleine as Muller's horse trotted alongside. Both men turned to stare at her.

'If it is Molitor, he'll recognise Wallace from the description provided by the villagers. They'll be glad to give him a reason to leave them alone,' said Muller.

'That's assuming he's found the village where we met,' pointed out the young woman.

'And that he knows it was me who killed Dubois,' added Wallace.

'But how could …?' said Madeleine. She put a hand to her mouth as comprehension arrived. 'Oh, that would mean that Picart and his men …,' she tailed off again.

'We could sit here all day discussing what might be. Let's get moving,' suggested Wallace. He turned towards Muller and said, 'How far is it to where we meet your master?'

11: A CHANCE ENCOUNTER

Alice Glanville wondered why she'd bothered going to the police station. In her heart, she'd known they wouldn't take her seriously. The Inspector had half-listened to her story, eyed her up and down and smirked when he asked her what she did for a living. Ignoring the slight warmth in her cheeks, she'd described herself as a struggling actress. He'd raised an eyebrow and made a great show of writing a single word against her name. The leer on his face made it abundantly clear what he thought she really was. The three words looked lonely on such a large sheet of paper, but they were all the man had bothered to record. As he wrote, she observed him from under her lowered eyelashes. His thinning grey hair looked almost comical when paired with the enormous mutton-chop whiskers. While he wrote, the podgy forefinger of his left hand tried to ease the shabby collar of his tunic away from his throat. All this achieve was to reveal an angry red blotch on the flaccid skin.

He blotted the word and replaced the pen in its holder, next to a large bottle of ink. Then, with much huffing and puffing, he struggled to his feet and offered to see her out. Embarrassed, she'd been in such a hurry to get away that she'd almost missed the young policeman, waiting to see his commanding officer. He too paid her little attention. But even though she'd been crying, she'd recognised the young officer as a regular visitor to one of her co-workers. *Perhaps he would be more willing to listen to her tale?*

Absorbed in her thoughts as she hurried away from the police station, Alice was oblivious to the tall figure who followed her. Although not especially interested in this woman, some instinct told it that it might be useful to find out where she lived. It was always a good idea to know where to find a potential source of fresh meat. More important, her stalker had noted the look of recognition on her face as she'd passed the young policeman. The possibility of some sort of link between the two made her even more interesting. She might be useful if the police began to ask awkward questions about recent events.

Whiston concluded his report, closed his notebook, and then waited for Inspector Johnson to react. His senior officer sat back in his chair. With great deliberation he opened a small drawer in his desk. Taking out a pipe and a pouch of tobacco, he carefully filled the bowl. Leaning forward, he tapped down the contents and set them alight with an old-fashioned flint. Puffing furiously on the stem clenched between his teeth, he said nothing. Soon, a cloud of noxious fumes had half-filled his small office.

The young policeman waited with growing impatience. He understood that this was Johnson's way of reinforcing his superior rank but struggled to keep his temper in check. The older man was regarded as a dithering old fool by his men. He commanded little respect when out of earshot.

At last, the smoker broke the silence. 'So Sergeant Mindelen has identified the culprit but you, a less experienced man, have some doubts?' His tone was dripping with sarcasm.

'With respect, sir,' said Whiston, 'I think it odd that a priest of all people would murder his landlady in cold blood and in such a horrible way. The doctor was certain that the killer must be deranged. Wouldn't people have noticed a priest who was acting in an odd manner?

Johnson stared up at him through watery washed-out grey eyes. As he spoke, he waved the pipe for emphasis. 'When you're older and more experienced, you'll learn that some men can be very clever at concealing their insanity. Madness lends them a special kind of cunning. I'm inclined to trust the judgement of your sergeant on this one. Take Blunt and Hallam with you and return to Mindelen.' Johnson resumed his slow and deliberate writing on the paper in front of him. Chewing his lip as he struggled to form the gothic script, he waved a hand in dismissal without bothering to lift his gaze.

Whiston hesitated for a few moments before coughing. 'I don't think you need the k in 'lady of the night' sir.

Johnson raised his eyes from the desk and stared with obvious distaste at the impertinent young man. Ignoring the advice, he snapped, 'Why are you still here, Whiston? I thought I gave you a very clear order?'

'You did sir, but my shift ends in another 15 minutes. I could pass on your instructions to my colleagues though, sir.'

Johnson let out a heavy sigh. 'Very well, go and do that. Now do you have anything else with which to waste my valuable time?'

As Whiston saluted and then turned to leave the room, the old man glared at his back. Once the door was closed, he scanned the sheet of writing and then rummaged in his desk drawer for a wedge rubber. With another sigh, he began to remove the offending letter k. He turned things over in his mind and reached a decision. His new friend might be interested to learn of Whiston's suspicions.

Stimulated by this thought, he pushed the sheet to one side and began to write on a new one. A few minutes later he called Isaac into his room. Still seated at his desk, he handed the clerk a sealed envelope. Isaac left with strict instructions to deliver it to a nearby address.

Once outside the Inspector's office, the clerk glanced at the envelope. He mouthed the name of its intended recipient before committing it to memory. Then he set off for the address he'd been given.

Whiston delivered the Inspector's instructions to Hallam, checked for messages, and finished his shift. He exchanged pleasantries with a few colleagues and then walked to his lodgings at a brisk pace. His treatment at the hands of the Inspector had annoyed him far more than the old man's crass arrogance normally did. He wasn't sure why. At the back of his mind he pondered his reaction. Perhaps it was the man's refusal to even consider the possibility that Mindelen might be wrong? That the missing Father Unwin was not the killer of the recently deceased Mrs. Crawford?

Edward Whiston continued to mull things over as he consumed a meagre supper of bread and bacon. He ate alone in his lodging room, oblivious to the faded and peeling wallpaper, the wind leaking through the rotting window frame and the threadbare carpet by his bed. The more he thought about it, the more agitated he became about the iniquity of his having to follow orders from Mindelen and Johnson. After pacing up and down for a few minutes he decided to visit Rose. She could always be relied upon to cheer him up and, since they'd started walking out, her services no longer came at the usual price.

He changed into his evening clothes and set off for the brothel, whistling a popular tune. The air was muggy with a fine drizzle and, as he pulled up his collar, he wondered whether the night would bring fog.

Half an hour later Whiston carefully surveyed the street. He was standing opposite the house of ill repute. The shabby building was well known in the area, and he didn't care to be seen going into it. Associating with a prostitute would do little to enhance his already slim chances of promotion.

Satisfied there was no-one he knew or recognised in the immediate vicinity, he crossed the road and was soon climbing the three flights of stairs to the floor where Rose worked. He'd nodded to Mistress Lydia and her two 'boys', neither of whom had challenged him. After all, he was a regular client.

At the top of the stairs, he paused to gather his thoughts and then walked the short distance to the door of her room. He tapped on the old wood and, without waiting for an invitation, turned the handle and walked into her room.

Mr Black observed Whiston from the safety of the shadows. His interrogation of the young woman from the police station had been as swift as it was brutal. Her information had led him to reconsider his plans. Black picked a piece of meat from his teeth. His upper lip curled in wry amusement at the good fortune that linked her and his next target.

With his eyes closed, he let his mind roam the local area, seeking a sleeper. He rejected the first two before settling on a small child. It was an easy matter to insinuate himself into the little boy's dreams and steer them towards a horrific monster. The child stirred and cried out, but there was no-one to help the frightened infant. Father was away on 'business', casing a local property from which he planned to liberate certain valuables. Mother was walking the streets in the hope of turning a quick trick that could be later exchanged for something in a bottle, something to ease her pain.

In the dream world of the innocent child, a grotesque shape raced across the ground, its eight limbs ending in razor sharp talons. Saliva dripped from a large fang-filled mouth and stubby horns protruded from its cheeks. The creature caught the dreamer and tore his sanity to shreds. Gorging itself on the violent emotions, it forced its way through the barrier between worlds. Moments later, a lizard-like shadow slid across the bedroom floor and through the open window. Headfirst, it appeared to run down the outer wall and then shot across the street.

Soon it was climbing another wall, using the suction pads on its feet to grip the rough brickwork. It paused to orient itself, before sliding across the wall to take up a position just above a window on the third floor of the building. Taking advantage of its incredibly acute hearing, the creature listened to the hu'man conversation drifting through the open window.

Rose lay on the bed which dominated the small room. Clad only in her underclothes, her back was turned towards the door, and she jumped as it opened. Turning to look over her shoulder, her face lit up in a beautiful smile when she registered the identity of the man walking in to greet her. She was still on the bed when he fell upon her, taking her slim body into his arms and showering her ruby red lips with kisses. Laughing, she pulled away and said, 'Edward, I wasn't expecting you tonight!' She used a slim hand to brush a loose strand of blonde hair from her face. A pale pink suffused her cheeks, and she lowered her eyes as she added, 'I have a client in about half an hour. I'm sorry.'

Whiston stood up, crossed the room, and sank with a groan into the only armchair available in the confined space. 'It's alright my beloved. I just needed to see you and to talk. It's been a trying day.' He smiled and said, 'If I could just get my promotion, you wouldn't have to stay here. We could marry and you could stay at home and raise a family.' It was now his turn to blush as he realised what he'd blurted out.

'Why, Mr Whiston. Is that a proposal?' she teased him. Then, seeing the earnest look on his face, her tone became more serious. 'My dearest, what do you mean, it's been a trying day?'

Her lover paused to collect his thoughts before starting to summarise the unusual murder case. He poured out his annoyance with his fellow officers in general and Inspector Johnson in particular. Rose listened, resisting the urge to ask questions or to offer soothing reassurances. She was smart enough to let him work out his frustrations in the telling of his story.

'Why, the man's a fool and barely literate!' he finished, with evident feeling.

Outside, still clinging to the wall, a dark shadow listened to the meaningless sounds from the room. But in its mind, a familiar visitor listened with growing interest as it considered a number of possible plans. The young man inside the room inadvertently helped it to select one.

'I cannot believe the priest is responsible for this atrocious crime. I suspect someone came to the house and murdered the poor woman for nefarious reasons as yet unknown.'

The effect of his words on the invisible listener was instantaneous. Here was a threat to be dealt with. Rose still reclined on the bed, propping herself up on one elbow and with her back to the window. Her full attention was focused on the occupant of the chair and she neither saw nor sensed the intruder, sliding in through the gap at the top of the window, until it was too late. Whiston started to rise from the chair, startled by the unexpected movement on the other side of the room. Panic flashed in his eyes. Alarmed by the sudden change in his demeanour, Rose started to turn towards the outer wall. Moments later, the huge jaws clamped down on the back of her neck, instantly severing the spinal cord. Whiston's eyes widened in shock as the nightmare creature came into the light of the candles burning atop a small table. He flung up his right arm and started to back towards the door as the creature launched itself at him from behind the falling figure of his sweetheart. A slashing claw ripped through his coat and shirt, tearing deep into the flesh of his forearm. Collapsing under the surprising weight of the creature and with pain searing through his nerves, Whiston started to yell for help. Tears blurred his vision. Tears for his loss and for the pain in his arm.

12: Crossing the line

Mysterious clouds roiled within her eyes as her lips parted to reveal a myriad of sharp teeth. Fumbling behind her back, he almost dropped the knotted thong before whipping it over her head, down around her throat and then began twisting the two ends tighter and tighter around her neck. Shocked, she paused for a moment before beginning a violent struggle. Her face twisted in fury, and she started to beat upon his arms with clenched fists as an unearthly scream erupted from her mouth.

Fearing that she might try to bite or punch him, he raised a knee and delivered it as hard as he could into her stomach. Forced to exhale and with the ligature tightening, she slumped forward, head-butting his chest in the process. The two of them went down in a heap and he struggled to get on top of her. A few moments earlier he had been imaging what it would be like to be penetrating her sex. Now, he was desperate to throttle the life out of her. The irony made him laugh – which was a mistake. As he relaxed, she surged upward and almost succeeded in dislodging him. In desperation, he took both ends of the thong into his left hand, bunched his right fist and smashed it into her face.

Much later, he would decide that The Gods were indeed on his side. By a stroke of good fortune, his fist struck the septum, breaking her nose and driving the splinters of bone up into her brain. Within moments, her frantic efforts to escape had subsided. Not willing to take any chances, he continued to apply pressure to the thong, desperate to choke the last vestiges of life from the creature which had come so close to bewitching him.

At last, certain that she was dead, he released the pressure and tried to stand. Looking down, he watched in fascinated horror as the once beautiful woman aged dramatically. The lustrous golden hair shrivelled to grey wisps, the skin sloughed off the bones and the teeth rotted away. Within less than a minute, he was staring at a torn and dirty blue dress from which extruded a number of ancient bones.

As he backed away in horror, a familiar laugh disturbed his growing sense of revulsion. He turned to find himself facing the Keeper. *'Well done, Novice. You have killed your first sentient being in this realm,'* said the voice inside his head. There was a distinct pause before the voice came again, *'Be assured, it won't be the last time you have to kill. The law is very simple here. Learn quickly or die. You have crossed a line and from henceforth there can be no turning back. You can either complete your search for the truth … or die.'*

Sensing that the being in front of him might be coaxed into revealing more, he asked, 'What was that creature?'

'A good question, Seeker – it seems you are acquiring a modicum of sense at last. In your realm they were once common enough to have a name. Your ancients called them Syrens. They are an ancient life-form, evolved to feed on the life-force of others. They are masters of illusion, offering their prey a vision of what they most desire. It takes a great effort of will to resist their allure, as I am sure Sagana has already told you. Now I have something to say to you.'

He braced himself, fearing another lesson or trick from the enigmatic creature. To his surprise, it was neither of these but more akin to some practical advice; *'It would serve you well to pay attention to something else I have to say.'* Not waiting for a response, the strange being continued. *'Your next test will take a different form. It falls to me to prepare you. But first, I have a little history lesson for you.'*

His face must have betrayed his emotions.

'You need not look so surprised. My … purpose … here is to both test and instruct you. Now, pay attention, for I do not repeat myself.'

The Keeper then began to explain how the hu'man's had been bred as pets for the mysterious beings now known as The Elder Gods. They'd been given a world of their own to inhabit as part of an experiment and also to provide entertainment for their masters. Over countless millennium, factional in-fighting among these Gods had weakened their ties to the hu'man plane until almost all contact was lost. Eventually, the Gods themselves had become so wearied by the endless conflict that an uneasy truce was called. Surprisingly, this held, and the remaining Gods were able once more to turn their attention to old hobbies and research. Inevitably, they rediscovered the plane of existence now occupied by their former pets. At first, they were delighted to see how much progress the creatures had made; but their mood soon turned to anger when they found that their former pets had also invented religion. Very few of them still worshipped their creators, having forsaken them in favour of other false Gods.

As his mind reeled from the shock of this revelation, he interrupted the Keeper. 'Wait! You're telling me that our mighty religions are wrong? That we owe our very existence to these Elder Gods?'

'Yes. And this leads me onto your next task.'

With a flash of inspiration, he interrupted again, 'You want me to kill another hu'man?'

The Keeper dimmed for an instant and then settled back into its normal colour and intensity. 'So you are not witless after all! Sagana was right to choose you. Yes, you have been selected to eliminate a meddlesome priest of your Christian faith in your own plane of existence.'

'Why?'

'Because this hu'man is trying to force his beliefs upon all of those around him and threatens to destroy one of the last settlements still loyal to the Elder Gods. Not only must you kill this creature but do it in a way that sends a clear message to his followers.'

There was a pause, and he formed the impression that the Keeper was listening to a voice it alone could hear. He jumped when the creature began to speak again.

'Your history lesson is over. It is time for you to return to your own plane, where Sagana will brief you more fully on this task.'

Still shocked, he stood in contemplation of what he was being asked to do.

'Why are you wasting time here? You should return to your realm whilst there is still light. This is not a good place to be at night for creatures like yourself.'

Without warning, the Keeper flared into a painful brilliance before slowly fading away. Taken by surprise, he stood a little longer, waiting for his eyes to adjust. Then he bent down to retrieve the thong and the direction pebble. A gentle breeze blew some of the dust away from the stone.

Deep in thought, he untied the pebble and set it in his hand. Concentrating as Sagana had taught him, he sought the way back to his own realm, barely conscious of the gentle heat radiating from the stone.

His mind whirled with the implications of what he'd just been told. After a while, he shook his head, trying to clear his mind. Unbidden, an image of the sleeping syren came into his mind and he stopped walking, as it seemed to pour out of his mind and form itself into a living being stood just a few paces in front of him. He'd last seen her as a rapidly decaying skeleton, clothed in a dirty and tattered blue dress. But now she was once more a vision of beauty, clad in a stunning scarlet dress that left little to his imagination. Lost in lust, he drank in her lustrous dark hair, then jumped back when she opened her eyes to reveal green eyes of an impossible shade.

Deep at the back of his mind, he knew that something was wrong. Yet he stood still, enraptured, when she spoke to him in a lilting voice that made him think of soft lace and honey.

'Do I please you, my lord? It would be a pleasure to serve you and to help you explore my world. Have you ever made love on a bed of rose petals?' Smiling, she held out her hand.

He gulped and found himself taking a step closer to this gorgeous woman. Then he cursed, as the pebble in his hand suddenly became so hot that it burnt his palm. The shock of the sudden pain jolted him to his senses, and he now saw that the woman in front of him wavered in and out of his vision, reminding him of the ripples spreading out from a stone dropped in a pond.

Sucking in air, he realised he'd been holding his breath. 'Be gone, witch,' he snarled. The flickering apparition hissed at him, then suddenly disappeared with an odd popping sound.

'Congratulations. You've passed the second part of the test,' said a familiar voice, behind him.

Heart pounding, he whirled to find himself once again face-to-face with the Keeper. 'You could have warned me!' he spat out.

'But then it wouldn't be much of a test, would it?' The Keeper made no effort to hide the amusement in his voice.

'How many of these damn syrens are there?'

'How many stars fill the night sky?'

'Don't play games with me. I thought you wanted me to kill someone for you?'

The Keeper made no reply at first, seeming content to simply study the creature in front of him. When he finally spoke, he said, *'I'm not asking you to kill for me. Your task was set by one of the Elder Gods and I serve their will. As you must learn to do and without question. It is not wise to demand explanations from beings more powerful than you can imagine.'*

The Seeker snorted in derision. 'If they're so powerful, why are these Gods so worried by one priest? Why don't they kill him?'

The Keeper flared a deeper red colour and his response boomed across the desert. *'Take care, fool, lest they decide to strike you down. Do not ever challenge the Elder Gods, for their ways are mysterious and unfathomable to a mere hu'man. They have honoured you with a task. Complete it and you will be rewarded well. Fail and the price is eternal suffering.'*

'And if I simply choose to walk away and forget any of this ever happened?' The pain in his head appeared so suddenly that he gasped and raised his hands to his temples. It felt as though an iron band had been wrapped around his brain and he began to panic when it started to tighten. The pain rapidly became excruciating, and he screamed, begging his companion to stop. Then, just as suddenly as it had arrived, the pain was gone. He glared at the Keeper through tear-stained eyes, his whole body shuddering in little spasms.

'Does that answer your question? If not, remember that I also fear the wrath of the Elder Gods.' The Keeper began to fade. *'It's your choice ...'*

As he approached The Rent, the Seeker was still deep in thought. A part of him regretted that he'd ever met Sagana but deep down he knew that he was no longer master of his own destiny. He'd already walked too far down a path whose goal still lay far away. Already, he was being forced to murder a priest and he wondered where else this strange path would take him. He 'd considered and dismissed the idea of asking Sagana what unspeakable acts he'd done in order to stay alive. It was clear that any indication of doubt or dissent could have very painful consequence sand he had no wish to repeat the lesson he'd been taught in the desert.

With a shrug of his shoulders, he dismissed his gloomy speculation and concentrated on the ritual which would allow him to return to his own plane.

Later, as he spoke of his experiences with his mentor, he was careful to keep quiet about the second syren and his experience with the Keeper. He had just taken a deep swig of ale from a jug when Sagana casually asked, 'Which syren did you like the best?'

Sputtering and choking, he tried to laugh as Sagana thumped him on the back. 'You didn't think I'd let you go there without keeping an eye on you?'

13: THE MASTER

They rode along in silence. Wallace turned to glance over his shoulder every few minutes, as if willing Muller to keep up. The warrior was clearly worried about being pursued and yet the old man seemed unconcerned about the potential danger. After less than half a league, Wallace reined to a halt. With his two companions alongside his own horse, he spoke, 'We need to find a hiding place. At this pace, it won't take Molitor and his men much longer to catch up and I can't fight them all. You know what will happen if we're taken by them.' This came out as more of a statement than a question.

Madeleine cast him a questioning glance, but he shook his head. Muller hadn't missed her meaning though and said, 'I've been through these parts before. It's not much further to the next village. Just beyond that, there's a thick patch of forest. We should be able to hide in there.' As he spoke, he pointed at a range of hills to their left.

'Let's get moving,' said Wallace. 'And for God's sake, ride faster,' he added, with a glare at the old man.

Muller muttered something under his breath then kicked at the ribs of his mount, urging it to greater speed. Behind them, the dust cloud kicked up by a larger group of riders was gaining ground.

As they breasted the hill, they saw the village nestled on its lower slope and, beyond that, a sizeable patch of forest. Wallace took another look behind and uttered a curse. 'If I'm not mistaken, I'd say that was Molitor and about 20 riders

101

with him. They're gaining fast. We'll be lucky to make it to the trees, let alone have time to hide from them. Damn you, old man. What have you led me into?'

Muller started to protest but was interrupted by Madeleine. 'Ride! It's our only chance and wasting time arguing won't save us.' As she said this, she urged her horse forward and set off at an angle, heading straight for the forest. After a moment's hesitation the two men followed her example, with Wallace's horse soon taking the lead.

Wallace veered towards the village and began to shout out, 'Raiders, bandits. Beware!' As he changed course back towards his two companions, he spotted signs of frantic activity among the huts of the settlement and smiled to himself. Offering resistance would almost certainly get the villagers killed, but he prayed that some of them would have bows and that the prospect of a few arrows landing among his men would force Molitor to delay the pursuit long enough for their little party to escape deep into the forest.

Reaching the treeline first, Wallace urged Muller and Madeleine to press on into the relative safety of the forest. He paused to take another look at the village and smiled as their pursuers charged into the press of huts. The sounds of battle reached his ears, but he turned away, knowing that the villagers would buy them but little time.

Resuming the lead, he used the weight of his stallion to force a way through the tightly packed younger trees that formed the outer edge of the forest, trusting that the other two would follow.

Muller called out, 'To the left. I think there's a path of sorts. It will make our going easier.' Not stopping to wonder how his companion could know this, Wallace pulled his horse in the suggested direction and was surprised to find that the old man was right. They pressed on for a little way before the stallion suddenly reared. On the narrow path ahead, a man dressed all in green stood facing Wallace. In his hands he held a large bow with a nocked arrow ready to fly.

Wallace was weighing the chances of running the man down before he could release the arrow when he realised that other shadowy figures were hidden among the trees. Behind him, Madeleine whispered, 'Are they outlaws?'

They both turned in surprise when a calm-voiced Muller said, 'Hold now, Frederick. Is the Master with you?'

The archer slowly lowered his bow and grinned before replying, 'Muller, you old rascal! Where did you spring from?'

'Aye, it's me sure enough. But we have little time to waste on idle chatter. Angry men of the Christian God are chasing us.' He turned in his saddle. 'This one,' he nodded towards the open-mouthed Wallace, 'killed a few of their friends.'

'Then we'll provide them with an appropriate reception,' replied Frederick. 'Quickly, bring your horses over here, where they're hidden from view. Then get behind me and my men.'

As they hastened to obey, Wallace heard shouts from the edge of the forest. He led the stallion away from the path and into the thicker undergrowth, patting its neck to reassure the beast that all was well. From the corner of his eye, he'd spotted a dozen or so archers and a smile formed around his lips. These weren't villagers but professional soldiers. He could tell by their positioning and the condition of their weapons that they would not prove easy pickings for Molitor.

It took just a few minutes before a nearby shout indicated that the Pope's little army had found the path. Wallace quietly unsheathed his sword and tensed, prepared for battle, scanning the trees and the path ahead. 'Stay hidden and quiet', he whispered to Madeleine.

Frederick allowed the riders to come on until they were almost upon his own men, then he gave a single piercing whistle. As Molitor and his men froze in surprise, feathered shafts flew towards them, taking down seven or eight in the first salvo. While the riders recovered from the shock and tried to locate the source of the ambush, a second flight of arrows took down another five or six.

'Back, fall back' screamed Molitor, an arrow protruding from the rump of his frightened horse. Less than half of his force remained mounted and now green-clad men, previously unseen, began to drop from the branches overhanging the path. Some landed behind the startled riders and held on to them as short blades were drawn across throats. Others knocked their target to the floor, where the archers now rushed forward to stab through the gaps between protective leathers or armour before their stunned opponents could gather their wits.

Molitor managed to evade the efforts of the man who landed behind him. The shock of the additional weight drove his already wounded horse down on its back haunches and his would-be assailant fell off backwards. With a curse, Molitor leapt from the dying mount as it collapsed on top of the other man. After a quick glance around, he started to run for the nearest horse. Around him, the remnants of his force were being sent to meet their maker.

He stopped in confusion when Wallace emerged from the side of the path, sword in hand, to block his intended means of escape.

'You!'

'It's time to find out if that Papal dispensation is worth the parchment it's written on,' said Wallace.

Molitor snarled as he launched himself at his former ally.

As his enemy charged forward, Wallace shouted out, 'No-one else touches him. This is personal.' He had no time to see Frederick's questioning look towards Muller, or the grin on the old man's face as he shook his head.

Two swords crashed together, the juddering impact sending shockwaves down the arms of their wielders. It soon became apparent that both men were skilled fighters First one, and then the other, pressed forward. Neither could find an opening for a killing blow, although each man managed to inflict minor wounds.

Panting heavily, Molitor said, 'Treacherous swine. I was right not to trust you. God lend strength to my sword arm ... to avenge himself upon a coward.'

Wallace grunted, narrowly avoiding a bludgeoning stroke aimed at his head, before replying, 'Oh, you were magnificent against helpless peasants.' He spat out a mouthful of dust, before continuing, 'but now you're facing me.' As he finished speaking, he kicked out, catching Molitor on his right kneecap and sending him crashing to the ground. Twisting as he fell, Molitor was able to get his sword arm up in front of his body. He parried the vicious downward sweep that would otherwise have finished the fight. Scuttling backwards, he used his left hand to pull a throwing dagger from his boot and hurled the weapon straight at Wallace's face. As the latter ducked under the blade, Molitor scrambled back to his feet and the swordplay resumed.

However, it soon became obvious that he was favouring his right leg, struggling to do much more than hobble. Wallace began to press his advantage, but just when it appeared that the fight must be almost over, he over-reached himself and Molitor, seeing the opportunity he'd been waiting for, rushed forward with a cry of triumph. It was all that Wallace could do to deflect the incoming blade onto his right arm, where it tore a deep wound just above the wrist. Molitor began to laugh. 'Not so confident now, my friend? How does it feel knowing you're about to lose?'

With blood pouring from his wounded arm, Wallace made no answer. His face revealed nothing more than pain as he gritted his teeth and seemed to lose heart. He began to back away, his sword held out in a warding position, even as his right arm dangled uselessly at his side, the hand seeking shelter behind his back.

Molitor pressed forward, using large, powerful, hacking blows to try to either batter his way through Wallace's defences or to tire him out. He knew blood loss would weaken his opponent and that he could afford to wait for him to make a fatal error. It wasn't long before each furious onslaught began to be met with weakening resistance as Wallace continued to yield ground.

Eventually, Molitor judged that the time was right to bring the fight to a close. Launching a furious volley of blows, he stepped in, past the other man's guard to deliver the final cut. Wallace went down on one knee and Molitor, raising his sword high above his head, yelled, 'Now you go to hell!'

As he spoke, Wallace surged up, dropping his sword as he used his left hand to plant the long dagger, taken from a belt pouch hanging behind his back, under Molitor's exposed armpit. As he drove the blade deeper, Molitor screamed in frustration, trying to bring his own weapon down even as Wallace used his right arm to keep it away.

With one last tremendous effort, he pulled the dagger free, only to ram it into Molitor's throat, before kicking his beaten enemy away. No longer supported by Wallace, the dying man fell to the ground, where he tried to speak through a mouthful of blood. As Wallace turned away, he collapsed before struggling to drag himself a short distance to where he could prop himself up against a tree. He was looking for Madeleine and took no notice when Molitor gave a throaty gurgle before drawing his last breath.

Madeleine raced towards Wallace, calling out for water and bandages as the wounded man slumped down further. Arriving at his side, she looked round to find that no-one had moved. Frederick and his men were all looking towards Muller, who ignored the woman's angry repetition of her recent demand and said, 'He has something of mine. Retrieve it for me and then we'll leave them here to fend as best they can. I need to find the Master.'

Frederick began to object, 'But he clearly has no love for the Papists, and he's injured.'

Muller walked towards the ambush leader and snarled, 'When I want your opinion, I'll ask for it. Now do as I say, before I report you to the Master.'

'There's no need for that, Muller,' said a new voice. Wallace looked up to see a middle-aged man, garbed in rich attire, who sat calmly astride a magnificent horse, nonchalantly twirling a small, thonged whip in his right hand. He noticed that the stranger had cat-like eyes, which

106

seemed to fluctuate between green and gold in colour. As others turned towards the newcomer, they bowed low before sinking to one knee. Muller alone remained in an upright position.

'Master,' croaked the old man. He turned, to point at Wallace, before adding, 'He has the statue you seek.'

The mounted man turned an unsettling gaze on the warrior. Wallace felt a strange sensation in his head, almost as if someone were examining his very thoughts and memories. After a long pause, the Master spoke again. 'Then perhaps it would be wise to show him a little more respect?'

He reached behind, pulled out a rolled bundle from a saddlebag and tossed it towards Madeleine. 'You'll find unguents to stop the bleeding in there and clean bandages after you've washed out the wound.' He nodded back over his shoulder. 'Frederick, send one of your men to fetch water from the stream.' Then he turned towards Muller. 'You're getting old and presumptuous Muller. Did you need this man to help you complete your mission?'

The old man sighed, as if bored with the conversation. 'Only because I was unfortunate enough to be trapped in a stinking village when,' he pointed at the body of Molitor, 'he and his friends attacked. That one,' and now he pointed at Wallace, 'was with them. I had to reach an understanding in order to prevent him from hacking me to death.'

'I see,' said his Master. 'In other words, you made a mistake and then had to make a bargain with this man in order to rectify the situation?'

Muller's eyes flashed as he digested this unwelcome assessment of his actions. He puffed out his chest and said, 'I was just unlucky, Master. Now why don't we kill him, retrieve the statue, and go home?'

'And the woman? What would you have me do with her?'

Madeleine began to rise in indignation, but Wallace used his good hand to pull her back down. 'Wait,' he whispered. 'I sense this Master is not as ill-tempered as Muller.

Follow my lead. But get ready to run into the trees if I say so. I'll try to buy you some time.'

His mouth writhing as though it were filled with something distasteful, Muller said, 'She's soiled goods, Master. No use to us, except perhaps as an offering. It would be simpler to kill her now though.'

The Master sighed. 'Indeed. You seem to have thought of everything.'

A look of triumph lit up Muller's face and he started to turn towards his former companions.

'Except that you haven't explained how you managed to be caught in that miserable village. Did your appetite get the better of you, again?'

Wallace's mind flashed back to the hut where he'd first met Muller. He remembered the cauldron and the odd smell of its contents as well as the sticky red liquid dripping from the overturned jug on the table. Sudden understanding brought with it a feeling of nausea.

Muller's cheeks had turned crimson, but he protested his innocence and swore that he'd done nothing wrong except to be unlucky. The Master's eyes met those of Wallace.

'Very well my old and faithful servant. Come closer and I'll let you have your reward.'

With a meaningful glance in the direction of Wallace, Muller shuffled towards the mounted man. Standing by the side of the horse, he was taken by surprise when its rider leant over and struck him across the cheek with his whip. For a few seconds, nothing happened except that Madeleine tensed and Wallace whispered for her to get ready to flee.

To their surprise, Muller fell to his knees and began to beg for forgiveness. He lifted his right hand to his face and grimaced when his fingers came away covered in blood. Madeleine watched the Master's reaction to the old man's pleas, noting the slight upturn of his lips and the scowl that disfigured his face. As Muller continued to whine, his master seemed to arrive at a decision. 'Stop mewling man. Try to show some dignity! Your ugly face will heal. Consider yourself lucky I'm feeling generous. But mark me well, Muller. This is the last time you make such a mistake and remain alive to smirk about it behind my back.'

Wallace had been observing the Master, sword gripped firmly in his left hand, as the latter sat impassively, while his servant prostrated himself on the forest floor. 'I'm sorry to have offended you, my lord. Please forgive me and accept my promise that I will strive harder in the future to make myself worthy of your praise.'

The Master ignored the old man and smiled at Wallace, revealing a mouth full of white pointed teeth. 'Relax. Please. I believe we have an agreement. You give me the statue and I give you 50 silver marks. I'm also willing to instruct you in the ways of the Elder Gods, if you so desire. If not, I can offer you shelter, hospitality and protection, while you recover. Then you are free to walk away. Oh, I almost forgot. My name is Sagana. And I've spent the last five years searching for someone like you.'

'You need a mercenary? They're not exactly in short supply,' said Wallace.

'Not a mercenary. I already have plenty of those at my disposal. No, I need a man with a certain attitude and set of skills. I suspect you fit my needs.'

14: SHATTERED DREAMS

Whiston tried to roll away from the hellish creature. At first glance it resembled an impossibly huge black spider. His mind struggled to process the image in front of him, refusing to believe that each of the hairy legs had a miniature head where the joint should be. Near the end of each leg, fingers on tiny hands writhed in constant motion. As Whiston struggled to make sense of what he was seeing he noticed that the hands ended in sharp, vicious-looking nails resembling talons. Worse, each of the eight tiny heads had an identical face resembling that of a small child caught up in a nightmare.

As the creature reared up Whiston was entranced by the horns on its cheeks. That fascination quickly ended as his eyes registered the saliva dripping from the fangs protruding out of the slit of a mouth. Raised voices and a hammering from outside the room distracted the creature and Whiston began to inch away from it. Moments later, the door crashed open and Lydia's two strong-arm's burst into the room. They skidded to a halt, taking in the scene in front of them and cautiously backed off. Later, Whiston would swear that the nightmarish thing had actually grinned at the new arrivals. With astonishing speed, it surged forward and spat a fine thread at the larger of the two new arrivals. As the stuff hit him in the face, the man raised his hands to try to pull it off, but his assailant used the hands on its two front legs to wrap the thread around the man's head, shoulders, and arms, thus rendering him immobile. In the few seconds this took to accomplish, his companion stood open mouthed, the club in his right hand hanging down by his side. Muffled sounds came from the region of the man's mouth.

'Help him!' cried Whiston, struggling to his feet.

'Not me. I'm not paid enough to face that thing.' He turned and started for the door. The creature shot forward and grabbed the coward in its four front legs. As the razor-sharp nails on the end of its fingers sliced through his clothing and skin, the man cried out in pain and shock. Whiston's escape was now blocked by the monster. In desperation, he scrambled backwards, trying not to look at the lifeless remains of Rose still lying on the blood-soaked bed. As if sensing that Whiston now posed no immediate threat, the monster casually bit off the right arm of the struggling man clutched tightly in its deadly embrace. It then used its talons to poke out both of his eyes. As the wretched man screamed and begged for help, new arrivals outside the room momentarily attracted its attention. Whiston heard a woman scream and then a dull thud. A man's voice cursed, even as he backed away. Other voices raised anxious queries.

Meanwhile, the spider-like creature began to dismember its hapless victim. As blood spurted in various directions, his screams stopped abruptly. Taking advantage of this brief

110

reprieve, Whiston looked frantically around the room, searching for anything he might use as a weapon. He had no doubt that as soon as the creature tired of playing with what was left of the strong-arm, it would turn its attention back to him. There didn't seem to be anything of any use – the battered side table held only a small glass bottle of holy water and a candle.

A strange gurgling sound made him look up to find the creature had dropped the pitiful remains of what had until recently been a man. It was staring at him. Panic took a firm hold and he felt hot liquid run down the inside of his leg. As the spider began to move towards him once more, the terrified man grabbed the bottle, smashed the top off on the edge of the table and tried to use the jagged edge of the neck as a knife. It was close enough that he could smell its fetid breath as he frantically swung the bottle at its gruesome face. To his surprise, some of the water in the bottom of the bottle splashed out causing an unexpected reaction. So confident moments before, the spider retreated, a hissing sound emanating from its mouth. To Whiston's amazement, where the water had splashed against it, the creature's flesh appeared to be melting. A rank odour began to fill the room and, seizing what might well be his only opportunity, Whiston grabbed the candle and threw it at his tormentor. To his disappointment, this didn't produce any obvious damage, but it did cause it to move slightly to one side and further towards the corner of the room. Praying to God, he raced around the bed and shot out of the doorway. Turning for the stairs, he went his full length over the legs of an unconscious woman lying on the landing.

Somehow, ignoring the pain in his left wrist, he scrambled over the woman and half threw himself down the stairs. His fall came to a sudden end against the legs of a man who was trying to climb the stairs. 'What the devil!' said a deep bass voice.

Whiston looked into the face of the man towering over him. 'Don't go up there if you value your life. Holy water is the only thing that will stop that monster.'

111

'Monster? What monster? What the deuce was all that racket just now? It damned well put me off my stroke, so you'd better have a good answer. And what's that awful smell?' Strong hands lifted Whiston to his feet. His new acquaintance took in his dishevelled state, eyes widening as he saw the blood on what was left of the sleeve of Whiston's clothing. 'Who did this? Was it that damned tomcat I've seen lurking about outside?

Whiston began to laugh. 'A cat? A cat? You fool, there's something evil up there and it's just killed two people and mummified a third. It's not a cat. More like a giant spider, but with a face and hands.'

The other man took a step back. 'K-killed two people?' His eyes narrowed. 'A spider with a face and hands? Oh come on. Are you drunk or do you take me for a complete idiot?' His cheeks flushed with anger, he pushed Whiston to one side and set off up the stairs.

The young policeman was torn. He didn't want another innocent life lost, but he was afraid to go back to the room of so much carnage. Rose's face swam before his eyes, the look of shock on her face marking the moment he'd lost her. He barely registered the small crowd that had gathered during his brief exchange with the other man and fought to hold back tears. Then he recognised an anxious-looking Mistress Lydia and turned to face her. 'At least one of your men is dead up there. Probably both. So is Rose.' As the realisation of what he had just said began to sink in there were several gasps and exclamations from those around him. Whiston felt hot tears trickle down his cheeks. He pointed up the stairs. 'That fool will probably be next.'

Lydia gave him a long hard stare. 'That fool, as you call him, is an important client. Oh, dear God, I can't let anything bad happen to him.' She turned to a small boy cowering behind her. 'Jack, fetch my pistol.' She turned back towards Whiston. 'A monster, is it? Well, let's see how it likes a taste of lead.'

Before he could respond, there was a startled shout from above, followed by a crash. 'The damn thing has jumped out

112

of the window,' said a deep voice from above. 'Bring a sharp knife. And hurry.'

Whiston ran up the stairs, followed by several men and women. At the top, the woman still lay in exactly the same position. He paused, and turned back, blocking any further progress by those behind. 'It's carnage in there. The women should stay well away. This is men's work.' He waited until the women began to edge back down the stairs then stepped over the prone figure and edged into Rose's bedroom. Inside, the sole occupant was desperately trying to unravel the thread from the first enforcer. He looked up and demanded, 'Do you have that knife?'

'No. It's coming. But I doubt it will do him much good. He must have suffocated by now.'

The other man glared at him then slumped to the floor in frustration. 'In the name of God, what was that thing?'

'I don't know. I was talking to Rose when it suddenly came through the window and … and … killed her.' He paused, fighting a growing sense of nausea, trying to force himself to stay calm. 'Mistress Lydia says you're an important man.'

'What of it?'

'Can you afford to be here when the police arrive?'

'Good point.' He looked at the strong-arm still lying on the floor, his upper torso wrapped like some grotesque parcel. 'I'd better go. Things to do.' He took a step towards the door, then turned back. 'How come you survived?'

'I've no idea.'

Another man entered the room, brandishing a large carving knife. He knelt down and started to hack at the strands around the dead man. After a few attempts he cursed in exasperation. 'Bloody hell. This stuff is tougher than the blade. It's not cutting through it at all.' As he rose to his feet, he noticed the figure on the bed. 'Is that … Rose?'

'I'm afraid so', answered Whiston. She was the first to … That thing, whatever it was, came in through the window. It all happened so fast.' Then he threw up.

By the time he'd finished retching, the room was full of people. Lydia was directing clean-up instructions and Jack had been sent for the police. Several of the establishment's customers had made their excuses and melted away, unwilling to be associated with its services. Whiston sat on the edge of Rose's bed, gently holding her hand while a young servant did her best to clean and dress his wounds. Rose's hand was cold, and it was already turning stiff. He felt empty inside and couldn't get his thoughts together.

A hand on his shoulder made him jump. He looked up to see one of the other 'girl's' watching him with a look of pity etched on her face. He realised that he didn't even know her name. His eyes turned back to Rose.

A stinging slap shocked him back to the reality of what had happened. 'I'm sorry, but you weren't listening. Rose told me a little about you, so I know what you do for a living. Perhaps you ought to think about leaving as well? You know, before the coppers arrive?' He took a last lingering look at Rose's corpse and bent down to kiss her blue lips. He made his way home through a blur of tears.

A few streets away from the brothel, a child cried out. It tried to tell its worried mother about the monster and the blood. She rocked it back to sleep, wondering if she ought to consult a priest or a doctor. No child at such a young age should have such a horrible imagination. When the candle in the room sputtered out, she thought she heard a strange sound.

The next day Whiston turned up for his shift with his right arm in a heavy bandage. He dutifully told his hastily made-up cover story about an attempted mugging in a back alley and asked if he was to continue the investigation into the missing priest, or if any other suspects had been found for the murder of the landlady. Sergeant Mindelen snorted and told him things had moved on while he'd been sleeping.

'There's been another murder. A young woman called Alice Glanville was found by 'er landlady early this morning.

She was mutilated after a terrible beating. And 'er eyes and tongue was missing.' The sergeant looked at Whiston with a look of triumph on his face. 'Remind you of anything?'

'Well, it's similar to the landlady, Agnes Crawford,' admitted the younger man. 'But I don't recall that Agnes had been beaten as well.'

'That's not important,' said Mindelen. 'It proves it was the priest that done it. Stands to reason.'

'So, we've got a double murderer to find,' suggested Whiston, choosing his words carefully.

'Maybe's more than that!' came the reply. The sergeant paused dramatically, waiting for the obvious question.

Whiston sighed, then asked, 'Why? What else has happened?'

'There was a triple murder at a brothel last night as well. Near to where you lives. The priest got a bit more inventive this time. Broke a whore's worthless neck, cut up one man with something real sharp and tied another one up with some sort of fishing line what choked 'im to death. The whore don't matter but now 'e's gone and killed two good men.'

The younger officer fought to retain his self-control. Every fibre of his body wanted to smash the sergeant to a bloody pulp but, deep inside, he knew that this wouldn't help him bring Rose's killer to justice. Feeling weak at the knees, he staggered to a chair and sat down.

'What's a matter? You don't look well.' A smile crossed the sergeant's face. 'Got an 'angover is it? Drunk on duty?'

'No, I'm not drunk. It must be the after-effects of being attacked last night. I lost quite a bit of blood.' He wanted to add that he'd also lost the woman he had been planning to marry but knew better than to reveal this to the sergeant. At the back of his mind he realised that Rose's best friend had been called Alice. A chill ran down his spine. Was her death just an unfortunate coincidence or was he missing something here? And where was the awful spider now?

'Snap out of it, boy. We've got work to do. We've got us a mad priest to catch and 'ang.'

115

15: THE HAND OF GOD

14 January 1208.

A lone figure stood on the tower battlement, squinting into the bright afternoon sunlight. He had been tracking a slowly approaching dust cloud for the last ten minutes, both eager and yet dreading to confirm that it was heading straight for the castle. At the centre of the cloud rode the fat legate, Pierre de Castelnau.

His most important mission to date was about to enter its final phase. The watcher shivered in a sudden chill wind and jumped when a barely audible whisper suddenly urged him to carry out his task. He spun round but found he was still alone – not that he expected the Keeper to reveal himself here and now. Judging that he still had an hour or so before the Papal party arrived, the watcher mused over the events that had brought him to this part of southern France.

A year earlier he'd been working as the court fool for the powerful Count of Tuscany. That lord's reluctance to oppose the growing Cathar heresy had earned him the disfavour of the Holy Father in Rome. It was whispered that Pope Innocent III had appealed to Philip II, the French king, to condemn those who, like Count Raymond, refused to prohibit the Cathar faith or persecute its leaders. Fearing the loss of his own authority over the southern nobility, the King was expected to lend his support to the Pope. It seemed certain that if Raymond refused to cede to the Papal will, he would be excommunicated as a punishment.

The man responsible for this outrage had been the same de Castelnau who now approached. It seemed ironic that Sagana had persuaded Raymond to release his fool and provide the necessary assurances for him to be engaged by his current employer, the Count of Roaix. Not for the first time, he wondered if this new arrangement had been an entirely innocent coincidence.

Snapping out of his reverie, the watcher began the descent back to the castle courtyard, his mind whirling with possibilities. Although he was not keen to take the life of another human, even one as depraved as the legate was rumoured to be, the would-be assassin sought a prize beyond value – immortality. This single act would, he was certain, considerably advance his cause along the path of enlightenment. He nodded to several other servants on the way to his tiny room.

A little over an hour later the Papal party rode wearily into the courtyard. Apart from the legate, there were four armed and mounted men plus a few servants on foot. The entire party was covered in dust. Watching from the shadows, the jester couldn't help but notice that all of the servants were good-looking – the young boys as well as the girls. All of them kept their eyes downcast as they stood waiting for orders.

The legate half slid, and half fell from his horse, a great plodding beast who looked more suited to the plough than to its current task. The horse was lathered in sweat, but de Castelnau paid it no heed as he snapped for one of his retinue to stable the beast. Spotting a servant of the castle, he beckoned the man over and demanded to be taken to the nearest roasting fire. 'I'm cold, hungry and thirsty,' he shouted. 'Get me food and drink and a thick cloak.' Turning to his own party, he ordered them to find lodgings, before pulling a pretty young girl back and whispering in her ear. The girl's cheeks turned a crimson colour, but she nodded her agreement, curtsied, and scurried off on whatever task she had been given.

The wily jester slid through the shadows and into the main hall, where his master sat on a large wooden throne, impatiently awaiting the Papal envoy. At his side, his ever-present lady sat on a smaller throne, a look of pained indifference on her face. Albert III, Count of Roaix, snapped his fingers and a servant came running towards him, before bending a knee in the customary manner. 'My lord?'

'Fetch me a jug of wine and something to eat.'

'And for your lady?'

'Nothing for me Xavier. I'll eat later when our guest arrives. As the servant set off to fulfil his order, Albert's wife, Cateline leant closer to her husband. 'Stay calm, my lord. He

117

can prove nothing against you and so will try to provoke you into making a rash statement. A clear head would be a useful ally this evening.'

The fool smiled to himself and stepped into the light cast by the fire in the huge hearth that dominated the hall. 'Your command, my lord?'

Albert seemed startled to find the jester in front of him. 'Where did you come from, Guiscard?' he demanded.

'I've been told I was hatched from my mother's egg, although I may have been dropped by a passing stork,' came the polished reply.

The Count hesitated for a moment and then burst into laughter. 'I sometimes envy you,' he said. Then, after a moment or two of reflection, he added, 'But not too often. Whilst it might be nice not to have to worry about affairs of State, it must be frightening to know so little of how the world works. Not for you the intrigues of a man of affairs, eh?'

'My lord, I do not need to know how the world works. That is why we have fine nobles like your lady and yourself to instruct a poor fool like myself.'

Before Albert could add anything else, another servant came into the room and announced, 'The Apostolic legate, Pierre de Castelnau.' Guiscard was waved away as the Papal envoy entered the room.

'It's unusually cold here,' he announced, dispensing with the usual honorifics. The Count bristled at the deliberate insult, but his wife laid a restraining hand on his arm.

'I welcome you to my humble castle, legate. The weather is, of course, under God's control and not our own. I have faith that he chooses wisely on our behalf.' The legate narrowed podgy eyes as Albert continued. 'My wife and I would be delighted if you would take your evening meal with us. It would be wonderful to have such a distinguished man of the cloth break bread with us and bless our humble repast.'

'Just so long as it's not too humble,' complained Pierre. 'I haven't eaten since a miserable lunch at the local monastery.' He patted his huge stomach and added, 'My poor stomach thinks my throat has been cut.'

It could be arranged thought Guiscard, watching from his hiding place behind a huge thick curtain.

Albert clapped his hands and servants rushed in and began laying out a banquet in honour of his guest. The legate frowned and moved closer to the throne. 'There are things we need to discuss.'

'Indeed. But we can turn to them after our meal.'

'You did say just moments ago that you were hungry, Pierre,' added Cateline.

The legate turned a cold glare in her direction. '*You* will address me only when spoken to. It offends me to be spoken to by a mere woman.' The duchess put a hand to her mouth, clearly discomfited by this unexpected reprimand.

An angry growl escaped from her husband as he surged to his feet, his right hand on the hilt of the short sword at his side. 'You forget yourself, de Castelnau. I'll thank you not to speak to my wife as though she were some ignorant peasant! This is *my* castle. I make the rules here.'

The servants pretended not to hear and made a point of focusing on their preparation of the food. But even the deaf would have been aware of the booming retort as the priest said, 'And you forget that I am the Pope's emissary. Mother Church is well aware of the heretics that infest this land and of the nobles who fail her in permitting them to flourish. Have a care, my lord, lest I judge you unworthy of your title.'

The room fell silent as everyone waited to see how Albert would respond to this threat. Long seconds passed before he suddenly burst into laughter. 'Continue' he ordered, waving at his servants. He turned towards his guest and said, in a quiet voice, 'So the games begin. Do not think to threaten me again in my own castle. I have a clear conscience, which is more than can be said for some members of the clergy, even those currently in favour in Rome.' The two men locked eyes.

De Castelnau was the first to blink as, with a studied air of indifference, he announced his intention to freshen up before the meal. 'Send me that servant,' he said, pointing to a pretty young girl who was busy setting bowls of apples on the table.

'What do you want with her?' asked Albert.

'Do you expect me to wash and dress myself?'

'I thought you preferred young men to assist you?' asked the Duke.

'Really. I don't know where you've heard that. Send her to me.'

Only Albert noticed as Guiscard eased out from behind the curtain and set off towards the castle's private chambers. The Count nodded to himself.

The young serving girl entered the legate's room with her eyes fixed firmly on the floor. 'You asked for me, your honour?'

'Come girl. The honour is soon to be all yours. Blessed are they who serve under me.' The fat priest laughed, then pointed to a large tub filled with warm water. 'Close the door then remove your clothes and bathe my aching body. You'll be like the Magdalene. What's your name, wench?'

The girl looked up but quickly turned her gaze back to the floor when she found the priest staring at her. 'They call me Jeanne,' she whispered. 'Please sir, but I'm only thirteen and I generally serve my lady.

'I don't care what you normally do, today you are here for my pleasure. I will instruct you and you will obey. I am a man of God, an important man, and you are clearly in need of instruction. Why are you still dressed?

Jeanne began to look around, searching for a means of escaping what she feared was about to happen next. A hard slap to her face jolted her out of her rising panic. Soft hands began clawing at her tunic, almost tearing it from her shoulders. 'Move, before the water cools.'

120

Tears blurring her vision, the girl obeyed, fearful of the consequences if she tried to defy this powerful man. She closed the door and turned back to discover that the priest had disrobed. She tried to look away from his corpulent body. Although still a virgin, she was not entirely innocent when it came to sex, and she knew what the stiffening of his manhood meant. 'Please sir, I'm untouched. Don't do this to me,' she begged. Laughter was her only reply.

'You'll do exactly as I say, or I'll denounce you as a heretic and see you hung from the nearest tree. Now use the cloth to wipe away the grime. Then I'll show you why a pretty wench like you was put on this earth by a benevolent God.'

After she had finished wiping him down and used a soft fleece to dry his body, the priest ordered the young woman to lie down, still wet, and naked, on the huge bed that filled one side of the room. She began to protest but her words, tears and begging all failed to move the determined de Castelnau. 'Stop whining' he demanded, adding a back-handed clout to her head as a physical warning. 'You should be honoured to perform this one little service. My need is great and what you do or don't want means nothing to me. Now, open your legs.'

Sobbing, she refused to obey but cried out as he climbed on top of her and forced her legs ever wider. Moments later, she felt his tongue rasping across her neck. Unable to move under his weight, the poor girl felt as though she were being crushed. She could hear him grunting as he thrust into her. Moments later and apparently satisfied, he rolled away and ordered her out of his bed. 'Fetch me my clean clothes from the table over there and then bring me some wine. And hurry up, lazy child.'

She did as he ordered, grabbed her clothes, and retreated to a corner. Dressing hastily, she staggered out of the room and made for the kitchens. Jeanne felt dirty and used and was in such a hurry to escape from the evil priest that she almost ran down the corridor. At the corner she bumped into someone and tried to go round them, muttering an apology. A strong hand on her shoulder slowed her progress and she looked up, fearing further ill use.

'Not so fast little one. What has happened to upset you so?' The speaker was the Count's fool - a man she'd barely spoken to before. He stood waiting for her answer, stepping back when she flinched and pushed his hand away. 'Has someone hurt you?'

He seemed to pose no threat, so she nodded her agreement before bursting into more tears. The jester frowned. 'Was it the Legate?' Seeing the look of confusion on her face, he tried again. 'The fat priest?'

She nodded. 'He ... he ... did things to me. I ... I asked him not to, but he said it was what I was for.' She looked down as she felt something trickle down the inside of her legs. The sight of her own blood made her feel feint and she clutched at the fool's arm, afraid she was about to pass out.

Guiscard frowned. 'And where is this not so holy man now?'

'In his room. He told me to fetch wine.'

'Bring it to me. I'll take it to him. I have a ... message for him. Then you can go and clean yourself up. Say nothing about this to anyone.' She started to move off, but he spoke again. 'And know this. God will punish him for what he has done to you.'

The girl started to thank him for his kindness but stopped when she noted the scowl on his face. 'Have I done something wrong?' she asked, close once more to tears.

'No. But it would be better if you went now to fetch that wine before his holiness comes looking for you.'

Jeanne returned in a surprisingly short space of time and offered a large jug of wine plus an ornately decorated goblet to her saviour. He smiled and told her not to worry; everything was going to be alright. She scuttled away, no doubt glad to be free of anything to do with de Castelnau. Guiscard composed himself and then set off for the priest's room.

A few moments later and he was knocking gently on the door. After a short wait he heard a foul-mouthed curse, then the door was pulled violently open. 'You took your time ....'. The priest paused mid-sentence, puzzled to find himself staring up into the face of a man dressed as a jester. 'Who are you and what do you want?' he demanded, trying at the same time to peer round his unexpected visitor. 'Where's the whore?'

'Whore? I know nothing about a whore. I was instructed to bring you this wine. One of the young servant girls has had an accident and is bleeding.'

'An accident? What sort of accident?'

'How should I know. I'm just a fool. Do you want this wine or not? Here, I'll put it on the table.' Guiscard pushed past the startled priest and walked over to a table positioned next to a small window. 'There you are my lord. I wish you good health. I'm sure a man of God must always walk in his divine favour.'

As he left the room, the door was slammed shut. The fool smiled to himself. He'd seen enough of the room to find his way round it in the dark.

The evening meal was a muted affair. Guiscard made an effort to play his part but after just a few minutes the priest peremptorily ordered him away. The fool looked to his master for confirmation and pulled a sad face when Albert said, 'Do as the Papal Legate commands.'

Guiscard withdrew by performing a backward somersault, waving to the Count as he regained his feet. Albert smiled, then reached for a goblet.

It took the fool just a few minutes to reach the secret hiding place that afforded him a view of the great hall, but in that brief time Albert and de Castelnau had contrived to be at loggerheads. As Guiscard carefully sat down on the small stool, their voices drifted up from the table below.

'Don't imagine the Holy Father is ignorant of your friendship with Raymond of Toulouse. That scoundrel has allies across southern France and Rome knows all of them by name.'

'Is it now a sin to be a boyhood friend of a fellow noble?' asked the Count.

'Of course not, but it is a sin to follow his example and allow the Cathar heresy to flourish,' snapped the priest. He paused to stuff a large chunk of meat in his mouth, dribbling juice as he chewed. Albert said nothing. The silence stretched out until de Castelnau suddenly said, 'He cannot win, you know.'

'Are we still talking of Raymond?' asked the Count in a mild tone.

'Don't pretend to be stupid – leave that to your fool. Think very carefully before you choose your side, Albert. I am on my way to Lyon, and I will be returning with soldiers. Those who stand against the Church will be made to pay for their blasphemy.'

The Count made no reply, preferring to gather his thoughts as he took a long pull from his drink. He smacked his lips then slammed the goblet down on the table. A smile creased the corners of Guiscard's mouth as the priest flinched. 'I've already told you not to threaten me in my own castle. You are a guest here and, as such, have certain rights and privileges. But don't confuse that with thinking you can do just as you please. Even a man of God must obey certain common courtesies.' He paused to glare at the priest. 'If you have charges to make then make them and provide your evidence. If not, I'll thank you to take a more civil tone in *my* home.'

The priest stared at the Count and then slowly put his hands together. He looked as though he were about to pray. 'I don't take kindly to threats, my lord. Have a care lest I denounce you to my friends in Rome. For now, I tire of this paltry meal and unpleasant conversation. I will retire to my bed and pray for your soul. Think on what I have said.' So saying, he rose and stalked out of the room, calling for a servant to prepare his room.

Albert looked to his wife. Cateline was pale and frown lines creased her forehead. 'Don't worry my dear, all will be well. The odious fat priest will not bother us for much longer.'

'He leaves tomorrow?'

'One way or another, yes. He *will* be gone tomorrow.' Albert looked up towards where Guiscard had been sitting and nodded his head.

Dark clouds scudded across the face of the moon, casting much of the castle into murky shadow. Here and there a lonely torch provided just enough light for the handful of guards to perform their sentry duties. Most of the castle slept, some more easily than others.

Jeanne lay awake, the pain between her legs a constant reminder of what the priest had stolen from her. Normally a timid girl, her whole being was consumed by a seething rage as her mind considered and dismissed various ideas in rapid succession. She could hear snoring from the other servants in her cell but still rose with great caution from her bed.

Slowly, making as little noise as possible, she edged her way towards the kitchen. Once she was satisfied that her movements had gone undetected, she crossed the room and eased a large carving knife from the basket where it lay. Holding it behind her back, she retraced her steps, out of the kitchen and down a corridor leading to the priest's room. She froze suddenly, halfway along the corridor, when she heard a woman's voice, followed by a man grunting. Moments later, came the sound of something crashing to the ground, quickly followed by an angry exclamation.

Jeanne fumbled behind her back, searching for the store-room latch. Her eyes were focused on a door further down the corridor. As she squeezed inside the small room, her elbow caught a basket, sending it crashing to the floor. Luckily, it hit her foot, just as a door further down the corridor opened, spilling a faint light. With the cupboard door opened just a fraction, Jeanne held her breath as one of the castle servants came towards her. The woman was half-naked, and she looked back as she walked. A muffled voice urged her to hurry back. As she passed Jeanne, the girl noticed the jug in the woman's hand.

Hardly daring to breathe, the young girl tried to calculate how long it would take the other woman to fetch wine and return to the priest's room. *A few minutes, no more*, she told herself. *Not enough time.*

The woman took longer than expected and Jeanne was starting to feel cramp in her legs when she sensed as much as heard movement nearby. Holding her breath once more she glimpsed the same woman heading back down the corridor and heard the door close. Letting out a sigh of relief she stepped out of the cupboard, pondering her next move.

A hand clamped across her mouth and her knife-arm was twisted up her back. As she struggled to fight the panic rising inside her and to free herself, a voice whispered in her ear. 'Stupid girl! Let well alone and go back to bed. I understand your motive but trust me, things will seem much better in the morning. I'm going to take my hand away. Make a sound and we both die. Now go!'

Jeanne trembled as she felt the pressure on her arm slacken and the hand slipped away from her mouth. She turned to find herself facing the court fool. 'You!' she said, her voice sounding dangerously loud in the still night air.

The man put a finger to his lips, then said, in a barely audible whisper, 'Go! Make no noise. Trust me.'

Jeanne hesitated for a moment before nodding her agreement. She started to tip-toe back to the kitchen, intent on replacing the knife before it was missed. What had Guiscard meant by his cryptic comment? Her mind was a whirl of conflicting emotions but above all it was hope that surged through her and she smiled in anticipation. *Perhaps there was a God after all?*

Guiscard watched the girl to make sure she really was leaving. At the same time his ears strained to catch any sound that might indicate their recent struggle and the girl's outburst had attracted attention. De Castelnau's guards were no problem because they were all lying in an apparent drunken stupor back in their own room. The drugged wine had done its job.

Satisfied that he was undetected, Guiscard crept further along the corridor and stopped outside of the priest's room. Putting his ear to the door he thought he could detect sounds of movement. Moments later this was confirmed by a woman's squeal. 'Oh you like that?' asked a man's voice. The woman giggled. 'Perhaps it is time to plant my holy seed?' asked the priest. The woman said something that the fool couldn't quite make out.

He shrugged and crept back to the storeroom recently vacated by Jeanne. It took him a while to rearrange the contents so that he had enough room to fit inside and still leave the door slightly ajar. It might be a long night, but he was in no hurry. Sunrise would not be for another four hours or so and he was certain the priest would order the woman out of his room once he tired of her. While he waited, he used the time to check the weapons at his belt.

16: THE BARGAIN

11 September 1213.

Wallace struggled to his feet, leaning heavily on Madeleine's shoulder. The loss of blood had left him feeling light-headed, yet he retained enough of his wits to realise that the next few minutes might well shape the rest of his life. 'I'm Wallace.' He pointed to the woman. 'And this is Madeleine.'

He paused as a wave of nausea swept over him, then rallied his thoughts once more. 'It is true that I have your statue and the old man promised me the option of both coin and your tutelage. Of course, I'll take the coin but as to the rest of the bargain, I think we should talk a little before I make up my mind.' He pointed to his horse and was surprised when Sagana ordered the nearest of Fredrick's men to bring it over to where Wallace stood. 'I take it you prefer to leave now?' was the warrior's only comment.

Sagana hesitated for a moment, glanced toward Madeleine, and then seemed to arrive at a decision. 'Despite your wounds, it is important that we make it to Muret before nightfall. However, we can take the ride at our leisure, and you can recover your strength as we talk.' He turned towards Frederick and ordered, 'Mount up. Close order with scouts ahead and two behind.' Pointing to the stiffening bodies strewn among the trees he added, 'I don't want to be surprised by any more of this rabble. The forward scouts stop in cover as we approach our goal.'

As soon as Wallace and Madeleine were mounted, Frederick's men wheeled about and set off back in the direction they had come from. Sagana urged his own horse alongside that of Wallace and said, 'Let us begin our discussion.' The tone of voice was friendly enough, but his eyes were cold and calculating. Wallace felt a shiver slip down his spine and knew that this was not a man to be taken lightly.

As the riders trotted along a narrow path, the local wildlife called out warnings and threats from the forest canopy, thus marking their passage. Sagana ordered Muller to join the rear of the company and raised an eyebrow towards Wallace whilst nodding towards Madeleine. The warrior turned in his saddle and asked the woman to leave the two of them in private. Uncertainty flickered across her face, and she frowned to express her disapproval. Easing back on her reins, she tried to engage Frederick in conversation.

'Do you trust her?'

Struggling to conceal his surprise, Wallace said, 'Yes. With my life.'

'Be careful when you make such rash statements, my friend. A pretty woman has turned many a man's head or stayed his sword arm at a vital moment.'

Neither man spoke again for a few minutes until Sagana looked skyward and muttered something unintelligible. To Wallace's amazement, the bird cries ceased, and the forest fell into silence as effectively as if it had been covered with a thick cloak.

'That's better,' said Sagana. Now we can proceed in peace and continue our discussion. I presume you wish to know more about what I can teach you?'

'Something like that, yes. The old man claimed that you are close to acquiring the secret of immortality. A proud boast and an impressive one if true. Isn't that what all the alchemists claim though?' He glanced sideways at his companion's face before continuing, 'I mean no offence, but many men have made similar claims. So far as I know, nearly all of them are now dead and mostly forgotten.'

His answer was a deep-throated chuckle. 'You are right to be sceptical, my new friend. The claim is easy to make but difficult to prove. Note that I say difficult and not impossible. I assume Muller told you that I need the statue for my research into the secrets of the Elder Gods?'

Wallace nodded his agreement.

'Did he also tell you that Lu'Ki'Fer is a jealous God who guards his secrets carefully? It has taken me many years of work and not a few ... sacrifices ... to reach this point in my studies. But now I am ready to strike my own bargain with this most powerful of the Elder Gods. You see, I can give him something he needs in order to regain his legions of disciples and, in return, I want the secret of eternal life. However, I also require someone I can trust to stand at my side and guard my back. Eternal life does not mean immortality, even those who cannot die from old age or illness can still have accidents or be slain by certain means. Muller is too old and too greedy of his own self-interest to be relied on any longer and I have been looking for a replacement.

'Meaning someone like me?'

'Why not? You are obviously an accomplished warrior and no fool. I assume you were originally planning to share in the plunder that the Pontiff's noble supporters are no doubt keen to avail themselves of at every righteous opportunity. And you could have killed Muller back in that village and kept the statue as a bonus. And yet, you chose to spare the

129

miserable wretch. I can only assume you were intrigued by his offer?'

Now it was Wallace's turn to laugh. 'You make a good point, Sagana.' He winced as his horse stumbled over a half-buried tree root, but then continued. 'Let's say I am intrigued. What exactly would you be teaching me and what precisely would you want in return?'

Sagana smiled. 'Straight to the point, eh? I like that. It makes a refreshing change after many years of Muller's devious circumlocution.'

'He's certainly accomplished at talking round things.'

'But you prefer bluntness? Excellent! That should speed up the learning process if you choose to join me.'

'And what happens to Muller?'

The question earned him a sharp look from his companion. 'He's free to find his own way in what little life remains to him. Although, given his somewhat unusual tastes, I very much regret that even 'little' may be a trifle optimistic in his case.' He adjusted his seat before speaking again. 'The old man was useful for a while, but he lacks patience and a sense of propriety. It will be his downfall one day. I can't always be there to protect him, as you well know.'

'Yes, I understand. Given his attitude towards the woman, I was tempted to kill him myself.'

Sagana started to speak but thought better of whatever he had been about to say. Instead he asked, 'The woman is important to you?'

Mentally, Wallace cursed, mindful that he'd just unthinkingly offered a tool to be used against himself to someone who was obviously a dangerous man.

'She helped me in a fight against some of Molitor's men. I owe her something for that.'

'Muller said that she was soiled goods. I presume she's no longer pure?'

'If you're asking have I bedded her, then the answer is no,' said Wallace.

'Too bad. Every man needs a good ...'

The comment was cut short by a shout from ahead. Sagana immediately reined to a halt and sat waiting for the man racing on foot towards them.

'Well, Symon?'

The new arrival fell to one knee, sucking in air, before blurting out his report.

'The armies are gathered my lord. Our spies report that de Montfort has around 1,600 men, some 900 of these being cavalry, including nearly 300 knights. Ranged against them, Peter of Aragon commands over 2,000 horse and around 25,000 foot, although many of the infantry are militia from Toulouse. Your orders, sire?'

Sagana paused to think, then turned to Wallace.' You're a soldier, what do you make of this?'

Wallace grinned, happy to be accepted as being of some value. 'De Montfort is a good commander with experienced men, but the odds seem stacked against him. He will probably try to charge and break the Aragonese cavalry, knowing that success will demoralise the militia. He can ill afford to let himself be besieged in the town where his horse has little value. If Peter is sensible, he will take up a defensive position and try to stem De Montfort's efforts with bow and spear.'

Sagana gave him an appraising look before turning towards Symon. 'Tell Frederick to post men just inside the forest cover. We must not be seen by either side, so no campfires and no ale tonight. Double lookouts. Keep the horses quiet. We go to work tomorrow.' He turned his attention to Wallace. 'Questions?'

'Only the obvious ones. What work do we go to tomorrow and on whose side?'

'Ah, that is for me alone to know unless you are ready to commit to me and accept my full offer. Until then, I will say only this. We fight for neither side tomorrow save our own.' He raised his voice, before finishing, 'Anyone seen breaking cover towards the town will be shot down. Frederick and his men are excellent archers.'

'You forgot my role, tonight. Do I sleep or take a turn as a look-out?'

'I advise sleep my friend – recover your strength. Tomorrow, you may need it.'

After gathering ferns to make a rough bed for each of them, Madeleine turned her attention to the warrior's wounded arm. She changed the dressing, declaring that there was no sign of the wound turning bad. One of the archers brought dried strips of meat and tough chunks of bread for them, which they chewed and then washed down with lukewarm water from a leather bag.

Dotted among the trees, Frederick and his men settled in for the night, protected by an outer circle of lookouts and both Sagana and Muller were located at the centre of the whole makeshift camp. Although partially screened by bushes and low-hanging leafy branches, Wallace could see enough to form the impression that the two men were engaged in some sort of argument. As they talked, Muller became increasingly agitated and was soon waving his arms about as if to emphasise his points. Eventually, Sagana shrugged and dismissed his servant by waving him away.

'Well! What was all that about?' asked Madeleine.

'I'm not sure,' said Wallace. 'But I'd be wary around Muller from now on.'

'You can rely on that,' said Madeleine. 'Haven't you seen the way he looks at me? He's a disgusting old man and what's worse is that he's also ... but that doesn't matter now. You need your rest, not idle gossip. I'll be safe with Sagana to hold Muller back.'

Wallace looked at Madeleine, wondering what she had been about to reveal. He didn't like the way they were both hiding things from the other but held his tongue. His arm ached and he was suddenly feeling exhausted. Struggling to stay awake, a sudden suspicion made him ask, 'Did you put a sleeping draught in my water?' With her face melting before his eyes, he was asleep before she could answer.

Fighting her own tiredness, Madeleine lay down alongside him, hoping that they really would be safe if she also fell asleep. Her anxiety would not have lessened if she had been aware of Muller's eyes on her.

The old man was stroking a small blade concealed in his right hand whilst the other hand gently caressed the ugly welt across his cheek. His eyes glittered and the tip of his tongue slipped back and forth between moist lips as he made a solemn promise to his own Gods. If they still favoured him, the warrior who was hoping to replace him would soon be dead and of no use to his Master. Then the woman would be his to play with as he wished. In his fertile but warped imagination, the fun had already begun. Seeing her settle down, he began to creep closer, keeping an eye out lest he be observed by another member of the party. A moment of doubt entered his mind. *Had he read Sagana's intentions correctly?* A fragment of their earlier discussion came back to him. 'The warrior has strong blood. He could be useful.'

17: A MYSTERY DEEPENS

Whiston was struggling to conceal his growing frustration at not being able to tell all he knew about the events of the previous night. Sergeant Mindelen had started their murder investigation by visiting the house of Mistress Lydia and questioning the owner as to whether or not a certain priest had been a frequent and recent visitor. Despite her denials, he continued to press her to admit that Father Unwin was one of her customers.

'And I'll tell you once more, Sergeant, that I have no memory of ever having seen this man.'

'Ah, no recollection is it? I knows 'ow you ladies can conveniently forget things'. There was no effort to disguise the sneer in his voice. 'Paid you extra to keep quiet did 'e?'

Mistress Lydia spat out, 'Pah! He didn't pay me anything, for the simple reason that, to the best of my knowledge, he has never set foot in the place!' She glared at Mindelen as she rose from the lounge chair before adding, 'Do you really think I would protect whoever murdered one of my best girls'?'

Mindelen also took to his feet and stared at the woman for long seconds before he replied, 'I think the priest threatened to expose you unless you keeps yer mouth shut.'

Mistress Lydia glanced towards Whiston then locked eyes with the recalcitrant sergeant. 'Then you're a bigger fool than I took you for. Shouldn't you be looking for clues upstairs or something? I fail to see the point in trying to make me say that this Father whatever-his-name-is was a visitor here. It's simply not true.'

'All right. 'Ave it your own way. Then I'll be needing a list of all of your visitors, as you calls them. Especially the ones what was 'ere on the night of the murders.' The Sergeant folded his arms across his chest, confident he'd struck a telling blow.

The woman coloured slightly but quickly recovered her composure. 'I'm not sure that will be necessary.'

Whiston had tensed at his sergeant's last comment, fearing his secret was about to be revealed. He relaxed when Mistress Lydia continued, with a faint smile playing on her lips, 'You might want to check that request with your Inspector?'

From the corner of his eye, Whiston watched the implications sink into Mindelen's inadequate brain.

'Oh, so you knows Inspector Johnson, does you?'

'We've met a few times at the theatre, and he's been good enough to invite me to one or two of his dinner parties. I think he might be interested in your line of questioning, sergeant.' She suddenly turned towards Whiston. 'And who is this fine-looking young officer who has so little to say?'

Whiston felt relief wash through him. *Lydia was not going to let the sergeant know that the two of them were already acquainted.*

'Who 'e is don't matter,' said Mindelen. ''E's 'ere to assist me with my enquiries and to do as I tells 'im.' He paused, searching his pockets for a notebook. 'Finding it in the breast pocket, he had another thought. 'Why don't you go upstairs and look for clues in the murder room, young Edward? That'll be things like blood or a weapon,' he added, always keen to demonstrate his intellectual superiority over his junior officer.

Mistress Lydia gave a wave of her hand. 'Are we done here, sergeant? I have other things to attend to.'

Yes, like warning your richer clients to stay away for a few days, thought Whiston. 'Excuse me Miss, which room should I be looking at?'

'I'll send my boy, Jack, to show you, officer.' She stepped out of the room and yelled for Jack.

'You go with this Jack fella an' see what you can find. I'll be writing up me notes and thoughts,' said Mindelen, licking the end of a stubby pencil.

A few moments later, Jack appeared in the doorway. He gave no sign of recognition but asked, 'Which one of you wants to see upstairs?'

'That would be me,' said Whiston, walking towards him.

Once they were in Rose's old room, Jack gave Whiston a sly grin and whispered, 'Mistress told me to pretend I don't know you.' He looked down at his feet before adding, 'I liked Rose. She was always nice to me. Not like some of the other whores. They're mean and shout at me.'

Whiston felt a surge of anger flush his cheeks at hearing his late lover described in such an unflattering way, but he checked himself. The youth didn't mean any harm and his description had been, technically, accurate. It was only himself that thought of her as a woman rather than as someone available for sex – at a price.'

135

Fearing that he'd offended Whiston, Jack started to back towards the door. 'I can see you're still upset, Mr Whiston. I'll leave you to do your job. I really do hope you find the bastard responsible for her death.'

Whiston looked around the familiar room. It was in a mess and not all the signs of the recent nightmare had been erased. There was a crusty brown patch on the floor and the window was boarded up with bits of rough-sawn timber. His mind drifted back to Rose's last moments and his own narrow escape from death.

A voice broke in on his thoughts. 'I said, what 'ave you found?'

Whiston blinked rapidly, then pulled himself together with an effort. 'Well that looks like blood down there and it seems the killer fled through the window. We ought to go outside and see if that's feasible. But I was pondering what the lad said.'

'And what did 'e 'ave to say?'

'He says there was talk of the killer being some sort of creature, like a giant spider.'

Mindelen stared at Whiston for a while, his mouth hanging slack. Then a crafty look entered his eyes. 'You're 'avin' a joke with me. Right? A giant spider? That's a good one.'

Whiston paused, then added, 'But suppose, just for a minute, that it's true?'

'Suppose it's true! 'Ave you gone daft?'

'So how do we account for this?' Whiston held out a piece of something which resembled a length of grubby white rope.

Mindelen took the object, sniffed at it, and then pulled on both ends. 'It's damnably strong, I'll grant you that. What is it? Some new sort of fishing line like I already reckoned?'

'I don't know,' said Whiston, remembering how the spider-like creature had wrapped one of Mistress Lydia's strong-arms' in the stuff before dismembering the unfortunate man. With an effort, he pushed the memory from his mind. 'I found it on the floor, next to the blood-stain.'

'Aah, I suppose it could be some sort o' rope, left behind by one of the dead tart's clients. I've 'erd as how some of the men wot use places like this can get creative with the girls. Forget about it.' Mindelen turned towards the door. 'Come on then. Let's see if the killer could 'ave escaped down a drain-pipe, or somethin'.'

Whiston followed the sergeant down the stairs and along a corridor leading to a rear exit. The door was locked, to the annoyance of Mindelen, who sent his colleague to find a key.

Whiston shouted for Jack and told him that they wanted to see the back alley. The lad grinned, scuttled off and soon returned with a large brass key. 'Mistress says the lock might be stiff. She hasn't opened that door in ages.'

Lydia's assessment proved to be correct, and it was with some difficulty that Whiston eventually persuaded the key to turn in the lock. When they heard the click, barged Whiston to one side but struggled to force the door open. ''Ere you 'ave a go, young Whiston,' he ordered. 'It's about time as you did somethin' to help.'

Hampered by his bad arm, Whiston still managed to force the door open far enough for him to be able to squeeze through. Outside, he found a pile of old leaves and assorted wind-blown rubbish that had built up against the door. Kicking most of this away, he pulled the door further open, allowing his colleague to join him in the narrow alley between the brothel and the house on the opposite side. The two policemen looked up at the boarded-up window, only to find no down-pipe within reach.

'So much for your idea that the killer escaped out the window!' said the sergeant, a smug grin playing around his lips. 'I reckon ae' must 'ave gone down the stairs and out the front door.' Whiston started to protest but then decided he would be wasting his time.

'Let's get back to the station,' said Mindelen. 'It'll be lunchtime soon.' Mistress Lydia glanced at Whiston before nodding towards the departing sergeant. 'Poor Edward,' she said in hushed tones. 'First you lose Rose and now you have work with that idiot.' She stroked down an imaginary crease in her dress, adjusted her favourite lace shawl and set off for the main lounge.

As Mindelen and Whiston neared the police station, Isaac caught up with them. He pulled at Whiston's sleeve. 'Can you spare a minute, constable?'

Whiston glanced at his sergeant.

'I expect 'e's probably after a loan,' said Mindelen, making no effort to disguise his dislike of the old man. 'Don't give 'im anythin', young Whiston. You can't trust a Jew.' He paused in the station doorway. 'Don't say as I didn't warn you. I'm off for something to eat.'

Whiston looked at Isaac. 'Ignore his cruel comments, Isaac. I know you're better than he ever gives you credit for.'

Isaac looked at the ground and shuffled on his feet. Then his indecision seemed to be resolved and he looked up. 'Can we go somewhere more private Mr Whiston? There's something I want to tell you but it's not for other ears.'

Whiston hesitated, then, noting the pleading look in Isaac's eyes, said, 'We could go to The Bull. Use one of the little back rooms. If it's as busy as usual, no-one will be able to eavesdrop.'

Isaac nodded his agreement.

Inside the tavern, business was brisk. Whiston paid for two glasses of porter and weaved his way towards the little table where Isaac sat, looking anxiously around. The pair were soon ensconced in a little alcove and able to talk quietly. Around them the swirl of various conversations, interspersed with outbursts of laughter, provided ample protection against being overheard.

'Your health, Isaac.' Whiston took a gulp from his drink.

'And the same to you, my young friend.' Isaac copied Whiston's example then placed his glass on the table. Whiston waited, while the old man gathered his thoughts.

'Let me begin by asking you a question. Am I right in thinking that you and the sergeant are investigating the murders at the brothel?'

'Indeed,' replied Whiston. 'Although I think the sergeant has already decided who he would like the culprit to be.'

'A man of limited imagination, in my experience,' said Isaac, a slow smile creasing his face. 'And are the pair of you also investigating the murder of another prostitute, namely one Alice Glanville?'

'Well,' said Whiston, wondering where Isaac was leading and how much to reveal. 'Mindelen thinks she was another victim of the same murderer. Of course, it would be very convenient if all these local deaths were the work of the same person.' He took another drink of his ale.

'That's what I'm coming to,' said Isaac. He paused to take a large gulp of his own, then continued. 'Glanville visited the Inspector the day she was sent to meet her maker. She was leaving the police station as you entered it.'

Whiston spluttered on his own drink. Did Isaac know about his visits to Mistress Lydia's and was he trying to blackmail him? 'Sorry, it must have gone down the wrong way.'

'Yes. Well, as I was saying, she was leaving, and I was returning from an errand. I followed you inside but as I did, I noticed a tall, well-dressed man follow after her. I didn't think anything of it at the time, assuming he was just another gentleman looking for a bit of fun.'

'Go on,' encouraged Whiston. 'Though I'm not sure why you're telling me this.'

'I'd only been in the station a few minutes when the Inspector called for me and gave me a letter to deliver. I took it to the address he wanted but the man I was supposed to deliver it to wasn't at home.' Isaac paused to drain his glass and then looked expectantly at his companion. Whiston grinned, followed the old man's example and then scooped up both glasses before setting off to purchase refills. When he returned, Isaac raised his glass in salute. 'Bear with me young sir, I promise you'll be interested in what comes next.

'The Inspector said I was to place the letter in the recipient's hand, but the landlady wouldn't let me in, so I waited around outside for nearly three hours. It was dark and getting a bit on the chill side when the man I wanted turned up at the house. He was none too pleased to see me and snatched the letter out of my hand before telling me to go away. Didn't even offer me a gratuity!'

Whiston leaned closer to the old man. 'Is this where it gets interesting? Only I need to get back to the station soon. Mindelen will be waiting for me.'

Isaac chuckled. 'Well, I was annoyed at the ingratitude, so I lingered at the corner of the street to see what this unpleasant man would do. He read the letter, stuffed it into his pocket and then let himself into the house. As he passed inside, the streetlamp let me see that he had a dark stain on his cuff and something red dried around his mouth. The man's name on the letter was Mr Black. He's the man who followed Alice Glanville.'

Whiston had been about to empty his glass but instead he put it back down. 'Are you sure, Isaac?'

'Oh yes. I may be getting old, and I know some of you officers think I'm just a stupid old man. But my eyes still work as good as ever. It was the same man, alright. I'd swear to it.'

Whiston was struggling to contain his excitement. 'Do you recall the address?'

Isaac beamed happily. 'Of course. It's the first thing a good messenger does.'

Whiston was struck by a sudden thought. 'Why have you told me this, Isaac?'

The old man snorted. 'Mindelen's a fool and the Inspector is obviously acquainted with this Mr Black. If he's involved in Alice Glanville's death, who else is going to bring him to justice?'

Instinct guided Whiston's next question. 'Did you know Alice Glanville?'

Isaac looked at the young policeman with tears in his eyes. 'She was my niece. No-one should die like that.'

18: BRISTOL

'I asked where you were going, sir?'

Unwin snapped out of his reverie and glared at the little man ensconced safely behind the counter. 'Bristol. One way. Second class.'

The clerk gave him a dubious look before reaching for a ticket and accepting payment. 'The next train leaves in 40 minutes but you're welcome to use one of the waiting rooms ... sir.'

The sarcasm implicit in the delayed use of the honorific was not lost on Unwin but he forced himself to relax, smile and say 'thank you' as he turned away. He still felt upset about the death of his friend but realised that it would be unwise to draw attention to himself. With a heavy sigh, he headed for the nearest waiting room.

This proved to be square with a single door providing access. Dirty large glass windows offered a murky view of the platform outside. Inside, a pair of small oil lamps flickered as draughts chased each other round the room. Uncomfortable-looking wooden chairs lined the three inner walls. Unwin selected a chair in the corner between the back and the right-hand wall as he looked at it. Here he was seated in the deepest shadow and could observe anyone entering the room. His right hand was free if he needed to fight. He glanced around the room. His companions consisted of two middle-aged women and an old Jew. The two women were holding an earnest conversation but talking in muted tones. Unwin decided the old man looked like a businessman of sorts although his attire was a little old-fashioned. His shirt still boasted a high upstanding collar, and his necktie was tied with a bow, with the pointed ends sticking out like wings. As he struggled to read a battered newspaper in the poor light, the old man squinted through a looking glass and muttered a few words now and again. Unwin recognised them as Hebrew but couldn't make sense of what was exercising the man's mind.

He leant back against the wall and continued to watch the door through half-closed eyes. To all intents and purposes he appeared to be dozing.

Ten minutes later, a young man paused outside the room and stared inside. Unwin felt a moment of panic, fearing that this new arrival was searching for him, but he relaxed as the young man's eyes swept across the old Jew and then flicked back to take a second look. Moments later, the door swung inward and the young man sauntered in. He pointedly looked around the room and then headed for a seat near to the old man. The latter continued to read his newspaper, oblivious to the new arrival.

Unwin feigned stirring in his sleep. His new position offered him a better view of the new arrival and he noted the younger man appraising him. After a few moments, he seemed to be satisfied that Unwin offered no threat and moved to sit next to the old man. The two women glanced towards the pair and stood up, one of them announcing in a loud voice that their train was now due.

The young man stared at the older man for a while and then leant closer towards him. For the first time, the Jew appeared to notice that he now had company and he slowly lowered his newspaper. 'What do you want with me, sir?' he asked in a querulous voice.

'Don't be alarmed old man. I simply 'ave some friendly advice for you.' The speaker paused to glance towards Unwin then, satisfied that he was still asleep, leant in closer towards his target.

Now half turned away from Unwin, the younger man couldn't see when the priest reached inside his coat and palmed something into his right hand before resuming his previous slumped position in his seat. Meanwhile, he continued to talk to the old man. 'You see, some folk round 'ere don't take too kindly to your sort. They might get nasty if they see the likes of you sittin' 'ere. Alone. But me, see, I'm more tolerant of your lot. Live an' let live, that's wot I says. And for a small reward, I could persuade 'em to leave you alone. What do you say?'

The old man suddenly stood, taking the younger man by surprise as he fled the waiting room before the latter could recover. The young man shook his head and chuckled to himself before turning his attention to Unwin.

Sauntering over to stand in front of his new target, the young man kicked the priest's feet by way of introducing himself. Unwin pretended to be startled into wakefulness and looked up at the younger man. 'Eh? Is something wrong?'

This produced a smirk before his visitor replied, 'A waiting room can be a lonely place for a man on his own. There are some nasty elements round 'ere'.' He smiled and brushed a loose strand of greasy hair back from his ear. 'I can see as you're tired. Perhaps I could keep an eye out for you and guard your valuables while you sleep. In return for a small consideration, of course.'

Unwin looked the speaker in the eye before shaking his head. 'I'm sorry, but I'm a little deaf. Could you repeat what you just said?'

The young man grinned and then leant in closer. His breath stank of gin and something that reminded the priest of rotting meat. As he began to repeat himself, Unwin surged upwards and clasped him closer with his left hand before pushing him away. This produced a frown and then the youngster started to speak. 'I ...' He paused, a look of surprise etching his face as he took an involuntary step backwards. When he looked down, his eyes struggled to focus on the stiletto blade protruding from his chest.

'Between the ribs and into the vital organs,' said Unwin. 'The wages of sin and may God forgive you.' He pulled the blade free and wiped it on the young man's coat tail. Moments later, his victim crumpled to the floor, drowning in his own blood.

Unwin stepped over the dying man, pausing to look back and around the room before heading for the exit. He felt better, almost relieved to have struck out at someone in revenge for Father Fulbright. Yet, at the back of his mind, he cursed himself for a fool. *Don't draw attention to yourself? Well, you couldn't have found a better way of doing that!*

Outside the waiting room he checked the station clock and set off for the platform where his train was due in the next few minutes. His mind whirled with conflicting emotions, but one predominated above all others. For the first time in his life he felt ashamed.

The train journey was uneventful, and Unwin spent most of it in his seat, musing on the events of the last few hours. He wondered how long it would take before someone found the young man and alerted the police. Would they link him to the killing? He couldn't bring himself to admit it was murder. He tried to console himself with the thought that the young man might well have attacked him if he hadn't acted first. And, of course, his self-appointed mission meant that no-one could be allowed to get in his way. His conscience told him that this was a poor excuse for taking another life.

The one time he left his seat was to seek out refreshment in the buffet car. He ate heartily but tasted little and, after paying his bill, returned to his compartment. Minutes later he was joined by a young woman who apologised for intruding upon him before adding that she found her previous travelling companions boorish. Unwin exchanged a few pleasantries with the newcomer before apologising that he needed to rest after a long and trying day. Once again feigning sleep, he watched the young woman as she first read from a small book and then followed his example and, after covering herself with a blanket, joined him in sleep. He was amused when she began to snore gently.

Unwin alighted at Bristol Temple Meads and paused to survey the platform before moving off. Seeing no evidence of any unusual police activity, he left the station and hailed a hackney. Once aboard, he gave the driver instructions to take him to a hotel near the city centre, then settled back to enjoy the ride. The driver tried to engage him in conversation, but his passenger excused himself by claiming tiredness and a pounding headache.

Dropped off at his destination, he paid the fare and added a small tip then strode purposefully towards the hotel entrance, whilst keeping one eye on the departing hackney. When it disappeared around a corner, he crossed the street and began to retrace his steps. As he walked, he kept his head down but continued to scan his surroundings, anxious to avoid recognition. After almost half an hour he turned onto the street housing his real destination.

Spotting his intended hotel up ahead, he moved into the shadows and stopped some 20 yards short so as to survey the entrance. He was relieved to see a familiar figure leant up against one of the marble pillars flanking the front porch and set off once more with a renewed spring in his step. A few feet from the porch he began to wonder if James, the young porter, had fallen asleep. He called out a greeting to his young friend and paused when there was no response. Hastening forward, he prodded the young man in the shoulder then leapt back as the cold body tumbled forward. He caught a glimpse of the ragged edge of the wound across the throat and the blood-soaked waistcoat before he started to whirl as some inner sense warned him of danger.

Unwin woke with a raging headache but soon realised this was the least of his problems. He lay naked on a cold metal table, with wrists and ankles held secure by sturdy chains. The dim light came from a solitary rush torch stuffed into a sconce and he could hear the steady drip of water nearby. The air smelt and tasted stale. He tried to marshal his thoughts, recalling the shock of finding Jeremiah dead outside what he'd thought was a safe house in which to rest and plan the next stage of his mission. He sighed, waiting for the next move from his captor. Feeling weary he decided to attempt to snatch some sleep while he could. For all he knew, this might be his last chance to rest before what he feared was coming and yet the thoughts racing through his mind suggested that sleep would elude him.

Cold water hit him in the face, and he spluttered as a second bucket was poured over him. His first sensation was that the light source had improved, and he turned his head to try to see what had changed. To his right, a tall man sat in a large and comfortable looking chair. Taking in the long grey hair he felt a stab of fear in his gut.

'Welcome to my chamber of delights,' said his new companion. I'd introduce myself but I'm sure you already know who I am?' His host chuckled, although there was no warmth in the sound. 'The question is, what to do with you? I suppose I could end this pointless game and kill you now, but where's the entertainment in that?' He rose and walked closer to Unwin's prone figure. 'Oh, don't look so shocked. Did you truly think I didn't know about your supposed safe lodgings? The Shield is not so secret as you like to think!'

Unwin made a mental note of this tacit admission that they had a spy or traitor in their midst but tried not to betray this deduction on his face. *Of course, there's no guarantee I'll live long enough to make use of this confirmation of my suspicions*, he told himself.

As if reading his mind, the other man laughed. 'Not that this admission is going to do you much good. But, back to business. Another option would be to find out everything you know. That might involve a little discomfort on your part but think of the fun I'll be having. His captor's hand moved in a blur and Unwin felt a stinging pain along his right forearm. His tormentor leant forward and slowly licked the blood oozing from the thin wound. Unwin struggled not to shudder at the intimate contact.

'This is just a little appetiser. I have to leave you for a little while but feel free to make yourself comfortable. You can spend the time trying to imagine what I have in mind for the main course.'

19: A FATAL DECISION

Guiscard was forced to wait for over an hour before the woman left the legate's bedroom. She crept out of the door, clutching her clothes to her chest and tiptoed along the corridor. Guiscard permitted himself a wry smile. At least de Castelnau would be tired after his recent exertions. And with a little luck, he might also be drunk.

The fool counted to ten after the woman's footsteps had died away and then slipped out from his hiding place. He moved with great caution, pausing after every step to listen for any sounds of activity. At last, a fine sheen of sweat plastered to his brow, he reached the door to the priest's room. After one last look up and down the corridor, he gently took hold of the latch and eased the door open. The hinges gave a slight squeal of protest and Guiscard cursed himself for not anticipating the unwelcome noise. However, there was no reaction from inside the room and he pushed the door a fraction further, creating an opening wide enough for him to slip through. Despite the gloom, he could make out the bed and the fat figure asleep upon it. Guiscard eased the door back into a closed position and then turned towards the bed. He allowed a few moments for his eyes to become accustomed to the darkness then crept closer to his target.

Reaching his objective, he stood looking down on the Papal envoy. He didn't care about the Keeper's motives for getting rid of this man, but he knew that Sagana also wanted de Castelnau dead. Above all, he felt sorry for the young serving girl and a slow rage begin to burn inside his chest. Moving with caution, he eased a curved blade from his waist belt. He'd worked on the cutting edge several days earlier and had no doubt of its sharpness - de Castelnau was already as good as dead.

Bending low, he plunged the blade into the legate's throat, making sure to strike below the larynx and severing his windpipe in one swift move. He stepped back quickly, not wishing to be drenched in blood. The priest opened his eyes in shock then clutched at his throat. He was struggling to breathe and taking in huge gulps of air. Blood gargled out of his mouth and was spraying out of the wound. The man had but moments left before he lost consciousness. As his body went into its death spasm, Guiscard bent closer and whispered 'That's for Jeanne. Rot in hell.' He couldn't be sure the legate heard him. It didn't take long for the spasms to cease, although blood was still pouring out of the wound.

Guiscard cleaned his knife on the priests bedding and sheathed it in his belt. He crept to the door and leant against it, listening for sounds outside. Satisfied by the silence, he eased the door open, slipped out and closed it once more. Then he set off for his own room, planning to grab some sleep before the storm that he knew would break in the morning.

He woke to a tapping sound and struggled to identify the source for a few moments. Then he realised it was coming from the door to his room. It was a little past dawn, judging from the illumination coming in through the slit of a window that provided his room with its sole source of natural light. He scanned around, making sure that there was nothing to link him to the events of last night. He'd disposed of the knife down the castle well and buried his blood-stained clothes in one of the stables. No-one would be keen to check Blackie's stall – the stallion was notoriously bad-tempered and had kicked several of the servants in the last few weeks. Unknown to anyone else, it was Guiscard who had taught him to do this.

He leapt out of bed and strode to the door. 'What is ...?' he began as he fumbled for the latch.

Jeanne looked at him, a mixture of awe and fear on her face. Guiscard pulled her inside and closed the door. 'What are you doing here?' he asked. When she didn't answer, he shook her, staring into her eyes.

'You killed him?' she whispered.

'Hush. Don't ever say that. If they find out it was me, they'll want to ask you some difficult questions. We must both say nothing. I hope you were suitably shocked by the news?'

'Oh, yes,' she said, nodding her head. I didn't think you'd kill him though. I thought you were just going to hit him a little.'

'Child, men like the legate don't take well to being hit, even if it is only a little. If you wish to chastise them, it has to be something a little more dramatic.' He paused to smile, hoping to reassure her. 'You'd best get on with your work. Try to say nothing but if pressed, express your shock at such an untimely death. Be careful ... and stay away from me.'

Guiscard found Albert pacing the north wall. The Count raised an eyebrow when his fool drew near and spoke in a low voice, mindful of the soldiers patrolling the wall nearby. 'So, it is done?'

'Yes, my lord. The legate will bother you no more.'

'True, but now, in the cold light of day, I wonder if this might not bring further difficulties down upon my head. Was I wise to listen to you? The Holy Father is not well known for his sense of forgiveness.'

'My lord, our mutual friends were certain that de Castelnau had to be removed. If you fear for your own future, I am prepared to leave here. Give me a three-day start and then, if pressed, you could mention your suspicions as to the timing of my departure. That should leave your loyalty to the Church beyond reasonable doubt.'

Albert smiled. 'And what of you? Such a ploy would make you their chief suspect and the Church has very long arms.'

'My friend, Sagana, has very deep pockets. He will know how to shelter me until the initial fuss has died down.'

Guiscard said nothing of the realms beyond the Veil. Although unpredictable, he knew he would be safer there than being hunted by an angry Church.

Albert pondered this for a while, then arrived at a decision. 'Very well. Take Blackie and there will be provisions for you in his stall. I'll also throw in some gold since you have kept your part of our agreement. Leave me now. Things will be ready by noon.'

In the great hall, Albert, Count of Roaix, frowned at the legate's guards. It seemed that some of them were nursing the after-effects of excessive drinking. He slammed a fist down upon the arm of his throne, making most of those present jump. 'Where were you when your master was being murdered in his bed?'

The four guards looked miserably at the floor.

'Well?'

The youngest of the four found his voice. 'My lord, I suspect our drink was laced with a sleeping draught!'

Albert frowned. *Damn this one for his perception!* 'Is that the best excuse you can think of? Do you expect me to believe such a preposterous story? Well, no matter. You can explain it to his Holiness.' He paused, waiting for the implied threat to sink in. 'I'm sending you back to Rome where, no doubt, your master will be less lenient than myself. You will leave now and take the poor legate's body with you. He deserves a decent and fitting burial, even if you couldn't provide him with a natural death.' As the disgraced soldiers shuffled away, Albert called after them, 'And God have mercy on your souls.'

Guiscard had told the guards on the gate that he was being sent on an errand. One of them had questioned why he was riding the lord's horse but had been satisfied with the explanation that the errand was urgent, and this was the fastest one available. 'Besides, I know better than to steal from the Count. He'd have my head!' Guiscard fancied he could hear the pair turning this over in their minds and jumping to the conclusion that his errand had something to do with the murder of the priest.

Once beyond the castle walls, he turned his mount to the west and urged him on. In his heart he trusted Albert to give him the three days he'd asked for, but his head urged caution. The Holy Church was a formidable enemy, and the Count was in no position to oppose its wishes for long. With these doubts in his mind, he urged the horse on, aiming to put as much distance as possible between himself and the Castle de Roaix.

Night was falling when he reined in Blackie and looked down the hill towards the little village nestling below. He was close to Saint-Jean-du-Pin and both horse and rider were tired. Guiscard decided to take advantage of the nearby forest and walked his mount towards the trees. They soon found a little clearing and he made a small fire to keep any wolves at bay. After seeing to the horse, he settled down to feed himself then prepared to sleep on a hastily made bed of leaves.

He woke with a start, senses straining to detect any sound that might indicate what had disturbed his sleep. Blackie snickered as Guiscard checked his sword and the throwing knives at his belt. A shimmering light began to glow in front of him and with a sinking feeling he recognised the arrival of the Keeper.

The strange creature stood regarding him for a little while and as the tension mounted, Guiscard felt the hairs begin to stand up on his neck. Eventually, he could stand the silence no more and asked, 'What brings you to my little camp, Keeper?'

'As if you didn't know!'

Puzzled, Guiscard tried to discern the meaning of this unexpected response. 'I accomplished my mission. The fat priest is dead.'

'Indeed. And you've left a hornet's nest behind you.'

'I don't understand. You didn't think I could kill de Castelnau, and no-one would take any notice? It was you who said that he was becoming a nuisance to our cause and must be killed. That's what I did, so what's the problem?'

The Keeper flickered and blood red ripples shimmered in front of Guiscard's eyes. Alarmed, he rose to his feet. 'Now wait. I did as you asked.'

'No, you fool! You were supposed to act in secret with the Count, yet you boasted of your part to the young woman. Your vanity has left us with a major difficulty. What do you think will happen when she is questioned about what she knows of the legate's death? Do you imagine her mouth will stay shut under torture?'

Guiscard began to back away, his hand edging towards his sword. 'Does it matter? They'll never find me once I'm beyond the Veil and even if the Count is implicated, how does that harm us?

The Keeper's colour abruptly changed back to the more familiar white. 'You're right. At least about them never finding you.'

Guiscard started to relax, confident that he was under no immediate threat. He felt rather than saw the net that dropped over his head. 'What the ...' he began. 'Is this some ...' Guiscard paused, conscious that the net, which now hung down to his knees, not only hampered his movement but seemed to be tightening around his shoulders. As realisation dawned, he started to panic.

The Keeper watched as the net tightened around the struggling hu'man. Its unbreakable threads began to bite into his skin and Guiscard screamed as he was sliced into ever smaller chunks of flesh. The sound cut off suddenly and within moments all that remained was a pair of lower legs surrounded by a small sticky pile of what had once been a living creature. The Keeper spoke a strange syllable and a ball of flame shot from his hand into the mound. Unaffected by the intense heat, he bent forward and retrieved the net, folding it up into a small package that was soon concealed within his cloak. He looked at the small patch of scorched ground. *Now there is no problem. Although Sagana will have to start training a new disciple. Too bad. I quite liked this one – it showed potential.* Then he faded out of existence. His work was only half done here.

20: A FALLING OUT

Overhead, the forest canopy fragmented the feeble light from the moon and many of the stars were obscured by massive banks of cloud. Muller edged closer to the vague outlines that marked the sleeping bodies of Madeleine and Wallace. He struggled to focus on his immediate task – the slaughter of the hated warrior – preferring to dwell on his plans for the woman. Not for the first time, he imagined tearing off her clothes, exposing the pale firm breasts and her flat stomach. He was uncomfortably aware of his stiffening manhood as his fantasy progressed and he watched himself entering her, enjoying her protests as he planted his seed inside her warm flesh. Later, when she was swollen with his brat, he would cut the unborn child from her womb and rape her again, timing his climax to coincide with the moment the light died in her eyes. Then he would dine on her raw liver, washing the feast down with her still warm blood.

He continued the mental struggle as he closed in on his target until he was almost within striking distance of Wallace. Crawling ever nearer on his hands and knees, he paused before raising the dagger, gripped tightly in his right hand, above his shoulder. 'One good thrust ...' he muttered to himself, before freezing as a twig snapped somewhere close behind. Torn between his desire to stab the sleeping man and his fear of what had stepped on the twig, he chose to risk a glance behind. He was still struggling to see anything in the gloom when something hard smashed down onto his right wrist. Muller yelped in surprise and pain, an involuntary reflex in his fingers allowing the dagger to tumble to the forest floor.

The old man started to rise, only to find himself looking up into the face of Frederick. The mercenary captain held a short sword in his right hand and a length of bough in his left. As Muller started to speak, Frederick threw the bough away and levelled the sword at the old man's throat.

'Stand up.'

Muller rose with great caution, all too aware of the blade that could end his life in an instant and trying to control the rage that threatened to consume him.

'What do you think you're doing?' asked Frederick.

'I was making sure our guests were safe,' said Muller, rubbing his wrist whilst looking at the floor.

'By stabbing them in their sleep?'

Spotting his weapon, Muller took a step towards it. 'No. I thought I heard something creeping up on them.'

'What an odd coincidence,' said Frederick. 'I had the same experience.'

'I was worried it might be a spy from one of the armies.' He edged closer to the dagger.

'Pick it up and you die. Two of my men have arrows aimed at you right now.'

Now Muller looked up, his eyes flicking to both sides as he tried to work out whether or not his captor was bluffing.'

'You should know better than to mistrust Frederick,' said a new voice. Muller winced as Sagana appeared out of the shadows. 'What's going on here, Frederick?'

'I caught this worm creeping towards the warrior and his woman. He was about to stab the warrior with the dagger that now lies at his feet.'

The silence that followed seemed to Muller to last an eternity. His mind racing, he searched for a way out of the mess he'd landed himself in before breaking the silence. 'The woman confused me. I thought she was an enemy sneaking up on Wallace.' His feeble hopes were dashed when Sagana laughed at this desperate claim.

'I warned you earlier that I would tolerate no more mistakes, my duplicitous servant. It seems you didn't take that warning seriously.' He nodded towards Frederick. 'Gag him and tie him to a tree. I'll deal with him later but, for now, he can contemplate the error of his ways.' To Muller he added, 'I doubt if you'll live to regret this latest mistake, although long before Death comes for you, I suspect you'll be looking forward to meeting him.'

Meanwhile, Wallace muttered something prompted by an uneasy dream as Frederick beckoned to one of his men and the two of them led Muller away. Sagana remained alone, staring at Madeleine for long seconds, before he too walked away. He smiled when he sensed her eyes on his back. *I knew you were pretending to sleep!*

As they walked, the old man tried to persuade them to let him go but his pleas and threats were ignored. After a few minutes, Frederick said, 'Enough. Do you think either of us would be foolish enough to copy your example and betray Sagana? Unlike you, he's a man to be feared by his enemies but generous to his allies. I'm not going to cross him just to save your worthless skin.'

Muller fell silent, not even protesting when they tied him to a great oak and left him to await the pleasure of their master. With his wrists tied together, an old rag stuffed in his mouth and thick ropes pinning his arms and legs so that he could barely move, Muller knew his prospects looked grim.

Carlos stirred in his sleep. He'd fallen into slumber almost as soon as he'd been relieved of sentry duty and was gently snoring his way through the night. Yet inside his mind, he quaked in terror. His dream of playing back in the village where he'd grown up had been interrupted by the arrival of a familiar face – a face from his worst nightmares. Sometimes, when awake, he wished he'd never listened to the promises of the old man or become embroiled with the Blood Cult. Now, he faced his real master, the demon known as Helr'ath, and was being ordered to help the old man. Carlos whimpered in his sleep. Helr'ath stood some eight feet tall and had four arms. Two held sharp knives and a third held a severed head. The demon used its last appendage to point a six-fingered hand adorned with cruel talons at the head. Peeking through terrified eyes, Carlos could see that the head wore his own features. Blood dripped from the neck. The message was clear – help Muller to escape or face the fury of the demon.

Carlos carefully opened his eyes and checked to see if any of his comrades were watching him before scanning the immediate area. At last, satisfied that no-one was paying him any attention, he got to his feet and slunk away in the shadows. In his mind, his real master provided directions, enabling him to take a zig-zag route to the tree that held Muller.

As he approached, the old man appeared to be asleep but just as Carlos extended a tentative hand to wake him, Muller opened his eyes. As Carlos pulled the stinking rag from Muller's mouth, the old man scowled at him, then hissed for more haste in setting him free. Pulling a knife from his belt, Carlos began to hack at the restraining ropes, pausing frequently to scan the area.

'Hurry, fool,' hissed Muller.

'If I'm seen, we're both dead,' snapped Carlos.

'If you don't free me, you're dead anyway,'

At last, enough of his bonds had been cut to allow Muller to escape the tree. He held out his wrists then grinned when this last restraint was also cut. Without bothering to thank his rescuer, the old man scuttled off into the night.

Carlos crept back to his sleeping place and settled down to try and rest. He dared not sleep again for fear that Helr'ath would send him a new task. Instead he prayed for the dawn to arrive.

The pale light of early morning greeted Wallace when he opened his eyes. His mouth was dry, his arm throbbed and his back ached. Sitting up, he glanced across at the sleeping Madeleine and tried to remember a strange dream. A jumbled mixture of images slipped away, and he shook his head, trying to clear out the cobwebs that had grown on his brain.

'Would you like some breakfast?'

Wallace looked up to see one of Frederick's men holding out a wooden tankard and a slab of bread, topped with some sort of dried meat. He reached for both, taking a huge gulp from the beaker before realising it held water. His frown prompted the other man to laugh. 'Don't worry, it's from a fresh spring. Sagana's orders. We all need to stay alert today. I'll fetch Frederick to tell you about last night.' With that, he turned and was gone.

Realising he was hungry, Wallace chewed on the rest of the victuals whilst wondering what had happened last night. He'd almost finished his food when Madeleine came to with a start. She looked confused for a moment before gathering her wits.

'How's your arm?'

'Painful. But I think it will heal. Are you hungry?'

She smiled. 'Yes. What are you eating?'

'I'm not sure. One of the archers gave it to me. He's gone to fetch Frederick. You can ask him for something to break your fast.'

Madeleine stood up, brushing leaves and bits of dirt from her clothing. She half turned away, then said, 'There was trouble last night. I was pretending to sleep when ...'

'I intervened,' said Frederick.

Madeleine spun towards the new arrival, her face turning crimson.

'Oh don't worry about your little deception,' said Frederick, his eyes twinkling. 'It doesn't matter to either Sagana or me.' Then the twinkle faded, and he turned towards Wallace. 'Last night, I caught Muller trying to creep up on you. He was armed with a dagger.'

Wallace surged to his feet. 'What! Where is the little weasel?' Then he seemed to realise the full significance of what he'd been told. 'I'm sorry. Where are my manners? I thank you for saving us from that treacherous assassin. I owe you a favour and won't forget it. If ever you need my help, then just ask.'

Frederick smiled. 'I'll send someone with food and drink for the woman. But I imagine you'd like to see Muller?'

'He still lives?' Wallace scratched at his cheek. 'Well, not for long.'

'Wait. Sagana knows what the old man was up to and ordered him gagged and tied to a tree. He plans to deal with Muller himself – and unlike you, I don't think he'll permit the worm a quick or an easy death.' Frederick paused, clearly weighing his next words. 'I can understand your anger, but I'd advise you not to cross Sagana. Be content with letting him exact revenge on your behalf.' Nodding to Madeleine, he started to walk away.

'Sorry,' said Wallace. The other man paused, turning back to face the warrior. 'Thank you for your advice. And I meant what I said about returning the favour one day.'

'I'll hold you to that. Meanwhile, shall we visit the prisoner?'

'Lead on.'

'How did he escape?' demanded Sagana in a voice that promised painful retribution.

The other man looked alarmed. He'd never seem his master look so angry before. 'I don't know, sire. Willem asked me to check on the old man and when I got to the tree, I found he'd gone. His ropes had been cut.'

Sagana spun round as Wallace and Frederick approached.

'Where's ....,' began Frederick.

'Gone. Escaped.' Sagana spat out the words.

'How?' asked Wallace, his nostrils flaring and anger colouring his cheeks.

'I'm not sure,' said Sagana. 'But it looks as if he had help. I should have killed him last night.'

Wallace frowned. 'But at least you now know you have another traitor in your midst.'

Sagana stared at him then burst out laughing. 'A good point, Wallace. Well it looks as if you may make an excellent student after all. And as an added incentive, I can promise you that if we ever meet Clovis Muller again then you can have the pleasure of killing him.' He waved the other man away. 'Now we must make plans for today.'

In the ensuing discussion, Wallace found himself astonished by Sagana's plan. Not the least of his worries was how this strange man could possibly know the outcome of the imminent battle. Even more odd was his instruction to Wallace.

A few hours later, and from the safety of the trees that hid them, Wallace and Madeleine watched as King Peter positioned his army. He nodded his head in approval as it became clear that the King was using the River Saudrune to protect his right flank whilst a similar role was served by marshy land to his left. However, his face wore a frown as a large number of the militia from Toulouse began to head for Muret itself, no doubt under orders to take the town from the defenders.

'Why the frown?' asked Sagana, a look of calculation in his eyes.

'The King underestimates de Montfort's men. Although they number something less than 1,000, they are mostly experienced fighters and will have been trained to a high level of discipline. True, the Aragonese have at least thrice their number and some infantry as well, but I wouldn't feel confident facing de Montfort and his men, even with those odds.'

'Let's wait and see, shall we? And don't forget your task if my expectations come to fruition.' With this reminder, Sagana left them to their own devices, striding off to check that Frederick and his men knew what they were expected to do.

Madeleine looked at Wallace for an explanation, but he shook his head. 'Trust me, you don't want to know. And before you ask, no, you can't help me with it. It'll be too dangerous, and I want you to wait here.' He smiled at her, trying hard not to laugh at the indignant look on her face.

It wasn't long before de Montfort appeared close by with his cavalry divided into three squadrons. Wallace was a little disappointed to see that their opponents made no use of their archers but instead prepared to charge. 'The King is a fool!' he exclaimed.

'Why?' asked Madeleine.

'He ought to be using his archers,' he replied in a distracted tone. To his amazement, the Aragonese King had shed his royal armour in favour of what appeared to be a plain suit of light armour, judging from the ease with which he walked to his horse before mounting it. Wallace swore under his breath – if King Peter were unhorsed or slain this unmarked armour would make him difficult to identify.

As de Montfort's men charged in a tight formation, King Peter led a ragged charge of his own. The two sides met in a tremendous crash of horse flesh, leather, and metal. The result was never in doubt and much as Wallace had anticipated. Madeleine put a hand to her mouth, clearly shocked by what she was witnessing.

'You don't have to watch,' said Wallace.

'Well I'm not staying back there.' She waved a hand behind her. 'We don't know who else might want us dead.'

The battle-hardened men behind de Montfort crashed through the Spanish ranks, dealing out death and destruction with very little resistance. In a matter of just a few minutes the Aragonese cavalry had been broken and the survivors began to wheel away in panicked disarray. Wallace saw their King unhorsed and shook his head as Peter disappeared in a mass of bodies. When this mass moved on, the King was nowhere to be seen. Wallace marked the spot in his memory before glancing at the knights pursuing what was left of the Peter's cavalry. A grim look crossed his face as he realised that de Montfort's other two squadrons, one of them made up largely of crusader knights and both still more or less intact, had turned towards the town. It crossed his mind that the militia from Toulouse would stand no chance if they allowed themselves to be trapped between the town walls and the cavalry soon to be at their backs.

Telling himself that their fate was no concern of his, he began to consider how best to carry out Sagana's wishes.

21: A NEW LEAD

Whiston could understand Isaac's pain as his mind jumped to an image of Rose, sprawled lifeless across her bed. He looked into the old man's eyes. 'Isaac, I promise you that I'll do everything in my power to bring her killer to justice.' He paused, then said, 'Is there anything you can tell me about her that might help me to identify who might have done this terrible thing?'

Isaac shook his head, using the back of his hand to wipe away the tears. 'She was my sister's youngest. There was some sort of row, and she ran away. That was the last time they heard from her.' He sobbed and reached for his glass, then changed his mind and withdrew his hand, folding it into the other one on his lap. He stared at his hands for a moment then, without lifting his eyes, said, 'I heard the desk sergeant talking about the shocking murder of a young woman and felt a premonition. Somehow, I just knew it would be Alice.'

Whiston interrupted his companion. 'Did she marry someone called Glanville?'

Isaac shrugged. 'I don't know. Maybe she just chose that name at random, so as to make it harder for the family to find her.'

'It might be worth trying to find out. If she had a husband, we ought to find him?'

Isaac looked up. 'Yes, I suppose he might be the killer?'

Whiston tried not to smile, mindful of his own suspicions. 'I'm truly sorry, Isaac. No-one deserves to die so young.' He wondered if the grieving uncle had any idea how Alice had earned her living in the last few years but decided to say nothing – there seemed little point in adding to the old man's grief and his revelation might invite awkward questions. When Isaac showed signs of pulling himself together, Whiston bought the old man another drink before hurrying back to the station.

Inside he found Mindelen, munching on a greasy meat pie, and reading a thin file about Father Lemuel Unwin. Looking up as Whiston approached him, the sergeant tapped the file on the counter in front of him. 'Not much 'ere to 'elp us catch the blighter. Says as the priest 'as no criminal record but hints that 'e might not be all what 'e seems. Apparently, there's been several unsolved murders in parishes where Unwin was working. Seems like 'e certainly moves around a lot for a man in 'is line of work.'

'That doesn't make him a murderer though, does it?' said Whiston, regretting the words as they sprang from his mouth.

Mindelen eyed the younger man with unconcealed scorn. 'Why is you so keen to defend 'im, Whiston? Not 'is partner in crime, are you?' The sergeant chortled at his own joke.

'No,' said Whiston with deliberate caution. 'But we can't arrest a man because he often changes his job, can we? If you're right, sergeant, we're going to need some real evidence.' He paused, as if a thought had just struck him. 'How's about you go back and put some more pressure on Mistress Lydia to tell all she knows, and I'll go and have a look at the Glanville place? We can cover more ground that way and you're better at wheedling stuff out of folks than me.'

As he'd expected, the sergeant rose to the bait, happy to wallow in the junior officer's belated recognition of his greater value. Whiston was relieved that it didn't occur to

162

Mindelen to bridle at the other's temerity in suggesting what he ought to be doing.

'For once you might be right, young Edward. And I rather fancy 'avin' another crack at that Mistress Lydia. She's a fine-lookin' woman but let's see 'er try her charms on me!'

Whiston gave him a slight smile. 'Yes, she'll have a job to try and outwit you, sergeant.' Inside his thoughts took a rather different line and for a brief moment he pictured the pair in bed together, locked in a passionate embrace. As Mindelen set off for the station front door, Whiston gave a slight shake of his head. Somehow, he figured the sergeant would always be out of his depth with the Mistress.

Whiston stood for a few minutes, surveying the street which Isaac claimed was home to the mysterious Mr Black. Summoning up his nerve, he approached the front door of the lodgings and rapped on the recently painted panelling. He was about to knock again when he heard footsteps approaching the other side of the door. As it swung inwards, he found himself face-to-face with a stern-looking elderly lady dressed entirely in black. A high collar hid her neck, making it seem almost as though her head somehow floated above the dress. His first thought was that she must be in mourning, perhaps a recent widow.

'What do you want?' Her voice was surprisingly deep and the tone, although not exactly hostile, certainly gave no hint of either friendliness or femininity.

'I'm sorry to disturb you, ma'am, but I'm making enquiries after a Mr Black. He's a friend of my Inspector and I'm given to understand that he resides in your establishment?'

Soulless, grey eyes stared at him for a moment before the woman replied, 'Then your Inspector is to be disappointed. Mr Black left us today. He has urgent business outside of London.'

'Aah,' said Whiston. 'That is a pity, since I was supposed to be picking up a package.' He paused, as if thinking, then stooping slightly added, 'I don't suppose he left it with your good self?'

'Certainly not. Is that all?' The door started to close.

'I'd be ever so obliged if I could just have a quick look for it in his study, Mrs ...'

'It's Miss and no you can't. There is no package, so you don't need to waste your time.'

Whiston could see that his main purpose in visiting the house had been defeated. 'Well, thank you for your time. I'm sorry if I've caused any inconvenience.' His shoulders drooped a little as he turned to leave.

'I'll mention it to Mr Black when he returns from The Royal Hotel in Bristol.'

Whiston turned back quickly, only to see the door slammed in his face. *Not that it matters, I've made some progress!*

With a spring in his step, he set off for the last lodging place of poor Alice Glanville. While it was possible that Mr Black had departed London for entirely innocent purposes, Whiston had developed a deep mistrust of coincidence.

Meanwhile a tall man was congratulating his landlady. 'You did very well, my dear. You can go back to sleep now.' The woman, dressed all in black, gave no sign that she had heard him but simply turned away and began to slowly ascend the stairs to the room where she would await his next command.

Alice had rented a room in a tall miserable looking dwelling that sat almost in the centre of one of London's most notorious slums. Whiston supposed the building had once belonged to a successful merchant but now its grimy façade spoke of long decay and neglect. He was surprised to see a brass knocker on the front door and made liberal use of it.

A scruffy adolescent answered his summons. 'What d'yer want?' demanded the youth.

'Are you in charge of this building?' replied Whiston.

'What if I am?'

'Stop messing me about or I'll take you off for a night in the cells,' said Whiston.

The youth looked him up and down in a defiant manner, doubtless trying to decide whether or not to call the policeman's bluff. 'Charlie, who's there? What do they want?' A woman's voice, from inside, saved him from his mental dilemma.

Whiston cocked his head to one side. 'Move, Charlie. Now.' When the youth continued to hesitate Whiston pushed him to one side and strode into the hallway, taking in the stairs to his left at a glance. He called out, 'Police. Here to see the landlady.'

The youth opened his mouth, as if to protest at being man-handled, but a middle-aged woman appeared from a side room before he could say anything. 'I'm Mrs. Cooper, the landlady. Go out the back and fetch some wood for the stove, Charlie, there's a good boy.' Charlie looked at her, scowled at the policeman and then headed down the hallway, muttering to himself as he went.

Whiston stepped forward. Mrs Cooper had long straggly blonde hair, showing signs of turning grey at the temples. Her dress had seen better days and the apron she wore was covered in smuts and other unidentified stains.

The woman patted down her hair and smiled, revealing a gap in her upper front teeth. 'My, but you're a handsome one. I might take you on myself if the price is right.'

'I'm not here for a room, Mrs Cooper.' He'd decided to ignore the bawdier interpretation of her offer. 'I'd like to see where the young woman was murdered.'

The landlady turned pale. 'Oh? It was a terrible shock, finding her like that, I can tell you. She'd been sliced like a kipper, from throat to her ... you know.' She pointed to the stairs. 'Alice lived up there. In the garret. Wait a minute and I'll fetch the key.' She didn't wait for his response but scuttled off towards the back of the house.

When she returned, she held out her hand, offering a small key to Whiston. 'Have a good look round young man. I'll be available, in the back sitting room, if you want me.' She placed it into his outstretched hand, her fingers lingering a little longer on his than was strictly necessary.

'Aren't you coming up to the room with me?' he asked.

'No, goodness me. I saw her after he'd done with her, and my nerves are all shot. I don't want to be reminded.' She gave a shudder. 'The police surgeon said the killer had removed her heart and kidneys. Who'd want to do something awful like that?' As she started to turn away, she paused, as if having second thoughts. 'Bring me the key when you've done, there's a love. I'll get Charlie to clean the place up. Can't afford to have rooms going unused when we need the income. My husband would kill me.'

Whiston watched her departing back, then set off up the rickety stairs. The garret was on the fifth floor, and he was slightly winded by the time he turned the key in the lock. The door swung inwards with a tortured creak. The tiny room was lit by a small and very dirty window in the roof, on the front side of the dwelling. Dust motes floated in the air and there was a lingering smell of urine, faeces, and blood. The bare floorboards were scuffed and dark from years of use.

There was very little furniture in the room, a bed, a chest of drawers, a small table, and a high-backed chair. There were no curtains to the window although, since it was not overlooked, there seemed little point in wasting money on such a luxury.

The bed had been left as it was found. Only the pitiful remains of Alice had been taken away, to be given a decent burial. Whiston had already skimmed through the medical report and recalling the emotionless description of the woman's wounds made him nauseous. As he opened the drawers, he was thinking about how she must have died an agonising and horrible death. Worse, the killer had then cut out some of her vital organs and, presumably, taken them with him. Whiston didn't want to think about the possibility that Alice might still have been alive when she was so ruthlessly cut open or speculate as to what the killer had done with these gruesome trophies.

How did the murderer keep her quiet while he was torturing the poor woman? And why inflict such appalling punishment on her anyway? What did she know or have that her killer wanted so badly? The questions flooded through Whiston's mind as he decided to begin by searching the drawers.

There didn't appear to be anything of value or significance in the first drawer. It occurred to him that everyone was assuming the killer had been a man. He shook his head in disbelief.

Surely no woman could have done those things to another woman? But having accepted that conclusion, what sort of man could have done them? In his mind's eye, he saw again the mutilated body of Agnes Crawford. Were these two murders carried out by the same person? Was there any motive behind either murder or were the police dealing with a dangerous lunatic? If so, where, and when would he strike next?

The second drawer also contained little of interest. He felt carefully along the seams of Alice's undergarments, wondering if she had stitched in something of value. His efforts produced nothing at all. Did she know something important or dangerous? Perhaps one of her clients was someone powerful or wealthy? Could Alice have been trying to blackmail the killer?

The bottom drawer was almost empty, save for a few small coins, a handful of letters and a small locket, engraved with 'To AG with all my love'.

Whiston let his eyes roam around the room, trying not to linger on the heap of blood-stained linen strewn across the chair. He was about to leave when he saw something almost hidden under the bed. Bending, he picked up a small and crumpled sheet of paper. Smoothing it out, he held it up towards the window so that he could read the copperplate writing. His blood froze as he read the three words. The first two were Unwin and Glanville. The last was his own name.

22: Unfinished business

It had happened so fast, and he felt ashamed that he'd been too afraid to do more than watch from his grimy attic window. Now, sitting on an untidy bed, absent-mindedly stroking the scars on his face, he wrestled with his conscience.

Thomas Farral was still undecided whether to thank or curse his God for the fluke chance that had saved him. His mind kept slipping back to that fateful night when he'd almost lost his life. The scars on his face would never let him forget how close he'd been to death.

He shivered as his mind drifted back to the fierce sword fight, high atop a metal gantry inside a large fertiliser factory. A woman's loud squeal had distracted him for a fraction of a second. Alas, that gave his opponent the opening both were struggling for, and he found himself barged off the side of the gantry, falling head first towards a large vat. Even as he fell, he saw the sneering triumph on the Black Blade's face as that accursed villain had set off in search of the woman.

Only divine intervention had allowed his left arm to brush a dangling rope which he'd then grabbed at. For a brief moment it seemed as though his weight would tear his arm out of the shoulder socket, but somehow, he'd managed to keep his grip despite the searing pain. He was still angry with himself for having dropped his sword – it had plummeted into the vat below, the impact throwing up a spray of liquid that made him cry out in shock. At the time, all he'd known was that it was burning his skin wherever it was exposed. Trying not to breathe the noxious fumes rising from the liquid too deeply, he'd abandoned any thought of retrieving his favourite weapon and used both hands to grip the rope. A couple of attempts to swing to the side of the vat were enough to convince him that his one chance of salvation was to climb back up to the gantry. As he pulled himself up and wrapped his legs around the rope, he felt a growing soreness in the back of his throat. It had felt as if his lungs were on fire.

Farral was exhausted by the time he'd reached the safety of the gantry and terrified that the Blade would come back to finish him off. He grimaced as he struggled to make it down the steps and into the welcoming shadows, at the rear of the factory, where he'd spent an anxious few minutes straining to hear any sound that would tell him if the Blade had returned.

Whatever he'd almost fallen into was still eating away at his flesh and the growing pain meant that he needed urgent medical treatment. In addition, His mouth and throat were getting worse, and he was finding it ever more difficult to breathe. There had been no choice other than to risk making the effort to reach his nearest 'safe house' and hope for the best.

Feeling as though he were walking through the torments of Hell, he'd somehow managed to stagger to his house, where he immediately doused himself with water before applying salve-laden bandages.

Over the next few weeks he'd hidden himself away, eking out his emergency provisions and using half-forgotten skills imparted by his trainers to begin the healing process. A cautious night-time revisit to the factory had confirmed his suspicion that he'd been close to drowning in a huge tub of oil of vitriol. Although this aided his self-administered healing lotions, it also caused him to worry about permanent damage to his throat and lungs. Gargling with an alkaline solution had helped to ease the burning sensation but he wasn't confident that all the damage could ever be repaired and weeks later he accepted that he would never be able to fully resume his old occupation. The scars on his face and arms would be almost impossible to disguise; worse, he could no longer hope to function as an assassin when serious physical exertion caused him to wheeze like an old man.

With time on his hands and little to do except rest and hope for the best, he contemplated two mysteries. The first was his last conversation with Lemuel Unwin. The enigmatic priest had hinted that he suspected a traitor in their ranks. The other issue that troubled him was the identity of the woman who'd so nearly cost him his life. Who was she and why had she been in the factory at night?

Thomas pondered both mysteries but failed to make any progress in their solution. He was almost relieved when he realised that his provisions were running low, and he would need to venture outside for fresh supplies. He'd made no contact with anyone – a half formed plan to let everyone assume he was dead would provide a perfect cover under which he could pursue the answer to one or both of his personal mysteries.

Farral reached out for the glass of water on the rickety lopsided table at the side of his bed. After several gulps of the cooling liquid, his memory jumped forward to a week earlier. Things had not gone to plan.

It was after midnight when he'd emerged from his bedroom window and crept across the roof of his secret hideaway. Descending silently down a rope ladder normally rolled up and stored among the chimney pots, he paused when his feet touched the narrow alleyway. As he waited for the pain in his arms and chest to subside and whilst he recovered his breath, his eyes became accustomed to the dark. Confident that his unconventional arrival in the alley had gone unnoticed, he set off for the backstreets that would take him to a grocer's almost a mile away.

It took him just a few seconds to open the back door with one of his picklocks. He was filling a sack with provisions when a scraping sound sent him scurrying behind one of the shop counters. He crouched down, listening for any sound of activity. After a short pause, the scraping sound resumed, and he realised that someone was attempting to jemmy the front door. Thomas hoped that the would-be thief would give up and go away but, to his dismay, he heard the lock click and the creak of the door as it swung inwards on its rusting hinges.

Peering round the corner of the counter, Farral watched as a large man sauntered through the door, followed by a scrawny youth who pushed it closed behind him. The pair started to head towards the back of the shop and the counter behind which Thomas was hiding. The big man suddenly stopped in the middle of the room, flinging out an arm to halt his companion. He raised his head and snuffled like a bloodhound. 'What's that funny smell?' he whispered.

'Dunno. What smell? I can't smell nuffin'.'

'Bah. You're useless. Sumfin' ain't right 'ere.'

Thomas slid a throwing knife from the top of his left boot.

'Can't you smell it? It's like sumfin' a quack would use.'

Thomas cursed himself for not realising that the lotions he'd been using smelt so strong.

The big man seemed to arrive at a decision. 'Freddy, I fink as we've got company,' he said. He pointed a finger the size of a sausage at the counter. 'Come out 'ere where I can sees yer.' In his other hand he held a cosh. Farral noticed the glint of metal around the business end of the weapon. He didn't doubt that its owner would know how to use it.

Thomas surged up and threw the knife in one smooth motion. It buried itself in the big man's chest, rupturing the heart. As his victim looked down in surprise, the younger man froze.

Even in the pale moonlight, Thomas could see the open-mouthed look on the younger man's face. 'Wrong place, wrong time,' he said, as he took a step closer to the Freddy.

Hearing Thomas speak seemed to snap Freddy out of his shock. 'Wot?' I ...'

A poisoned dart, fired from the tiny crossbow strapped to Thomas' right forearm, took him in the throat and he slumped to the floor without finishing his sentence.

'Sorry,' said Thomas, 'but I can't afford for you to see me. You should have stayed at home. Or chosen somewhere else to rob.'

He calmly retrieved his knife and the bolt, checking that both men were dead. The big man looked like a hardened thug, but Freddy was little more than a boy. Thomas didn't feel sorry for either. He couldn't afford to allow either of them to live long enough to talk about a scarred man. The Blades had spies everywhere and one of them might connect such a tale to himself. Adding a few more items to his sack, Farral then set off for the back door and home. The shopkeeper and the police would struggle to work out what had happened here but, in the end, they'd conclude that a gang had fallen out with each other and that two less thieves to worry about wasn't such a bad result after all.

As his mind returned to the present, Thomas arrived at a decision. He'd moved to Bristol and into his current room a few weeks ago, having decided to keep an eye on who went in and out of the hotel. It was a regular haunt for members of the Shield, and he'd recalled Unwin saying that he needed to go to Bristol soon. If he was going to break cover, then Unwin was the one man he could trust.

Sure enough, the priest had turned up outside the building. But, to his astonishment, Farral had watched as Unwin was attacked from behind and dragged, apparently unconscious, into a cab. Thomas had no idea where he'd been taken but he'd recognised the cab driver and knew which drinking dens he patronised.

Moving a small rug to one side of the room, Thomas used a kitchen knife to prise up a loose floorboard. Lying full length on the floor, he used his left hand to feel down unto the opening he'd revealed and groped around for a few seconds before pulling out a canvas bag. He placed the bag on his bed, then put the board back in its usual place and pulled the rug back to cover it. Sitting on the bed, he untied the cord around the neck of the bag and emptied out its contents. Within minutes, he'd assembled a pistol and checked the firing mechanism before loading it with ammunition. Donning a coat and a large scarf wrapped around his lower face and neck, he checked his other weapons as he headed for the door. Thomas Farral had finished with feeling sorry for himself.

Farral had no intention of entering the timber framed Llandoger Trow. The tavern had stood on King Street for several centuries among the filth of the docks. Its regular patrons were a motley selection of thieves, pickpockets, whores, and assorted ne'er-do-wells. Many would cut your throat for a few pence and fights were common, if generally confined to one of its many nooks and crannies. The beer was foul and the food worse – the meat pies often contained horsemeat scavenged from the local abattoirs or, even worse, rat-meat. He didn't want to think about or know where the latter might have come from. But he did know that the local police rarely set foot on the premises, preferring to see it as a cesspit where their natural foes gathered to drink, quarrel and fight themselves into oblivion.

Although it had several exits, most could be observed from a pawnbroker's shop doorway, and it was here that he took up temporary residence. The streetlights outside offered little illumination but, even so, Thomas pressed himself back against the door, eager to minimise the chance of being discovered by anyone who passed by. He frowned as he heard a church clock strike the tenth hour. It might be a long night ahead.

Farral turned up his coat collar and tightened the scarf as the temperature fell, although he was protected from the worst of a chill wind by the doorway. He stamped his feet from time-to-time, always watching as various men emerged from the tavern before staggering homewards in a cloud of oaths, boasts, threats and promises.

At last, his wait was rewarded when, a little after two in the morning, he spotted his target. He emerged in company with another, and the pair had stood for a few moments in deep discussion. Both wore a dark greatcoat but only his target wore a hat - one of the ubiquitous bowler hats so beloved of the lower classes. After a brief handshake, they had taken different routes.

As the man he was after approached the doorway, Farral scanned the immediate vicinity. There was no sign of anyone else in the vicinity and he eased out of the shadows and fell in behind the other man, taking care to move with as little noise as possible. Judging from his gait, the target was the worse for wear and Farral allowed himself a quick grin. If the other's thoughts were clouded by drink, then that made his own task so much easier.

Soon, their route turned left down an alleyway. Farral paused for a few moments, peering round the corner. A curse rent the night air as the first man stumbled over an old crate, losing his hat in the process. As he stooped to retrieve it, Farral surged forward, wrapping an arm around a scrawny neck as its owner returned to an upright position. In his hand, Thomas held a long-serrated dagger, which he pressed firmly against his victim's throat. The overpowering stench of sweat and ale made him want to gag.

'Quiet now. You and I are going to have a little talk. Tell me what I want to know, and you live. Try anything else and ...' He pressed a little harder, dragging the edge of the blade across the skin and drawing a thin line of blood.

'You don' know who yer messin' wif.' The other man tried a gentle arch of his back, looking for a means of escape.

'Do that again and you die,' hissed Farral.

'Wot does yer want? I ain't got no money. Spent it all.'

'I don't need money. I want information.'

'Eh?'

'The man who was kidnapped outside of the hotel last night. You were driving the hansom cab that took him away. Where did you go?'

The other man shrugged. 'I can't tell ye that. It's more'n my life's worth.'

Farral quickly reversed his grip on the dagger and smashed the pommel into the man's temple. He stepped back, releasing his grip, as the other slumped to the ground. He swallowed a few mouthfuls of the cool night air before, with a sigh, he secreted the weapon back in its hiding place and bent down. He hoisted the unconscious man to his feet and, supporting the weight, set off for the waterfront. Before they set off, Farral kicked the bowler hat into a foul-smelling puddle. To any casual observer, the pair looked like two drunks staggering home after a night of heavy drinking.

It took Farral almost thirty minutes to make it to the old, deserted warehouse. A quick look round confirmed that everything was as he had left it and he set to work after removing his coat. The effort of half-carrying his unwilling companion had taken its toll and Thomas was breathing heavily through his damaged lungs.

Minutes later, a bucket of cold seawater roused the captive back to the waking world. He came to with a start and his eyes widened as he found himself securely tied to a chair. He started to struggle.

'Allow me to explain your predicament,' said Farral. 'You are my prisoner here in this abandoned place. There is no-one within earshot. Now you have one last chance to answer my question. Or ...' He waved the dagger in front of his prisoner's face.

'I told yer. I'm sayin' nothin'.'

Farral moved to the bound man's left side and casually sliced off the tip of his ear.

A howl echoed around the room as blood spurted from the wound.

'You were saying?' prompted Farral.

His captive looked into eyes that betrayed no hint of mercy. Tears ran down the wounded man's face. 'If I tells ye, I'm as good as dead. Please.'

Farral smiled and took hold of the man's right hand, splaying the fingers against the arm of the chair. 'Which one do you want to lose first?'

23: ANGELE

Wallace watched the victorious soldiers looting the bodies of their fallen opponents. His face betrayed no emotion, although his attention was fixed upon a specific part of the battlefield. At last he stirred into motion.

Madeleine sat with her back against an old oak tree. She had spent several hours patching blankets, looking up at Wallace from time to time. Her efforts at engaging him in conversation had been brushed aside. But now she spoke again. 'Where are you going?' She lay her work to one side, preparing to accompany him.

'Don't get up. I have a small task to carry out, but it might be dangerous. You'll be safe here until I return.' He smiled at her before lowering his voice, 'And I've asked Frederick to keep an eye on you.'

Madeleine frowned and started to speak, but then reached for another blanket. 'Be careful.'

Without replying, Wallace walked away, heading for the edge of the trees and towards the battlefield.

A voice at her side made Madeleine jump. 'Don't worry. My men will cover him.'

She looked round at Sagana. 'Cover him? Why? Where's he going?'

'There's someone he needs to meet, and we've just lured him over here. But you don't need to know more than this or to worry about it.'

Wallace came out from behind a large tree just as one of de Montfort's soldiers walked past. He mimed relieving himself and grinned at the startled man.

'I don't recognise you. Who's your lord-commander? What are you doing in the trees?' asked the soldier.

Wallace held up a hand. 'Slow down. Fighting always makes me want to empty my bladder. I'm one of the mercenaries. Although, to be honest, I don't think you needed us.' He shrugged, then looked back towards the trees. 'I thought I saw a couple of those Aragonese cowards run in here. And when I saw you heading this way, I thought you might have seen them as well.'

The other gave him an appraising look. 'And thought you might help yourself to some booty, eh? I didn't see anything except a flash of sunlight on metal.'

'Well, you can't blame me for trying! And I'm happy to share. There might have been three of them. We could split it, say half and half?'

De Montfort's man pondered this offer for a few seconds then grinned. 'Alright. But I'm not going too far into this wood. There might still be spoils ripe for the taking back there.' He waved his left arm at the bodies strewn behind him.

Wallace chuckled. 'I doubt the scavengers have left much for either of us. Let's try our luck.' He started towards the trees, hearing a twig snap as the other man followed him. As planned, he led the way along a narrow trail, pausing now and then to study the ground, as if looking for signs of passage.

After a few minutes, he entered a thicket. His companion followed, then realised he'd lost Wallace. 'Where are you?' he hissed. When there was no answer, the man reached for the sword at his hip and started to back away.

Seconds later, three arrows took him from behind and he pitched forward. Wallace suddenly reappeared in his failing vision. He looked down at the dying man and shook his head from side to side. 'Sorry, but you have something I want.'

'Bast ...' said the man, just as the last flicker of light died in his eyes.

Wallace bent and sliced the ties holding a purse to the man's belt. He undid the cord and upended the contents into the palm of his right hand. He took a small oval-shaped blood-red jewel from his hand and dropped it next to his foot, then poured the rest of the contents back into the purse, before retying its cord and throwing the bag to a watching archer. 'Here, you can split this with the other two as a reward for your help.' The man deftly caught the purse, grinned at Wallace, and then disappeared into the trees.

The warrior glanced around then bent down to pick up the jewel. He added it to his own purse before hurrying back towards Sagana's camp.

Madeleine leapt to her feet when Wallace reappeared. 'Who did you meet?'

Wallace frowned. 'What makes you think I met someone?'

'Sagana. He said – '

'I see. Well, it's nothing for you to worry about. I'm back now. And hungry. Let's go see if any of the men have something we can eat?'

'In other words, you're not going to tell me?' She had her hands on her hips and a scowl on her face.

Wallace grinned. 'Trust me. It was nothing important and there's no harm done. Are you hungry or not?'

Madeleine hesitated. 'When everyone keeps telling me not to worry? I hope you know what you're getting yourself involved in.'

'I can look after myself. And I promise that I won't let anything bad happen to you either. I haven't forgotten what you did back at that tavern and although I don't claim to be the best of men, I do have some honour. I owe you and I won't risk my soul by ignoring that debt.'

Madeleine relaxed, a smile replacing the scowl. 'Very well, but I don't like secrets.'

After they'd shared a meal of dried meat, cheese, bread and fresh water with Frederick and his men, Wallace asked the mercenary captain where he could find Sagana.

'Oh, he left a little while ago. Said he had urgent business in Clermont-le-Fort. It's a small village roughly due east of here and a few hours' ride. He took some of my men and said the rest of us should follow him there once you've completed your business here.'

'Could we make it before nightfall?'

'I don't see why not. It might be a good idea to get away from here anyway.' Frederick raised an eyebrow as his eyes betrayed a flicker of mirth. 'Let's get going then.'

With Frederick in the lead, their little column headed away from Muret. The other soldiers gave Wallace and Madeleine some privacy, although there were always men on all sides of them. As they rode, Madeleine spoke softly to Wallace. 'You do know that Sagana left Frederick and his men to make sure we don't just ride off?'

'The thought had crossed my mind. But it's not surprising. Once again, I have something he wants and he's testing me – to see if I can be trusted.'

'Providing us with an armed escort seems an odd way of trusting someone!'

'Or … he places great value on what I'm carrying.'

Madeleine gave him a sharp look. 'And *what* are you carrying?'

Wallace sighed, then fished inside his purse. After a few moments, he held the jewel between his thumb and forefinger. 'This. I think it's another object that he needs for his religious quest.'

Madeleine pursed her lips and the colour drained from her face.

Wallace reined up his mount and put the jewel back into his purse. 'What's the matter?'

Madeleine struggled to control her own horse and before she spoke Wallace could see that her eyes had grown wide and round. 'You don't know?'

'Know what?'

'That jewel. It has a religious significance but not in the way you think. It's a blood stone. It's used by high-ranking members of The Blood Cult.'

Wallace frowned. 'The one's you mentioned back at the tavern? You thought they'd had a hand in your father's death.'

179

Madeleine looked around, the tension in her body making her horse skittish. 'I've heard that they practise vile things, including human sacrifice. I thought that Muller might be one of them but ...' she paused as a rider approached.

'Is something wrong?' Frederick looked concerned.

'It's nothing. The lady just felt a little faint, but I think she's alright now.'

'Then we need to keep moving.'

As Frederick rode back to the head of their little column, Wallace glanced across at Madeleine. 'We'll talk more. But not now. Somewhere where we can't be overheard.'

The group rode on in silence. Madeleine stole the occasional glance at Wallace, but he seemed to be lost in thought.

Frederick led them on, staying close to cover whenever he could, although Wallace could detect no signs they were being followed. It was dusk as Frederick led them into the small village of Clermont-le-Fort. He urged his horse into a canter and was soon dismounting outside a dilapidated hut that was almost twice the size of its companions.

Madeleine slid down from her own horse, complaining about the soreness of her thighs. Wallace followed her example but said nothing as he handed both sets of reins to one of Frederick's men. Madeleine nodded her agreement when he inclined his head towards the larger hut and the pair set off towards it.

As they approached its entrance, Madeleine commented on the unusual number of small bones strewn around. Wallace responded with a non-committal grunt. Stopping just outside the tattered cloth that covered the entrance, he called out 'Sagana? Are you in there?'

There was a pause and the sound of a chest being closed before a familiar voice replied, 'Yes. Come on in. There's someone I'd like you to meet.'

Madeleine followed Wallace into the hut, wrinkling her nose as the smell hit her. It was gloomy inside, with little light provided by the rush torch that hung from the ceiling, sputtering smoke and sparks. As their eyes adjusted, the new arrivals could make out two others standing in the room. Madeleine flung a hand across her mouth, trying to supress a gasp as she identified Sagana and an old woman.

A low chuckle broke the silence. 'Surprised little lady?' The old woman held up a hand. 'Not pretty enough for you? Well, never mind. It's what's locked in here,' she tapped her head, 'that matters.'

Sagana coughed to draw their attention. 'Don't mind Angele. She's an old friend who has offered to help me with the statue you delivered into my keeping. The locals think she's some sort of enchantress but that's because they don't understand what she can do with a few herbs and a bit of old lore.' He smiled at Madeleine before adding,' She's harmless. Unless you cross her.' As he said this, he exchanged a meaningful glance with Angele.

The old woman let out another laugh before dragging a tattered sleeve across her mouth. 'True enough,' she agreed, spitting out a gobbet of something dark.

Wallace looked pointedly at the foul-smelling mess that had landed just short of his left boot. Looking up, he snarled, 'I've killed men for less than that.' He took a step towards Angele.

Sagana stepped between the pair. Turning to look at the old woman he said, 'Now Angele, that's no way to treat my friends.' He looked Wallace in the eye as he continued, 'She didn't mean anything by it. Angele isn't used to receiving visitors and sometimes forgets her manners.' He turned back towards her. 'Perhaps some wine would help to settle everyone?'

Angele stared at Sagana for a few seconds before blinking. 'I've got a bottle somewhere. Took it in payment from a tavern owner whose daughter was poxed. He gave it me when she recovered, even though I couldn't do anything about the scars on her face. I told him – '

'The wine?' prompted Sagana.

'Yes, of course.' As she shuffled deeper into the shadows at the back of the room, Angele continued to mutter to herself. 'No-one cares to hear about my work these days. People think I'm just a stupid old hag.' She lifted a piece of blanket from a small table, revealing a solitary bottle laid on its side. 'Here it is. Don't know if it's still ... '

Frederick burst into the hut, almost knocking Madeleine over in his haste. 'My lord, you'd better come outside.'

24: Personal investigation

Whiston sat on his bed, deep in thought. A greasy mess of gravy-soaked meat had congealed on the plate bearing his half-eaten meal, which had been left on the floor by his feet. He'd not mentioned the note to Mindelen when they met up again in the police station, simply confirming that he too had found nothing useful to throw any light on the identity of the man responsible for killing either Alice or the three victims at Mistress Lydia's establishment.

Numerous thoughts revolved in his head. What was it that linked Glanville and Unwin to himself? The first was dead – horribly murdered – and the second had lived in the same house as another recent murder victim who'd also been mutilated in a gruesome manner.

He put his head in his hands. Thinking was getting him nowhere and yet ... if Mindelen is somehow right in believing the priest is the killer, why is he interested in me? How does he even know that I'm investigating the murders? And where do the deaths at the brothel fit in? Was I the real target and not my poor beloved Rose? Would she still be alive if I hadn't visited her that dreadful night?

An image of the spider-creature sprang into his mind, unbidden and unwelcome. What had the evil thing been? How could it be related to the priest? Was it some sort of devil spawned from the pits of Hell?

A half-born plan which had been brewing at the back of his thoughts chose this moment to take shape in his mind. 'Yes, I'll do it!' he said out loud to the empty room.

The next morning Whiston arrived at work a little earlier than was necessary. He hovered outside until he saw a familiar figure heading towards him.

'Good morning, Inspector. Would you be able to spare me a few minutes of your time, sir?'

'Eh? What? Oh, it's you, Whiston! What the devil do you mean by waylaying me like this?'

Inspector Johnson was clearly unhappy to see him, but Whiston wasn't about to let his idea drop. *Not if it helps to find Rose's murderer.* 'I'd appreciate a few minutes of your time, Sir. I might have a lead on the person responsible for the recent spate of murders, but I wanted to get your opinion before I do anything about it.'

The Inspector consulted his fob watch. 'Oh very well. I'll give you two minutes. This had better be good though; I don't make a habit of listening to every half-baked idea my junior staff come up with.'

'Thank you, inspector.' Whiston held the door open for Johnson. Once inside the station, Whiston followed the Inspector straight into his office, noting the surprised look on the face of Mindelen as he set eyes on the pair of them.

Johnson removed his coat and hat, then sat down at his desk. He pointedly didn't ask Whiston to sit, while he parted his watch from its chain and set it on the desk. 'Well?'

The younger man cleared his throat. 'I've had a tip-off from a local snitch. He's usually dependable. The thing is, it seems our suspect has fled to Bristol under a false name.' He watched the seated man, praying that Johnson would assume he was talking about Unwin.

After a slight pause, the Inspector looked up from his watch. 'And ...?'

'I'd like a few days to follow up this lead, sir.'

Johnson frowned. 'Why you? It would make more sense to send a more experienced man, such as your sergeant. Or we could just send a message and the details to the local force.' He sat back. 'You've got 30 seconds.'

Whiston had anticipated this reaction. Now he played what he hoped would be his trump card. 'For some reason, my snitch says he'll only divulge the false name and Bristol address to me when we both arrive in the city, sir. He doesn't want a reward, just his train fare.'

The Inspector took a while to digest this last piece of information. Whiston distracted himself by imagining the cogs turning in the other man's head. He half expected to see small puffs of dust erupting from Johnson's ears as little used bits of the man's brain came to life. 'Why does he want to go to Bristol?'

Whiston felt a sense of elation. *I've got him!* 'I'm not certain, Sir, but I think he's upset somebody here in London and wants to lie low for a while. At least while he's in Bristol he won't be making any work or trouble for us here.'

'Very well. You have three days. But this had better not be a waste of time, Whiston. Do you understand me?'

'Yes Sir, Thank you, Sir. I will of course report back to you as soon as I return.'

'Very good. And take Mindelen with you.'

Inside, Whiston let out a string of profanities.

'Bristol? Bristol! Why in the name of all that's 'oly would you want to go there?' Mindelen was far from happy, and he had Whiston pinned up against a wall.

Whiston felt flecks of spittle hit his face. 'Calm down, sergeant. It's the Inspector's orders, based on information from a snitch.'

'What snitch?' yelled Mindelen, causing heads to turn in their direction.

'Whiston swallowed. 'You're attracting attention. Why don't we discuss this in a more civilised manner, somewhere more private?'

'Giving me orders as well now, are we?'

'Of course not. But we don't want the whole of this side of London to know where we're going, do we?'

Mindelen glared at the younger man, then released his hold and stepped back. 'So who's the snitch and 'ow does 'e know where the priest 'as gone?'

'The tip-off was that we should take a look at The Queen's Hotel in Bristol. The Inspector thinks it's worth a shot.' Whiston knew that he was playing a dangerous game here, but his deliberate ploy of letting both Johnson and Mindelen jump to their own conclusions was the only way he could think of that would allow him to hunt for Mr Black. If his suspicions were correct then he'd be the hero of the hour; if they were wrong, then it would probably be the end of his career as a policeman.

'Suppose that's some expensive place, then?'

'What makes you suppose that sergeant?'

'Stands to reason. A priest isn't going to slum it when 'is church is stuffed to the rafters with gold and treasure.'

Whiston shook his head. 'The valuables don't belong to the priests, sergeant. They belong to God.'

'Same thing, in my book!'

'Well, let's not waste time arguing theology. We've a train to catch if we're going to Bristol. There's one in a little over two hours, out of Paddington.'

'Yeah, I suppose so. I'd better go and pack a few things then. We can meet at the railway station in an hour and a half.'

Whiston spotted Mindelen scanning the crowded station concourse. The sergeant was carrying a surprisingly smart-looking overnight bag and wearing his best topcoat and hat. 'Over here,' he called as Mindelen was walking past him.

The sergeant's head turned towards Whiston. 'Oh, there you is. I was startin' to think as you'd got lost.'

'No sergeant, I've been here for a good ten minutes or so. I've already purchased our tickets. Second class.' He paused, aware that Mindelen was more interested in scanning the crowd around them. 'Are you expecting someone else to show up, sergeant?'

'Eh? No, I was trying to see if I could spot this snitch of yours. To be 'onest, I'm surprised an officer as green as yourself even knows a snitch.'

Whiston ignored the jibe. 'Indeed. So there are some things you don't know about me, sergeant?' He forced himself to make the comment sound jocular. Even so, Mindelen gave him a long hard stare.

'If I thought you was mockin' me, there'd be 'ell to pay young Whiston.'

'Mock you, sergeant? The thought never entered my head.' He stooped to pick up his own bag. 'Here's our train.'

As the train chugged out of the station, the two policemen sat in silence. The peace was broken by an elderly stooped man who entered their compartment with two large bags of his own. 'Sorry gents.' He paused, weighing up the other occupants with furtive glances in their general direction. 'Is there room in here for one more?'

Whiston looked up with a weak smile on his lips. 'It would appear so.' At his side, Mindelen gave a low growl of discontent.

The newcomer stowed one bag on the overhead rack before parking the other under the carriage window. 'Name's Smythe,' he announced to no-one in particular. 'Travelling salesman. I deal in old books.' He hesitated for a fraction of a second then continued, 'Either of you two fine gentlemen interested in books?'

'No,' said Mindelen.

'Yes,' said Whiston, at the same time.

'Then permit me show you my wares, young sir,' said Smythe, a wide grin on his face.

186

'You got a licence to sell on this train?' asked Mindelen, leaning towards the suddenly alarmed salesman.

'Well, I ...'

'That'll be a 'no' then?'

'Sir, I'm merely trying to earn an honest living.'

'Aren't we all. We're policemen, see, but as I'm in a good mood, I'll let you off with a warnin' this time. Now clear off afore I changes my mind.'

Smythe gathered his bags and left to look for another seat.

'You were a bit harsh, sergeant,' suggested Whiston.

'I let 'im off, didn't I?' Mindelen folded his arms across his chest. 'Now keep quiet while I 'as a nap.' Moments later, a gentle snoring filled the carriage. Whiston sighed. It was going to be a long journey.

Whiston was having a bad dream. A giant spider with a human face had him trapped in a corner and was about to make him its next meal. As he felt a sharp fang sink into his ribs, he gave a yelp before opening his eyes to find Mindelen peering at him.

'Wake up lad, you was squealin' like a girl.'

'Sorry, sergeant. Bad dream I suppose.' He sat up straight. 'Something evil was trying to eat me.'

'Hmmph. That's what comes of readin' stupid books, with their fancy stories and daft ideas.'

'Makes a change from the bad cheese theory.'

'Eh? What you on about now?'

'It doesn't matter. Anyway, I'm awake now. Where are we?'

'Darned if I knows. Somewhere near Bristol I suppose.'

Whiston consulted his timepiece. 'If the train is on time, we should be there in about 20 minutes.'

'Good, I've 'ad enough of listenin' to you whimperin' in me right ear'ole.'

'Should we take a cab to the local police station?' asked Whiston.

'Well I ain't walkin'! All this sittin' down 'as made me tired.'

Alighting from the London train, the two police officers headed for the cab rank, paying little attention to their surroundings. A pair of dark eyes picked them out of the crowd. Satisfied that the identity of the younger man corresponded to a description supplied by their master, the owner of the eyes lingered near the waiting cabs. Here she had no difficulty in over-hearing the older man instruct a driver to take the pair to the Western Division police station. As soon as they had set off, she hailed a cab of her own, giving the driver a private address in the southern part of the city.

Mindelen strode into the police station as if he owned the place. He pushed aside a young officer who was struggling to keep hold of a street urchin and demanded the immediate attention of the desk sergeant.

'See here, now, sir. You can't just walk in and expect to be dealt with immediately. The officer here was about to book in this young miscreant for pickpocketing.'

Mindelen ignored the rebuke. 'I'm Sergeant Mindelen from London and I'm 'ere with my young assistant,' he pointed over his shoulder to a spot roughly where he'd told Whiston to wait for him, 'in pursuit of a murder suspect. So, I'd like a word with your Inspector if it's not too much trouble.'

Whiston saw the look this elicited from the desk officer and winced inside.

'Is that right. Then, as I'm sure you know, sergeant...?'

'Mindelen.'

'... Mindelen, it's customary to first offer some proof of identity.'

If Mindelen registered the rebuke, he did an excellent job of hiding the fact. 'Very good, sergeant. I'm pleased to see you country officers are acquainted with proper procedure.' He fished inside his coat and produced a battered warrant card. Without looking for his colleague he barked, 'Whiston. Show the officer your card.'

Whiston picked up both overnight bags and made his way to the desk. Depositing the luggage, he also produced his card.

The desk sergeant gave both cards a cursory glance then smiled. 'Welcome to Bristol, gentlemen. I'm sorry to have to tell you that our Inspector is out at the moment.' He turned to look at Mindelen. 'And no, I don't know when he'll be back. You're welcome to wait in the back office if you like. Or you could find your hotel and try again later.' With that, he turned to the young officer who still held the struggling pickpocket. 'Now then young Barraclough, where were we before the interruption?'

Mindelen started to protest, but Whiston pulled him away from the desk. 'Sergeant, we're not in London now and it might be a good idea not to antagonise the locals?' As Mindelen strode away, muttering to himself, Whiston caught the desk officer's eye. 'Sorry about that, sergeant. My colleague meant no offense. He just wanted to let your Inspector know we were on his patch and following up a lead on a murder suspect.'

The desk sergeant nodded, a smile playing around his lips, then returned to the task of booking-in the young pickpocket.

Mindelen had paused halfway to the station door and dropped his bag. He glared at Whiston before picking up his luggage and heading once more for the exit. Whiston followed, anticipating the angry ticking off that he suspected would be coming his way outside. To his surprise, Mindelen shrugged his shoulders. 'Guess you're right, for once. I let me impatience get the better of me. Let's find somewhere to stay.'

25: A PRAYER IS ANSWERED

As soon as the door closed, Unwin tested the restraints. It didn't take him long to realise the futility of this exercise. The wound on his forearm still stung and he wondered if the blade had been coated with something. Struggling to see the wound proved yet another waste of time, so he tried to consider the limited options available. He was surprised to find this difficult, and his vision began to blur. 'Sleeping drug?' he asked as the room began to spin.

Unwin came to with a start. Something had aroused him from an uneasy slumber, and he feared that it could be the return of his captor, keen to make a start on the delayed interrogation. The priest was cold and stiff, hungry, and thirsty and expected to die within the next few hours. The only uncertainty was whether he would reveal any of the Shield's most precious secrets. His gloomy musing was interrupted by the sound of the cell door being opened.

A familiar tall figure appeared at the periphery of Unwin's vision and seemed to be studying him before it bent closer. He felt a warm hand on his thigh.

'I apologise for being away longer than planned. I hope you're not too comfortable idling away your time here.' McNulty gave a lop-sided grin, impressed with his own wit. When Unwin made no reply, the other's face creased into a frown. 'Cat got your tongue? Well, my friend, you needn't worry about that. I'll leave your tongue alone, else how are you going to tell me what I want to know?'

The tall figure moved out of view, then reappeared at Unwin's other side a few moments later. 'Don't worry, it won't be much longer before I'm ready to begin. But first, let me explain what's going to happen. I'll ask a question and you'll give me an answer. If I even suspect that you are being less than entirely honest, then you'll be punished. We can't have a dishonest priest now, can we? Of course, I'll already know some of the answers.' A finger caressed Unwin's left ankle but still he maintained a stubborn silence, aware of the beads of sweat on his brow.

Wallace McNulty grinned once more. 'Each time I think you're lying I'll remove a little of your skin. How much depends on the size of the lie. And, of course, if you maintain this petulant silence then I'll be forced to remove even more of your worthless hide.' He paused, waiting for Unwin to digest this information, and watching the priest's face for any reaction. Unwin fought to give nothing away but knew he'd failed when he saw the gleam of triumph in the other man's eyes.

Pressing home this advantage, McNulty continued. 'Of course, I won't just remove random pieces of skin. Oh no. That would be both messy and pose no challenge. No, I'm going to use your body in the way an artist uses a blank canvas. Can you guess what I'm going to attempt?'

When Unwin didn't answer, McNulty moved away and began to hum a popular music hall song to himself. The significance of the song abruptly hit Unwin when he found himself mentally supplying the lyrics and reaching the line about peeling an orange. Unable to prevent himself from shivering in apprehension, he found his captor peering at him once more.

'Good. I knew you were a man of the world. And you're right. I *am* going to peel you like an orange.' He paused. 'Well, not quite like an orange. You see, I've set myself the challenge of peeling your skin in one piece. The ancient Assyrians used to be quite good at it – I believe they could keep the victim alive for up to three days.'

Unwin gave an involuntary shudder.

'That's right. I'll start with your feet, work my way up your legs, skin your crotch and then start on your buttocks, back and chest. I'm not sure how far I'll get before you die but then again, I don't see that as a problem. It will be fun finding out.'

The priest bit the inside of his mouth.

'Excuse me while I get my best scalpel. In the meantime, you can prepare your first answer. With Cox and Farral dead and you enjoying my hospitality, which leaves just one of your accursed assassins unaccounted for. So where is George Hunt?'

Unwin's mind raced. If he deliberately lied to McNulty and the latter carried out his threat, then the price would be excruciating pain. But it would also bring him a step closer to death. The question was, how much could he endure? If he succumbed to the torture, he might be forced to give away vital secrets. He decided to test the limits of his pain threshold. 'George who?'

For a moment, his captor stared at him. Then he began to chuckle. 'Oh very good. You think to cheat me by dying?' He moved to the foot of the table. 'Very well, let's play your game for a little while. His hand moved and Unwin watched as the scalpel disappeared from sight, only to re-emerge clothed in a red substance. Moments later, the pain receptors in Unwin's foot gave vent to their anger.

'Instep, just in case you were wondering. When I'm annoyed with you, I'll remove a toe – makes it easier to peel the leg without having to worry about little complications like that. I'll just get a napkin to wipe my implement clean. Wouldn't do for dried blood to degrade the effectiveness of the blade.' McNulty stepped towards the door and disappeared from Unwin's view.

It wasn't long before he reappeared, bending over the priest's chest. He waved the scalpel close to Unwin's face. Wallace McNulty appeared to be pondering something but then shrugged. 'No, on balance I think I'll leave you your sight. I was wondering whether to stick this scalpel through your left eye – purely in the interests of science, of course – but I'm in a generous mood tonight. I'm sure you want to be able to see inside your own body just as much as I do.'

Unwin struggled to maintain his stubborn silence when McNulty suddenly patted the priest's wounded foot, sending lances of fire surging up the leg.

'Now, let's try again. Where is George Hunt?'

'I don't know.'

'Hmmm. I suppose that could be true.' McNulty grinned. 'I know though. He's currently languishing in a cell as a guest of a good friend of mine. The poor fellow isn't in the best of health.' He paused, head cocked to one side. 'Don't you want to know what's wrong with him?'

'Would you tell me even if I cared?'

'That's the spirit. Since you've decided to play along, I'll tell you. It seems poor George has unwittingly ingested the eggs of an organ beetle. A curious creature and not really a beetle, but then again, it's not native to this realm.' Wallace McNulty paused, clearly enjoying himself.

Despite himself, Unwin felt compelled to ask what his captor meant.

'You mean to say that you haven't discovered this is not a unique realm of existence? Oh dear. No wonder your precious Shield is such a weak opponent. But where was I?' Feigning momentary confusion, Wallace took up the narrative once more. 'The organ beetle. Unusual form of life. Vicious too. You see it lays its eggs in water. Other creatures drink the water, and the eggs then incubate inside their gut. When they hatch, the larvae feed on the internal organs of their host as they burrow their way out. What is really fascinating is the way that the young beetles manage to time their exit just before the host dies.'

Unwin felt tears begin to form. George had been his apprentice and was still a young man. No-one deserved such a disgusting death.

'Anyway, I've given you a piece of information, so now it's your turn. Let me see ... ah, yes. Where is the Blade of Banishment?'

Unwin was genuinely confused. 'What?' he blurted.

McNulty stepped back. 'You really don't know? Disappointing, although your ignorance suggests you may be of less value to me than I'd thought.' Almost as an afterthought, he added, 'I need to ponder this and consult with an ally. But don't worry, I'll be back soon.' He started to walk away but turned back as if struck by an afterthought. There was a brief impact then Unwin screamed.

A scalpel stuck out of Unwin's right eye.

'I did say I'd leave your left eye alone. But I didn't give any assurances about the other one.

Unwin was still thrashing about on the table as the cell door closed.

The priest mourned the loss of his eye through gritted teeth. He had no way of measuring time but knew that blood loss and hunger were slowly weakening him. It was with some degree of shock that he realised he still wanted to live. 'Oh mighty God, please hear my prayer. Help me to escape this place and I swear I will devote my remaining days to bringing your righteous punishment down upon the head of Wallace McNulty.' He repeated these words a number of times before lapsing into quiescence, trying to conserve as much strength as possible. If God had favoured him, he believed there would be just one opportunity to escape this predicament.

The cell door opened once more. Unwin tensed, expecting to see the smirking face of Wallace, and mentally preparing himself for more pain. Instead, the light level in the room began to increase, slowly at first but then more rapidly. Confused, Unwin used his remaining good eye to watch as a ball of pure white light hovered at the foot of the table. It was revolving at an ever-increasing speed and also seemed to be growing larger. As the intensity of the light increased it became painful to watch and Unwin was forced to lower the lid, although this didn't entirely blot out the brightness. In growing terror, he lay still, sensing rather than feeling something soft and warm touch his injured foot, right forearm, and mutilated right eye. A gentle voice murmured close to his right ear, and he realised that the brightness had now diminished. Through a half-lowered lid, he risked a glance towards the light source and blinked in astonishment.

A strange humanoid creature stood smiling at him. Without thinking, Unwin sat up, still not registering that the shackles around both wrists and ankles had been removed.

'Who or what are you?' he whispered in a voice tinged with both awe and fear.

'*There is little time to waste. You may call me The Guide. I represent those of the Elder Gods who wage eternal war on the group you know as the Black Blades. One of your allies comes to rescue you but he will need help. This is your chance to escape the fate planned for you. Take it.*' With these words still echoing in Unwin's head the creature began to fade.

Unwin now realised that not only was he free, but his wounds had been healed. He was still weak and naked though. Eyes roaming the cell, he sought some sort of weapon. They came to rest on a small table which held a neat row of sharp implements. He smiled. A God had answered his prayers, although he wasn't sure who this God was. Right now he didn't care. Climbing from the table, he walked stiffly towards the table, outstretched hand reaching for a large cleaver that looked as if it would be more at home in a butcher's shop.

Unwin began to perform a few exercises to work the stiffness from his joints. He was halfway through these when he heard faint sounds and a muffled but raised voice. Some instinct told him that help had arrived.

26: BETRAYAL

Wallace stepped to one side as Sagana strode past him, closely followed by Frederick. By the time both he and Madeleine had followed the pair outside, Frederick was waving towards a hut on the edge of the village.

'My men found it behind that hut over there.'

'And you interrupted my meeting to tell me this?' said Sagana, a cold edge creeping into his voice.

'It's what else they found that justified the interruption, my lord.'

Sagana sighed then said, 'Very well. Show me what all this fuss is about.' Over his shoulder he added, 'Wallace, you come with me. Madeleine, please wait with Angele.'

Wallace heard an exasperated intake of breath, followed by the sound of footsteps fading away behind him. He allowed himself a wry smile, then set off after Sagana.

Behind the hut, two of Frederick's men stood at ease. Sagana glanced at them and then asked Frederick, 'Why have you posted this guard?'

Frederick pointed to a large bush and then hesitated, glancing towards Wallace.

'It's alright. I would have preferred to delay this part of his education a while longer, but there's no harm in his finding out now.' It was Sagana's turn to smile as Wallace tensed, ready to fight. 'Relax my friend. Frederick is asking if you are to be permitted to share a secret.' Turning towards the other man, he said, 'Show him.'

Frederick parted the stems of the bush to reveal a pile of stones lying in a rough circle around what appeared to be some sort of altar. Wallace threw a questioning glance at Sagana.

'This is a portal. It acts as a door to other realms of existence. Their location and purpose are a closely guarded secret.' He held up a hand as Wallace started to speak. 'Wait. I'll explain. You recall that I've already mentioned the Elder Gods?' The warrior nodded his head. 'Well, they are ancient beyond our comprehension and have travelled between many worlds. The portal is a tool that allows us to do the same – if you know how to use it.' His next comment was addressed to Frederick. 'I knew it was here, so again I ask, why have you brought me to it?'

Frederick swallowed, looked at the ground, then seemed to recover his nerve. He looked up, straight at his master, and said, 'I think it has been used very recently. There is blood on the altar, and I found this.' He held up a smooth pebble and offered it to Sagana.

To Wallace's surprise, Sagana studied the pebble with obvious interest. Both men flinched when he let out an oath. 'Muller!' He paused then said, 'Now I understand your concern. You did right to bring this to my attention. Post men around the village and tell them to be vigilant. Wallace, with me.'

A puzzled Wallace followed Sagana back towards Angele's hut and almost bumped into him when the Master suddenly stopped. 'This is unwelcome news and forces me to change my plans. I didn't realise that the old man had absorbed so much of the old learning and would know how to use a portal. I can't let him roam at will – there's no knowing what mischief the sly old fox could get up to. But first, we have unfinished business to attend to. Stay close to me, follow my lead, and be prepared to fight for your life.'

Madeleine entered the hut as Wallace, Frederick and Sagana strode away. She was muttering to herself about the arrogance of men and not paying attention, so that her assailant had little difficulty in wrapping a scrawny but surprisingly powerful arm around her throat from behind. 'What ...?' said the startled young woman, struggling to free herself.

'Be quiet,' hissed Angele, close to her ear. 'Call for help and you die.' As if to emphasise that this was no lame threat, Angele stuck the point of a dagger against Madeleine's ribs. 'That fool Frederick has likely gone and ruined everything.'

'I don't understand,' said Madeleine in a low voice.

'Of course you don't. A foolish little whore like you can't be expected to understand. But I'll tell you this. There's more blood to be spilt soon and if you don't want it to be yours then you'll do exactly as I say. Now move over there, towards the back of the hut.'

Madeleine began to inch into the dark shadows as instructed, hoping the old woman would ease the pressure on her throat and give her an opportunity to try to escape. However, there was no letting up of the grip that held her, and she found herself bumping into a low cot. 'Stop!' hissed Angele. 'Now stand very still for a moment while I think what to do next.' The brief hope that flared in Madeleine was soon extinguished as she felt the grip around her throat loosen, only to have her hands yanked back and swiftly tied with some sort of cord. A shove completed the old woman's plan as Madeleine found herself sprawling face down on the foul-smelling cot. As she started to protest, fingers grabbed her hair, forcing her head back and a rag was stuffed into her mouth. Another cord secured the rag so tight that it bit into her cheeks. Angele then pushed her prisoner's head back down as she issued another warning, 'Move or speak again and you die.'

She felt the other woman settle onto the cot alongside her. Moments later, something sharp made contact once more with her ribs. Fearing for her life, Madeleine lay very still, her mind racing through numerous scenarios as to what might happen next. She prayed that Wallace would somehow save her but could see no way in which to warn him of her predicament. For all she knew, he might even now be riding away with Sagana.

'Now we wait.'

Madeleine offered no reaction, mindful of her last warning from the old woman.

As they hurried towards Angele's hut, Wallace asked Sagana to explain what was going on. Sagana slowed his pace and replied, 'Fresh blood is required to make a portal work and I doubt whether Muller would have been able to use this one without Angele's knowledge and assistance. I fear I may have made a foolish in trusting her. Don't be deceived by her looks – she's a formidable opponent and I – we – need to find out what game she's playing. I'll explain the pebble later – it doesn't matter right now.'

Wallace frowned. 'And you sent Madeleine back to her?'

Sagana shook his head. 'Yes. I thought she'd be safe there. Quickly now – she may need our help!'

Almost afraid to breathe, Madeleine became aware that the light level inside the hut was increasing. Puzzled, she risked turning her head towards the door – only to flinch as a shimmering white light began to coalesce into a dark-robed figure. Angele chuckled low in her throat and stood up. As she rose, a small pebble fell out of her shawl, but the old woman didn't seem to notice. 'Welcome, Keeper, to my humble abode. Now, time is short, so I want you to take me ...' she turned to point at her captive '... and this *thing* to the fortress of Helr'ath at once.' The new arrival seemed to ripple before the startled gaze of Madeleine. Angele snapped, 'Because I demand it and because even you must bow before the God of Chaos. Now stop wasting time and do as you have been instructed. There are those close by who would try to stop me from delivering his new toy.'

Fear coursed through the younger woman's veins and gripped her heart as the old woman forced her head back. When Madeleine started to scream, Angele poured a vile-tasting liquid down her throat. The young woman was still gagging when her world began to spin at an ever-increasing rate, while the light became so bright that she was forced to shut her eyes for fear of being blinded.

As Sagana and Wallace burst into the hut they were greeted by a brilliant but then rapidly fading light. Peering through tears of pain, Wallace thought he could make out three human-looking forms, but these quickly vanished, leaving just an image on his retinae.

Sagana let out a curse. 'That wasn't supposed to happen. I've seriously underestimated the old woman and now I fear she's taken your friend.'

Wallace scowled. 'Taken her where? We must go after her. Now!'

'It's not that simple. I suspect Angele was aided by The Keeper – which means they could be anywhere.'

As his eyes adjusted to the gloom, Wallace approached the cot and began to feel around as he said, 'We have to hope Madeleine found a way to leave us some sort of clue. Who is this Keeper? If he hurts her, I'll kill him.'

Sagana shook his head. 'I doubt she had the slightest idea what was happening or where she was being taken. I'm sorry, but there's no easy way to follow them. If there was, I promise you I'd take you there along with some of my men.' He shrugged. 'She's probably no longer in this realm. And, trust me, you don't want to cross swords with The Keeper.'

Wallace spun round, anger evident in his stiff posture. His scabbard brushed across the top of the cot, dislodging something which fell to the ground. Bending down to pick up whatever it was, Wallace spat out, 'What does that mean? Not in this realm? And what's so special about this Keeper person. He bleeds when cut doesn't he? I'm not afraid of anyone.'

'The Keeper isn't a hu'man. He works for the Elder Gods, and no-one knows what he is, let alone whether he bleeds or not – no-one has ever managed to get close enough to find out. That one has many strange powers and skills. You attack him at your peril.'

Wallace sighed. 'What have you got me into, Sagana? And why was this on the old hag's cot?' He held up another pebble. 'What sort of person sleeps on a pebble? It looks similar to the one Frederick found.' He lifted his arm, preparing to toss the pebble to one side.

Sagana grasped the other man's wrist. 'Let me see that!' He snatched the pebble and took it over to the doorway, turning it over in the evening light. He spun round to find Wallace watching him. 'This is a clue. It looks like any other pebble but it's something much more valuable. We of the old faith use these pebbles to help us navigate towards an objective. If, as I suspect, this one belonged to Angele then I can use it to track her movements.'

Madeleine felt sick as she lost all sense of up and down. The world seemed to be rushing past in a blur and although she tried shutting her eyes for a while, when she re-opened them things weren't any better. Angele was watching her, upper lip curled in amusement at the younger woman's distress. 'We're approaching The Veil. Once we pass through The Rent, your friends won't be able to help you. Old man Muller thinks I'm taking you to him, but I have a more grateful master in mind. I think the Lord Helr'ath will be amused by you for a while and will reward me well for delivering you into his not-so-tender clutches. And if you don't like his caresses, consider this; once he grows tired of a new toy, he has a habit of tearing it to pieces, like a small child ripping the wings from a butterfly.'

The old woman paused to let this information sink into Madeleine's consciousness. Seeing the young woman turn even paler, she grasped her by the throat. 'Yet, if he decides to breed with you, your life might be extended for a little while longer. Not that you are likely to survive the birth of any bastard child he might give you – his offspring have a nasty habit of becoming impatient in the womb and often use their baby fangs to tear their way out.' She bent down and removed the rag from her prisoner's mouth before pushing the terrified woman away with one final mocking taunt. 'Either way, you'll soon be glad to welcome death. The Lord Helr'ath is not a gentle lover.'

Madeleine spat in the old woman's face. Angele reacted with fury, backhanding her across her right cheek and then tearing at the younger woman's hair. Madeleine could feel sharp nails scraping across her scalp as the old woman tugged at the roots.'

The Keeper spoke inside Angele's head. *'The Lord does not like damaged goods. You would do well to remember this.'*

To Madeleine's surprise and relief, the assault ended as abruptly as it had begun.

Angele let go of her hair and stepped away. 'Yes Keeper, you're right. I mustn't damage her before he has a chance to play.' The old woman added something else, under her breath. There was a slight pause and then she said, 'At least, no damage of any consequence.'

Madeleine said nothing but inside she wondered how the old woman could know what the Keeper was thinking. So far, she couldn't recall his having uttered a single word. Around her the world was growing darker and her head started to spin. She felt sick and a rising sense of panic. Would the warrior and his new master even bother to look for her or was she already doomed to the fate Angele had so gleefully outlined to her? She fought to stifle hot tears of regret, unwilling to let Angele see her despair.

27: AN EVENTFUL EVENING

Whiston led the way towards a place near to The Royal, armed with directions and the name of a cheap hotel, courtesy of Inspector Johnson. They arrived outside an early 19th century building, probably dating from the reign of George III, whose exterior suggested The Grand Hotel had seen better days. This initial impression was confirmed by the dilapidated state of the lobby and reception area. Whiston was not in the least surprised that it had two vacant rooms or that the desk clerk asked for payment in advance as he registered them in a large leather-bound book.

The two men agreed to deposit their bags in their respective rooms and to meet in the lobby in ten minutes.

As they climbed the stairs, the clerk was busy summoning a small boy. He scribbled a note and told the boy to deliver it promptly, threatening dire retribution if he wasn't back within five minutes.

Whiston turned the large brass key in the lock and pushed open the heavy wooden door on its squealing hinges. *Well, I suppose no-one will surprise me in the night* he told himself, with a frown. *And I won't be able to creep out either!* The room was small, with a single bed, washstand, and a small chest of drawers. Two coat hooks had been fixed to the back of the door. Fading prints in cheap frames covered the walls, no doubt intended to distract the occupants' attention from the ancient wallpaper that was peeling away from the walls in several places. He dumped his bag onto the bed and crossed to the dirt-smeared window. Peering out he realised he was in a room at the rear of the hotel. His view was restricted to the back of another building on the opposite side of the narrow alley running between it and the hotel.

Whiston struggled with the window before it relented and allowed him to slide the bottom half up as its counterweights decided to work. He stuck his head out, glancing left and right before allowing himself a wry smile. To the right, a cast iron drainpipe suggested an alternative way of leaving his room unnoticed. Or it might, if not for his bad arm.

Mindelen was waiting for him in the lobby. 'You took your time. I was just wondering if I should come and see if you'd managed to get lost.' He grinned then said, 'Do you know this place at all? Only I'm starving and I can't think on an empty stomach.'

'I've never been to Bristol before. We could eat here I suppose, although it might be cheaper to venture out. My expenses allowance won't go far.'

Neither of them took any notice of the slim young man sitting quietly in a corner of the lobby, apparently reading a newspaper.

'So we're working blind? Didn't your snitch offer any advice about where to eat?'

'Hardly. I doubt their advice would have been useful, anyway.'

'We could ask 'ere. Tell them we want to stretch our legs and work up an appetite.'

'I suppose. Or we could ask for directions to the theatre area. There's always somewhere to eat near a theatre.'

Mindelen laughed. 'Well ain't you the clever one?'

Whiston went to talk to the clerk and returned with a happy look on his face. 'Apparently, if we turn right out of here, walk to the end of the street, then turn left, there's a decent hostelry down the third street on the right.'

Moments after they had left their hotel, a slim young man with a rolled-up newspaper followed them out and along the street.

Half an hour later found Mindelen and Whiston seated and enjoying a glass of beer in a small hostelry. They'd already ordered some food and were discussing their murder case in low tones. Their waitress was engaged in a rather lengthy conversation with a thin young man who had followed them into the place and was now seated alone in a dark corner. If they had been watching, they might have noticed how the waitress cast several glances in their direction before finishing with her new customer.

'I'm looking forward to arrestin' this priest,' said Mindelen. 'It's a stroke of good luck that your snitch so 'appened as to know where he was runnin' to.' The sergeant paused to take another swig from his glass. He gave his companion an appraising look then shrugged. 'Come on, lad, you can tell me the name of this snitch. We're a team, you and me, and we should be able to trust and 'elp each other.'

Whiston reached for his own drink. Taking a long slow draught, he put the glass down in front of him and smiled. 'Sorry, sergeant, but this particular snitch insists on keeping their identity secret. I don't know why but suspect they may be scared of someone in the station.' He prayed that this explanation would satisfy Mindelen.

Mindelen frowned and was about to say something when the waitress arrived at their table, clutching two plates laden with generous portions of stew. Depositing the plates and retrieving utensils out of her apron pocket, she beamed at Whiston. 'Mind the plates gents, they're rather hot. Can I get you anything else?'

'No, thank you,' said Whiston, feeling his cheeks blush as the maid leant over him to swat away an imaginary crumb. 'Not just now.'

The waitress, straightened up, patted her hair, which was tied up in a bun and walked away, pausing after a few steps to turn back and wink at Whiston.

Mindelen laughed. 'You could 'ave 'er for puddin'.'

Whiston concentrated on his plate, forking a chunk of meat into his mouth.

'Oh come on, she's not bad-looking and 'as evidently taken a shine to you!'

'We're here to work, not enjoy ourselves,' mumbled the younger officer.

'All work and no play is bad for your 'ealth,' said Mindelen. 'I wouldn't turn 'er down.'

Whiston was shocked. 'I thought you were happily married, sergeant?'

Mindelen gave him a hard look. 'Married I may be but that don't mean I'm 'appy about it.' The sergeant looked away and fidgeted in his chair.

'I'm sorry, sergeant. I didn't mean to pry.'

Mindelen took a mouthful of carrot and chewed thoughtfully. The silence between the two men stretched out. Then, suddenly, 'It's alright lad. You weren't to know. But keep it to yourself, right?'

'Sure, sergeant. It's not my business to be gossiping in the station.'

'Good lad. Now, eat your food afore it goes cold.'

The waitress returned to clear away their empty plates. She smiled at Whiston as she asked, 'Is there anything else that tempts the young sir? Mindelen snorted.

Whiston felt his cheeks burning and he shook his head. 'Another time perhaps? We have work to do.'

As he stood to leave, Mindelen grabbed the young woman around the waist and whispered in her ear. She giggled, before casting a knowing look towards Whiston.

Once outside, Whiston stopped so suddenly that Mindelen almost walked into him. The younger man turned and demanded, 'What did you say to her?'

'Calm down lad, I simply told 'er where we was stayin'' She likes you and it's about time some woman made a man of you!'

'And how do you know one hasn't already?' snapped Whiston.

Mindelen gulped, backing away. 'I'm sorry, lad. I didn't realise.' He held up a placatory hand. 'Anyway, she might be entertainin' for one night and you don't 'ave to let 'er into your room if you don't want to. I was just tryin' to do you a favour. Sorry.'

Whiston was already beginning to calm down. 'Oh never mind. She might distract me from other things.'

'That's the spirit. What other things?'

'Like killing you for interfering in my life.'

Mindelen saw the look on Whiston's face and burst out laughing. 'Come on young Edward, I'll buy you a pint to fortify you for later.'

As the pair left the hostelry, another customer picked up his newspaper and called for his bill.

One drink turned into several more and by the time they were heading back to The Grand both men were feeling relaxed and happy. As they entered the lobby, the desk clerk looked up with a frown. 'Gentlemen?' he said.

Mindelen stepped closer to the desk. 'A key for me and one for 'im, as well, if you please, my good man.'

The clerk looked down his nose at the sergeant. 'There's a young lady been asking after your friend. I told her she could wait in his room.' Reaching behind himself, he selected two number-tagged keys from the row hanging on the wall. 'Here you go, sir. And this is for your companion. Mind the stairs, they can be a bit tricky at this time of night after a few drinks.'

Mindelen peered at the keys before selecting one and handing it to Whiston. 'Time to greet your new friend,' he said, adding a conspiratorial wink. 'I'll see you tomorrow at breakfast. Don't stay up all night.' He staggered towards the stairs, chuckling to himself at his own wit.

Whiston stared at the key, wondering who this new friend could be. Then his slightly befuddled memory supplied a picture of the waitress from the hostelry. With a sigh, he too set off for the stairs. 'Don't fret, Rose,' he muttered. 'I'll get rid of her.'

Whiston paused outside his door before struggling to put the key in the lock. He was still fiddling with it when the door opened to reveal the young woman he'd met earlier. She frowned when she saw him, then peered out of the doorway, glancing left and right along the corridor before pulling him inside.

'You fool! I came to warn you that both you and your friend are in serious danger if you stay here. And now you finally turn up half drunk.'

Struggling to make sense of her words, Whiston sat heavily on his bed. 'I'm ... I'm very flattered by your interest, Miss, but I belong ... '

A stinging slap across his face stifled the end of his sentence. He looked at the young woman in anger. 'What did you do that for?'

'Didn't you hear me? Your life is in danger if you stay here.'

A loud bang from further down the corridor made both of them look towards the door. A hand flew to the woman's mouth. 'Oh God, it's too late. They'll kill me as well if they suspect I've betrayed them.'

Whiston shook his head, still trying to understand what was happening. 'Who'll kill you? Don't worry, I'm a police officer.'

Another loud thud, followed by a muffled oath, almost drowned out her next words. 'You're sitting there whilst I fear your friend may be fighting for his very life!'

Outside, in the corridor, Whiston heard Mindelen cursing someone, followed by the sound of scuffling. The young woman grabbed Whiston's arm, panic in her eyes. 'You have to move. Sit here and we both die!' Her desperation began to motivate Whiston just as his room door flew open with a crash.

Mindelen backed into the room, waving his cosh about as though it were some sort of sword. Blood poured from a wound to his scalp. 'He risked a glance behind him, then shouted, 'Whiston you fool, get out of here while I hold 'em off. Use the window. Fetch help.'

Whiston saw two figures in the doorway, one armed with a curved dagger, the other with a club. Thinking of the drainpipe outside his room, he remembered his weakened arm and then stiffened with a sense of duty towards his sergeant. He pushed the woman towards the window and looked around for something to use as a weapon. Spying a poker in the hearth, he grabbed it and strode towards the door. Mindelen was busy trying to evade both the dagger and the club but was fighting a losing battle as he was being forced further into the room. Soon, his two assailants would be able to attack him from both sides.

Whiston was nearest to the man with the club, and he set about his foe with relish. Taken by surprise, the unknown assailant backed up, giving a little ground, before launching a ferocious counterattack of his own. As the two struggled back and forth, Whiston could see that Mindelen was tiring. Already he was bleeding from several more cuts and it seemed only a matter of time before the sergeant suffered a mortal wound. Then, to his horror, Whiston saw the young woman step behind Mindelen's attacker. From the corner of his eye, he caught a brief flash of movement, before being forced to concentrate on his own fight once more.

To his surprise and relief, his own attacker suddenly turned and fled out of the room. Puzzled, Whiston turned towards his partner, only to find both Mindelen and his opponent slumped to the floor. The woman stood with a hand over her mouth, staring at the hat pin protruding out of the dagger-man's neck. Even as he looked back, the body toppled sideways, driving the pin in even deeper as it caught against the floor.

Mindelen was moaning softly, blood streaming from his various wounds. One to his left shoulder looked nasty and Whiston sensed that his partner was in a bad way. 'Sergeant, try to stay awake. I'll fetch help. You'll be alright.'

Mindelen gave him a weak grin. 'I'm done for. We must 'ave been set up.' He slumped lower, then rallied a little. 'You try to get away.' He nodded towards the young woman,' She knows about this.' Pausing to coughing up a mouthful of bright red blood, he continued. 'Find who did this. Make 'em pay. I know I ...' He passed out.

Whiston was fully sober and awake now. He turned towards the woman, a menacing look in his eyes. 'You have some explaining to do.' He stepped towards her.

'Not here. Your sergeant was right. We have to leave and I'm willing to bet the clerk was in on it. Let's see if there's a back way out of here and I'll take you to meet someone who can protect and help you. I'll explain along the way.'

'No!' He pointed towards Mindelen. 'I'm not leaving him here. What if they come back? He wouldn't stand a chance.'

The woman stamped her foot in frustration. 'What do you suggest?'

Whiston studied her face. He bent to pick up the blood-stained dagger, wiping it quickly on its previous owner's trousers, before shoving it into his waist band. 'Alright. You go down and ask the clerk to come up here – tell him there's been an attempted burglary and I was injured. I'll ambush him in here, then we leave with my friend and seek medical help.'

The woman gave him a half-hearted smile, then headed for the corridor.

28: A Timely Resurrection

Unwin hesitated by the cell door. Although he was armed, he was also naked and doubted the wisdom of charging into a potential fight. He put his ear against the door as the sounds outside grew in volume. There were voices and hearing the familiar clash of steel on steel made up his mind. With the cleaver ready in his right hand, he eased the door open, ready to jump back in an instant.

The sound of battle flooded into the cell. When nothing happened to indicate that anyone had noticed his action, Unwin risked a quick glance outside. He took in the dimly lit corridor and the figure standing with his back to him just to the right of the door. Whoever he was, his right hand held a pistol which was pointed further down the corridor. A quick look towards the intended target almost wrung a shouted warning from Unwin. Two figures, armed with swords, were engaged in a desperate fight against a lone swordsman. More to the point, this lone figure was supposedly a dead man. Realising that the shooter was searching for an opening through which to fire at his resurrected friend, Unwin's rigorous martial training took over.

'Pssst.'

Startled, the gunman turned towards the unexpected sound from the cell doorway. Raising the cleaver high, Unwin brought it down with all his might upon the outstretched arm, severing it just below the elbow. His victim gave a strangled cry of pain, turning towards the new attacker. The gun bounced once as both it and the limb hit the floor in a spray of blood. Unwin had allowed the cleaver to complete its downward swing past his right hip and now he brought it forward in a vicious over-arm swing before burying it in the forehead of his opponent. As the dying man fell, Unwin stepped out into the corridor, just as the nearest of the two swordsmen turned and charged towards him. Reasoning that there wasn't enough time to extract the cleaver from the man's ribcage, he dropped to one knee just as a blade sliced through the air where his neck had been moments earlier. Grabbing the blood-covered pistol and the severed arm from the floor, Unwin scrabbled backwards as he wiped the pistol on the sleeve covering the flaccid limb. The swordsman was stepping forward, preparing to deliver a downward thrust, when Unwin squeezed the trigger. There was a loud explosion as bits of bone, tissue, brain, and a fine mist of blood erupted outwards. Unwin's assailant fell backwards, a gaping hole where his face had once been.

Unwin glanced down the corridor. The remaining opponent, perhaps distracted by the gunshot, reacted too slow to a feint, and was punished by being skewered through the heart by Farral. As the final enemy fell, Unwin stood up and waved towards his old friend. 'I thought you were dead!' Tears began to cloud his vision and he angrily wiped them away.

Farral rammed the tip of his sword through his opponent's eye, leaning forward to press down with all his weight so as to drive the point deep into the dead man's brain. Satisfied with this seemingly pointless act, he leant against a wall, panting for breath. 'I thought you had better dress sense. Give me a minute. I'm not as fit as I used to be.'

Unwin heard the rasp in Farral's voice and guessed that his comrade was not fully recovered from an earlier ordeal. 'I'll see if any of these men have something I can wear.'

As Unwin knelt down alongside the man he'd shot, Farral was shaking his head. 'They're not men. They're near-men.'

Unwin looked up with wide eyes and an open mouth. 'Near-men? But they've been nothing more than legend for centuries.'

Farral, his breathing a little less laboured now, grinned. 'Well they're not a legend now. Fortunate for us that you dispatched those two the way you did, eh? I met another one when I first entered this place and had time to take a close look. Trust me, these things were near-men a few moments ago. What the hell have you got yourself into?'

Pulling on the tight-fitting shirt and trousers of the deceased, Unwin gestured back down the corridor. 'There'll be time to catch up later. Our first priority should be to get out of this place. I don't want to meet the owner when he comes back.'

'That should be easy enough. I used the front door.'

'You did what? That was either bold or very foolish!'

As the pair set off, Farral took up his story. 'I saw someone leave while I was scouting the place and figured that anyone left inside would never expect someone hostile to approach that way. I was right.' He pointed the way ahead as they came to a junction. 'I knocked on the door and a servant opened it. I asked if his master was at home, and he seemed a little confused. While he thought about it, I stabbed him in the chest and then pushed him inside, where I cut his throat.' He pointed up some stairs to the left. 'Since there was no obvious reaction to my entry, I searched his pockets and that was when I noticed the puncture marks on his neck. I was quite shocked when I realised that he wasn't human. Well, not anymore. I hid the body in a side room and came looking for you.'

At the top of the stairs, a right turn would take them deeper into the ground floor of the building, a left terminated at the front door. Unwin strode towards the door, planning to take a quick look out before they could safely leave. He was halfway there when he heard voices outside and saw a shadow fall across the small pane of glass. 'Back, we've got company,' he signed to his friend.

Farral pointed to the right and set off for the back of the building. Unwin hurried after him. The pair turned into a sitting room just as the front door opened. Voices drifted down the corridor.

'It's perfectly safe. He can't escape and I'll put you in a small side room. You'll be able to hear everything he says but

212

he won't even know you are there. This way, you can corroborate what he tells me.'

A deeper voice replied. 'I'm not entirely happy about this, Professor McNulty. I mean, as a man of God, I don't think I should be condoning torture.'

The professor laughed. 'Come now, Archbishop. It's not as though your church has an unblemished record in this respect. Or have you forgotten the excesses of your Inquisitors?'

'But that was a long time ago. I've never personally – '

'Enough. You're in too deep to start worrying about your conscience.'

Unwin gave Farral a meaningful look. 'This confirms one of my suspicions.' he whispered.

'This way, my Lord.'

'Must we rush into this unpleasantness?'

'No time like the present. Besides, I have a lecture to give later, and I'd like to make some progress with this enquiry before I leave this evening.'

The sound of footsteps descending the stairs down to the cell where Unwin had been held soon echoed along the corridor.

'We move, now,' said Unwin. The pair crept out of their hiding place and along the corridor towards the front door. Unwin grabbed a cloak from a stand, figuring it would help to hide the poor fit of his blood-stained stolen clothing. A loud curse gave them fresh impetus, signalling that McNulty had discovered the dead bodies of his guards. As Farral opened the door, footsteps sounded on the stairs.

Once outside, Farral grabbed Unwin's arm, dragging him along the street towards a corner. There was an angry shout from behind, but the two friends quickened their pace. After a few yards, Farral turned left into a maze of back alleys. 'Stay close to me,' he panted. 'We'll lose him in here.'

McNulty turned left just in time to see his prisoner disappear into the maze of slums that bordered his own more respectable neighbourhood. He peered after them, cursing inwardly at the lost opportunity. It was clear the priest had received help but from what quarter he couldn't guess.

Once he was satisfied that they were no longer being pursued, Farral slowed his pace. Noting that he was breathing heavily, Unwin suggested they stop and rest, but Farral shook his head. 'No. ... We need to ... keep moving. ... I have a ... safe house.' A fine drizzle meant that there weren't many people about and the few passers-by cast curious glances in their direction but hurried on to their own affairs. It wasn't long though before Unwin became aware that two men were following them. He mentioned this to his friend. 'I'm unarmed,' he added.

Farral glanced behind then moved closer to Unwin, passing him a dagger as they almost collided going around a bend. 'I still have my sword under this cloak,' he said. 'After two more turnings we wait in the doorway on the left side and ambush them.'

'Why? They may mean us no harm.'

'The smaller one has a distinctive tattoo on his left hand. They're part of a gang of footpads and I'd wager they see us as their next mark. If they continue to stalk us, we'd be well advised to strike first.'

The men continued to follow them round the next corner, gradually closing the distance. At the next turning, Farral bundled his friend into the rubbish-strewn doorway of a deserted shop. With ears straining they heard the two footpads approach the corner. Seconds later, the pair walked straight past the doorway then paused. A confused voice whispered, 'Where'd they go?'

It was the last thing the man ever said as a strong arm grabbed his long hair, forcing the head back and exposing the vulnerable throat to a razor-sharp blade. His companion hesitated in shock, before starting to advance on his friend's killer, a heavy cosh in his left hand. From the doorway to his right a sword snaked out and sliced deep across his ribs before flicking up to embed itself under his armpit. The man

214

gulped, then staggered. Meanwhile, Unwin had finished his own grisly work and now stepped forward to drive the dagger into the other man's chest.

As the second man fell dying, a small boy came round the corner. His eyes widened as he took in the scene and looked at Farral and Unwin with undisguised horror.

Farral stepped forward, clasping the boy by the shoulder. 'Are you a good boy?' he asked, his breath coming in ragged gasps. Too scared to speak, the boy could only nod in the affirmative. Farral produced a shilling and flipped it towards the startled child. 'Then be a good boy and forget what you've just seen. Understand?' Again the boy nodded before turning to run back the way he'd come.

'Do you really think we can trust the child?' asked Unwin.

'Yes,' said Farral. 'This is a tough area and children who blab about what they see tend to disappear. The boy was old enough to know that.'

With nothing else to slow them down, Farral led the way by a complicated route to his safe house, doubling back several times to make sure they were not being followed. Once inside, he collapsed onto his bed, worn out by his recent exertions. Unwin took the single worm-eaten chair, marvelling that it still retained enough strength to hold his weight. Over the next hour the two talked, filling in their recent histories' and planning their next move. Farral was especially intrigued to hear about the mysterious Guide. Unwin was concerned to learn about the permanent damage to Farral's lungs, whilst the latter was worried about Unwin's theory that their organisation had a traitor in its ranks. Neither man had seen McNulty's companion in the house but the fact he'd been referred to as an Archbishop was both worrying and useful – it certainly narrowed down the list of potential suspects.

Under his host's instruction, Unwin assembled a meal of cold meat, cheese, and bread together with some apples. This was washed down by a couple of bottles of beer before they decided to get some rest. Whilst one acted as sentry, the other slept in the bed for four hours at a time.

As he slept, Unwin dreamed about his unexpected ally. If he could find some way to contact the Guide than he had a lot of questions.

Farral glanced towards his friend as the priest muttered in his sleep. His own thoughts followed a darker path. *Had he been wise to reveal himself in this way? Would helping Unwin prove to be a costly mistake? Could he still trust his old friend?*

29: QUESTIONS AND ANSWERS

Wallace listened in fascination as Sagana tried to explain how the pebble, which he called a tol'agr'un, could be used both to communicate over long distances and to help locate someone travelling in another realm beyond that of the Earth. 'But where do you find these tol'agr'un?' asked Wallace, stumbling over the unfamiliar word, his eyes still locked on the pebble.

Sagana gave him an odd look. 'Not in your world,' he said.

Wallace pressed the point. 'I don't understand what you mean.'

Sagana sighed. 'This is going to take longer than I thought. These pebbles come from the home world of the Elder Gods. A place so far from here that if you set off on a good horse at the age of twelve and rode all day, every day, for the rest of your life, you still wouldn't be close to it.'

'Then how can you travel between these places?'

'There are short cuts if you know where to look and how to use them. It's all to do with the mind. The pebble helps you to focus on where you want to go.'

Wallace seemed to ponder this for a while. Then, abruptly, he said, 'How do you know where you're going if you've not been there before?'

Sagana laughed. 'Excellent, Wallace. I knew my instinct about you was right.'

Wallace gave him a hard look. 'Are you mocking me?' he asked, a menacing tone to the words.

'Not at all; in fact, I'm praising you. It takes a smart man to pose your last question and it's a very good one.'

'So what's the answer?'

'There are markers, a bit like the way-signs you're already familiar with, but only visible if you're using one of these pebbles. You can travel, very fast, between these markers, even if you've never been to one before.' He paused, then added, 'Of course, you don't know what sort of place you're going to the first time. And some of these places are not very welcoming.'

'And how many people know how to use these pebbles?'

Sagana laughed again. 'Slow down. You can't learn everything at once. It takes years to acquire the knowledge I hold and for good reason. Some of it is very dangerous.' With this, he turned and strode out of the hut. Wallace shrugged before following Sagana, a troubled look in his eyes.

Sagana finished giving his orders to Frederick and then turned to Wallace. 'We two will go after the young woman. You'd best make sure your weapons are sharp – I doubt our passage will be easy.'

'Why are you helping me to rescue Madeleine? She's nothing to you.

'True. But she matters to you and you're my apprentice. Think of it as a gesture of goodwill. But, more important to me, is that Angele has betrayed me. I can't allow her to get away with that.' Sagana shrugged. 'So, we may have different motives, but we have a common cause.'

Wallace made no comment. Retrieving a whetstone from a small pouch inside his gambeson, he sat on a large boulder and began to run it along the length of his sword.

Sagana stood looking at the pebble Wallace had found in Angele's hut. From time to time he turned it over in the palm of his hand. The corners of his mouth turned up and his eyes glittered in the sunlight. He was still studying the stone, lost deep in thought, when Wallace stood up and coughed.

In an instant, Sagana snapped back to the present and raised an eyebrow. 'If you're ready, I know where they've gone. Here, drink this.'

Wallace eyed the small vial with a scowl on his face. 'Things like that usually contain poison.'

Sagana chuckled. 'My, but you're a suspicious one. It's not poison but it will help you across The Void. Without it, you could arrive a gibbering wreck.'

Wallace took the vial and swallowed the contents in one gulp.

The two men were tied together, opposite ends of a rope uniting their belts. Wallace had started the journey wide-eyed and apprehensive but had soon elected to squeeze his eyes shut against the bright light and the sickening sensation of spinning through a never-ending vortex. He was drenched in sweat when he felt a bump, solid ground under his feet and a tug at his waist. 'We're here. Crouch down and untie the rope. We'll wait a few moments for your senses to sort themselves out.'

'I'm fine,' growled Wallace, peering out through narrowed slits. 'But that stuff tastes awful.'

'No you're not. Travelling through The Veil is disorienting even for those of us who've done it many times and that was your first. If we have to fight, you need to be fully recovered from the experience. And not everything here is as it first seems. This is not your world.'

Wallace chose to ignore the implications of that last statement. 'But Madeleine is in danger!'

'And you can't help her if you're dead. Trust me. Besides, there's a reception awaiting us up ahead although I don't think they've scented us yet.'

218

At first Wallace could see nothing but an empty grassland rolling away to the horizon. His head spinning slower now, Wallace opened his eyes wider. The air was hazy, as if a light fog lingered, and small clumps of bushes and stunted trees broke the monotony, but the land boasted no hills for as far as he could see. They were crouched among tall grasses in a small hollow. Wallace was about to ask Sagana what he meant when he caught a flicker of movement where his companion was pointing.

A small creature stood sniffing the air. Details were scarce at this distance, but Wallace could see enough to make him think of the devils that featured so much in the teaching of the Church. The creature was four-limbed, with a long tail and horns protruding from the top of its head.

'Gol'bin' said Sagana in a low voice. 'Vicious meat-eaters. They live and hunt in packs; as many as thirty at a time. If it scents us, it will alert its friends and they'll come straight at us.'

'A good job the breeze is blowing towards us then,' offered Wallace.

'Indeed. But we need to head in their general direction. They're armed with sharp teeth and even sharper claws. On the other hand, they're neither clever nor especially brave. Once we've killed a few, they should melt away and leave us alone.' Sagana drew his sword. 'Are you ready?'

Wallace grinned as he unsheathed his own weapon. The two men started to climb out of the hollow, Sagana on the right. It wasn't long before the sentry gol'bin noticed them and a sharp bark rang out across the plain. More of the creatures appeared from the grass and soon a pack of around twenty-five was charging straight for them. Their yips and barks rose in volume as they closed on their intended prey.

As the gap between them narrowed, Wallace began to discern more detail of the creatures. Their bodies were covered in fine, pale brown fur and their tails whipped around from side-to-side, helping them to maintain their balance. They ran upright but leaning slightly forward, driven by powerful hind legs. Their long narrow front arms were held close to the body, and he could see no evidence of weapons. As they drew closer, Sagana broke his silence. 'Decapitate them.' He moved further away, giving both men room to swing their blades without getting in each other's way.

The first creature to reach Wallace almost took him by surprise as it used its tail to execute an impressive leap and launch itself at his head. He barely got his sword up in time to impale it, before flicking his wrist to free the weapon and bringing it round in a wide arc that separated the gol'bin's head from its shoulders. Out of the corner of his eye he saw Sagana calmly kill his own opponent before the main horde closed in. Teeth snapping and claws rending, the creatures attacked en masse. Wallace planted his feet and swung his sword in great powerful sweeps, chopping through bone, sinew, and soft tissue with almost reckless abandon.

The battle didn't last long. Within a few minutes, almost half of the gol'bin lay dead, piled in a heap around Wallace and Sagana. Their kin were already racing back the way they'd come. The victors hastily examined their own wounds but neither found more than a few small bites and scratches.

Wallace gulped in a lungful of air and re-sheathed his sword. 'That was different. You might have warned me they could jump.'

Sagana narrowed his eyes. 'I've never seen them do that before. I wonder ...'

Wallace was about to ask what Sagana was wondering when his companion shook his head and held up his left hand, palm towards the warrior.

'I don't think we have time to waste on answering your questions. We need to move on.' So saying, he set off across the open land, looking as if he knew exactly where he was going.

As they walked, Wallace asked what was so important about the gol'bin's new ability to launch itself into the air. 'They're not supposed to learn anything. Their role in this world is to act as scavengers and to kill the weak. In this way they help the process of natural selection by ensuring that the strong alone live long enough to breed.'

'I don't understand,' said Wallace. 'What difference does it make whether a creature is strong or weak? It can still breed.'

'Not if it dies before it becomes an adult.'

'So these gol'bin kill the weak? A bit like a farmer selecting the best cattle or sheep to breed and eating the rest?'

'Yes, you could think of it that way.'

A thought struck Wallace. 'How do you know so much about the gol'bin?'

Sagana paused before replying. 'I created them.'

Madeleine feared she was going to be sick. She eased one eye open to find Angele staring at her, a crooked grin on the old woman's face. A quick survey of her surroundings indicated that she was in a small tent, with bare earth for a floor, branches providing a frame and animal pelts supplying the coverings. A small opening around a central pole provided a little light, such that Madeleine thought it must be either dusk or a little after dawn.

'So, you don't like to travel? Well, don't worry. A short trip to the fortress of Lord Helr'ath and you'll never travel anywhere again – except to the realms of delight the Lord chooses to introduce you to. At least, until he finds a new distraction. Then you'll be begging the release of death rather than endure the places he keeps his trophies and broken toys.'

Madeleine stared at Angele, watching the old woman's face crease into a frown as the latter tried to gauge what sort of reaction her words had induced in the young woman. The frown gave way to a narrowing of the eyes and a pursing of the lips, confirmation that Angele hadn't discerned the tremendous effort it cost Madeleine to keep her own facial muscles under control.

'Well? Say something. Do you understand what lies in store for you?'

Now Madeleine smiled. 'Are you jealous because this Lord never chose you?' As soon as the words had left her lips, she knew she'd made a mistake.

Angele gave a screech and uttered a string of strange syllables. Madeleine felt as though some unseen creature was crawling across her skin and then her whole body went rigid. Panic started to set in as she found herself unable to move. Angele laughed at her discomfort and walked slowly towards the younger woman, brandishing a small knife in her right hand. Dirty claws scratched at Madeleine's arms and Angele's face was contorted in fury. 'You sneering bitch. Do you think you're better than me?' She slapped Madeleine hard across the cheek, then grabbed a handful of her victim's hair. 'The Lord has use for me. He values my skills.' Madeleine involuntarily exhaled as she was punched in the stomach. Angele stepped back, then spat in her prisoner's face, her own features looking more composed now that she had reasserted her control of the situation.

Without warning, she stepped forward once more and used the knife to cut away Madeleine's blouse, exposing the young woman's breasts. To Madeleine's disgust, Angele proceeded to run her hands across both breasts, before poking out a forked tongue and licking between them. 'Not so smart-mouthed now, are we? If you think this is bad, wait until you meet my Lord. He won't be so gentle – and he bites!' The old woman stepped back, cackling to herself.

Madeleine threw up.

'What do you mean, you created them?' demanded Wallace as he laid a hand on Sagana's arm. The Master turned towards him, his eyes flashing anger.

'Take your hand away? Now!' Wallace stepped away, only now becoming aware of the cold tingling sensation in his fingers. 'I have powers you cannot even begin to imagine, Wallace. I have travelled many worlds and across many planes. And, just as I have decided to trust you, to take

222

you on as my apprentice, so you must trust me.' Sagana locked eyes with Wallace. 'You have much to learn. One of the first, is never to touch me. Later I will explain why this must be so, but for now, suffice it to say that it could be detrimental to your health.'

Wallace sucked air through clenched teeth. He was unaccustomed to being treated this way and from any other person might have seen such an instruction as a challenge. But something in Sagana's eyes made him check his natural instinct. 'Very well. But at least tell me where we're headed.'

Sagana gave him an appraising look and then nodded his agreement. Pointing slightly to the left of dead ahead, he asked, 'Do you see that tiny dot on the horizon?'

Wallace looked in the direction indicated and screwed up his eyes, desperately trying to make out whatever it was Sagana was pointing at. In a voice tinged with frustration he was forced to admit,' No. What tiny dot? What is it you see?'

Sagana smiled.' I would have been surprised if you had been able to see it. My eyesight is much better than yours.' He lowered his hand before continuing. 'We are headed for a great forest. It is many of your leagues from here but ... with my powers I can encourage it to come towards us.'

Wallace laughed. 'You jest!' Seeing the look on the other's face, he swallowed hard. 'You really can make an entire forest move?' he asked in an awed voice.

'Not in the sense you mean,' said his companion. 'I know how to manipulate space so as to make it seem as if the trees move towards us. What I actually do is too complicated to explain right now but try to think of it as opening up a short-cut.' He paused to see how Wallace was reacting to this revelation. 'I know, I keep telling you things are too complicated to explain, but you'll have to accept my word on this. It has taken me many years to acquire my knowledge and powers and you can't expect to learn everything in just a few hours.'

Wallace grunted, his mind opening up to new ideas never before considered. 'So how long will it take before we meet this forest?'

'A few hours, but don't be quite so keen. When we get there, the real fighting is going to begin. The forest is home to the tra'll. They only welcome visitors when they're hungry and few have ever been there more than once.'

Wallace gave him a shrewd look. He felt a chill run down his back as he realised the import of Sagana's last comment.

30: A NEW ALLY

Whiston watched the departing woman for a few moments before hurrying to retrieve the club. He scanned the room, debating whether or not he had time to move Mindelen or their unknown assailant. The sound of a woman's voice drifted into the room, followed by the deeper tones of a response. Shaking his head, Whiston took up position behind the half open door, gripping the club in his right hand. At the back of his mind, a tiny inner voice urged him to abandon the club in favour of the dagger at his belt. A different voice warned him that the clerk might not have been involved at all and that it would be difficult to kill the man in cold blood.

Louder voices brought an abrupt end to this dialogue and Whiston also heard footsteps approaching his room. 'It happened in here,' said a familiar female voice. 'I think one of them is in a bad way.'

'I'm shocked, young Miss. To think that such a thing could happen in my hotel.'

Whiston judged that the clerk was just outside the room.

'It happened so quickly. Oh, please help him.'

'Are you sure the attackers have gone?' The deeper voice sounded uncertain. Whiston heard the sounds of a hand brushing against cloth.

'Oh! I didn't realise you had a gun, Mr Barrington.'

'Good girl,' thought Whiston. 'Thanks for the warning.'

Moments later, the barrel of a pistol began to enter the room. Whiston tensed, waiting for the outstretched arm to follow it. He brought the club down as hard as he could.

There was a cracking sound and a yelp of pain. As the pistol tumbled to the ground, Whiston grabbed at the now empty hand and jerked Mr Barrington into the room. The clerk gave another yelp. 'You've broken my arm,' he complained, tears running down both cheeks as he cradled his right arm against his chest. Whiston glanced at the injured arm, noting the spreading red stain on the jacket sleeve.

'That's not all I'm going to break if you don't start talking.' He raised the club again, watching the clerk flinch as he did so. 'Who were the men that attacked us?'

Barrington's upper lip quivered before he said, 'Why ask me? It was nothing to do with me!'

Whiston stepped closer to the clerk. 'I'll ask you again. I don't have time to waste, playing games. Last chance.'

A look of desperation came into Barrington's eyes. 'I can't tell you,' he whined. 'Please, they'll kill me if I talk.'

Whiston swung the club, smashing it into the other man's jaw with a sickening sound as the bone splintered. Barrington fell to the floor, out cold. 'Now you can't talk to anybody,' he said. He stooped to pick up the pistol before turning towards the young woman, who was standing just inside the doorway, wide-eyed and with a hand to her mouth. 'Right, you can start by telling me your name. And as you've doubtless just realised, I'm not in the mood for tricks.'

She stared at him for several seconds, swallowed hard and then seemed to gather her wits. 'I'm Lizzie Cobham.'

'And why are you so interested in me and my friend?'

'I wasn't until you came to where I work. The young man who followed you in is a nasty piece of work. He keeps trying to persuade me to walk out with him but ... he has some powerful friends.' She paused, choosing her next words carefully. 'I've been warned not to trust him.'

'And ...?'

'I have a friend who is interested in the young man and his associates. I keep this friend informed when young Christian eats at the hostelry and who he meets there.'

225

'This young man you talk of is Christian?'

Lizzie started to wring her hands. 'Yes. Christian Figulus. Or at least, that's the name he gave me.'

'What makes you think he was interested in us?'

'He asked me to find out where you were staying.'

Whiston replayed the meal in the hostelry through his mind. 'Is that why you started to flirt with me?'

Lizzie looked at the floor, a slight flush colouring her cheeks. 'No. He hadn't spoken to me then.'

'So why did you come here?'

'He followed you out of the hostelry. I've seen him do that before and ...'

Whiston was becoming impatient. He glanced at the unconscious Mindelen. The sergeant's chest rose and fell but the man's breathing seemed shallow. 'And what?'

'People have been found beaten or worse in a back alley.' She paused again. 'I told you, he's a nasty piece of work.' She glanced at Mindelen. 'Shouldn't we be getting him some help. I know people. Good people.' She looked Whiston straight in the eye. He saw concern and no evidence of guile.

'Ok. I'm going to trust you. But remember, I now have a pistol.'

Lizzie shuddered.

Between them, they managed to get Mindelen on his feet, although they had to half carry him out of the room and down the stairs. The dead weight of the sergeant almost toppled them down the steps and Whiston was puffing heavily when they reached the hotel reception area. 'You go check outside. I'll keep hold of him.'

Lizzie went to peer out of the door, scanning in both directions before she beckoned Whiston towards her whilst keeping her eyes on the street. As he struggled to manoeuvre Mindelen across the room, the sergeant stirred and muttered something. 'What?' said Whiston.

226

The sergeant shook his head and tried to stand straighter. 'I said, get our things. From the rooms.'

Whiston laughed, causing Lizzie to turn towards him, a puzzled expression on her face. 'He wants to take our belongings with us. As if he wasn't heavy enough!'

The woman paused, then nodded her head. 'I'll fetch what I can.' Before Whiston could respond, she was running towards the stairs.

As she disappeared from sight, Mindelen spoke again, this time in a whisper. 'Don't trust her lad.'

Whiston hoisted the sergeant higher. 'We don't have a choice. You need help.' The sergeant groaned and his head fell forward. Drops of blood fell to the floor from the wound in his shoulder.

A few minutes later, Lizzie came back down the stairs, dragging Mindelen's overnight bag behind her. 'I stuffed what I could in here.'

'Now we're both over-laden,' observed Whiston. We'll have to leave the bag behind unless you can find somewhere nearby to leave it.'

'Or I could go and fetch my friend. Come back with a carriage?'

Whiston eyed the young woman thoughtfully. 'How long will it take?'

'About 20 minutes, if he's at home.'

'And if he's not?'

'Then I'll have to come back and help you do what we can.'

'You've got 20 minutes. Then I leave on my own.'

Whiston watched Lizzie's departure with mixed feelings. He shook his head, still wondering if he really could trust her. Then he struggled to settle the sergeant in an armchair that stood to one side of the reception area, before settling himself down behind the counter. He'd arrange Mindelen to look, to any casual passer-by, as if he were sleeping. Blood continued to ooze from the sergeant's shoulder and the man's face was now deathly white. Whiston was worried about Mindelen's chances of surviving much longer. He kept glancing at a clock on the wall, willing the minute hand to move faster around its face. Tiring of this, he started to search through the drawer at the back of the counter. Its meagre contents didn't distract him for long. There was a guest register, a couple of well-worn quill pens, a half empty bottle of black ink and an almost empty bottle of cheap gin. He finished the contents of the bottle in one long gulp.

His head jerked up at the sound of wheels clattering on the cobbles outside. Snapping out of his doze, Whiston felt guilty and quickly surveyed the lobby. Mindelen was still slumped in the comfy chair, his breath sounding more ragged and laboured than before. The noise stopped outside, to be quickly followed by the sound of a carriage door closing. Whiston picked up the pistol from the counter and pointed it towards the hotel door. He heard the sound of whispering from outside, then the door slowly opened.

'It's only me,' said Lizzie, stepping into the lobby. A small, well-dressed man followed her. Once inside, Lizzie went to check on Mindelen, while the man executed a slight bow and removed his top hat. 'You must be Mr Whiston?' A pleasure to meet you, sir. I'm Doctor Barclay.' His voice was a rich baritone, with a strong hint of his native Scotland. A well-trimmed ginger beard also hinted at his ancestral roots. 'Is this the wounded colleague?' He nodded towards Mindelen.

'Yes. I think it's the cut to his left shoulder that has done the most damage.'

'I'll just fetch my bag from the carriage,' said Barclay.

'Oh hurry, Mitchell,' urged Lizzie as the doctor returned. She stepped away from the chair, giving her friend room to examine Mindelen.

As Barclay worked on Mindelen, Whiston drew Lizzie to one side. In a quiet voice he asked, 'Are you sure we can trust him?'

'I'd stake my life on it,' she said, her eyes flashing anger.

'You might have to if Barrington's friends come to investigate. Whoever ordered this attack, will be expecting a report. They aren't likely to sit around forever.'

Lizzie turned pale as the import of Whiston's words sank in.

'Mitchell, can we move him? My friend is worried about another attack.'

Barclay looked up, halfway through applying a dressing to Mindelen's shoulder. 'We could take him to my rooms. Although I'm concerned that jolting him over the cobbles could reopen the wound again. It's pretty deep. He's lucky it missed the main artery.'

'Can he survive the journey?' said Whiston.

'Probably, but I can't guarantee it. If the wound tears further things could get difficult. And he's already lost a lot of blood.'

Whiston hesitated for a moment, weighing his options, before speaking again. 'Then we have to risk it.'

Barclay shrugged before starting to put his instruments back into his bag. 'What about the other man? The one upstairs?'

'Leave him. He was part of the attack. We don't have time to waste on him.'

Barclay glanced towards Lizzie. She shook her head.

'Alright,' said Barclay. Let me help you to move the patient into my carriage. We'd best lay him out and I'll need to keep an eye on him. Can you drive the carriage, Mr Whiston?

'I'm happy to try. Besides, I have a pistol if we're attacked again.'

The two men struggled to get Mindelen into the carriage, while Lizzie fetched the doctor's bag and Mindelen's overnight bag. As the doctor sat fussing over the sergeant, Whiston helped Lizzie to store both bags in the trunk before offering his hand to help her up into the carriage. Satisfied they were not being watched, he hauled himself up and into the dickey box, took up the reins and clicked his teeth. The horse began to move forward.

At the end of the street, hidden in the shadows, a scruffy looking dog lay flat on its belly. It was uncomfortable with the presence inside its head and whined softly as it saw people emerge from a doorway and load things into one of the moving things humans sometimes fitted to the back of a horse. Its ears went flat, and it raised its muzzle to scent the air, before locking its eyes onto the activity outside of The Grand Hotel. When the carriage moved off, the dog gave a series of yips.

Nearby, in another hotel, a guest lay fully clothed on a king-size bed. This guest appeared to be sleeping, although a close observer might have noticed how the lips moved from time-to-time, without warning, the guest opened his eyes and sat up. A wide grin transformed the face for an instant, as a smile revealed oddly shaped teeth which appeared to have been filed into razor-like points.

'So, Figulus was right in his surmise. It is time for you and me to meet, Mr Whiston.'

31: THE RECKONING

Farral woke Unwin just after dawn. His friend seemed refreshed and eager to begin implementing the plans they'd discussed the previous evening.

'Wait, Lemuel. We need to be sure we know who and what we are dealing with. There's nothing to be gained by rushing around.'

'But we know he's here! I have to kill him. I promised to do it for Artie's sake.'

'You're letting your desire to avenge your friend over-rule your common sense.' As Unwin scowled, Farral continued, 'Don't you think he'll be waiting for you to try something? Right now, he's doubtless setting a trap for you.'

Unwin shook his head and raised both hands in frustration. 'We can't just sit here. Don't *you* think he'll come looking for us?'

'Now we're getting somewhere. Our first priority should be to find a new hiding place. Then we can scout out his house and try to figure out what he's doing.'

Unwin sighed, then smiled. 'Yes, you're right. I know that here,' he tapped his head, 'but in here I want to see him die.' His right hand thumped his chest.

'Farral raised an eyebrow. 'I thought you said you'd already dealt with Brother Fulbright's killer?'

'That's right, but McNulty has long been my main target. If I'd acted sooner, Artie might still be alive.'

'Or not. We'll never know for sure, and you can't change the past. But if we don't get moving soon, I suspect we may not have much of a future.'

When both men were armed and ready, Farral led the way out of his bedroom window and across rooftops made slippery by overnight rain. The early morning sun peeped between the chimney pots, but it would be many hours before its rays reached the alley where Unwin stepped off the homemade rope ladder. Shouts from the main street mingled with the softer sounds of people stirring in the nearby houses. The alley walls, made from the backs of badly constructed houses, were covered in grime and soot. A woman cursed nearby, and a dog began to bark. A horse whinnied as it pulled a cart across the cobbles and the cries of a hawker carried from around the corner and down the alley. An infant's cry added to the growing cacophony. Farral and Unwin cautiously set off for the end of the alley, narrowly missing being drenched by the foul-smelling contents of a chamber pot as they crept towards the main street.

At the junction, Farral peered out in both directions before signalling to his friend that he should follow him out. A casual observer might well have taken the pair for moderately successful businessmen taking a morning constitutional before returning home for a hearty breakfast. A wizened old woman approached Unwin, gnarled hand held out as she begged a coin. The priest waved her away and walked on, ignoring the colourful invective aimed at his back.

'She likes you,' said Farral.

'Ignoring her meant she had less time to register our facial details.'

Farral chuckled. 'You're back in control then?'

'Of course. But I will complete this mission or die in the attempt.'

'That's what worries me.'

The pair walked on, already having to dodge the growing number of early risers and those yet to find their beds. The smell of burning meat assailed them as they passed a street vendor.

Christian Figulus fiddled with his collar. His face was flushed, and his mouth was dry. He stood in front of a large desk, his eyes drawn to the strange swirls and patterns carved into its surface. On the other side of the desk sat his employer. Mr Black was playing with a stiletto, using its point to pick at his cuticles and offering no indication that he was aware of the trickles of blood forming on his long nails.

At last, Black looked up at his servant. Placing the stiletto to one side and with both hands on the desk, he said, 'Tell me again, what happened at the hotel. And this time, don't forget to mention whose idea this attack was and who chose the men charged with carrying it out.'

Figulus swallowed and shuffled on his feet. 'Well, sir it was like this. I knew you were interested in these men and so I decided to follow them to the hostelry where they dined. Mr Barrington made sure they went to that place, knowing that I was acquainted with one of the serving wenches there.' He paused, trying to gauge how his master was reacting to this new version of events. Seeing nothing to encourage him, he took out a large kerchief and mopped at his brow. 'Anyway, there was some chat between one of the men and the wench. I drew her to one side to find out what she knew but this didn't amount to much. When they left, I followed them to a tavern.' His voice faded to a whisper as he added, 'That was when the idea of dealing with them came to, erm, came to me.'

Black took his hands off the desk and folded them, fingers interlaced and with the palms resting on his stomach. 'Go on.'

Figulus glanced at the stiletto, then found his voice once more. 'It was clear they were going to stay put for a while, so I left the tavern and went and found two acquaintances of mine who I knew would be drinking nearby. They're good men who've worked for me before and know how to keep their mouths shut. I outlined my plan and they agreed to take the job.'

Black held up his left hand. 'So let me see if I've misunderstood you on any point. I instructed you to keep an eye on the two men and report their movements to me. You took it upon yourself to show some initiative, for once, and decided to have them killed. Did I misconstrue anything?'

Figulus hesitated, then shook his head. He stepped back, his face turning crimson.

'Ah, Figulus, don't leave yet. You haven't finished your story. What happened next?'

'I went back to the tavern and found the two men still drinking. Later, I followed them back to the hotel, nodded to my two friends and kept on walking round the corner. I waited for them to bring news of success but, instead, one of them returned alone. He told me that Eddie was dead, but both of the targets still lived – although one was badly wounded. Uncertain as to what I should do, I paid Bert, as agreed, and set off for my lodgings. I stayed there until I received your summons, Master.' Figulus took out his kerchief again.

Black leant back, his eyes locked on the uncomfortable servant. 'It is well then that the unfortunate Mr Barrington alerted me to the mess you left behind.'

'Sir, I ...' Seeing the look in the other's eyes, Figulus decided to hold his tongue.

'Christian, Christian, now *what* am I going to do with you?' Mr Black smiled. 'Should I commend you for showing a rare spark of initiative? Should I reprimand you for disobeying my explicit instructions?' He stood, picking up the stiletto. 'Or should I discipline you for failing me?' Figulus started to back away.

Farral surveyed the dilapidated house from the other side of the road. There was no sign that anyone was at home, although both he and Unwin knew that this meant very little. The man they wanted to talk to was not known for advertising his whereabouts.

'Well?'

Farral interrupted his survey long enough to frown at Unwin. 'He's there. See the vase in the top left window?'

Unwin tilted his head back a little and glanced up at the window. ''What of it?'

'It's in the centre of the sill. That's the code.'

Unwin shrugged. 'So what are we waiting out here for?'

'We need to be sure no-one is watching us.'

'Apart from the flower seller by the right-hand junction?'

'Don't worry about her. She works for Molay. Come on.'

As Unwin raised his fist to hammer on the door, it swung inwards on silent hinges. He peered into the gloomy interior then stepped inside, Farral following close behind. As the door swung shut behind them, a smooth voice, emanating from the top of the dimly glimpsed staircase ahead, ordered the pair to stop. Unwin wrinkled his nose, trying not to sneeze. The smell made him think of camphor.

'Do as he says,' whispered Farral.

'Leave your weapons on the table to your right. All of them.' Unwin looked towards his companion, one eyebrow raised. He'd noticed the unfamiliar accent of the speaker.

Both men unloaded pistols and a variety of small knives.

'Thank you, gentlemen. Please come up the stairs and we can discuss terms, like civilised men.' His eyes now becoming more accustomed to the low light, Unwin could just make out the figure of a small man standing at the top of the stairs. He covered his guests with what looked to be a shotgun held in the crook of his left arm. A bandaged hand held the trigger guard, one finger poised to set loose death and destruction should its owner feel threatened.

As Farral and Unwin neared the top of the stairs, their strange captor retreated a few steps into the light cast from a small candelabra. 'You can put the gun down now, Jannes,' said Farral. Unwin glanced at his companion.

A guttural laugh erupted from the lips of Jannes Molay. 'Is that you, Thomas? I heard you were dead!'

'A common but fortunately erroneous belief,' said Farral. He pushed past Unwin, as Molay propped the shotgun against a wall, and embraced the smaller man in a bear hug. When they separated, Farral gestured towards a bemused Unwin. 'Jannes, this is my colleague, Lemuel Unwin.'

Molay offered his hand. As they shook, he said, 'I've heard of you, of course. People think you're the last surviving senior assassin of the Shield.'

Unwin grinned. 'Not quite. Young Thomas here is most accomplished in the art of removing our opponents.'

Molay waved a hand then turning said,' Follow me, gentlemen. Let's see if we can help each other.'

Figulus took another step away from the desk, wincing at the thought of what his master might do. He'd heard rumours of what happened to those who crossed Black and feared that he might very soon be able to confirm some of them. That was if he was still alive. 'Master, I'm sorry if I have offended you or let you down. I'll never use my initiative again, I swear.'

Black stood statue-like, studying the squirming hu'man in front of him. His blood ire was running strong, and he knew that the only way to satisfy it was through violent action. He debated within himself the best option – should he kill the fool now or damage him as a lesson to others? Reaching a decision, he smiled, noting the effect this had on the pale faced Figulus. 'Come here. I'm not going to kill you, but you may find the next few minutes ... instructive.' As the other hesitated, Black surged forward, grabbing the young man by the throat.

Figulus tried to wrench himself free but found he couldn't loosen his master's grip. Black half dragged his reluctant servant back to the desk and released the throat, only to take a new grip on the young man's left hand. 'You are right-handed, are you not?' Figulus responded with a reluctant nod as he sucked in air, tears forming in his eyes.

Black slammed the captive hand down on the desk, eliciting a sob from his servant as knuckles met unyielding hardwood. Moments later, Figulus screamed as the stiletto was driven through the palm of his hand, pinning it to the desk. Blood started to well up as Black thrust his face into that of the petrified young man. 'Now look what you've made me do! That's going to leave a hole in the surface. What am I going to fill it with?'

'I don't know, master. I'm sorry.' Figulus knew that he was whining as he tried to placate his master, alarmed at the continuing grin on the latter's face.

'You don't know? I have an idea. How about I cut off your manhood and ram it into the hole. Do you think it would be large enough to fill that pinprick?

Figulus wet himself. 'Yes master. I mean no. Please don't do that.'

'Yes? No? Not very decisive now?' Black took a dagger from an inside pocket. 'I have a better idea.' With astonishing speed, he used his free hand to yank Figulus' little finger sideways as he slammed the dagger down across it, severing the digit forever from its fellows. His victim screamed, louder this time and the smell of excrement was added to that of urine. Black calmly picked up the severed finger and popped it into his mouth. As he commenced to chew, he pulled the stiletto from the wounded hand and ordered its owner out of his study. As Figulus fled, cradling his mauled hand to his chest, Black said, 'Next time I won't be so merciful. Find me that policeman!' He spat out a small piece of bone and gristle as the study door slammed shut.

Molay offered his guests a glass of ale then seated himself behind a large, plain desk piled high with scraps of paper. Candles flickered around the room, which held enough books and parchments to fill a small library. 'Are you serious?' he asked.

'My friend is very serious,' said Farral. He sipped at his drink and then leaned forward in his chair. 'We are, of course, willing to pay for this information.'

'I would hope so,' laughed Molay. 'What you seek will be difficult and dangerous to acquire. Not to mention expensive.'

'How expensive?' said Unwin.

Molay sat forward, elbows on the desk and hands steepled together. After a slight pause, he said, 'Two pounds now and another two when I have it.'

Unwin stared at him for a moment and then smiled. 'Agreed.' He took a small package, wrapped in a piece of silk, from inside his jacket and pushed it across the desk towards the Dutchman.

Molay picked up the package and opened a drawer in his desk. He dropped the payment inside, ignoring the chink of coins, closed the drawer, and offered more ale from a large pitcher. 'I would have taken less.'

'I would have paid more. But the deal is settled.'

Molay chuckled then held up his beaker. As Unwin and Farral clinked their own beakers against his, Molay said, 'The deal is done.'

'How long?' asked Farral.

'Give me three days. Now finish your drinks and get out of here. I have other things to do.' He turned his attention to the top piece of paper on the nearest pile.

Unwin and Farral looked at each other, downed their drinks and rose.

'Use the back door,' said Molay, without looking up.

'Three days, 'said Unwin, heading for the weapon-laden table at the foot of the stairs.

32: Tra'll

Wallace stared at the forest edge, enjoying the cooling breeze blowing into his face. The trees were enormous, with many branches and large, spiky leaves almost twice the size of Wallace's hand. Strange throaty calls echoed among the higher branches, where the feathered but flightless duk'en lived in nests made of twigs, woven, and held together by a sticky oil secreted from glands on the creatures' legs. Sagana had said the duk'en were harmless and timid, although their cries of alarm would warn any other creature for miles around that something was moving through the forest. As far as Wallace could tell, they were about the size of a turkey and looked like a bird, albeit with a beak lined with teeth. His master had said that they mostly lived on the hard nuts which grew on the trees, although they would eat rotting meat given the chance.

Sagana too was surveying the forest. His head was cocked a little to one side, as though he were listening to something. He glanced at Wallace then said in a low voice, 'The duk'en are too active for my liking. There's something nearby and it may be waiting for us. Keep your wits about you.' He started to walk closer to the treeline, his hand resting on the hilt of his sword.

Wallace shrugged before copying Sagana. As they reached the first trees, he discovered how effectively the canopy limited the natural light inside the forest. 'It looks like dusk already,' he whispered. Sagana said nothing but nodded his agreement, eyes fixed on one particular tree. 'Be ready,' he muttered, as they slowly approached the thick trunk.

He'd reached about four feet from the tree when a sudden cacophony of raucous cries burst out. The leaves on the branches burst into frantic activity and Wallace glimpsed more than a dozen duk'en running along the branches, crashing through the leaves in their haste to hop and jump to the safety of the higher branches. He stood watching in amazement before a low hiss attracted his attention. Sagana pointed at Wallace and then to the left of the trunk before tapping his own chest and pointing right. His sword was in his hand.

Wallace drew his own sword then crept forward, heading slightly to the left. The two met around the other side of the tree, where they found what was left of a strange-looking six-limbed creature. At its side lay a badly made and broken axe, the shaft snapped almost through. Resembling a squat human, the creature was still wearing a crude form of metal armour. Its head was covered by short pale fur. Exposed flesh had been torn away in places. Sagana knelt to examine the corpse more closely, while Wallace stood guard, anxiously scanning the nearby trees.

Risking a quick look of his own, Wallace could no longer contain his curiosity. 'What is it?'

Sagana looked up, frowning. 'It's what's left of a Fram'ska warrior, although I have no idea what she was doing here.'

'She?'

'Yes. The Fram'ska are a warrior race, organised into small nomadic clans on their own world. They spend most of their time fighting each other, except during the breeding season. The females are larger than the males, so they are the main fighters and protect the eggs laid by the males.

These are incubated for around three of your months before they hatch. During that time, raiders from other clans will try to steal or destroy them.'

'What killed her?'

Sagana used his boot to turn the corpse over. Long rents in the warrior's back had pierced the armour and opened the body to the bone before severing the spine. 'She was running away from a tra'll.'

Wallace felt a cold shiver down his back. 'She should have faced it then!'

Sagana shook his head. 'I'd wait until you 've faced one before being so quick to judge. The Fram'ska are not cowards.' He stood up, sniffing. 'The wind has changed direction. We should get moving before anything else comes to investigate.' He pointed deeper into the woods.

Angele scowled at Madeleine. 'I'm going to release you from my magic now, but only so that you can lick that slop up before we go.' In her hand, she held a coiled whip. Madeleine felt the stiffness leave her body to be replaced with a burning, tingling sensation in her limbs. Angele grabbed the young woman by the hair and started to pull her head down, tugging so hard that Madeleine was forced to kneel or risk having a handful of hair torn out from the roots. Still gripping the hair, the old woman moved behind her captive and pushed her forward, face down into the pile of vomit. 'Now lick the floor clean, like the pig you are!'

Madeleine tried to push herself up, earning the unwelcome reward of a stinging sensation across her shoulders, as the older woman lashed them with her whip. 'Lick it up, you worthless little whore,' demanded Angele. And don't think I won't use this again – the Lord doesn't care what your back looks like. He likes to watch your face while he pleasures himself inside your stinking body.'

The young woman groaned, earning another lashing, this time lower down. She hesitated, almost retching at the thought of what Angele was demanding. Without warning, the whip was coiled around her throat and the old woman was hissing in her ear. 'Do it. Now. Or would you like me to use my magic again and play with your body for a while?' The pressure on her throat eased a little and Madeleine bent forward. The tingling sensation was fading and as she forced herself to start licking the disgusting mess on the floor, her mind was seeking a way to escape from the evil old woman. Sensing victory, Angele started to cackle.

Several hours later, Sagana called a halt. Wallace was keen to press on, but his Master insisted they take a short break, explaining, 'We must be vigilant against a surprise attack. One careless mistake due to tiredness could be our last.'

Wallace sat with his back to a tree, sipping water from a leather pouch. Nearby, Sagana fiddled with the pebble they'd found in Angele's hut. He started to mutter something but stopped abruptly, his head turning to his right. Rising, he waved Wallace closer. The warrior hurried to his side. Sagana whispered, 'We have company. Over there.' He nodded to his right. 'Follow me and try to make as little noise as possible. I sense more than one visitor.' Without waiting for a response he set off, heading away from the direction in which he'd just nodded.

Wallace hurried to catch up, taking care where he put his feet. Coming alongside Sagana, he whispered, 'I'm not happy about running from something at my back.'

The Master didn't respond at first, seeming to be more concerned with scanning the path ahead through the trees. When he did speak, he too kept his voice low. 'You might be even less happy to face it if my suspicions are correct.' He pointed to a huge tree off to the left with low hanging thick branches. 'Can you climb?' Wallace nodded. 'Then follow me and keep quiet.'

The pair soon reached the tree, and both pulled themselves up, scrabbling to find a secure footing before they started to climb higher towards the thicker foliage. Unlike the majority of the forest, this particular tree had large, straight-edged, pale-yellow leaves which offered little

obstruction to a determined climber. Wallace followed
Sagana to a height of around thirty feet. Here the two men
crouched among the leaves where two thick branches grew
out, side by side, from the trunk. 'Watch,' whispered Sagana.

Wallace peered out from their hiding place, back along
the path they'd followed. He was about to protest that
nothing was happening when a four-legged creature the
size of a small horse burst out from among the trees. Light
brown in colour and smooth-skinned, it bore two powerful-
looking pointed tusks along either side of its chin. As it pawed
at the ground, it turned to face back towards the way it had
come and lifted its head, revealing small red eyes and a
large flat nose. It seemed to be scenting the air when
suddenly and without warning it let out a tremendous bellow
of unmistakeable rage, a battle challenge like none Wallace
had ever heard. 'Po'glet,' muttered Sagana, pointing to the
creature.

Moments later a shaggy goliath burst out of the trees. It
stood half as tall again as a man and was wearing the skin of
some large beast. This newcomer had long straggling hair,
deep-set eyes, and a hooked nose. Its eyebrows
disappeared into its hairline, covering a large portion of the
low forehead. In its right hand it gripped a crude axe, little
more than a rock tied to a short branch with some sort of
vine. Tilting its head back, the creature offered its own
challenge as the po'glet charged towards it, bellowing with
fury.

The two creatures met in a tremendous collision that
shook the ground, almost dislodging Wallace from his perch.
Sagana grabbed him by the arm, pulling him back to safety
as he started to fall. 'Watch! Don't join in,' was his saviour's
unnecessary advice.

Turning his attention back to the battle, Wallace could
see that the po'glet had impaled two of its tusks into its
opponent's left leg and was now frantically shaking, trying to
free itself. Meanwhile the axe was being smashed down
around its head as the second creature struggled to retain its
footing. There was a loud cracking sound and then the
po'glet pulled back beyond the swing of the axe, thick

cream-coloured blood pouring from the right side of its jaw. The tusks remained embedded in the other creature's leg and Wallace thought he could see exposed bone. Its enemy staggered towards it, then went down on one knee. It made a strange keening sound and tried to throw the axe at the wary po'glet before tumbling sideways, where it now lay very still. The po'glet approached warily, before lowering its head and again charging at the prostrate form. This time they collided head-to-head, but the po'glet alone started to back away. It now circled its fallen opponent, sniffing every few seconds before finally emitting another bellow as it walked away and disappeared among the trees.

Wallace prepared to climb down, eager to examine the fallen creature. Sagana put out a restraining hand. 'Wait. Give it five minutes. Let's be sure the po'glet has gone and that thing is dead.'

'If we must wait, tell me what that other creature was?'

Sagana chuckled. 'That, my friend, was a young tra'll. A child.'

Wallace sat with his mouth open but said nothing until a few minutes later, when he was examining the dead tra'll. The creature's left leg was swollen and almost black around the sites where the tusks had speared its flesh. Sagana watched him for a while before offering an explanation. 'The po'glet carries a deadly poison in sacs attached to the roof of its mouth. It can release this, through its tusks, into any wound it has inflicted on its foe. Once impaled, the tra'll never stood a chance.'

'But why didn't the axe smash the creature's skull?'

'The po'glet's skull is made up of dense bone and harder than most rocks. An older tra'll would have known this but I'd guess the youngster had never encountered a po'glet before.'

'So how do you kill one of those things?'

'A sharp thrust through the eye usually works – if you can get close enough and avoid the tusks. It's a pity we don't have Frederick and his archers. Bringing them was too much of a risk.'

'Why?'

'The more life forms accompany me, the easier they are to detect. Like the tra'll, Lord Helr'ath seldom welcomes visitors to his realm.'

'Are you mad, woman? What is she doing?' The familiar voice caught Madeleine's attention. She looked up to see Muller glaring at Angele.

'The bitch threw up. I told her to clean it up. She must be hungry.'

Muller narrowed his eyes, taking in the young woman's torn blouse. He licked his lips, his gaze lingering on her breasts. His obvious lust wasn't lost on Angele. She stepped between him and the younger woman. 'Oh no you don't. The Lord Helr'ath wants her, and I don't think he'd be happy with used goods.'

Muller turned pale. 'It's good to see you ... wife,' he said.

Angele performed a mocking bow. 'Wife in name but not in practice, eh, you scheming old goat?'

'I always come back, don't I?'

'Hah. When you want something. Or somewhere to hide.' She turned suddenly and kicked the still kneeling Madeleine in the ribs. 'Did I say to stop?'

Muller stepped towards her and pushed Angele to one side. 'No. You didn't my sweet. But I will.' He turned towards Madeleine. 'Get up, girl.'

Madeleine glanced at Muller and back to her tormentor.

'Oh, do as he says,' snapped Angele. 'The old fool is doubtless impressed by your teats, but I suppose I can't offer you to Lord Helr'ath if you're too damaged.'

Madeleine thought back to her experiences at the hands of Dubois and his men but decided to hold her tongue. If Angele found out she wasn't a virgin, there was no knowing how the old woman might react. Then she recalled

244

that Muller knew and wondered why he didn't say anything. Her next thought brought both an explanation and made her shudder. If she were left alone with the lecherous old man, would he force himself upon her as the price for maintaining his silence? Angele or Muller? Madeleine didn't like either option. As for the mysterious Lord Helr'ath ...

33: TIME HEALS

Whiston flinched when a hand clasped his shoulder. Peering through blurry eyes, he struggled to recollect where he was. Memory came flooding back when he managed to focus on the pretty face of the young woman offering him a cup of tea. 'Miss Cobham,' he began, struggling to extricate himself from the blankets that had kept him warm through the night. Although comfortable, the chair he'd slept in had given him a mild cramp in his right leg. 'Is he ...?'

Lizzie Cobham smiled as she shook her head. 'Your friend is still sleeping. I sat with him until sunrise and then the doctor took over, so I could snatch a little sleep.'

Whiston stood up with exaggerated care, mindful that he needed to stretch out the aching calf muscle. Looking at his visitor, he was fascinated by the dimples in her cheeks and wondered why he hadn't noticed them before. The oval face was framed with auburn ringlets and warm brown eyes twinkled with a hint of amusement. He realised he was staring and took a sip of the hot tea to hide his embarrassment before blurting out 'Thank you for your help. I wasn't sure I could trust you, but I see my doubt was misplaced.' She rewarded him with another smile.

He sat once more and tried to arrange his thoughts. Lizzie busied herself with drawing the thick velvet curtains, letting strong sunlight flood into the well-furnished sitting room. Whiston squinted in surprise as he looked up. 'What time is it?'

Lizzie looked towards a large clock on the mantelpiece. 'Why, I do believe it will soon be noon.'

'Noon! How long have I been asleep?' Feeling a moment of panic, he leapt to his feet.

'Dr Barclay had his servant cover you up around 3am. He was confident your friend would live and ordered you to get some rest. After last night and the late hour when you retired, it's not surprising you've slept all morning. I take it you don't normally sleep this late, Mr ...?'

Whiston blushed, took another sip of tea too quickly and started to splutter as some of the liquid went down his windpipe. Recovering, he put the cup down on the corner of a small table and said, 'Edward Whiston at your service', whilst bowing from the waist.

Lizzie laughed and then, seeing the puzzled look on his face, said, 'Very formal Mr Whiston. I'm not used to young men having manners in my line of work. Most think it's acceptable to grab me wherever and whenever they can. Although my place of employment is a hostelry, most of the customers seem to mistake it for a brothel.'

Whiston held up a hand to stop her. 'Not me. That's why I was upset with my friend.' He fell silent for a few moments before continuing, 'I used to know a young lady who worked in a brothel.'

Something in his tone made Lizzie give him a hard look. 'Used to know? That sounds rather final.'

Whiston's eyes fell to the floor. 'She died. She was murdered.'

'Oh dear. Forgive me, Mr Whiston, but you do seem to attract death and his friends.'

He sighed. 'I suppose it comes with being a policeman. But please, call me Edward.'

'And you must call me Lizzie.' She put a hand to her mouth. 'Oh my goodness! Here we are talking, and I was meant to tell you that cook has prepared some breakfast. It's waiting in the dining room.'

After a hearty breakfast of bacon, eggs, and slabs of bread, generously covered with butter, Lizzie took Whiston upstairs, to visit his friend. Mindelen was propped up in bed, talking with Dr Barclay, who was in the process of opening the curtains. The sergeant was very pale and his hair, normally slicked down with cheap oil, stood up at various random angles. A variety of bandages bore mute testimony to his recent experiences. He smiled a little sheepishly upon seeing his colleague. 'Well, well, young Whiston. The doctor's been tellin' me as 'ow you and the young lady 'ere saved me.' He paused to cast a suspicious look at Lizzie. 'She looks even better in the daylight.'

Lizzie coloured at the compliment and tried to hide her discomfort by offering to plump up the bed cushions.

'I've told you before, it's about time you found a nice young woman to settle down with.'

'Steady on, sergeant,' said Whiston. 'Just because she helped us last night, it doesn't mean I'm about to propose to Miss Cobham.' Dr Barclay smiled, enjoying his patient's rough humour.'

'Oh, *Miss* Cobham, is it?' said a grinning Mindelen, winking at Lizzie.

Desperate to change the subject, Whiston turned towards the doctor. 'We owe you our thanks, sir. I don't carry much money with me, but I'd be happy to give you a written note confirming my acknowledgement of your fee, if that's acceptable to you.'

'I wouldn't dream of charging you for my services,' said Barclay. 'Sergeant Mindelen has already explained that you are policemen from London and I'm always happy to help the agents of law and order. Miss Cobham's late father once helped me out of a very awkward situation, so I was delighted to be able to answer her plea for assistance.' He paused, as if about to add something, but then coughed. 'The sergeant is out of danger, but he'll need to rest for a few days, and we shouldn't tire him. Let's leave him to take a nap for now and you can visit him again before dinner.' He gestured towards the door.

Back downstairs, Barclay led the way to his private study. Whiston and Lizzie settled themselves into large and comfortable leather-covered armchairs as the doctor rang a small bell on his desk. A few moments later, a maid came into the room. 'Bring three glasses of my best sherry, please, Nancy.' Barclay moved to the seat behind his desk.

As the maid departed, closing the door behind her, Barclay looked at Whiston and asked, 'Would now be a good time to enquire as to how your friend came to receive his injuries?'

Whiston paused for a few moments before answering. 'We're here as part of a murder investigation. My sergeant and I have different theories as to who the killer might be – but we both believe they could be here in Bristol. I'm not sure why we were attacked though. The men who fought with us were total strangers. They could have been simple robbers, or they could have been set on us by a suspect. Or the explanation may be something else entirely.' He paused, wondering how much to share with the doctor. 'It seems odd though. We arrived yesterday and, as far as I know, no-one knew we were coming.' In his own mind, a niggling thought pointed out that the Inspector had known about their visit. He tried to shake it off.

Lizzie came to his rescue. 'The two gentlemen dined where I work and, unfortunately, left a wallet behind. There was a card inside with the name of the hotel. I took a gamble and was taking the wallet back to them when the attack on the sergeant began.' She smiled at Whiston.

'That's right. She'd just entered my room to ask if the wallet was mine when we heard a shout and the sounds of a scuffle. The rest happened so fast, I'm still finding it hard to believe it was real and not a bad dream.' He shook his head, as if struggling to recall the exact sequence of events. 'I suppose it was lucky for us that Miss Cobham was there and that she knew you. Otherwise, I'm not sure what would have happened.'

'Didn't the night clerk hear anything? I'm surprised he didn't try to help you.' Before Whiston could answer, a knock on the door signalled the return of the maid. He used the opportunity to buy himself some thinking time and went to open the door. The maid seemed surprised to find him in the doorway but said nothing as she deposited a tray on the doctor's desk.

'Will that be all, sir?'

'Yes, thank you for now, Nancy. I'll ring if I need anything else.' As she left, Barclay stood and took up two of the small glasses sitting on the tray. He handed one each to Lizzie and Whiston, before resuming his seat and taking a sip from the third glass. 'Where was I? Oh yes, the night clerk.'

'Towards the end of the fight, he did put in an appearance,' said Whiston, before Lizzie could say anything. 'Unfortunately, I thought he was another attacker and laid him out with a stout cudgel, dropped by my assailant. I don't think he'll be suffering anything worse than a sore head though,' Whiston finished with a smile. 'I suppose I ought to go and apologise to the poor man.'

'Oh. I wouldn't worry yourself,' said the doctor. 'It won't be the first time he's been involved in a brawl at that place. You couldn't have picked a more disreputable place to stay if you'd tried!' laughed Dr Barclay.

'Really? I wish we'd known,' said Whiston, with a laugh of his own. The niggling voice was back in his head – hadn't Inspector Johnson made a point of recommending the place?

'You seem a little preoccupied,' suggested Barclay. 'Are you sure you're alright?'

'I'm fine, thank you. Just a little shocked I suppose. You don't expect to be attacked in your hotel bedroom!' Whiston temporised. He grinned at Lizzie as she came to his rescue.

'I would imagine that unfortunate experience and worrying about the sergeant would be enough to make most people feel a bit out of sorts,' she suggested.

'I suppose so,' agreed Barclay. 'Anyway, drink up and we can make arrangements for you to sleep more comfortably tonight. I have several spare rooms here, so I'll get my housekeeper to make up two beds and freshen the rooms before tonight.' He waved away a protest from Whiston. 'No please, it isn't any trouble and I'll enjoy the company. Meanwhile, I'll check on my patient before making a few house calls. I'd recommend the pair of you take a short stroll and get some fresh air. Work up an appetite for tonight. My cook is rather good, even if I say so myself, and she hates to see food go to waste.'

Sensing that they were being subtly dismissed, Whiston stood and offered his arm to Lizzie. 'That sounds like good advice.' A sudden thought made him frown. 'Are you working tonight, Miss Cobham?'

'Unfortunately yes, but just for a few hours. I'll be free after nine, so I can join the two of you later, And I don't have to be there until six.'

Strolling arm-in-arm along the city centre streets, Whiston found himself humming a happy tune for the first time since the awful night of Rose's death. With a start, he wondered if he was being unfaithful to the dead woman's memory. Lizzie must have noted the sudden change in his demeanour for she stopped dead and asked, 'Are you alright Edward?

'What? Oh, yes, Sorry, I was just remembering an old friend and thinking how life can always take you by surprise.'

Lizzie gave a shy smile. 'Indeed. Often when you least expect it.'

'I guess it wouldn't be a surprise if you *were* expecting it?'

'Oh Edward, you know what I mean!'

Whiston looked at the blushing young woman and took her hand. 'Forgive me for being forward, Miss Cobham, but do you believe in love at first sight?'

Lizzie's cheeks turned an even deeper shade of scarlet. She snatched her hand away. 'Mr Whiston! We've only just met.'

250

'And yet I feel we've known each other forever. I'm sorry. I apologise if I've offended you. Come, let us resume our walk and talk of something else.'

She gave him a shy look. 'You haven't offended me, Edward. It's just that I'm not used to such directness.'

'Then we'll say no more and give you time to compose yourself. Come, is that a coffee house I see across the road? Let's partake of some light refreshment and watch the world go by, for just a little while.'

She smiled at him and then turned very pale, putting a hand to her mouth.

'What is it?'

Lizzie was pointing behind him. Whiston spun round, to find a young man emerging from a narrow side street and staggering towards him. The source of Lizzie's concern was immediately obvious – the new arrival was clutching a blood-drenched left hand to his chest, His shirt was stained crimson and his face was contorted in pain. Wild rolling eyes completed an unsavoury picture.

'My God. It's Figulus!' said Lizzie. Other passers-by were now starting to notice the young man. Whiston was struggling to recall where he'd heard the name before, but stepped towards the young man, aiming to put himself between the young woman and the man she seemed to know. Then recollection supplied some context and he realised this was the young man she'd spoken about back in the hotel.

At Lizzie's mention of his name, the young man's eyes seemed to gain some focus. He stared at her and then at Whiston, his eyes now growing wider. 'Oh,' he said and then his legs seemed to fold under him, so that he abruptly sat down.

Whiston took the few short steps needed to close the gap between himself and Figulus. Glancing at Lizzie, he turned his attention back to the wounded man. 'What happened to you?'

'Figulus looked up, his face contorted with misery and pain. 'Who are you?'

251

'I'm Edward Whiston. I don't think we've formally been introduced. What happened?'

'Figulus let out a sigh. 'My employer, Mr Black, is what happened.' At the mention of this name, Whiston stepped back. 'The bastard wants to meet you, Mr Whiston.' Then he passed out.

Whiston felt a gentle tug on his sleeve. 'What are we going to do, Edward?'

34: KILLING TIME

The back door let them out into a narrow alley. Glancing up, Unwin wasn't surprised to see there were no windows overlooking the little-used passageway. It terminated in a high brick wall at one end, whilst a pale oblong of light showed the way out at the other. 'Your friend likes his privacy,' he said.

'In his line of work it's not surprising,' said Farral. 'Snooping into the affairs of others isn't often well received and there are plenty of folk who would pay a lot of money to be rid of Molay. Let's get out of here.'

They emerged from the end of the alley and turned right, following the street at a leisurely pace back towards the junction where the old woman was still hawking her flowers. Farral paused to inspect her wares, selecting a large bunch of violas wrapped in plain paper. He paid the woman a few small coins before he and Unwin set off towards the city centre and away from the harbour.

Once they were out of earshot, Unwin asked 'Why did you buy those?'

'She could be useful if there's any threat when we go back. She may be old, but her eyes and ears are sharp. Plus, she'll tell Molay which way we were headed. He trusts no-one and neither do I – present company excepted, of course.'

Unwin smiled but said nothing. He was thinking about what the pair of them were going to do for the next three days. It wasn't in his nature to let revenge wait and he was eager to have a taste of its satisfaction.

Farral led them on a long and winding route, tossing the flowers into an unattended cart as they turned into a maze of narrow streets. Unwin had lost his bearings but wasn't surprised to find they were heading for the harbour. It was the sort of place he'd chosen for a hideout many times in the past and he trusted his companion to know what he was doing. Even so, he was a little taken aback when his friend stopped them near a shed-like structure that looked as though its only means of viable support was the rubbish piled up against three of its wooden sides.

'We can rest in there tonight, but I suggest we move on and come back after dark. I've scouted it out and it's clean enough inside. There are no windows, so we can light a small candle without fear of detection and the door can be barred from the inside.'

Unwin raised an eyebrow. 'And if a fire should happen to take hold ...?

Farral grinned. There's a trapdoor in the floor. It gives access to a tunnel built long ago by smugglers. I doubt many even suspect it exists now. It doesn't appear to be a good place to hide – which makes it perfect for our purposes.'

'I like it,' said Unwin. 'Let's find somewhere to eat.'

If the tavern had once seen better days, it hid the fact well. But much to Unwin's surprise, Farral had insisted the food here was good and the ale acceptable. As a bonus, the dimly lit interior made it impossible to see much and, according to his companion, most of the customers were the sort of people who liked to keep to themselves. 'Don't do anything to attract attention and we'll be left alone.'

His musings were interrupted by a woman who resembled the surroundings insofar as she was no longer in her prime. 'Yes gents. What can I get you?'

'We'll start with two pints of your finest ale,' said Farral. 'And then we'd like pie with all the trimmings.' He pushed a shilling towards the woman. 'Keep the change.'

Unwin waited for her to reach the bar before he asked, 'Pie? What sort of pie?'

'Stop worrying. Now that I've given her a tip, she'll bring us one with real meat in it. And it won't be rancid. I told you, the food here is good, provided you know how to ask for it.'

Unwin shrugged. 'Alright. I suppose you know what you're doing.' He looked around, noting that the place was filling up.

Farral watched him and said, 'Most of the regulars are dock workers. Hard men but fair enough. I told you, leave them alone and they'll return the favour. Relax.' He leant forward and took off a boot, upending it to dislodge a small stone. 'That's better. Damn thing has been annoying me since this morning.'

Unwin tutted. 'So why leave it until now to do something about it?'

'Pain is good for the soul. Isn't that what our instructors used to say? He shrugged, looking towards the bar. 'And we might need to move fast.'

'What?'

'The tall, bearded man who just walked in. We know each other. Last time we met, I broke his arm.'

'I thought you said this place was safe?' Unwin started to rise.

Farral grabbed his arm, pushing him back down. 'Sit still. He hasn't spotted me, and I doubt he came in here looking for me. With a bit of luck, he'll not head this way and we can dine in peace. Besides, I've just paid for our food and drink and the landlord doesn't like trouble in here.'

Unwin lowered himself back onto the bench but kept his eyes on the bar. A few moments later, the waitress blocked his view as she deposited two mugs of foaming ale on the table. 'There you go, gents. Food's coming soon.' She turned away, heading for another table where four new arrivals were calling for ale. Unwin glanced at the bar. The bearded man had disappeared. Frowning, he tried his ale.

Half an hour later, he was tucking into his pie, potatoes, and carrots. His food swam in a sea of rich gravy, and, despite his misgivings, he was forced to admit that it was every bit as good as Thomas had promised. The filling turned out to be beef and although no expert, he felt sure that he was eating a decent cut and not the scrag ends from a local slaughterhouse. He nodded to Farral, his mouth too full to speak. On the table, a thick wedge of bread sat waiting to help him mop up the last of his gravy. His companion was already halfway through his own bread. Without warning, a huge fist slammed down on the table, making the plates jump and spilling the top from a second jug of ale.

Unwin looked up in surprise, to find himself staring at the bearded man.

'So, you've the nerve to come back then?' This was addressed towards Farral, who sat with a chunk of bread in his right hand and a fork in his left.

'I'm sorry. Do I know you?' Farral's face was a picture of innocence.

The bearded man ignored the question and pointed at an arm bent out of shape by having been badly set. 'Last time we met, you broke my arm with an iron bar. I don't forget something like that.' The tavern had suddenly gone very quiet.

From the corner of his eye, Unwin could see the landlord heading towards their table. In his hand he carried a heavy cudgel.

'Ah, I remember now. You tried to mug me,' said Farral. He paused, using the fork to spear a last bit of carrot. 'As you

255

can see, I'm trying to enjoy my evening meal,' he continued in a steady voice, suggesting he wasn't the least bit worried by the menace in the new arrival's eyes. He slid the carrot into his mouth.

'Now then, what's the problem here?' The landlord stood just behind the bearded man. 'Come on gents, you should know I don't allow fighting in my place of business. If there's bad blood between you, take it outside.' Unwin watched as Farral's former inquisitor turned and shot out a ham-sized fist, catching the unfortunate landlord a massive blow to the jaw, knocking him over like a skittle in an alley.

The bearded man turned back and lay both palms on the table, then leant in closer towards Farral. At this distance, Unwin could smell the foul breath seeping out of the bearded man's mouth. Farral was just wiping up the last of his gravy with the remaining morsel of bread. He popped it into his mouth and started to chew.

'Big mistake,' said Unwin to the bearded man.

'Eh?' He glanced at Unwin 'Who asked you?

There was a blur of motion as Farral shot out of his seat and planted his fork in the back of the bearded man's right hand. The man cursed as he tried to jerk his hand away, then screamed as Unwin produced a knife from his pocket and pinned the left hand to the table. At almost the same time, Farral leant forward and used his weight to force the fork deeper into the other hand. By now, Unwin was on his feet and had grabbed the cudgel from the landlord's unresisting hand. He swung it and there was a sickening sound as it connected with the back of the bearded man's head. The unlucky recipient slumped forward over the table, unconscious and with blood pouring from his various wounds.

No-one else had moved, but now, with both Unwin and Farral standing and watching them, a few men turned back towards their drinks and resumed their conversation. Others soon followed suit. Unwin knelt to check for a pulse in the landlord's wrist. 'He'll live,' he announced to no one in particular.

Farral walked towards the serving woman, who started to back away. 'It's alright. We're finished here, anyway. Excellent pie and sorry about the mess.' He tossed a shilling towards her, smiling as she plucked it out of the air. Digging in his pocket, he produced two half crowns and placed them on the bar. 'Drinks on the house.'

As men surged towards the bar, Farral and Unwin slipped away.

Later, having made sure they weren't being followed, the pair stood in shadow, surveying the wooden hut for a while until happy there was no-one else around. Farral produced a skeleton key and a bit of wire, fiddling with a rusting old padlock until he'd persuaded it to release its grip on the hasp.

With a final look round, the two men entered the shed and closed the door, taking care to bar it from the inside. Farral lit a small candle.

'We worked well together, back there in the tavern,' said Farral.

'The fool never stood a chance. Hard skull, mind.'

'Did you need to hit him that hard?'

'I hadn't finished my gravy.'

'Fair enough.'

Unwin was surprised to find two cots lined up against the walls. 'It seems you've been here before,' he suggested.

'It pays to be prepared,' smiled Farral. 'You never know when a place like this might be useful.'

'So what happened to the padlock key?'

'Lost it, a year or more ago. I only ever had the one. Knew it wouldn't be a problem.'

'Got anything to drink?'

'Funny you should mention that.' Farral strode over to a pile of battered wooden cases and removed the top two before rummaging around inside the third. 'Here we are,' he announced. 'Sorry, no glasses though.' He offered the bottle to Unwin.

'Whisky?'

'Why not?'

'I don't suppose a drop would hurt.'

They tossed a coin to decide who would take the first watch. Unwin lost, so he waited until his friend was settled, then blew out the candle and prepared to keep watch in the dark. Unable to see out, all he could do was keep alert and listen for anything unusual. It wasn't long before his friend began to snore in a gentle but regular rhythm. Unwin smiled in the dark, contemplating the plan they'd set in motion.

Unwin was beginning to feel drowsy and starting to regret the generous amount of whisky he'd consumed, when a dog began to howl. He stood up, head tilted a fraction to one side. From the darkness, Farral spoke in a whisper, 'I hear it too. It's probably nothing, but I think I'll take a look.'

'Be careful. Don't take any chances.'

The younger man slipped quietly out of the door and disappeared into the night. Unwin was fully awake now, ears straining for any sound that might indicate the imminent arrival of a threat. Long seconds dragged into minutes. The priest jumped when a dog yelped, just once, before silence returned.

Unwin's nerves were strained almost to breaking point. He was on the verge of leaving the hut when a soft scratching sound outside the door made him pause. A familiar voice said, 'Easy now. It's me,' as the door opened a fraction before Farral slid back inside. He pushed the door shut. Anxious to be doing something, Unwin groped in the darkness for the candle but then struggled to light it. Farral coughed a few times.

As the gentle glow appeared, Unwin could see that his friend was covered in mud. 'What happened out there?'

Farral grinned, patting at the drying dirt clinging to his trousers. 'I found the dog. The weird thing is it appeared to be watching this hut. I circled round behind it before cutting its mangy throat.' He paused, as if uncertain what to say next. 'The stupid animal just sat there, looking straight at the door. It made no effort to escape.'

It was Unwin's turn to pause. He shook his head and then held up his left hand. 'You remember I spoke of Artie's death?

Farral looked up in surprise. 'What has that to do with a damned dog?'

'His killer was a sig'areth disguised as one of us. They have the ability to control lower life forms, such as the chyvol that attacked me at the church. I'm wondering if there are more of them here and, more worrying, if they're using animals to keep track of our movements?'

Farral frowned. 'That's a big assumption to make. It was just a stupid dog.' He gave up trying to remove the rest of the mud from his clothing. 'At least, I hope that's all it was.' He found the half empty whisky bottle, removed the cork, and took a long swig. 'You might as well get some sleep. I'm wide awake now.'

35: BELKA

Sagana held up his hand for Wallace to stop. The two had been making good time through the forest, following a trail that the Master claimed had seen very recent use. He'd laughed when Wallace suggested they might be following another po'glet or even a tra'll. Wallace had shrugged. 'This trail was made by hu'mans,' was all Sagana had offered by way of explanation.

Wallace watched his companion scan the trees ahead. He was becoming bored and started to fidget, eager to press on after Madeleine, when Sagana surprised him. 'What do you notice about this part of the forest?'

The warrior looked around, seeking inspiration but found none. 'It's full of trees?' he said. 'It's a forest. Why are we wasting time?'

'Because something is waiting for us up ahead.'

Wallace's hand fell to his sword hilt. 'So? Let's go and kill it then.'

Sagana shook his head, a wry smile on his lips. 'Not so fast, my friend. The birds no longer sing here and that suggests they don't want to draw attention to themselves. Birds are sometimes smarter than you think.'

Wallace's mind flashed back to the time he'd accompanied Sagana through a very different forest. The Master had muttered an odd phrase and the forest had fallen silent. Was this some sort of trick? His musing was interrupted by the sound of a dry twig cracking up ahead. 'Whoever or whatever lies up ahead, they aren't doing very well at hiding from us.'

Sagana made no response but pursed his lips and pointed in the direction from which the sound had originated. 'Perhaps they want us to know they're here?' As he spoke, three Fram'ska stepped out from among the trees. They stopped beyond sword reach and openly stared at Wallace. Sagana spoke in a low murmur and without taking his eyes from the new arrivals. 'Stay calm. Don't make any sudden moves and keep your hands away from your weapons.'

He took one pace forward and began to speak in a language unlike any Wallace had ever heard. It seemed to be a random mix of guttural snarls, clicks and whistles. One of the new arrivals appeared to be listening to Sagana but the other two continued to stare at Wallace. Both were equipped with swords and short spears and as he stared back, he noted the muscular physiques, part hidden by basic armour made from what looked like crude metal discs sewn together. The one who'd been listening responded at some length and Wallace found himself wishing he could follow the conversation. The language was so strange that he had no idea what was being said and this made him uncomfortable, a feeling not improved when the speaker pointed his own spear at Wallace and continued in a tone that sounded aggressive.

Sagana interrupted the speaker with a short comment. To Wallace's amazement, all three of the Fram'ska fell to their knees, heads bowed towards his companion. Birdsong began to fill the silence hanging over the forest and Sagana sighed. 'They are willing to help us find your friend, but it was difficult persuading them to do this. These life-forms are wary of you and fearful of the idea of opposing the Lord Helr'ath. I reminded them that I too was a powerful magician and that they should also fear my anger. To be honest, though, I don't know how dependable they'll be if we have to fight for our lives.'

Wallace shrugged, as if the matter were of little consequence. 'If they're going to help, fine. But can we get moving? Madeleine needs us to rescue her from the old woman.'

Sagana gave him an appraising look. 'Our new friends have others of their kind up ahead. They number about a dozen in total. Most are females, so be careful not to upset them. Remember, they're the larger ones and their head fur is paler than that of the males. I've told their leader you're my bodyguard but to them you're just another intruder and not to be trusted.'

'I thought it was the tra'll we needed to worry about. What other surprises does this forest hold?'

'A good question to which I don't have a definite answer. It's a long time since I was last here.'

'Don't these Fram'ska know?'

'Why would they? They're not native to this world either.'

Wallace frowned. 'So where, exactly, are we?'

'In another world that sits alongside your own. That's why we had to travel here.' He paused, as if choosing his next words with care. 'Your Holy Church leaders know about these worlds but choose not to share that knowledge for fear of creating panic among the ordinary hu'mans.' Sagana held up his hand, stifling whatever Wallace had been about to say. 'There'll be time for this later. But for now, your friend Madeleine awaits us.' He said something to the still kneeling Fram'ska as he set off towards the rest of their band. Wallace hesitated just long enough to see the three warriors rise before setting off after him.

They soon found the rest of the Fram'ska. After another brief exchange, most of their new allies formed a protective screen around Sagana and Wallace, whilst two of them pushed ahead as scouts and trail-makers. The whole group pressed on at a steady speed, pausing every so often for reasons Wallace couldn't quite fathom. Despite his queries, all Sagana would say was that they needed to detour around a potential problem. Hunger pangs started to gnaw, and he thought the light was fading as he scanned the treetops for a particularly noisy bird. He was so intent on finding the source of prolonged and raucous cries that he walked straight into one of the Fram'ska.

The warrior snarled at Wallace as several of her comrades levelled their spears at his chest. The one he'd walked into unsheathed her sword and started to advance towards him, menace evident in the pale red, narrowed eyes. As Wallace reached for his own weapon, Sagana spoke in the language of the Fram'ska. With evident reluctance, they lowered their weapons as he now addressed Wallace. 'Stay where you are and sheathe your sword. Say nothing.' The Master turned his attention back to the Fram'ska, issuing another string of snarls, clicks, and whistles.

The creature Wallace had bumped into glared at him before answering. Wallace glared back, trying to ignore the sweat running down his back and the urge to draw his sword. Apart from Sagana and the Fram'ska he'd walked into, Wallace was all too aware that he was the focus of everyone else's attention. He could almost taste the tension in the air. At length, the discussion seemed to be over and Sagana was speaking again. 'Wallace, you must take more care. It's my fault for not telling you earlier, but any physical contact with a Fram'ska is taken as a challenge. Such challenges are often settled when one side draws blood, although these disputes can be fatal.' He paused to stare at the belligerent warrior Wallace had unintentionally offended. 'For now, Belka has accepted my explanation that you meant no harm or threat; that your challenge was made through ignorance. But take care, for she won't back down again. Ignoring or refusing a challenge invokes massive loss of status among their kind and she won't miss an opportunity to right the wrong you've done to her.'

The party set off again, with Wallace very much aware of the quiet discussion taking place among his strange new companions. Meaningful looks were cast his way from several of the Fram'ska and he made sure not to let his left hand stray too near to the scabbard on his right hip.

Wallace judged it to be about an hour later when the lead Fram'ska stopped and gave a low whistle. The rest of her comrades froze and Sagana also halted, his left hand held up to his shoulder. Wallace tried to peer through the foliage ahead but said nothing until Sagana came to join him.

'The scout has sensed danger ahead. Be prepared to fight but stay vigilant. There are creatures here unlike any you've met before, and one false move could be your last.' Whilst Sagana was whispering his advice, the scout slowly dropped on to her back four limbs and, spear in hand, began to creep forward towards a dense clump of young trees. Wallace held his breath, hand on the hilt of his sword, fascinated by the way the Fram'ska's back was jointed so as to allow its upper torso to stand erect while the lower half lay almost parallel to the ground.

Without warning, a huge shape burst out from among the trees and charged straight at the scout. 'Tra'll' yelled Sagana as the other Fram'ska moved into a semi-circle, facing the threat. Wallace registered the size of the hairy creature, the huge arms and the massive axe held in its right paw. For the first time in many years he felt a sense of fear as he craned his neck to view the low-browed shaggy head atop a monster he judged to be over twelve feet tall.

263

Stunned, Wallace watched as the tra'll swung its axe at the scout. The latter had drawn itself up to its full height and now stood on two legs, its spear projecting forward as if such a puny-looking weapon could stop the tra'll's mad charge. As the axe swept towards the Fram'ska's head, she launched the spear at the tra'll's neck, before diving, a split second later, to the right and rolling away. The sharp point of the spear embedded itself in its target but, to Wallace's amazement, it seemed to have no obvious effect on the monster, except to enrage it even further. With a mighty bellow, it turned towards the scout in mid-stride. A strange clicking sound engulfed Wallace as the tra'll stomped down hard on the midriff of the luckless scout, snapping bones before large claws tore away part of the flesh. Greenish fluid began to spurt from the wounds as Wallace noted that the other Fram'ska were now closing in.

Most of them held spears, intending to bring the tra'll down from the relative safety of standing beyond range of its axe. The plan might have worked if, at that moment, deafening bellows hadn't heralded the arrival of two more of the giant tra'll. These smashed into the nearest Fram'ska, scattering three of them like chaff on the wind. One struggled to regain her feet, only to be almost decapitated by a swinging axe. Her body fell to the ground in a mangled heap, the head resting at an unnatural angle.

Surrendering to the familiar icy calm of battle, Wallace noted how the remaining Fram'ska now backed away from the small group of tra'll, sliding with practised ease into a tight formation of bristling spears. A grim-faced Sagana stood in their midst, his eyes locked on the wounded tra'll, and his hands held up, palms outward, as he uttered a strange chant.

Realising that the three tra'll were focused on Sagana and the Fram'ska, he moved carefully to one side and worked his way behind the largest of the tra'll. For long moments, nobody else moved and then, as if at an agreed signal, all of the tra'll charged. The one with the spear still protruding from its neck was slower than the others. Sagana had seen this too and he shouted something to the Fram'ska.

Several of them ducked as he cast a small dart at the creature. It continued its charge for several paces before stopping as the axe slid from its grasp. Clutching at its throat, it uttered a choked cry before toppling sideways to lay twitching on the ground. Bubbles of white froth began to escape from the tra'll's mouth, but these soon turned black.

At the same time, the Fram'ska hurled their spears at the largest of the remaining tra'll. Most hit their target and with a howl that set Wallace's teeth on edge, their victim staggered and then crumpled to its knees. As it crumpled, a bolt of green light seemed to spring from Sagana's hand and hit the same tra'll in the face. It roared in pain, clutching at its ruined face and shaking its head as it staggered off to one side, where it collided with a tree and sat down, seemingly stunned by the unexpected impact.

Wallace leapt forward and swung his sword in an arc, using all the strength at his disposal to bring it down on the outstretched leg of this second tra'll. His grinned when he felt as well as heard the bones break under the impact. The wounded creature tried to grab him, but Wallace was too quick, leaping back and out of reach. Moments later, a second green bolt slammed into the tra'll's chest, and it gave a mighty roar before starting to cough up a thick black viscous liquid.

Turning his attention towards his allies, Wallace found the last uninjured tra'll was almost within striking distance of them. Hoping it had forgotten about him, he raced to hamstring it. As he tugged in desperation, trying to free his sword from the creature's leg, it turned with surprising speed and aimed a huge blow at his head. Wallace ducked under the axe and fell backwards as his sword came free. He scrabbled away, expecting the tra'll to stamp on him. Instead, it resumed its earlier charged towards the Fram'ska, using its axe to sever a spear head before the nearest warrior could throw it and leaving her holding just a splintered stump. Snarling, the wounded tra'll raised the axe once more, preparing to kill the now unarmed warrior. Then it yelped in pain as Wallace sliced a chunk from the muscle on the back of its remaining good leg. It tried to turn on its tormentor, but fell forward, its two wounded legs no longer able to support its great weight. Wallace leapt to one side as the beast crashed past him and stood panting for a few moments. He raised his sword high above his head, preparing to deliver a killing stroke, only to pause in confusion when Sagana called out, 'No! We need to take it alive. It might know where they've taken your friend.'

Wallace reluctantly lowered his sword as he half-turned towards Sagana, keeping one eye on the growling tra'll as it struggled to rise. 'How do we persuade a thing this size to help us?'

Sagana laughed. 'We don't. But the Fram'ska know how to make these creatures co-operate.' He paused and said something to the warrior with the splintered spear. The warrior glanced at Wallace before replying. Sagana said something else then switched back to a language Wallace could understand. 'Belka says you saved her life. You are no longer an outlander, fit only to feed their pigs. The feud between you is over.'

Wallace sighed. 'It's well you didn't tell me about the pigs or the feud before the battle. I might have let her die before crippling that thing.'

As they spoke, the surviving Fram'ska were circling the tra'll. It looked up and gave a scream of fury. One of the warriors said something and Sagana laughed. 'He says they'll ask it about your friend before they roast it for supper.'

Wallace couldn't tell whether or not he was serious.

36: Stormy weather ahead

Whiston knew he needed time to think. More important, he had to get Lizzie to safety. He looked at the gathering crowd and took in the shocked faces of the women and the uneasy frowns of the men in a single glance. A well-dressed middle-aged man started to move towards Whiston. 'I say, this man seems to know you. What the devil has happened to him?'

Lizzie clung to his arm, and he could feel her involuntary sobs. 'Not really. I'm acquainted with his employer, but I have no idea how he came to be in this condition.' On an impulse, he grabbed a soot-encrusted street urchin who'd moved to get a closer look at Figulus and held him while he fished inside a trouser pocket. 'Boy, do you know of a nearby doctor?'

The boy nodded his head in affirmation, even as he struggled to break free of Whiston's grasp. 'I din' do nuffin'.'

Whiston held out his hand, displaying a coin. 'Go and fetch the doctor and I'll give you this sixpence when you return with him.'

Several couples began to walk away. It seemed the drama was less interesting than they'd hoped for. Whiston raised his voice, 'Let's give this young man some air. I've sent for a doctor and there's nothing more anyone can do for him. I'm no expert, but I think he'll live. He looks to have suffered some sort of accident.' The small crowd began to disperse.

Lizzie looked up at Whiston, her skin an unnatural shade of grey. In a low voice, she asked, 'Who is Mr Black?'

'Not here. I suspect he's a dangerous man.'

Lizzie's eyes went wide. 'Must we stay? Can't we go back to Dr Barclay's?' Her eyes darted up and down the street, as if she were afraid someone might see her.

'As soon as the doctor arrives. I promise.' He took her hand and gave it a gentle squeeze. 'What are you afraid of?'

She swallowed and a pink hue suffused her cheeks. 'Figulus knows some very unpleasant people. People talk in the hostelry, and I know hard men who fear to cross him. I'm scared his friends might see us and think we did something to him.'

Whiston gave her an appraising look and was about to say something when the urchin returned with an elderly man in tow. 'This is the quack. Where's me money?'

Whiston flipped the coin towards the boy. It was plucked out of the air with a deft hand and the youngster took to his heels. The new arrival stood looking at Whiston.

'You're a doctor?'

'Used to be a barber. But I know something of the restorative arts.'

Lizzie pointed to Figulus. 'Can you help him?'

'What's it worth?'

'What's your usual fee?' asked Whiston.

'Depends.'

With a scowl, Whiston thrust a florin towards the old man. 'Here. That's all I've got. I gather the young man has some influential friends who might take it badly if you don't do your best. Now the young lady and I must leave. Pressing business. Good day to you, sir.' He pulled Lizzie along the street, walking briskly away. 'Don't look back,' he whispered.

Black sat in his study. On the desk before him was an unusual collection of objects. A small statue sat in the middle of a circle of blood red stones. In turn, these sat on a large golden platter decorated with ancient and largely forgotten symbols from a much earlier time. At each corner of the desk, a black candle fluttered in a gentle breeze, sending clouds of murky, foul-smelling smoke up to the ceiling, where it gathered in a growing cloud, spinning anti-clockwise in a lazy manner. The statue depicted a winged figure with four arms and webbed feet, each of which ended in three massive talons. Its head resembled that of a bird, the elongated mouth mimicking a beak, but from which sprang razor sharp spines. The body and lower limbs were covered by coarse-looking fur, whereas the upper limbs were massively muscled and smooth.

In a dark corner a small boy, aged perhaps nine or ten, sat tied to a chair, his hands and feet bound by padlocked chains. A large rag had been stuffed in his mouth and a strong black silk cord, secured through the back of the chair, prevented him from moving his head. His dirty face was streaked with the tracks of copious tears. The child wore a scruffy pair of trousers, too large for his small waist, plus what had once been a shirt, although it now resembled pieces of frayed cloth and thread seemingly held together by holes of various sizes. His bare feet rested in a puddle that smelled strongly of urine. His emaciated body had been painted with some of the symbols found on the platter. To one side of the chair stood a metal bowl, decorated with yet more strange symbols that seemed to writhe of their own accord in the dim light.

Uttering a strange phrase, Black sprinkled a pale crimson powder over each of the stones then looked up at the child. The boy tried to squirm, to no avail, and Black smiled. 'There's no point trying to escape. You are mine now and I will use you as I see fit. This is the price you pay for stealing a crust of bread.' He stood and came round the desk, walking slowly towards his prisoner. The boy's eyes widened in horror as he registered the scalpel held in Black's right hand. Muffled words came from behind the gag as he pleaded for his life.

'You should be honoured that a worthless piece of scum like yourself has been chosen. Soon, very soon, you will meet my master. He is coming a very long way to see you. True, he can be a little hard on his tools but then your hu'man bones are so fragile. There, there. It will all be over soon.' He leant over the terrified child and placed his left hand under his chin, pushing the head up and exposing the throat. 'Such a small throat.' The boy tried to shrink from his grasp and more tears came.

With a sudden move, Black used the scalpel to slash a deep but not fatal wound in the child's chest. The boy tried to scream, earning himself a back-handed slap to his head. 'Hush now, it's not so bad. I'll let you know if and when I need more blood.' Stooping, he picked up the bowl and used it to catch some of the hot red liquid spurting from the child's wound.

After a few minutes, he calmly walked back to his desk and took care to pour three drops of the congealing blood over each of the red stones. After a brief inspection of his handiwork, he returned to the petrified child and this time made a small nick in the radial artery of his left wrist. The boy turned his head away horror as his life blood dripped into the bowl. Black ignored him and returned to his desk once more, this time pouring the bowl's contents over the statue. He placed the bowl to one side and began to recite a long invocation, never taking his eyes from the statue.

Above his head, a murky cloud began to whirl faster, and streaks of golden light flickered here and there. At last Black fell silent and the cloud began to glow with a sickly green light. A foul smell filled the air. Without warning, a large figure seemed to step out of it and glide down to the carpet in front of the desk. This new arrival resembled the small statue and now stood naked in front of Black. He showed no fear and leant back in his chair. 'Welcome to the hu'man plane, my Lord.'

The figure looked about the room, its glowing yellow eyes resting on the child. It spoke in a deep voice and with an odd accent. 'Well, why have you brought me here?'

Black steepled his fingers across his chest. 'Apologies my Lord. I need your help in finding a meddlesome hu'man. I set a trap to capture him, but my idiotic assistant failed to carry out my instructions.'

'I trust you have punished this fool?'

'Indeed. He won't make the same mistake again. And he's already made partial amends for his stupidity.'

'What is so special about this hu'man that you summon me to find?' The eyes glowed with a malevolent fire, threatening retribution.

'He is an enforcer of the law among his own kind. I had arranged for a White Shield assassin to take the blame for killing another hu'man and this particular hu'man's master was happy to accept that explanation. I thought it would be amusing to have the hu'mans execute this assassin. But the one I seek expressed doubts about the assassin's guilt and has been asking questions about me. I ... we ... need to remove this meddlesome being before he ruins my plans.'

'I see you have prepared a suitable tool for me.'

Black glanced at the boy, who was feebly attempting to free himself from his bonds. 'Yes, my Lord. He is unused – so far.'

'Good.' This single word was accompanied by a bestial laugh which hinted at the depravity of Black's visitor.

'Very good. I'll find this meddlesome hu'man for you. Then we can discuss the cost.'

'As you wish, my Lord.'

The boy wet himself as the new arrival walked towards him, a look of hunger in its eyes. His young mind froze in terror at the prospect of what this evil creature might do. The last thing he saw before passing out was a grey forked tongue as it flickered in and out of the creature's beak.

Behind him and still seated, Black smiled to himself. Things were going better than he'd dared to hope – Lord Oln'ik was notoriously unpredictable, and he'd been worried that he might need to offer something more to secure the demi-God's aid. His mind briefly considered the two other children imprisoned in one of his cellars.

As Oln'ik began to caress the poor unfortunate boy's head, Black permitted his mind to turn to planning the demise of the young policeman. He wanted it to be something special, to both rid himself of a potential nuisance and to serve as a warning to others. The child would provide a useful, if unwitting, tool towards this end.

Whiston rapped on the front door to Barclay's house. His anxious eyes scanned the street in search of anything unusual and he heaved a sigh when Dr Barclay's housekeeper opened the door. 'Oh it's you, Sir,' she said, before moving to one side to let them in. 'I wasn't expecting you back so soon.' Her eyes took in the pale cheeks and timid manner in which Lizzie still clung to his arm. 'Why, whatever has happened? You look as if you've seen a ghost, Miss Cobham.'

Lizzie gave a strangled shriek before putting a hand to her mouth and fleeing upstairs. Whiston watched her through narrowed eyes then turned his attention to Mrs Carpenter. 'We met a young man known to Miss Cobham. He seems to have been attacked. I sent for a doctor but deemed it wise to bring her back here, where she can be safe.'

Mrs Carpenter stared at him for a few moments. 'Safe? Why would she need to be somewhere safe? What's going on Mr Whiston?'

Whiston let out a sigh. 'I'm not sure I know, Mrs Carpenter. Miss Cobham says the young man in question has some unsavoury associates and I suspect he may have been involved in the attack on Sergeant Mindelen and myself. If I'm correct, then it seemed wise to remove Miss Cobham from the scene rather than risk her being caught up in more unpleasantness.'

The old lady turned on her heel. 'I'll have some tea sent up to her room. That should help to calm her nerves.' She hesitated.

'Don't worry. I'll inform Dr Barclay.'

'You can't. He's gone out to see a patient and won't be back until supper. I think he's also calling at his club.'

'In that case, I'll pop in on my sergeant.' He handed his hat and gloves to the housekeeper and began the climb to Mindelen's room. Mrs Carpenter watched him until he was halfway up the stairs, then set off for the kitchen. As she walked, she shook her head in disbelief. 'The good doctor ought to choose his associates with a good deal more care,' she muttered to herself.

'Stormy weather ahead, mark my words,' she said, frowning at no-one in particular. By the time she reached the kitchen she had composed herself. She ordered the kitchen maid to make a pot of tea and to take it up to Miss Cobham's room, along with a plate of sweet biscuits. Then she returned to her own room, where she was soon engrossed, once more, in her crochet-work.

37: Tunnel rats

By midday, Unwin and Farral were beginning to irritate each other. It was bad enough having to share the confined space offered by the hut, but the lack of anything to do sat uneasily with both men. They'd gone over Unwin's plan numerous times but could refine it no further without the vital information Molay had promised.

Unwin broke the strained silence. 'You mentioned the smuggler tunnels. Where do they lead?'

Farral looked up from the short dagger he'd been sharpening with a whetstone. 'I haven't explored all of them, but I know the way to the old jail, a disused warehouse and the cellar of the sort of inn we probably shouldn't be seen in.' He tested the edge of the blade with his index finger. 'We could both use some exercise.'

Unwin smiled. 'What do you have in mind?'

'There's one tunnel I've never investigated. Rumour has it that it leads to the vault of an abandoned church. Smugglers supposedly still use it from time to time when the Excise men are a little more zealous – or a little more honest – than usual.'

'Well, what are we waiting for?'

Farral stood, returning the dagger to a leather sheath. 'We observe but don't get involved in anything. Right? We can't afford to reveal our presence here while we wait for Molay. Remember, our primary target is the Blade.'

Unwin raised his eyebrows. 'Of course. Killing him comes before everything else. But we need to be doing something before we start attacking each other from sheer boredom.'

'You could always pass the time in prayer?'

Unwin waited to see how long Farral could keep a straight face. Both started to laugh at the side time.

The tunnel had been high enough for them to walk upright at first, but after veering to the left the ceiling soon began to dip and it wasn't long before they were forced to crawl towards the intersection Farral had described. Sure enough, they eventually came to a rough crossroad. Years of training meant that the pair talked in a whisper and Unwin took care to shield the small candle he was carrying as he adjusted his position, seeking to ease the pressure on his mud-stained knees.

'That one leads to the warehouse, this one to the jail. Further up the warehouse tunnel is a fork that provides a way to the tavern cellar.' Farral pointed to the remaining opening. 'This one is supposed to terminate in the church vault – if my source was telling the truth.'

'You don't sound totally convinced.'

'Have you always trusted everything your informants tell you? Such people have a habit of exaggerating or telling you what they think you want to hear.'

'Good point. I guess if we trusted them without question, neither of us would still be here.'

'Let's press on and see what we find. But no excitement, eh?'

Unwin said something under his breath. 'I agreed, didn't I?'

Farral shook his head. 'I know you too well, Lemuel. Any chance to right a perceived wrong and you wade straight in.'

Unwin sighed. 'That was the old me. Remind me to tell you about Paddington Station and my instinct for justice. For now, let's just say that I may have learnt the wisdom of exercising caution.'

Farral took a sip of water from a small hip flask. He held it out to his friend. 'Let's see how far this new-found caution takes you then.'

Unwin shook his head. 'Lead on.'

They'd halted for a rest when the tunnel opened up above them, grateful for the freedom to stand and walk upright once more. Unwin had been about to speak when Farral's keen hearing caught a faint sound. He held up his hand,

274

then pointed in the direction the pair were headed. After listening for a few seconds, he held up his left hand with two fingers raised – suggesting there were two people up ahead.

Unwin extinguished the candle, plunging them into darkness. As they waited for their eyes to adjust, both men noted the faint glow of light that was almost cut off by a curve in the tunnel ahead. More sounds came to them in the form of a low grunt followed by a muffled curse. Whoever was in the tunnel seemed to be carrying something heavy.

Farral carefully unsheathed his dagger and Unwin's fingers curled round the hilt of a short sword. If it came to a fight in the confines of the narrow tunnel, both men wanted to be well prepared.

'How come I always have to carry the heavy stuff?' whined a plaintive voice. 'It ain't fair.'

'Because I says so,' said a deeper voice. 'You wants your share of the profit, don't you?'

'Of course, But why can't you take a turn? This barrel is damned heavy.'

'Quit moaning. It can't be much further to the junction.'

'So what?'

'So we set the fuse and get out of here. When the powder goes up, we want to be well away and preferably back topside.'

'Seems crazy to me. What's the point of destroying these tunnels? They've served men like us well over the years.'

'McNulty's orders. He's the smart one and we just does as he says. Leave the thinking to him and you'll do just fine. Here, we can catch our breath for a few minutes.'

Unwin tapped Farral's arm and leant close to his friend's ear. 'I don't like this. It sounds as if he knows about the hut and wants our escape route blocked. I bet it was that damned dog that gave us away.'

Farral shook his head. 'So what do we do now? If we kill the men ahead, he'll know we're on to his plan. And if we return to the hut, who knows what could be waiting for us?'

Unwin thought quickly before answering. 'We could head back to the junction and take one of the other tunnels. Maybe the church vault?

There was a thump and another curse. 'Watch what you're doing! We don't want the damn thing to blow up in our faces.'

'My arms is aching. I need a rest. Of course, you could carry it for a bit if you're so bothered.'

'Not likely. We'll stop here for a little rest.'

'We could head there after we dispose of those ahead. It would be a shame if they accidentally blew themselves to hell. And I don't fancy crawling on my hands and knees with potential enemies behind,' whispered Farral.

'And you were worried about my habit of wading into things! You make a good point though. I say we kill them, set up an accident and then head for the vault.' So saying, he started to inch his way forward, taking care not to make any unnecessary noise. Farral followed, timing his steps to match those of Unwin.

Ahead, a static, faint glow suggested their quarry was not far away from the curve. As Unwin and Farral edged closer, the deeper voice spoke again. 'Hush! Did you hear somethin'?'

'No. Probably a rat.' There was a short chuckle. 'You ain't scared of the little blighters, is you?'

'Me? Course I ain't scared of rats. But it din't sound like no rat to me.' There was a scuffling sound. 'You waits here and I'll go and 'ave a look.'

'Leave the candle then. I don't want to fall over this blasted barrel.'

'Ok. The light would give me away, anyhows. I won't be long.'

As the sound of approaching footsteps came down the tunnel, the two assassins flattened themselves against either side of the wall, doing their best to blend into the darkness. They could see the man in faint outline as he came around the curve, the shadow of a knife in his left hand whilst his right trailed along the wall. He hadn't waited for his eyes to adjust to the darkness and almost walked into Farral. Too late, he opened his mouth to warn his companion. At the same instant, a razor-sharp dagger slashed across his throat and a hand clamped across his mouth.

Unwin helped his friend to lower the ruffian to the floor while Farral kept his hand clamped in place until the body ceased to spasm. 'One down, one to go?' he whispered.

Farral made no reply and both men resumed their former positions, prepared to let the other man come to them. They didn't have to wait long.

'Bill.' There was a slight pause, then the dead man's companion hissed, 'You there?' When this elicited no response, the other man spoke a little louder. 'Stop messin' about. You're not funny. Get back here.'

There was the scuffling sound of someone struggling to their feet and straining to lift a heavy object. 'Come on, Bill. Let's get this job finished. I'm gettin' a thirst on here.' There was a grunt and the light started to move, slowly, towards Unwin and Farral. The latter held up the dagger, then grasped it in his right hand, ready to launch it at the target coming round the curve.

The man staggered into view, a barrel hoisted up on his right shoulder and a candle in his left hand. 'Who the ...' he began, before noting the body sprawled face down between the two men blocking his path. 'Hey ...' He tried to put the barrel down. As soon as it touched the floor, Farral threw the dagger, taking the man in the chest. As he staggered back, Unwin leapt forward and slashed at the man's head, slicing the blade of his sword through the jawbone. Dropping the candle, the man crumpled to his knees, his eyes already starting to glaze as his lungs filled with blood. There was a brief choking sound, soon followed by a long sigh.

Farral stepped forward and stamped on the candle. 'A bit too close to the barrel,' he said. Unwin walked several paces back down the tunnel then calmly lit his own candle.

He set it down on the floor then wiped the blood and flesh from his sword on the dead man's shirt.

Meanwhile, Farral had retrieved his dagger and cleaned it on the man's trousers. 'I suppose we'd better arrange for these two to have that accident now.'

It took the two assassins a little while to drag the two bodies back up the tunnel and well beyond the junction. They draped the dead pair over the barrel and then lit the fuse, before racing back the way they'd come. Waiting by the entrance Farral hoped would lead to the church vault, they heard the sullen boom as the barrel ignited. 'A blow for the Excise men,' said Unwin. 'Now we find out if we've just cut off our best means of escape.'

Farral grinned. 'Even if it's not the vault, this tunnel must lead somewhere.'

'Ever the optimist,'

The two men trudged on in silence, pausing every few steps to check for sounds of any other presence. At last they could make out what appeared to be a solid wooden door ahead. Unwin snuffed out his candle and approached the door with caution. Putting his ear to it, he listened intently for a few seconds before running his hand across the surface. The candlelight had revealed that the door was made from a single huge piece of wood and held in place by rusty iron hinges. It seemed solid enough, although here and there the surface was scratched, as if a giant cat had tried to claw its way through the barrier.

Unwin continued his search on his hands and knees and suddenly gave a low grunt that startled Farral from his reverie. 'What?'

Unwin looked up towards his companion but kept his hand on the door. 'There are ancient markings near the bottom. If I didn't know better, I'd say they were ancient Greek letters. Let me concentrate.'

Farral began to grow impatient. 'Hurry up!' he hissed. 'I've got a bad feeling about this.'

Unwin ignored him, determined to unravel the meaning of the letters carved into the door. At last he stood up. 'It's some sort of riddle. If I've recalled my lessons well, it says "press me close to push me away." Any ideas?'

Farral snorted, 'Which word is "me"? Is it this one?' He knelt down and pressed on the letters. There was a whirring noise and the sound of something moving, then the door swung inwards.

Unwin groaned. 'I was expecting something a little more challenging.' He peered into the darkness and fumbled for his candle. 'What's that smell?' Moments later, they were looking into a large room. Dust sheets covered lumpy mounds on tables that ran around the edge of the room. Directly ahead of them a narrow flight of stairs led upwards through a gap in the wall. But it was what lay in an untidy heap in the middle of the room that held their attention.

38: HELR'ATH

Wallace almost felt sorry for the wounded tra'll. Almost, until he remembered that this creature might provide their only way to find and rescue Madeleine. He ground his teeth when he thought of what might be happening to the young woman.

The remaining Fram'ska had used lashings made from a tough vine to bind the creature and then the interrogation had begun. With its feet and hands bound, the tra'll could do little to defend itself as the warriors took it in turns to approach and slice tiny chunks from its flesh with small, curved knives. From time to time one of its tormentors asked a question but the tra'll stubbornly refused to speak.

Sagana watched the proceedings as he leant against a tree, cleaning his nails with a long delicate blade. 'The knives are coated with the sap of a leaf. It burns the skin.' Watching Wallace's face, he shrugged. 'The pain becomes excruciating. You want to rescue your friend, don't you?'

Wallace sighed. 'Of course. But is this really necessary?'

Sagana smiled. 'How else would you persuade a tra'll to tell you what you want to know?'

'Why not just ask it?'

Sagana shook his head. 'You have much to learn, my friend.' He gestured towards the Fram'ska. 'They are unreliable allies at best. And they hate the tra'll. I couldn't stop this even if I wanted to.' He paused. 'Besides, the signal from the tol'agr'un is fading. I suspect Lord Helr'ath has found a way to hide his location from me.'

'So? I thought we were here to rescue Madeleine, not find this Helr'ath?

Sagana sighed. 'I'd wager that Angele is taking your friend to Helr'ath. As a gift.'

'What!'

'If we're going to rescue her from his clutches, we need to know where his fortress is. And that's why we have to persuade the tra'll to tell us.'

Wallace suddenly recalled something that had been niggling at the back of his mind. 'The green light you used against the tra'll. What was it?'

Sagana shrugged. 'A simple weapon. It is made from ingredients contained in a small globe. I press a pin and throw the globe at the target. A few seconds after I release the pin, the globe shatters, the stuff inside mixes together and the light is released. It destroys anything it touches before it dissipates into the air.'

'It looked as if a beam of light sprang out of your hand!'

Sagana laughed. 'Life would be much simpler if that were possible.'

Wallace frowned then turned away. 'I'm going for a walk, to clear my head.'

'Take care. This forest isn't safe for a lone novice who is unfamiliar with its denizens and ways. Death can come suddenly to the unwary.'

Wallace paused. 'Fair enough. Then I'll wait here and take a nap. I'm not comfortable with torture.'

'You'll learn to appreciate its value though. Sometimes it's the best way.'

Wallace said nothing but sat down with his back against a tree. He closed his eyes and thought about what Sagana had said. He sensed a subtle change in their relationship and wasn't sure he was happy about what this implied. Of course he'd been intrigued by the possibility that there might be a way to extend his lifespan and he knew he was no angel – he'd killed many men and often for no better reason than because somebody had paid him to do it. He was desperate to rescue Madeleine and not just because she'd saved his life. *And yet ...*

Muller and Angele dragged her from the tent; her hair wrapped around Muller's right fist and Angele's whip giving her encouragement from behind. Outside, Madeleine gaped in horror as she took in the two great hairy brutes waiting for them.

'These are my pets' said Angele. 'They're dumb beasts, called tra'll, and it's their fear of me that stops them from tearing you in half and feasting on your flesh and bones.' Her eyes flashed and her mouth turned up in a crooked smile. 'So don't make me angry, because they're hungry and it would take just one word to release them.'

Madeleine glanced at Muller. He stood with his arms folded across his chest and a blank expression on his face. Aware of her attention, he shrugged. 'I never come between my true love and her pets.' Angele rewarded him with a withering look before spitting on the floor.

With her hands bound behind her back, Madeleine was prodded towards the tra'll. The nearest one stooped to sniff at her and pushed a huge paw in her face. As she staggered back, the creature snarled and took a step towards her, before halting when Angele spoke to it in a firm voice. Madeleine noted the brief look of concern that flashed across Muller's face.

'Let's be going,' said Angele. She said something else to the tra'll and pointed to a gap between large trees. 'The fortress is that way. If you try to escape, I'll send these two after you. You'll die and Lord Helr'ath will be angry, but he'll take it out on my pets, not on me. So I don't much care what you do.'

Muller muttered something under his breath.

'What?' demanded Angele.

'Nothing, my dear. I was wondering how long it will take us to reach the fortress.'

Angele shot him a murderous scowl before answering, 'With luck, we'll be there before nightfall.'

Madeleine had travelled in a daze, unable to do much more than put one foot in front of the other. She was afraid of the brutish tra'll and scared to contemplate what Helr'ath might do to her. Without hope of rescue her future seemed to hold nothing but pain, suffering and death. Although they stopped several times for a brief rest and nourishment, she refused to eat or drink. Angele found this amusing, although her mood turned to anger when she caught her husband trying to persuade the young woman to drink some water.

With the light beginning to fade, they emerged from the forest to gaze down on a vast plain of wavering tall grass. Small clumps of bushes and young trees dotted the landscape and large birds floated on outstretched wings overhead, riding the thermal currents with practised ease. A large dark, fortress stood in the centre of the plain and even at this distance Madeleine could sense the presence of something unnatural about the place. She shivered.

'Cheer up, slut,' said Angele. 'You'll be in a warm bed tonight.'

Angele had quickened the pace as they approached the fortress, using the tra'll to herd her captive forward. Soon their small group stood in front of a massive wooden gate banded with horizontal iron bars. Madeleine sensed eyes watching them as Muller hailed the gate, demanding entrance. There was a long silence, then the gate began to lower towards them on massive chains looped through the stone walls and attached near its top on the inside.

With the echo of the crash still ringing in her ears, as the gate hit the ground, Madeleine was prodded forward and into a grim courtyard. Filth and bones littered the floor. Half hidden by shadows, armoured creatures stood in alcoves, their burning eyes taking in the new arrivals. Madeleine risked a quick look at one of the nearest creatures and instantly regretted her curiosity. Squat and standing a little more than five feet in height, the creature had scaly skin and long talons on the end of its hands. It clutched a long-handled axe, and a small metal-braced wooden shield was strapped to its arm. Its eyes glowed red and large tusks sprouted from its lower jaw. Sensing her gaze, the creature snarled.

Angele barked out something, unintelligible to Madeleine, and one of the guards replied, before turning to head up a small flight of steps and through a small wooden door. Muller hissed at Madeleine, 'Stand up straight! The guard has gone to inform the Lord that we have a present for him.' At a command from the old woman, the two tra'll withdrew into the shadows.

Tiring of their sport, the Fram'ska had ended their tormenting of the tra'll and huddled together in a short-lived conference. Belka had approached Sagana and, after casting a sideways look towards Wallace, began what proved to be a lengthy discussion. As soon as she turned away and re-joined her friends Wallace demanded, 'What was all that about?'

'Tactics,' said Sagana. 'Watch and learn.'

One of the Fram'ska disappeared into the undergrowth. The others sat around, sharpening their weapons or eating.

'I'm sure this is scaring the tra'll into talking,' said Wallace, his voice dripping sarcasm.

'Patience.' There was a rustling and hands went to weapons, before relaxing when a lone Fram'ska warrior emerged from the trees. In her left hand she held a long sack, which moved of its own accord. The other warriors greeted their comrade, but Wallace noted how they kept a respectful distance from the sack.

'What's in the sack?'

Sagana glanced at the sack and then back to Wallace. 'It's an adult kr'omk. A very nasty type of ... worm.'

'And?'

'It burrows through the flesh of a living creature and lays its eggs inside their stomach. Then it gorges itself on the host's body fat before curling up to die.'

'That's disgusting!'

'Isn't it? A few days later, the eggs hatch and the young feed on their mother's dead body, before burrowing their way out of the host. Of course, this kills their host. It's a slow and painful way to die.'

'Does the tra'll know this?'

'There'd be no point in capturing the kr'omk if it didn't.'

So the Fram'ska will offer the tra'll its life, if it tells us what we want to know?

'Don't be naïve. The offer is the kr'omk or a quick death in return for supplying the information we seek.'

Wallace shrugged. 'Not much of a choice.'

'But the only one on offer. You don't have to watch if you're squeamish.'

His upper lip curled as Wallace's hand leapt to the hilt of his sword. Sagana took a pace back and then held up his left hand, palm outwards. 'Calm down. I apologise for my poor choice of words. I know you're not a coward, but if I'm to guide you on the old path you need to lose some of your finer sentiments.'

Wallace let his right hand fall away by his side, although there was still more than a hint of fire in his eyes. 'I guess you're right. I've done more than my share of killing but I've never tortured anyone.'

Sagana stepped towards the warrior and clasped him on the shoulder. 'It's part of the price of near immortality. You don't have to like it, but you do have to accept it.'

Madeleine shivered in the cooling air. She tried to ignore Angele, who talked in a low voice and in graphic, disgusting detail about what Helr'ath liked to do to young women. After a few minutes Muller ordered his wife to be quiet. 'Don't spoil the surprises that lie in store, my sweet. Let her discover them for herself. Anticipation works better than knowledge in a situation like this.'

Angele stared at him and then, lightening quick, struck him around the head with her fist. 'Did you anticipate *that*, my sweet?' she mocked. Muller growled and started towards her but halted when a deep voice boomed out across the courtyard.

'What is this?'

All eyes turned towards the speaker. Madeleine took a backward step as she looked upon her new master. Helr'ath stood seven feet tall. He wore a dirty green loincloth, which did nothing to hide the bulging thigh muscles that, in turn, were dwarfed by his massive arms. A gold circlet adorned each arm, and another hung around his neck. The image of power was spoilt by the folds of fat that hung around his waist, but there could be no doubt that before her stood a powerful being. Short spiky hair stood out from the scalp above a large, hooked nose, yet the feature that most drew Madeleine's attention was the single glowing red eye that sat above the nose. Lidless, the eye moved constantly as it scoured the courtyard.

'Lord Helr'ath ...' began Angele, but he cut her off with a sweep of a hand as he strode towards a guard slouched in one of the alcoves. Seeing his master approach, the guard stood to attention, looking straight ahead. Helr'ath stopped in front of him. 'You dare to slouch on duty?'

The guard started to speak but managed only a few syllables before Helr'ath took him by the throat with his left hand and lifted him off the ground. As the guard squirmed,

Helr'ath clamped his huge right hand on the guard's head and savagely twisted. There was the sound of breaking bones and a short gurgle before the irate Lord threw his victim to the ground, in front of Madeleine. She gasped at the sight of the corpse, with its head facing the wrong way and a look of surprise in the lifeless eyes.

Her gasp attracted Helr'ath's attention. He stared at her for a few moments, then licked his thick, rubbery lips. A thin trail of drool hung from the corner of his mouth as he asked, 'Are you my present?'

Angele stepped forward and bowed. 'She is, my Lord.'

Helr'ath turned his eye in her direction. 'Ah, Angele. So you think this gift will make me forget your past failure?' Madeleine noticed Muller take a small but significant step away from the old woman. 'Is she sullied?' Helr'ath turned his gaze on the old man.

Angele swallowed, a fleeting look of uncertainty on her face before she rallied. 'She is untouched, my Lord.' She pointed to Muller. 'Although I had to prevent this old fool from testing her.' A sly grin curled her mouth as Helr'ath now turned towards her husband. Her hands made small gestures and her pets ambled away and into the shadows by the outer wall. All eyes in the fortress were busy watching its lord and master.

Beads of sweat stood out on Muller's forehead as he shuffled his feet and rubbed both hands down his thighs. He kept his eyes glued to the ground. 'My Lord, I thought it wise to check that she was still clean. For you.' He turned a sickly look towards his wife. 'But she mistook my motives. So, I cannot myself guarantee the status of the present and must trust that my wife speaks the truth. I hope my trust in her is well-placed.'

Madeleine thought rapidly. Muller knew Dubois and his men had raped her, so why did he play this dangerous game? As her mind raced through possible answers, she began to discern a possible motive. Unpleasant as the prospect might be, here lay a glimmer of hope – perhaps she could turn the old man against Helr'ath. She shivered as she contemplated the payment that he would undoubtedly demand of her. It seemed her only choice was between the unwelcome attentions of Helr'ath or Muller. Her spirits sank again.

'Bring her to my bed when the moon appears over the Black Tower. But wash and prepare her first.'

39: Loose ends

McNulty paced the floor of his study, his fists clenching and unclenching as he waited for news. He stopped, mid-stride, as his ears caught the sound of his front door opening, followed by a muffled conversation. Footsteps outside warned him of the approach of a servant. As knuckles rapped on the study door, he shouted, 'Come.'

A tall, stringy man entered the room. The newcomer clutched an old bowler in his hands, nervously playing with the rim as he spun the headgear slowly round. His downcast eyes hinted at bad news.

McNulty's gaze took in the tear in the left sleeve of the jacket and the dark stain lower down. 'Well? Must I beat it out of you?'

The man looked up, wincing as he straightened his left arm, the hand still clutching at his hat. He swallowed and brushed a grimy hand through his unruly hair. 'We did as you said, sir.' He paused, then in a rush, 'We went to the 'ouse what you told us and paid a visit to the old Jew. 'E didn't want to talk, so we 'ad to rough 'im up a bit. Then, from nowhere, some of 'is men tried to jump us.' The man looked down at his feet. 'There was a pitch battle, sir, an' I lost two of my best men. Well, we won, of course, but in the middle of all the fightin' the Jew tried to escape us. 'Arry, my brother, sir, tried to stop 'im. 'E didn't mean to do it, sir, but he hit the old man and wounded 'im.'

At this news, McNulty's eyes narrowed, just as the visitor risked a glance at his face to see how his tale was being received. The man flinched and stepped back a pace. 'Arry hisself took a mortal blow from a cudgel. Damn near split his skull in half. Anyways, we took the old Jew to the place like you asked and left 'im with your friend. 'E was in a bad way, what with the blood and like.' The man shuffled on his feet, then, in a low voice, 'If as you don't mind sir, I'd like paying please. I've got two funerals to pay for. They was good men. An' me and my missus 'as to eat.'

McNulty said nothing. His eyes glittered as he struggled to control his temper. His visitor looked alarmed, then relaxed when McNulty smiled. 'A reasonable request, even if you didn't do the job as discretely as I'd hoped. Still, you captured the target, which was the main priority.' He walked behind his desk, opened a drawer, and took out a bag which clinked as he set it down. 'Ten guineas, as agreed. Now go and keep your mouth shut about this affair. Make sure your men know to do the same. If I hear anyone has spoken of this, they'll not live to see another sunrise.' Picking up the bag, he tossed it toward the other man, who caught it in his right hand.

'Thank you, sir. We knows what 'appens if we don't keep quiet.' He turned to leave.

'Oh, Mr Smith?

McNulty fired the pistol as the man turned back. The first shot hit him in the face, and he screamed, once. The second shot ploughed through his chest and struck the heart. Watching the man's last convulsions, McNulty bent down and retrieved the bag of coins. 'I don't reward failure with gold,' he said. 'I pay for failure with lead.'

Straightening up, he returned the bag to the drawer then rang a small bell. A few moments later a huge Sikh appeared in the doorway. McNulty gestured to the cooling corpse. 'Clear this mess away and tell Jeremiah to take care of the other loose ends. There should be two of them. I'm going out.'

Dusk was falling as a brougham pulled up in front of a large house, set back among immaculate gardens in one of the richest parts of the city. McNulty alighted from the carriage and turned to speak to the driver. Satisfied that his servant understood the instructions, he reached inside for a silver-handled cane and then walked up the driveway and rapped on the door.

As he stepped back, the door opened to reveal a young maid. 'Good evening, sir. His Excellency is entertaining. I'll let him know you're here. You can wait in the front parlour.' As she scuttled off down the grand hallway, McNulty permitted himself a wry smile. The archbishop was reputed to engage some of the prettiest young women in Bristol and gossip suggested an ulterior motive. He removed his hat and gloves, laid them on a small table and stepped into the parlour. Seeing it was empty, he crossed to a small cabinet and helped himself to a glass of claret before taking it to a large comfy chair. Depositing the glass on a small ivory-inlaid table, he wandered over to a large mahogany bookcase and selected a volume at random.

When the maid returned, McNulty appeared to be engrossed in a book. If she was perturbed by this apparent familiarity with her employer's property, she had the sense to give no sign. 'His Excellency asked if you would mind waiting for a few minutes. His other guests are about to depart. Can I get you anything while you wait, sir?'

'No. Thank you. This claret is rather good and the book most convivial. I'm in no hurry.'

The maid retired towards the back of the house. McNulty stretched his legs out and made himself comfortable.

It was nearly half an hour later when the last of the archbishop's guests finally took their leave. Their host bustled into his front parlour, apologising profusely to the man slouched in his favourite armchair, a book open on his lap.

McNulty looked up. 'Ah, here you are. This book is really rather interesting. I didn't know you were a student of ancient religions, Archbishop.'

The clergyman looked rather nonplussed by this observation. 'I like to keep my mind active, McNulty. I wasn't expecting you this evening.' He turned to close the parlour door. 'Is there a problem?'

'A problem? Should there be?'

The colour drained from the archbishop's face. 'I wondered about the intruder. In your house.'

McNulty stood and walked over to the drinks cabinet. He poured two glasses of claret and offered one to his host.

As his host started to gulp at the wine, McNulty raised an eyebrow. 'I thought you would have more faith.'

The archbishop spluttered, spraying red liquid down his pale pink waistcoat. 'I ... er ... I don't follow you.'

McNulty sat back in the armchair and gestured for his companion to sit in a seat opposite. 'I hear you've been snooping round my special store.'

The other man, ineffectually brushing at the growing stain on his clothing, turned pale. 'I wouldn't call it snooping exactly.' Recovering his composure, he added, 'It is *my* church after all.'

'Tut tut,' said McNulty. 'I made a very generous donation in return for that space. I thought I also made it very clear that no-one was to pry into my private affairs?'

'I wasn't prying. I was looking for a particular chalice. It's worth a lot of money and the church needs ... repairs,' he finished lamely. 'I won't say anything to anyone. You have my word as a clergyman.' His face had turned a brighter shade of red and he pulled at his collar. 'I say, it's rather warm in here, don't you think?'

McNulty smiled and sipped at his own wine. 'Not really. I rather think it might be the stuff I took the liberty of coating your glass with.'

'What!'

'I'd like to say I was sorry, Archbishop. But that would be a lie. Mea culpa and all that.'

The clergyman was struggling to breathe, and foam flecked his lips. His face contorted in agony. He tried to speak but couldn't get his words out.

'I did warn you not to pry. You've ingested a lethal dose of an interesting South American plant extract. As we speak, it is destroying your heart and lungs. I'd give you the antidote but I'm afraid I left it at home. Goodbye Archbishop and look on the bright side – you're about to meet *your* God. Perhaps.' As he spoke, his victim slumped in his chair. McNulty put down his drink, rose and checked him for a pulse. Finding none, he nodded and carefully picked up a small handbell from its position on a side table.

Taking care not to let the bell make any sound, he crossed the room to the door and eased it open. A quick glance reassured him that there was no-one in the hallway. He rang the bell then quickly placed it on the floor and took up position behind the door, invisible to anyone entering the room. He took a thin cord from his pocket.

McNulty heard footsteps coming down the hall. The same maid who'd opened the door came into the room and gave a little squeal when she saw her master. As she turned to fetch help, a thin cord looped over her head and tightened around her throat. Despite her desperate struggles, she was no match for McNulty, and he had little trouble in throttling the life from her. Satisfied that she could provide no help to the police, he picked up the handbell and returned it to its usual position. A smile creased his features as he unwrapped the cord from the maid's neck and stuffed one end of it into the hand of her employer, forcing the fingers apart as he wrapped this end around the dead man's hand. He checked the room to make sure he'd left no evidence of his presence, returned the book to the shelf, and let himself out of the house.

He raised a hand and casually donned his hat and gloves as his brougham came down the street and stopped alongside him. Instructing the driver to take him home, McNulty sat back in his seat and contemplated his next move. Frowning, he decided it was time to arrange a meeting with the unpredictable Mr Black.

Back home, McNulty summoned Jeremiah Mason to his study. While he waited for his chief henchman to arrive, he poured himself a large measure of whisky from a crystal decanter on a tray with four accompanying glasses. Then he took up his customary position behind his large desk.

Mason was a small but dangerous man, skilled in knife-work and familiar with most aspects of criminal life. Short in stature, he had an oval face dominated by a large, crooked nose and an ugly scar above his left jawline. Bald since his youth, he habitually wore black clothing and was rarely seen without his favourite overcoat. Not even McNulty could be certain what he kept in the many inside pockets, although picklocks, a razor and a nail-studded cosh certainly formed part of his armoury. He strode into the study with his usual nervous energy.

McNulty decided to get straight to business. 'Any news of our two mutual friends, Jeremiah?'

Mason grinned, making his scar writhe. 'It seems they've both 'ad unfortunate accidents.'

'Good.' McNulty nodded towards the decanter. 'Help yourself to a drink and tell me the details.'

Mason poured himself a large drink and downed the fiery liquid in one gulp. 'One of 'em fell down a stairs and broke 'is neck. About an hour later the other tripped and smashed his 'ead against a brick wall. Both died quickly.'

McNulty chortled. 'You're an artist, Mr Mason. An artist who understands the virtue of brevity.' He sipped at his own drink. 'There'll be a large bonus in your pay at the end of this week. Keep your head down for the next few days. But be ready if I should need your skills at short notice. I have a feeling one of my interests is about to become a nuisance.'

Mason took his cue, bowed, and left McNulty in peace. The latter topped up his glass and then sat at his desk in deep contemplation. The meddling priest had presented an unnecessary complication but one that he had personally resolved with his usual efficiency. If his other servants were as successful as Mason, then both Unwin and Farral were either bottled up in a small shack or buried under tons of earth following an unexplained underground explosion. He half hoped they were still in the shack, where his men would soon cut them to pieces. That left only the annoyingly ambitious Mr Black to deal with. He would not underestimate that strange creature but, with Black out of the way, the path was clear for McNulty to become the undisputed leader of the Black Blades. He'd worked many years for this and now, with his goal in sight, he could almost taste the sweet rewards of victory.

His mind drifted to the prisoner down in his cellar. Perhaps he could cheer himself up by interrogating the old man.

40: MESMERISM

The doctor knelt down and bent closer to the young man sprawled on the street. 'Check his pockets for valuables, give him a quick sniff of the salts and then I'm done,' he muttered to himself. He was reaching for the man's jacket when a hand shot up, grabbed his lapel, and jerked him closer.

Figulus opened his eyes and whispered in the startled doctor's ear. 'You do that, and I'll gut you. Get away from me while you can still walk.' He pushed upward.

The doctor got to his feet and stepped away from his patient. 'It's alright,' he assured the small crowd who'd stopped to witness the drama. 'He's coming round and will be fine. Just passed out, I think.' He risked a glance at his supposed patient. 'Take it easy for a day or two, young man, and stay away from strong drink.' He raised his hat. 'Farewell.'

By now Figulus was back on his own feet and anxiously scanning the crowd and the street. He spotted Whiston and Lizzie striding away and a plan formed in his mind. Black might be a nasty employer, but Figulus instinctively knew that he would be even worse as an enemy. Ignoring several inquiries from the bemused crowd, he barged through them and set off in pursuit.

Black watched as Oln'ik stroked the boy's head. The demon was surprisingly gentle, and he stepped back as the boy began to wake. The child's eyelids fluttered and then he gave a start as memory came flooding back. His eyes widened as he took in the figure in front of him.

'Would you like this?' asked a soft-voiced Oln'ik. He was twirling a shiny, sparkly disc suspended on a chain in front of the boy. The boy looked at the disk but shook his head, clearly expecting some sort of trap. He flinched when the demon moved towards him, then frowned when the gag was removed from his mouth. 'That's better. We can talk now.'

The boy glanced towards Black and then at his injured wrist and back to the disc.

'Oh, don't worry about him. I won't let him do that again.'

The boy's eyes were beginning to glaze. Oln'ik continued to talk softly to him, still spinning the disc. Soon, the child's head drooped forward on his chest. Oln'ik grinned and stepped closer to whisper in the child's ear.

Whiston was talking to Mindelen and urging him to rest for a few more days. The sergeant was fretting about their case and anxious to learn of the Inspector's reaction to recent events.

'Don't worry. I've written a long letter to him, explaining what happened and why our return has been delayed,' said Whiston.

Mindelen leant back against this pillows, recently plumped up by Lizzie. 'Well, what about funds?'

Whiston smiled in what he hoped was a reassuring way. 'Dr Barclay has offered to lend me some money,' he lied. I can pay him back from my savings after we return to London.' He was grateful that Mindelen didn't see the way Lizzie's head jerked up. She was sewing by the window, sunk into a large chair, and surrounded by cushions. Noting Whiston's mute look of appeal, she raised an eyebrow a fraction but said nothing before resuming her task.

Mindelen was running out of objections. He was also becoming drowsy after his latest dose medicine. Whiston coughed gently to attract Lizzie's attention. She looked up once more and he said, 'We should let my colleague rest. It'll help his recovery. Perhaps we could retire to the parlour?'

As they negotiated the stairs, Lizzie put a hand on Whiston's arm. 'Why did you lie to him about money?'

'I don't want him agitated or to give him an excuse to get up. If he discovered that we were running out of money he'd insist on returning to London.'

Lizzie smiled. 'Is that the only reason, Edward?' she asked. Her voice was sweet and innocent.

Whiston stopped on the stairs, a crimson flush racing towards his ears. 'Well ... I mean ... that is ...'

Lizzie went on tiptoe and kissed him lightly on his cheek. 'Does that help?'

Whiston's face lit up. 'I think it does, Miss Cobham.' He lent forward and put one arm around her waist as he returned her kiss but with more passion. As they parted for air, he said, 'There's something I ...' A loud banging on the front door interrupted him. 'Now what?'

Black was talking with Figulus in his study. The young man seemed more comfortable than on his previous visit to that room. 'Your initiative served you well this time. Following the policeman to his current abode means we have a second chance of dealing with him.'

Figulus grinned. 'I won't mess up again, Mr Black. Just tell me what to do.'

Black held up a hand. 'I don't want you do anything, this time, Figulus. The matter is already in hand. Not because I doubt you've learnt your lesson. It's simply a matter of expediency.' He sat down behind his desk. 'I will have some work for you soon, though. In the meantime, take today off – but stay away from Whiston.' He looked down at a paper on his desk. Figulus turned and left, his mind whirling. He liked the young waitress. And she was with Whiston. The same man who was about to be subjected to some sort of attack. What if ...? As he left Black's house, Figulus shook his head, still trying to order his thoughts and shake off a sense of foreboding.

It was Nancy's day off, so it was Mrs. Carpenter who answered the summons to the door. Whiston and Lizzie heard her exclamation of annoyance. 'Be off with you. We don't give anything to street urchins. Away before I call the master.'

A child's voice drifted up the stairs, but it was too low for the words to carry.

'There's no-one here called Mr Whiston. Go away.'

'Wait,' shouted Whiston. At the sound of his voice, the housekeeper turned. She was taken by surprise when a young, scruffy-looking boy barged past her and into the hallway.

The child looked up from the bottom of the stairs and asked, 'Is you Mr Whiston?' There was something odd about his tone and Whiston hesitated before answering. At the same time a door opened quietly, and Dr Barclay poked his head out, frowning at being disturbed by Mrs Carpenter's squeal of rage at this uninvited visitor.

'I'm Whiston.'

The child said nothing but started to reach round his back at waist height.

Whiston took a step down. 'I don't know you. What do you want?'

The child looked up, his arm coming back round to the front. 'Lord Oln'ik sends 'is best regards.'

For Whiston, time slowed. He saw the barrel of a pistol moving up from the child's hip and being levelled towards his own chest. He heard a sharp intake of breath behind him and saw the puzzled look in the eyes of Mrs. Carpenter as she turned back towards the hall. There was a blur of movement, followed by a loud bang and a puff of smoke at the foot of the stairs. Then time sped up and back to normal. Whiston was charging down the last few steps as Dr Barclay knocked the boy sideways.

Both stood looking down at the child. The boy had a quickly growing welt just under his right eye and a heavy book lay by his feet. He sat up and looked around with a dazed expression. 'Where am I?' he asked, putting a small hand up to his right cheek. 'Ouch, that hurts.'

The doctor knelt down and moved a forefinger horizontally in front of the boy's eyes. He followed this action by putting his hand under the boy's chin and tilting his head back. He stood and pulled the boy to his feet.

'Well?' said Whiston, stooping to retrieve the pistol.

'I can't be sure, but I think he's been a victim of mesmerism. Bring him into my study, please.' He turned towards his housekeeper, who was watching the proceedings with her mouth open. 'Mrs. Carpenter, some tea please.' As she scuttled off towards the kitchen, Lizzie came down the stairs, a look of concern etched into her face.

'My God. He was going to shoot you!'

Dr Barclay suggested, 'Perhaps you'd like to help Mrs. Carpenter?' as he took her arm and steered her towards the back of the house. He looked at Whiston and nodded towards his room before pulling the child inside and firmly closing the door.

'I don't pretend to understand what's going on but I'm going to need an explanation from you, Mr Whiston.' Before Whiston could respond, he continued, 'But first, let's see to this child. If my surmise is correct, he's probably as confused as I am right now.' He proceeded to examine the child, checking his pulse, respiration and paying particular interest to his eyes. Whiston watched in silence, trying to marshal his thoughts into some sort of order while the doctor worked on the unresisting child. Nodding to himself, he started to speak but then paused at a knock on the study door.

'Your tea, sir. Should I bring it in?'

'Yes please, Mrs. Carpenter.' Whiston opened the door to admit the housekeeper, who was laden with a tray on which sat a large teapot, a jug of milk, a small bowl of sugar and three each of cup, saucer, and small spoon. She paused to look at the boy before asking, 'Will that be all Dr Barclay?'

'Yes, thank you. You may return to your duties for now, Mrs Carpenter.' As she closed the door behind her, he added, 'I think I'm in trouble. She only calls me that when she's upset with me.'

'Before you say anything else, I must thank you for your prompt action out there. If you hadn't thrown that book, I might well be dead now.' A thought struck him. 'Or he might have missed me and hit Miss Cobham.'

The doctor shrugged. 'I couldn't let him shoot anybody. It's bad enough the bullet's ruined the ceiling paintwork in the hall.' The grin fell from his face. 'I think this child has been mesmerised, but the effects seem to be wearing off. I think he's harmless now. Some warm, sweet tea will help. Would you mind pouring?'

As Whiston poured tea into the cups, he was taken aback by Barclay's next question.

'Who is Lord Oln'ik?'

'I'm afraid I have no idea. I've never heard of him. From his title, he sounds like a foreigner.' He handed one drink to the boy, who sat looking at it, and another to Barclay.

The doctor stirred some sugar into his tea then took a small sip. Putting the cup back on its saucer, he openly studied Whiston's face. 'What's going on? That's two vicious attacks in the space of a few days. Is policing always this dangerous?'

Whiston shrugged. 'I don't know what's going on, but somebody is obviously rattled by my presence here.' His mind flashed back to Rose's last evening. 'No, policing isn't usually this difficult.' He sipped at his own tea, gathering his thoughts but still uncertain how much to divulge to Barclay.

Barclay turned back to the boy. 'Do you remember who told you to come here?' The boy looked miserable and shook his head. The doctor started to say something else when there came the sound of a loud knocking on the front door.

'Now what?' said Whiston. His hand closed on the pistol in his pocket as he looked at Barclay. Footsteps sounded in the hall and Whiston opened the study door at the same time as Mrs Carpenter was reaching for the front door handle. Before Whiston could speak, she opened the door to reveal Figulus framed against the street, cradling his left hand, wrapped in a blood-stained bandage, against his chest. Lizzie was halfway down the hall. As soon as she caught sight of the new arrival, she let out a shriek.

Whiston strode towards the door, irritated by this latest interruption, and worried for the young woman's safety. 'What do you want? And how did you know where to find us?' he demanded.

Figulus shot a look over his shoulder. 'Can I come in for a few minutes? I've something important to tell you. I mean no harm. I can't stand by and see Lizzie get hurt.' He looked miserable.

Behind Whiston, Lizzie said, 'What do you mean, you can't see me get hurt? Who wants to hurt me?'

The policeman reached a sudden decision. 'You can come into the hallway but no further. You've got two minutes to explain yourself. Any funny stuff and I'll shoot you.' The boy's pistol was in his right hand and pointed at Figulus. Whiston raised his voice. 'Dr Barclay, I suspect you ought to hear this.'

Barclay emerged from his study and pulled the door shut behind him. After another backward glance, Figulus edged into the hall and closed the door. He took off his hat and stood looking at Lizzie, a wretched, half-smile on his face. Mrs Carpenter uttered a loud 'tut' and set off back to the kitchen. 'Really!' she muttered as she swept past her employer.

'Two minutes,' reminded Whiston.

Figulus tore his gaze away from Lizzie and looked straight at Whiston. 'I work for Mr Black. He's a nasty piece of work and if he finds out I've been here I'm a dead man. For some reason he doesn't like you, Mr Whiston. He doesn't like you at all. I think he's planning some sort of attack with the intention of killing you. He knows you're here.'

Whiston studied the young man with care. 'Why are you telling me this?'

Figulus groaned. 'I'm no saint, sir. But I care about the young lady, and it occurred to me that she too might get injured or worse in any attack on yourself. And you could have just walked away back there on the street, last time we met. But you tried to help me. It's been a long time since anybody did that unless they wanted something from me. I came round just after you left, and I followed you here.' He hung his head. 'I told Mr Black where to find you. I thought it would put me back in his good books. But then I found out that you're not safe from him. And Lizzie's here as well.' He shot a sorrowful look at Lizzie.

'You'd better come into my study,' said Barclay.' I'll take a look at your hand while we decide our next move.'

As they all trooped into the study, Whiston let out a curse. The window over-looking the street was open and the urchin nowhere to be seen.

41: THE BLACK ALTAR

Farral and Unwin stood in shocked silence. In front of them, a heap of heads, limbs and torsos lay scattered in various stages of decomposition around a blood-stained, cross-shaped black altar.

Farral found his voice first. 'What is this? And in a church!'

Unwin frowned as he walked closer, taking care not to step on any of the skulls, and bent to look at carvings on the altar. 'It appears to be some form of perverted black mass.' He pointed to the left arm of the altar. 'This is ancient Greek.' But I don't recognise the writing on the other arm at all.'

300

Farral joined him and glanced at his companion. 'With human sacrifice? It's more than a black mass. It's sick. It's depraved.'

'More to the point, who - or what - is using this basement for these rituals? He pointed to the stairs. 'We might as well go up and see if we can find out.' Unwin gestured for his friend to lead the way, his face set in a grim smile.

Halfway up the narrow stairs, a door was set into the wall on their right. After a short, whispered conversation Unwin tried the handle. It gave easily under his pressure. There was a click and then the door swung inwards. He gently pushed it flat against the wall. Both men started to wretch as they struggled to see anything beyond the dark that awaited anyone entering the room.

'What's that smell?' Farral poked his head inside and just as quickly pulled back, narrowly avoiding the double-bladed axe which swished past where his head had been moments before. He raised an eyebrow and gave a soft cough as he wiped away the sheen of sweat from his forehead. Unwin was watching the rope-suspended axe as it swung back and forth on an ever-decreasing arc.

'Nasty. And just the sort of trap I'd expect from our friends the Black Blades. It's well that your reactions are still as sharp as that axe appears to be.'

'It was the sound of the rope being released that warned me. Even so, that was a little too close for comfort.' He paused, one ear cocked towards the room. 'We have to risk a light. There's no knowing what else awaits an unwelcome visitor in there. Although whatever it is, I don't like the way it smells.'

'Are they protecting something important or is it just a decoy?' Unwin mused aloud. 'Stay alert.'

'As if I needed that advice.'

'I spotted some candles downstairs. You wait here and I'll go fetch a couple.'

As Unwin set off back down the stairs, Farral thought he heard something from the room. It sounded as though someone, or something, was trying to move in a stealthy way. He tightened his grip on the long knife in his hand and shrank back from the doorway before ascending one more step. 'Might as well have the higher ground,' he muttered.

The sound came again.

'Hurry up Lemuel. I think I'm going to need that light.'

A faint sound made him tense. He couldn't identify it but moments later he recognised a new sound as the pattering of tiny, clawed feet. 'Rats!' he muttered, glancing down the stairs. A pool of light was moving towards the bottom step. Tearing his gaze from the doorway, Farral exhaled as he recognised Unwin.

I think there's rats in there.' He gestured towards the dark room. 'And maybe something else. Something that smells very unhealthy.'

Unwin transferred the candle to his left hand and took a firm grip on the hilt of his sword. 'Let's get it over with.' Holding the candle high, he stepped into the room and hissed in anger as the illumination revealed the source of both the smell and the noises.

Chained to the back wall were the remains of what had once been George Hunt. Most of his chest was missing, little more than a gaping hole with ragged edges. Plump rats scurried away from the body, squeaking their annoyance at being disturbed from the feast of decaying flesh. One of his eye sockets was empty and half the nose had been chewed off.

'Poor George,' said Farral in a voice choked with raw anger.

Unwin skewered a rat which, bolder than the rest, had moved too close to his right foot. He flicked his wrist, sending the carcass hurling among its fellows. 'While he held me prisoner, McNulty boasted about knowing where George was and what was being done to him.' He glared at the rats, fighting for a share of their recently deceased companion.

302

'When I find McNulty, I'm going to kill him. Very slowly,' he said in a quiet voice.

'There's nothing else we can do for your student,' said Farral. Let's see what's at the top of these stairs.'

They backed out of the room and Unwin closed the door before following Farral up the remaining stairs. At the top he paused to listen for sounds of activity beyond the old oak door that blocked further progress. After a few tense seconds, he shook his head and reached for the latch. Easing it up with great care, he pushed against the door, opening it a fraction, and squinting through the gap. His eyes took in a small room, with a bench along one wall and clerical robes hanging from pegs on the wall. A well-thumbed bible sat on a battered lectern and a small table supported a variety of collection bowls, hymn-sheets, and candles. Several small jars held incense sticks. He turned back towards his companion and whispered, 'It looks like a vestry. And it's empty.' Pushing the door open further, he squeezed through the gap, followed by Farral.

The pair took in the contents of the room. 'Catholic church.'

Unwin nodded his agreement and pointed to yet another door in the wall opposite the head of the stairs. 'That must lead into the church itself.' He took one step towards it and then froze. From the other side of the door came the sound of approaching footsteps. Unwin signalled for Farral to stop but the younger man had also picked up the sounds. Farral lifted one upraised finger and the pair took up position, flattened against the wall on either side of the door.

The footsteps came closer and then stopped. The door handle began to turn. A rough voice broke the silence. 'You could give me an 'and, priest. He's bleedin' 'eavy for an old man.'

From the other side of the doorway, a younger voice answered. 'The only reason I let you in here was because his Grace instructed me to facilitate your nefarious comings and goings. I'm prepared to turn a blind eye, but I simply will not dirty my hands as well. Now, stop wasting my time and get on with whatever it is you're doing. I have an elderly parishioner who needs my spiritual comfort.'

There was a brief chuckle before the other replied. 'Oh, you're 'igh and mighty right now, with the fat priest to protect you. But don't come all pious with me. I knows about your little 'abits and 'ow you clergy fleece the old and gullible with your fancy words.'

'I must protest. I'm a man of God. Whereas you, you're nothing more than a common criminal. A hireling.'

There was a grunt and the sound of something heavy being dragged closer to the door. Unwin and Farral heard the sneer in the rough voice. 'Mind yer mouth, priest. The streets at night can be dangerous around 'ere.'

'Don't threaten me, you odious little man!'

This prompted mocking laughter. 'If you won't 'elp, then get out of my way.' The scraping sound resumed as footsteps moved away, followed by the slamming of a door. 'That's right. Clear off, you namby pamby. Go an' prey on some other poor soul.'

Unwin nodded to Farral as both tensed for action. Moments later a small bald-headed man wearing a black overcoat came backwards through the doorway. He was bent over, grunting with the effort of dragging a lifeless body he held under its armpits. Farral moved slightly, attracting his attention whilst Unwin brought the hilt of his sword down on the man's head. The heavy blow laid him out cold and he crumpled over the body he'd been dragging. Unwin closed the door. The two assassins looked down on a scar-faced man, making sure that he really was unconscious.

'What have we here?' muttered Unwin, rolling their victim off the other body. He stepped back in shock and uttered an oath, 'My God, it's your friend Molay!'

Farral had been using the small man's trouser belt to secure his arms behind his back. 'What!' He finished his task, making sure the bonds were secure then stood to get a better view of the other unconscious body. 'This doesn't bode well.'

A groan diverted his attention back to the other man in time to see him trying to sit up. A trickle of blood from the wound in his scalp ran down his face. As his eyes focused, the man snarled. 'You fools don't know who you're messin' with. Set me free and I might let you both live.'

Farral laughed then delivered a vicious kick to the man's mouth. Scar-face spat out blood and bits of broken teeth, a look of fear in his eyes. He glared at Farral.

'What were you going to do with this man?' said Unwin, pointing to Molay. A large circle of dried blood covered most of the old man's left shoulder and his face was ashen. His breathing was laboured and the rise and fall of his chest was shallow.

Their prisoner spat out more blood. 'Nothin'. I was just takin' 'im to a nice little room where he could rest.'

'A room furnished with manacles and hungry rats?' asked Farral in a menacing tone. 'Was it you who shot him?'

'Nah. If'n I'd shot 'im, the old fool would be dead.'

'Who are you working for?' said Unwin in a mild voice.

'Can't say.'

'Oh I think you will. Unfortunately for you, we know the old man and don't take kindly to him being shot.' Unwin stepped closer and produced a small cut-throat razor from the inside of his coat. 'The only unknown here,' he continued, 'is how much of you will be left when you decide to talk.'

The small man turned pale but snorted in a show of bravado. 'It'll take a better man than you to make me talk,' he boasted.

'No matter,' said Farral, walking behind the prisoner. 'Send our regards to McNulty when you meet him in hell.' He knelt down.

'How ...?'

Jeremiah Mason never finished his question. Farral wrapped his left arm around the man's head, forcing it back and exposing the throat. He dragged his knife across the flesh and then pushed his victim forward. Mason tried to speak but he was already starting to gargle blood. It didn't take long for him to die.

Unwin smiled. 'I was going to suggest we leave him to the rats downstairs but, on reflection, your approach has more merit. At least we can be sure he won't escape, and we didn't need his information. However, ...' he gestured towards Molay.

Farral frowned. 'He's still breathing. Just.'

'But what can we do for him? If we leave him here, the clergymen will presumably hand him back to the tender mercies of our friend McNulty. And we can't take him with us.'

Farral knelt again, this time at the side of the old man. 'I wonder how McNulty found him?'

He leapt back when Molay spoke. 'Traitor.' The voice was weak and reedy. Molay put out a hand and pulled Farral closer. 'Somebody ... betrayed me. McNulty's men attacked ... my house ... Tried their best ... but no match.' He ceased speaking and drew a series of shallow breaths before continuing. 'I tried to escape ... shot me.' A rasping cough racked the old body and Molay fell silent again, this time for several long minutes. His hand slid from the lapel he'd been clutching. Farral was about to stand when the old man spoke again. 'Water.'

Unwin signalled he'd look for water in the church.

'In a dungeon ... McNulty ... questioned me ... weak ... blood loss. He gave ... up ... ordered me ... Torture me ... later.' A trickle of blood oozed from the corner of his mouth and the frail old body was wracked with a coughing spasm.

Unwin returned with a small glass and a jug full of water. He handed the glass to Farral, who gently lifted Molay's head and pressed the glass to the old man's lips. Molay took a few sips and then pushed the glass away. 'Not long. Failed ... information.' He sighed and coughed again. Blood began to trickle from his nose as well as his mouth. Unwin, standing behind Molay, shook his head.

'Know ... useful to ... you.' Molay's voice was growing weaker, and he pulled Farral's head closer to his mouth. He managed to whisper a few words before giving one final convulsion and falling limp against the assassin's supporting arm. Farral ran his hand down the old face, closing Molay's eyes for the last time.

Unwin watched his friend with a raised eyebrow. 'Another one to add to the list of McNulty's debts.'

'It's long enough,' said Farral. He glanced at Molay. 'But he told me something interesting. It seems McNulty is in the habit of attending one of his clubs every Tuesday evening.'

Unwin grinned. 'Then let's see if we can arrange for him to regret tonight's outing.'

42: A DESPERATE GAMBLE

Angele couldn't resist taunting Madeleine before she was led away. 'Pray he impregnates you tonight. Or do you hope to try and keep him entertained by performing whatever sluttish acts he demands?'

The young woman made no response as she was escorted off by two guards, but she heard Muller berating his wife. 'Why do you hate her so? She offers no threat to you and we both know the Lord will soon tire of her. Her fate is sealed, yet you seek petty victories that are unworthy of a woman of your talents.'

'Oh be quiet, you lecherous, old fool. I don't need advice or chiding from you!'

As they moved out of earshot, one of her guards poked a stubby finger against Madeleine's left breast and said something to his companion. The other guard sniggered and slapped Madeleine's rump. She stopped and whirled towards him, anger lending her a bravery she didn't stop to consider. With an open hand, she slapped the second guard across his face. There was a moment while all three were frozen in shock, then the guard she'd hit snarled and reached for a knife from his belt. As he raised his arm to strike, the other guard grabbed his wrist and said something that made him pause. Both guards looked towards the main hall. The one who'd poked her breast shrugged and the other muttered something. Then both of them pushed her in the back, urging her to start walking once more. She could feel their eyes on her as she headed towards a dark tower.

A solid wooden door barred entry to the tower and one of the guards took hold of her arm while the other used the handle of his axe to hammer on a panel covered in unfamiliar symbols. Madeleine blinked, telling herself that it must be the poor light playing tricks with her imagination. Yet, when she looked at the panel again, the symbols still appeared to be moving and changing shape. Her inspection was interrupted when the door opened inwards and she met her new gaoler, the keeper of the tower. At the same instant, an overpowering stink of mould and putrid decay hit her nostrils.

Madeleine cringed as the guards exchanged words with the gaoler, a creature from the realm of nightmare. Short and fat, it had leathery wings protruding from its back and four small teats on her chest. Sparse tufts of thick, wiry hair stood straight up from the scalp. Two arms ended in pincer-like protrusions. The creature was clothed in some sort of animal pelt, girded at the waist with a thick rope. A necklace of bone fragments provided the remaining adornment. Madeleine lowered her eyes to the ground and instantly regretted it. Smooth legs. Large, clawed feet. The gaoler was some sort of lizard!

A clicking sound made her look up – to find the odd creature staring at her from its tiny, oval-shaped black eyes. One of the guards said something in harsh, guttural tones, prompting a long string of clicks in reply. The other guard shoved Madeleine towards her new keeper and turned away. As she hesitated, the gaoler grabbed her wrist between one of its pincers and pulled her inside.

Madeleine shrieked, earning herself a hard blow to the side of her head. As her eyes struggled to adjust to the gloom, she could hear incomprehensible clicks from the creature beside her. Madeleine fought to hide the tears brimming in her eyes and almost leapt out of her skin when a voice to one side whispered 'Over here. To me.'

As she turned towards the unseen speaker, the gaoler grabbed her again, pulling her down some sort of gently sloping corridor. The creature continued to click to itself as it dragged her along. Madeleine made out slight, door-shaped indentations along the corridor walls but was given no time to examine them. Without warning, the gaoler stopped and did something she couldn't see with its free hand, never relaxing its grip on Madeleine's arm. She watched in a mixture of fascination and dread as it began to push against the wall. A door opened and Madeleine was pushed into a small room. Before she could recover, the door slammed shut behind her and a key turned in the lock.

Clovis Muller was bored with his wife's never-ending monologue on what she hoped Lord Helr'ath would do to Madeleine. Angele had started as soon as the guard left the pair alone. Muller had taken in the contents of their guest room – a tiny and poorly furnished chamber - from a single glance. It was bereft of all but the most basic objects - a bed, small table, two stools and a badly cracked pot whose foul smell suggested its intended use. Angele had been so full of gleeful malice that she didn't appear to have registered these details, preferring to concentrate instead on her own hopes for the young woman's imminent fate. As she prattled on, Muller pondered the significance of their surroundings and wasn't happy at what he concluded might be Helr'ath's plans for the pair of them.

Sensing that Angele was unlikely to stop her monologue soon, he held up a hand. 'Enough!' As Angele's head whipped round and her eyes narrowed. Not wishing to be on the receiving end of another tongue-lashing, Muller continued. 'I've got a headache, doubtless triggered by the stench of that pisspot. I need some fresh air.' Stepping towards the door, he added, over his shoulder, 'See if you can't get us something to eat and drink, my dear. Then you can finish telling me all about the noble Lord's bedroom habits.' Without waiting for a response, he pushed his way past the startled guard outside their room and headed towards the door leading into the courtyard. He allowed himself a small smile as Angele's indignant curse followed him down the corridor.

Once outside, Muller took care to keep to the shadows. Although he appeared to be studying something in his right hand, he was watching the various guards with more than his normal curiosity. He'd crossed about half of the courtyard when he saw a small door set into the brickwork of a dark tower. One of the Sna'bor guards stood to attention at one side of the door. Muller could feel its eyes tracking him as he approached. He steeled himself as he drew near, gesturing to the symbols writhing on the door. As the guard turned to look, Muller brought up his right hand and blew across his palm. A small cloud enveloped the soldier's head, and his body went rigid, before falling forwards. Muller stepped closer, catching the body, and easing it back against the wall. The flesh was icy cold. The guard's eyes glared at him with impotent rage.

Muller used the back of his hand to wipe sweat from his forehead and turned to scan the courtyard behind him. He heaved a sigh of relief as he reassured himself that none of the other guards had observed his actions. Easing the door open, he slipped inside and then turned back towards the entrance, taking just a few seconds to insert a small dagger between the ribs of the paralysed guard. Removing the dagger, he wrapped it in a cloth, taking care not to touch the blade. The poison would kill the guard in about 20 minutes. There was little time to waste.

Inching down the dimly lit corridor, Muller found his way to the gaoler's watch-room. Guessing that Koyl would be in her favourite part of her realm, he risked a quick peek round the door and grinned when he found himself looking at the gaoler's back. Fumbling in a pocket, he armed himself with another handful of imoybil powder before scuffing a foot along the floor.

He heard the soft scrape of a stool. Moments later, the gaoler peered cautiously around the door, seeing Muller at the same moment as he blew his powder in her face. Koyl clicked and reached for a long whip, coiled at her waist. She took one step towards him and then froze. As Koyl started to topple over, Muller caught the falling figure and propped it up against the wall. With deliberate care, he extracted another dagger from inside his blouse and spoke softly to Koyl in a short burst of clicks. Her eyes widened as Muller stepped closer and plunged the dagger into her chest. Blood spurted over Muller as he tried to manhandle the dying body back into the watch-room, whilst liberating a bunch of keys from the belt around her waist. In disgust, he dropped the body and headed back up the corridor, pausing when he came to the cell holding Madeleine.

Madeleine was slumped with her back against the wall, facing the door to her cell. She heard a faint hiss. Fearing her gaoler had returned, she shrank back, wishing for some sort of weapon. She'd been wondering how to anger the creature enough that it would kill her, deeming this preferable to having to submit to whatever Helr'ath had planned. Another hiss came, followed by a familiar voice.

'Keep away from the door.'

'Muller?'

'Hush! Do you want to bring the guards down on us?'

She heard the scraping sound of several keys being tried in the lock before the cell door swung inwards. Madeleine leapt to her feet. 'What trickery is this?

Muller glanced along the corridor than answered her. 'I may be an old fool and I've done things you couldn't imagine. But I'm damned if I'll let Helr'ath use you just to please my wife.' He took another look along the corridor before continuing, 'I don't trust that fat bastard and I figure if I can save you then your friend might persuade Sagana to take me back. If not, well at least I'll have the satisfaction of thwarting that old hag.'

Madeleine looked doubtful. 'Why should I trust you? And how can we escape from this place?' She scowled at the blood soaking into the old man's clothes.'

Muller showed his teeth as he grinned. 'I know a secret exit that Koyl used to satisfy her nocturnal urges. She won't be using it anymore.'

Madeleine interrupted him. 'Who's Koyl?'

'The gaoler. Or ex-gaoler to be accurate.' He stared at her, irritated by her lack of trust. 'Your choice is simple. Follow me and at least live a little longer or stay here and wait for Helr'ath to take his anger out on your body.' With this ultimatum, he turned and set off down the corridor.

Wallace, Sagana and the rest of their group surveyed the fortress from the safety of the forest edge and mindful of the setting sun at their back. The Fram'ska scout had warned them about the patrols of Sna'bor which guarded their lord's home from surprise attack and Wallace had already counted more than a dozen of the creatures. 'How do we storm that place with so few allies?'

Sagana frowned. 'We don't. Even if we could storm the place, do you think Helr'ath would let Madeleine live long enough to be rescued?'

'Then why are we here?'

'We need to create a diversion. Something to draw Helr'ath' and his forces out of the fortress. Then we can think about storming it.'

'And how do we do that?'

'I don't know, yet. Give me time to think.'

Wallace sighed. 'A fine rescue party we make. Hiding here while Madeleine suffers who knows what? Assuming she's still alive.'

Sagana's mouth twitched into a smirk. 'Stop fretting. The Gods are about to help us.'

Wallace glared at Sagana. 'And what makes ... '

He never finished the sentence, distracted by sudden activity from the fortress. There were shouts and snarls and a deep drum note began to sound. To Wallace's surprise, Sagana hushed him and rapidly outlined a plan he was going to put to their companions. Wallace nodded his agreement and Sagana spoke loud enough for all of their party to hear. 'Lord Helr'ath and his soldiers are hunting for the woman we came here to rescue.' He gestured towards the warrior before continuing, 'The two of us are going to follow them. If you honour your pledges to me, you will come with us. I promised you rich pickings and with your help we intend to kill the Lord and his men. The fortress will then be easy prey for you and your fellow tribespeople to do with as you please. The two of us want nothing but the woman.' He paused and looked around the group.

There was silence for a few moments as the Fram'ska looked at each other. It was broken by Belka. Sagana softly translated her answer. 'We will honour our pledges provided you guarantee that we can destroy the fortress and keep its treasures.'

'Agreed. As I said, all we want is the woman. And her guardian. Follow me.'

Wallace gave a quiet cough. 'Her guardian?'

'An old acquaintance.'

43: THE NATURE OF THE BEAST

Barclay tended to Figulus' wounded hand in a silence broken only by the periodic moans of pain from his patient. Lizzie gave a start when the doctor spoke. 'That's the best I can do for you, young man. At least the wound is now clean and should heal without further complications. That is, provided you keep it free of dirt and get this dressing changed frequently.'

Figulus looked at his bandaged hand and then at Barclay. 'I'd like to thank you, sir. I know I don't deserve your help after putting you and your home at risk, but I swear I've done with Black. I'm no saint, but I do have some scraps of honour left and I won't do any more to discomfort you after you've been so generous in helping me.' He turned towards Lizzie. 'I'm sorry, Miss. I didn't mean for things to turn out like this.' His face flushed a deep shade of crimson, and he took a step towards Whiston. 'I was all set to help in your murder. I realise you'll never really trust me now, but if you like, I can tell you where Black lives. That seems only fair given the trouble I've caused you.' He paused, as if collecting his thoughts. 'Either way, I know I have to try to kill my former master. Before he finds and kills me. I'd appreciate your help, sir, but, if necessary, I'll try it alone.'

Whiston raised his hand. 'Mr Figulus, you ought to know that I'm a policeman. You've just told me that you plan to murder someone ...'

Figulus stood his ground, a defiant look in his eyes. 'It's him or me, sir. One of us has to die. That's the way he works.'

Whiston frowned. 'I can't condone a plot to murder someone! Although I can see why you might hold such a grudge against this man.' He glanced at Barclay and at Lizzie. 'I'm prepared to visit Black's residence with yourself but only with the intention of arresting him. I have a suspicion he may be guilty of more than a vicious assault on yourself and the attempted murder of myself and my colleague.'

Figulus swallowed and tried again. 'With respect, sir, you don't know him like I do. He won't let you take him alive. It's not in the nature of the beast. And he has servants at his command who won't hesitate to use violence against you. Visiting him at his home would be like walking into a lion's den.'

Barclay interrupted the pair. 'You can count on me to help, Whiston. And I know a few men who might be willing to assist us in return for a small recompense. They owe me favours which I can call in.' Whiston still looked sceptical.

'You're not dealing with a normal man, Mr Whiston,' added Figulus. 'In fact, I'm not entirely certain he even is a man.'

'What do you mean?' asked a nervous Lizzie.

Figulus paused and his eyes took on a glazed expression. Then he snapped back to the present. 'His private study is full of strange objects. I've never seen their like elsewhere. And his teeth ...'

314

Whiston shot him a look. 'What about his teeth?'

'They look as if they've been filed into points. I saw a picture of a negro cannibal once, in a book. Black's teeth reminded me of the cannibal. The book said they file their teeth to make it easier to tear human flesh.'

'Wait. Wait!' said Whiston. 'You've just reminded me of something.' He muttered under his breath. 'Agnes Crawford. The doctor said some of her was missing. Bits of her had been nibbled. Sharp teeth.' He looked up to find his three companions staring at him. 'Mr Figulus, I think you've may have given me an important clue to an unsolved murder.'

This provoked a storm of questions, which Whiston's next comment did nothing to abate. 'I'm not prepared to say more until I've spoken with Mindelen.' He backed out of Barclay's study with a chorus of protests ringing in his ears.

In his study, Black paced before his desk. 'How is it my fault?' he demanded. 'It was you, my Lord, who placed the spell on the boy. It was the boy who failed. My watchers have dealt with the little brat.' He made little attempt to conceal his anger.

Lord Oln'ik frowned. 'You dare to speak to me thus? Why did you not know that there were others in the house? Their intervention ruined the plan. The boy told me this. Before he died.'

Black paused. The veins in his head stood out as he wrestled with his immediate problem. Coming to a decision he softened his voice. 'I apologise. I should not allow my frustration to cloud my judgement. You delivered your side of the bargain and now I must deliver mine.' Walking to the other side of his desk, he took a tiny key from his waistcoat pocket and opened a small drawer. Pulling out a small cloth bag, he untied the string around its neck and poured out a small pile of desiccated leaves.

He glanced up in time to see Lord Oln'ik licking his lips. 'I gathered these myself. They are from a very rare plant which can only be found at high altitude in this blighted realm. The dreams they produce are most remarkable.'

Oln'ik strode to the desk and scooped up the leaves before pouring them back into the bag. 'You had better hope they work as well as you claim. If not, I will consider the debt unpaid.' Black blanched and fingered his collar. 'As you say, my Lord.'

The room grew darker, and the demon lord began to waver before his eyes as a murky cloud started to take shape above Oln'ik's head. Black averted his eyes when lightening lashed out from the cloud, leaving a lurid image on his retinae. A few moments later the light level in the room returned to its natural level. Lord Oln'ik was gone.

Black stood staring into empty space. His plan had failed, and he cursed softly. His instinct told him that Whiston would now attempt to seek him out, forcing a confrontation. The thought cheered him a little. 'Let's hope you don't wait too long, my gullible friend. I'll be, waiting for you,' he said to the empty room.

Whiston fidgeted in his chair, ignoring the brandy glass in his hand. 'How much longer must we wait?'

Barclay raised an eyebrow and took a sip from his own glass. 'Didn't you say that your sergeant advised that you take some men with you? And that you wait until nightfall? From what you've told me and the things I've seen in the last few days, this Mr Black is not a foe to be taken lightly or with ease.' He glanced towards the window, where Figulus stood, peering round a heavy drape.

Without taking his gaze from the street outside, Figulus added, 'Listen to the doc, Mr Whiston. I know Black better'n any of you and I would be happy if I never saw him again. But that's not an option. Once he learns I've betrayed him, he'll hunt me down.' He sighed, then wandered over to a leather wing-back chair set close to the fireplace. 'It'll be dark soon.'

'What about these men you thought would help?' said Whiston, looking at the doctor.

'Well, I've sent a note to both of them. We can only wait to see if and how they respond.

Whiston glanced at the clock on the mantle-piece. 'They've got another hour. Then Figulus and I will be on our way.'

'But what about me?'

'You stay here sir. If this is going to be dangerous, then I don't want you involved. Besides, somebody has to guard Miss Cobham.' Barclay started to protest but Whiston spoke over him. 'You've already done more than enough, Dr Barclay. If this evening goes badly, you may have to move both the sergeant, Lizzie, and yourself quickly, for your own safety.' The doctor continued to protest, but his face betrayed his relief at this new arrangement.

Black had pondered his options and decided on a new course of action. He summoned several of his staff and gave clear and detailed instructions. Within minutes, his household had erupted into furious activity, while its master sat and brooded in his study.

Down in his cellar, two young children looked up fearfully as the door at the top of the stairs opened. Holding hands, they cringed against back wall as footsteps approached. The youngest, a girl aged perhaps six or seven years, started to whimper as first a pair of boots and then a pair of legs came into view. Her companion tried to comfort her, but his own heart was now beating faster as he gained sight of the approaching figure.

Dressed all in black and wearing a cowl, the figure stood in front of the cage and tapped a small club against its left hand. A thonged whip was curled around its waist. Neither child had ever seen the hidden face, nor did either of them wish to.

The boy watched in horror as a bony hand, clasping a large key, emerged from the right sleeve of the cowl. As the key was inserted into the lock of their small cage, the young girl squealed in terror and wet herself.

'Oh I do love the smell of fear.' The voice was deep and rasping. 'It's time to play a little game.'

The boy tried to position himself between his sister and their tormentor.

Ten minutes before Whiston's deadline, there was a knock at Barclay's front door. The doctor leapt to his feet and hurried to answer the summons, waving Mrs Carpenter back down the hallway. Whiston, his right hand grasping the pistol in his pocket, watched from the study door, exhaling when the doctor said, 'Ah. Welcome gentlemen. Please, come in.' As the doctor stepped back, two men entered the house, each doffing a cap as he crossed the threshold.

Whiston saw two very different specimens of humanity. The first man was small and wiry with a ferret face and a shock of blond hair. He looked to be in his late twenties and had roving eyes which constantly scanned the hallway. His posture suggested he was permanently poised for action. The other man was much bigger, both in height and girth. A shaven head topped a muscular frame which hinted at tremendous physical power. He stared at Whiston through small piggy eyes lined with wrinkles. Whiston guessed the big man was a little older than his companion.

'Edward Whiston. Meet Nathan and Michael Dungannon.' Whiston stepped forward, offering his hand to the smaller man. 'Pleased to make your acquaintance.'

The new arrival gave him an appraising look then quickly shook, before glancing at his brother. 'I'm Nathan.'

'Hello' Michael's grip was like iron and his hand was cold.

Whiston was relieved when the big man let go, clearly happy that he'd asserted his physical dominance by almost crushing Whiston's fingers.

'Let's all go into my study where we can have a brandy while we get down to business.' Barclay ushered his guests out of the hall. Once they were all seated, he busied himself pouring out four large measures of the fiery liquid. He handed the glasses round and said, 'A toast. To a successful night.' Four glasses were tipped in almost perfect unison. 'And now to business.'

A light drizzle dampened spirits just as it contributed to the prospects of a misty evening. The earlier crowds had thinned out to become little more than a few stragglers, some hurrying to the shelter of wherever they called home, others hoping to drown sorrows or cheer themselves in an ale house. Whiston stamped his feet and blew on his hands, still watching a large, detached house across the road from the safety of the alley mouth. His two companions stood motionless, a mismatched pair of statues largely hidden by the last fading light of evening. 'Where is he?' asked the policeman.

Nathan gave him a sideways look. 'No point asking us. He's your friend, not ours.'

Whiston pondered that for a moment. 'I wouldn't really call him a friend. More of an ally.'

'Makes no difference to us. We're here because we owe the doc a favour.' He paused, then continued, 'And because we know of this Black. He owes us.'

Intrigued, Whiston couldn't resist asking, 'Really? What does he owe you?'

'One of his men killed our sister. She rented a room from him and got behind with her rent. He sent one of his men round to see her. The bastard stuck a knife between her ribs, then raped her as she was dying. In front of her kids.'

'Did you tell the local police?'

Michael laughed. 'No point. We made a few enquiries but realised men like his employer shield their hired thugs and they're beyond the reach of the law.'

'So her killer got away with it?'

'Not for long. He met with an unfortunate accident down a back alley and ended up feeding the fishes.'

Whiston was shocked again. 'You killed him?'

'Don't be stupid. We couldn't do it ourselves. But we've got friends.' He paused, locking eyes with Whiston. 'We never had this conversation.' It was a statement, not a question.

Whiston started to speak again. 'Of course. As a policeman, I can't condone your taking the law into your own hands. But as an ally and a brother myself, I can understand why you did what you thought was necessary. As you say, we've never ...' He was interrupted by a slight cough from behind. All three men whirled to find Figulus standing in front of them. Seeing their faces, he stepped back.

'My apologies. I didn't mean to startle you. I came back the long way round just in case I'd been spotted.'

'Never mind that. What did you learn?' Whiston was trying to read Figulus' face in the gloom.

The new arrival grinned, revealing tobacco-stained teeth. 'The house is occupied. There's a light in the hall and in one of the upstairs bedrooms. There's also a light in Black's study. It's at the top of the house.'

'What's your plan?' asked Nathan, looking intently at Whiston.

'Michael will go round the back and prevent any escape in that direction. Figulus will knock on the front door – that should throw them off their guard. When it's opened, we'll all force our way in. If anyone tries to stop us, we use the coshes. I've also got a pistol, but I hope I won't need it.' He saw Nathan frown. 'Don't worry. I will use it if I have to. And I want Black alive if possible. But if not ...' He shrugged.

Figulus put a hand on Whiston's arm. 'Are you sure you're a copper?'

Whiston's face hardened. 'Oh yes. But this man Black has a lot to answer for. And trust me, one way or another, he will answer tonight.'

'Let's get started then,' said Nathan. 'How long will my brother need to take up his position?

Figulus pointed to an alley on the other side of the road and a little to the left of where they stood. 'Down there. Right at the end. Fourth house on the right. There's a high wall with an iron gate. The gate was locked but I've taken care of it.' He held up a ring of picklocks for a few seconds, before stuffing them into a pocket. 'Through the gate a path leads straight the back door. Five minutes should be enough.'

Nathan rubbed his hands together.

44: Uninvited guests

Farral clambered to his feet. 'What do we do with these two?'

Unwin shrugged. 'I don't suppose we can leave them here for someone to find. We don't want McNulty warned that his plans are unravelling sooner than necessary, although I assume he'll know something is wrong when his henchman fails to return.'

'We could put them with George.' Farral's eyes sparkled. 'He might welcome some company.'

'Not funny. But it's not a bad idea.'

'I'll bring Molay if you can handle the other one.'

By the time they'd half-dragged and half-carried the two bodies back down to the cell, both men were covered in bloodstains. They held a brief conference, trying to think of a plan that would furnish them with new clothing without arousing suspicion. It was Farral who proposed what seemed the best idea, once he'd stopped wheezing from the exertion. Now, under cover of late evening, they stood outside the back entrance to Molay's house.

Unwin kept watch at the end of the alley while his companion struggled to pick the lock which had denied them access for the last half hour. He was concerned by the lack of people and the quietness that surrounded the immediate vicinity. Of course, it could be that the locals had learned of Molay's disappearance and were keeping their heads down. On the other hand, they might be aware of an unpleasant surprise awaiting Farral and himself inside the old Jew's home. That was assuming the younger man ever managed to open the stubborn door.

A short, sharp bark made him jump. He glanced back down the alley to see Farral beckoning him.

Unwin grinned. 'Success then? I was beginning to expect the mewling of a cat!'

'It was tricky. A challenging lock.'

'Were you expecting a simple one?'

'Enough talk. Let's find what we came for.' Farral gestured for his friend to enter, following him inside, but only after carefully checking behind him for any signs of movement or surveillance.

They found themselves in a dingy passageway, with broken furniture littering the floor. Even in the light from a full moon, streaming through a small window above the door, they could make out dark blotches on the walls; marks which hadn't been there a few days earlier. Both men walked with care, anxious not to make any sound. Their progress was delayed by a cursory search of two downstairs rooms. Both were an odd combination of office and sitting room; the first also served as a library while the next contained two tables piled high with papers. To Farral's surprise, neither room showed any obvious evidence of having been searched. 'It seems McNulty's men knew exactly where to look for whatever information they were after,' he whispered.

'Or perhaps they were only interested in capturing Molay?' came the response.

A slight sound from the room overhead made both men freeze. 'You hear that?' whispered Farral, pointing upwards.

Unwin nodded.

The two men crept towards the door and out into the passageway. Farral pointed up and they set off for the stairs, stopping at the bottom to check for further sounds and to study the steps. Unwin pointed to himself then placed a foot on the bottom step, taking care to position it as close to the wall as possible. He placed his other foot on the next step and hard against the baluster. Farral allowed his friend to climb the first four steps then followed his example, avoiding the more commonly used and probably creaky middle of each step.

Near the top Unwin paused again. Another faint noise made him half-turn and point towards the first room. When nothing else disturbed the silence, he exhaled slowly and resumed his ascent. Gaining the landing, he inched towards the nearest room and took up position to the hinged side of the door. Farral joined him moments later, a long knife in his right hand. The two men looked at each other and Farral nodded.

Unwin leant towards the handle and slowly began to turn it. There was a click, and he pushed the door open as Farral surged forward, already scanning the room for enemies. A small, dark shape launched itself from a chair. It hit the startled Farral in the chest. He winced as he felt sharp claws pierce his clothing and skin. Before he could react, his assailant was racing down the stairs.

Unwin was struggling not to laugh. 'Are you alright?'' he asked, wiping his eyes.

'Very funny. That damn cat almost gave me a heart attack.' Farral looked around the room. 'I think this might have been Molay's bedroom.' He pointed to large dark oblong shapes lined up against one wall.

Unwin meanwhile groped around on the top of a small chest of drawers and found a candle. He lit it, shielding the nascent flame with one hand, then smiled as the light level in the room increased a little. 'It looks as if you're right. Why would anyone need two large wardrobes though?'

'He kept a selection of clothes for both his spies and himself to use as disguises. Not that he went out very often in the last few years.' Farral paused before adding, 'Said he'd made too many enemies and couldn't trust the streets.'

'So that's why you were so confident we might find fresh clothes here?'

'Let's take a look.' Farral walked towards the left-hand wardrobe and pulled the door open, then leapt back with an oath as a body fell towards him. Unwin wrinkled his nose as he crouched down to examine the corpse. The remains of the brain spilled out from the ruined back of its head. 'It looks as if they were shot at almost point-blank range.' He used his foot to nudge the body over and swore. 'It's Molay's flower-selling lookout!'

Farral shrugged. 'At least she would have died quick. There are worse ways to depart this life.'

'I wonder what she was doing in here though?'

'Well I doubt we'll ever find out, so there's little point in speculating about it. Let's get on with what we came for.'

Unwin gave him a hard look and seemed to be on the point of responding when Farral pointed to the second wardrobe. 'Your turn.'

Unwin walked over to the second wardrobe, reaching for the door handle. Some instinct made him pause, even as his fingers closed on the wooden knob. Glancing at Farral, he said, 'You might want to move out of the direct line of fire?'

Farral took the hint, moved off to side of the room and stood by the other wardrobe. He now held a throwing knife in his right hand.

Unwin knelt to one side of the door, put the candle on the floor and stretched his hand towards the knob. As he gave it a sharp tug, he threw himself sideways. The door swung easily on its hinges. There was a blur of movement, followed by a thud as something embedded itself in the wall opposite. Unwin stood as Farral asked, 'How did you know?'

'Experience. Let's see what we have here.' He moved over to the wall and called back, 'It's a crossbow bolt! Nasty.' Turning, he found Farral looking inside the second wardrobe.

'Rigged to fire when the door was opened. Whoever came for Molay, they weren't messing about.' There was a pause as he adjusted the flickering candle. 'Ho. Here's our treasure trove.'

324

There was no-one else in the house and they left by the same door they'd used to gain access. Both men were now dressed in very different attire. To the casual observer they would pass for two middle-class gentlemen and were unlikely to attract much attention – not wealthy enough to be worth robbing unless any potential robbers were truly desperate. The weapons hidden inside their long coats were much less obvious.

Emerging from the alley at the back of the house, they turned towards the wealthier part of the city and set off at a brisk pace. Farral led the way, displaying a surprisingly detailed knowledge of the streets. Neither man said much apart from the odd muted comment about other people walking the streets. Both made a point of scanning ahead, hoping to sense any possible trouble. From time to time one or the other would pause to check they weren't being followed.

It was close to an hour later when they turned into a quiet crescent which was home to some of the most affluent citizens of Bristol. Gaslights offered some slight relief from the darkness, but they were hung so far apart that they provided only small oases of light rather than continuous illumination. Unwin and Farral made their way down the road in a zig-zag pattern, flitting from one pool of darkness to the next. At last, Unwin held up a hand, pointing to one of the houses. Farral nodded and the pair continued down the road, searching for a side alley that might give access to the rear of the property.

The road petered out in a dead-end and the pair were forced to retrace their steps. 'It seems McNulty chose his home well,' whispered Unwin.

'I think the rear must be bordered by a park,' said Farral. 'Do you want to try it, or do we risk going in at the front?'

'I'm assuming he'll be expecting us. He must be missing the man we dealt with back in the church by now.'

'So the question comes down to this. Will he be prepared for us to enter through his front door?'

'Or he might have gone to his Club and still be there?' Unwin's upturned mouth suggested he didn't really believe what he'd just said.

'The Devil looks after his own. We'd never be that lucky!'

Unwin pointed to a first-floor window. 'He's been kind enough to leave us another way in, provided we can climb that drainpipe without being seen by any of his neighbours or casual passers-by.'

'And provided we're stupid enough to accept the invitation!'

'Yes, it does seem rather fortuitous in the circumstances.' Unwin quickly surveyed the street. 'It's very quiet here. Perhaps a little too quiet? But this isn't getting us any closer to a decision.'

Farral showed his teeth as he smiled. 'I have a plan.'

Twenty minutes later, two drunken men staggered into a dingy tavern and ordered rum. With practised ease, they surveyed the other drinkers before, as if at random, choosing a table occupied by three scruffy looking men who were talking to each other in low voices. The newcomers appeared to pay no attention to the unsavoury trio.

During a lull in conversation, the smaller of the two started a heated discussion with his companion. Both men were slurring their words and although they were trying to whisper, the gist of their discussion was overheard by their neighbours at the next table. To the listeners, it soon became clear that some rich toff owed money to one of the men. He was so angry about this, he was trying to persuade the other to help him break into the toff's home. His companion, perhaps a little less drunk, wasn't too keen to help. 'How would we get in?' he asked, in a plaintive whine.

'Easy,' came the reply. 'I went round to see him earlier, but no-one answered the door. I spotted an open upstairs window.'

The nearby trio continued to drink but their conversation had now ceased.

'So? How does that help? We can't fly.' The speaker started to flap his arms, as if to emphasise his point.

'No, we can't. But we could climb the drainpipe.'

At the adjacent table, one of the customers nudged his nearest companion and cast a meaningful glance at the two drunks.

The would-be bird imitator pondered this idea for a while, took another swig of his drink then said, 'Well I can't come with you.'

'Why not?' demanded his friend, irritation in his voice.

'Cos, I don't know where he lives, that's why.'

'No but I do. It's one of those big houses.' As he continued to provide details of the address, the three men at the table next to him finished their drinks, stood, and headed for the door.

Farral took another sip of his rum and grinned. 'I told you it would work.'

Unwin shook his head. 'Unbelievable. Drink up. We'd better follow them.'

'Give them a few minutes. After all, we know where they're going. Don't forget we're meant to be drunk.'

'A few more of these and I would be. What sort of rum is this anyway?'

'Best not to ask.'

45: MY ENEMY'S ENEMY ...

Sagana called the whole group together to discuss their tactics. This took a while because he had to say everything twice in order to include both Wallace and the Fram'ska. He began with a warning. 'Lord Helr'ath is an arrogant and evil creature. He's ruled this world for so long that he thinks he's untouchable. Never forget though, he is also a dangerous foe with a violent temper.'

Sagana's plan assumed that Helr'ath would deploy both an advance screen of the Sna'bor and a small rear guard as he headed through the forest. 'However, I've seen how he does things several times, working both with and against him. He's a creature of habit.'

And what exactly is my role in all of this?' asked Wallace.

'Once we've hit the rear guard, he'll take an interest in us and that's where you come in,' explained Sagana.

As the master translated his reply for the Fram'ska, Wallace was puzzled to see a few smiles among them. Then his intuition supplied an explanation. 'Wait. You want to use me as bait?'

'That's right. He's never seen you before, so he'll be intrigued.'

'Intrigued to find out how fast he can kill me?'

'His soldiers are fearsome fighters at close range, but they scorn the use of ranged weapons. Whereas the Fram'ska here,' he pointed to Belka and her comrades, 'are excellent with a bow. When they catch a glimpse of you, the Sna'bor will give chase, but they'll soon give up.'

'And if I can't outrun them?'

'With your long legs?'

The discussion continued for a while longer until Sagana ordered two Fram'ska to act as scouts. The wily master knew it wouldn't be difficult to follow the path taken by Helr'ath and his soldiers, but their small group couldn't afford any surprises.

Wallace walked alongside Belka. From the corner of his eye he saw her watching the path ahead but noted how she gave him the occasional glimpse when she thought he wouldn't notice. He smirked but said nothing.

Madeleine hardly dared breath as she followed Muller. He led her down a corridor before pausing alongside a solid wall. Muttering a few odd sounds, he beckoned her closer as

328

a rectangular part of the wall faded away. 'How ...' she began but the old man waved a dismissive hand.

'We don't have time to waste on your education. If we're caught, we both die. Slowly and with a great deal of pain. Come *on*.' He disappeared into the gloomy tunnel behind the wall.

Madeleine hesitated for a moment then stepped through the strange doorway. She'd taken several steps before she thought to look back and let out a little cry of surprise. The wall was reforming itself. She spun round just in time to see Muller's outline disappearing into the gloom. Steeling herself, Madeleine set off in pursuit, still uncertain if she should trust the old man.

In the Black Tower, Helr'ath reclined naked on a huge bed. He drank in huge gulps from a jewel-encrusted goblet and contemplated what pleasure he would soon wring from his new toy. The old witch had assured him she was unsullied, and it had been a long time since he'd had a young female hu'man to play with. He imagined himself thrusting deep inside her and her squeals of pain as he planted his own special seed. Just the thought was making him stiffen and he took another mouthful of his favourite wine.

His good mood fled in an instant when a slave entered the room and looked nervously around, as if seeking an escape.

'Well, where is she?' he demanded.

The slave fell to the floor, prostrating himself. 'Oh master, the hu'man has escaped. Spare me, please my lord.'

With a roar of anger, Helr'ath leapt from his bed and swept past the slave, not forgetting to smash the creature's head with a mighty fist as he raced past. As he burst out of his bedroom, a pair of startled guards sprang to attention. 'Kill the slave,' he said as he pushed them out of his way. A wail arose from his bedroom. It cut off abruptly before he was halfway down the stairs.

Still naked, Helr'ath gave orders to his soldiers. Four were dispatched to fetch Angele and Muller. Another four were sent to check the cells for any clue as to how his gift had manged to escape. While he waited for these instructions to be obeyed, he had two body slaves dress him in his finest battle array.

Clad in golden armour, he glared at his men when they returned with the old woman but claimed to be unable to find her husband. 'His eyes flared deep red as he turned toward Angele. 'Where are they?'

She returned his gaze, trying but failing to hide her alarm. 'Where are who, my Lord?'

Helr'ath shot forward, grabbed Angele's right arm, and snapped it like a dry twig. The woman howled in shock and pain, her face contorted into a grimace.

'What did I do wrong, my lord?' she hissed through clenched teeth whilst cradling her wounded arm.

Helr'ath thrust his head close to hers and stared down intently at her for a few moments before stepping back. 'You expect me to believe you don't already know?'

The old woman blinked away tears. 'Know what, my lord?' she sobbed.

'Where are your husband and my gift?' He noted the look of surprise in the woman's eyes. 'Ah, now you understand?'

'My lord, I had nothing to do with this.' She made the mistake of shrugging her shoulders and gasped as renewed pain lanced through her broken arm. 'Has my useless husband has taken your present away?' She adjusted her grip on the damaged limb, still trying to ease the pain. 'I warned you he had his own designs on her.' Tears streamed down her face.

As soon as she'd uttered the words, the look on Helr'ath's face told her she'd made a terrible mistake.

'You warned me? YOU WARNED ME?'

Angele stepped back in alarm. 'My lord, I meant no disrespect. The fault is mine if I didn't make myself clear.'

Helr'ath smiled. 'So be it. You admit you are at fault.'

Angele licked her lips, uncertain what game he was playing now. Her face had turned a puce colour and she wavered on her feet.

The Lord nodded to two of his soldiers. 'Cover her in mud and then roast her on a spit. Slowly. And make sure she has a breathing tube.'

Angele turned pale. 'But my lord ...'

'And feed her cooked flesh to my po'glets.'

Angele turned her head back and forth, seeking escape from this sudden nightmare. She screamed when a soldier grabbed her broken arm. Her pleas for mercy fell on deaf Sna'bor ears as she was hustled away. Helr'ath's mocking laughter followed her as she tried to focus her thoughts.

In the shadows, forgotten by everyone else, two large, dark forms stirred.

Helr'ath now issued fresh orders. With the exception of a garrison of two dozen of his best fighters, the rest were to follow him into the forest. 'I will have my present,' he roared.

The gate swung down and a number of Sna'bor warriors poured out before taking up a loose formation around the much larger and fearsome looking figure who strode into their midst. Wallace didn't need Sagana's muttered comment to realise that this was Lord Helr'ath. The master of the castle spat out orders in a booming voice. Wallace noted several of the Fram'ska cowering lower in their hiding places. As soon as Helr'ath had completed his orders, the whole group set off at a trot as he strode into the forest.

Sagana sent a small group to follow them.

One of the scouts was waiting for them, hidden in the thick undergrowth. Sagana spotted her first and held up a hand for the main group to stop. The heat in the forest was stifling

331

and Wallace took the opportunity to swig water from a cloth bag hung at his waist.

Sagana exchanged brief words with the scout and then explained to Wallace. We've caught up with the rear-guard. 'Darus'ka here says there are six Sna'bor. We'll wait here while she and her friends take care of them.'

'I could use a short rest,' said Wallace, 'so I don't mind.'

Sagana smiled. 'Don't get too comfortable. If this goes wrong, we may have to move fast.'

'I thought you said the Fram'ska would take care of them with their bows?'

'Complacency, my friend, has caused much regret.'

A few minutes later, their allies returned, faces lit up with delight. Belka nodded towards Sagana, who said, 'Now we wait until Helr'ath realises he's lost his rear-guard.' He signalled for the Fram'ska to move out, then watched with Wallace as Belka and her comrades split into two groups and moved away at right angles to Helr'ath's path.

As soon as they were out of earshot, Sagana turned to Wallace. 'Now we need to hide before the Sna'bor come to find us.'

Wallace struggled to hide his surprise. 'I thought we were going to let them chase us?'

'There's no point taking risks. I told you before that we can't entirely trust the Fram'ska. It would go ill with us if they betrayed our position to Helr'ath.'

'After they just killed half a dozen of his soldiers?'

'Helr'ath doesn't worry about methods. So long as he gets what he wants, he doesn't care who else pays.'

'So why should I trust you?'

'Because Helr'ath and I are sworn enemies. The next time we meet, one of us will die.'

Wallace frowned. Had he heard Sagana correctly? He shook his head, trying to fathom what he thought had been the master's last muttered comment. *No,* Wallace told himself, *this time it will be forever didn't make any kind of sense. Sagana must have said something else ...*

Helr'ath growled. His forward scouts had just reported a large group of untamed tra'll ahead and the fools in the rear-guard had lost touch with the main force. He summoned a squad leader and told him to find the stragglers. This left him with nearly a hundred Sna'bor – surely that would be enough to deal with the tra'll and allow him to resume his hunt for the hu'man female? A vision of the gift he'd been robbed of swam before his eyes as a sudden new fit of temper made him throw caution to the wind.

'Forward,' he ordered. 'Kill the tra'll.'

Belka held up a hand, signalling for her group to take cover. Moments later, a Sna'bor trotted out from among the trees, pausing to sniff the air. Its scaly skin glistened in the humid heat of the forest as the creature turned its head back and forth. Without warning, it stopped its scanning and stared straight towards the hiding place of one of the Fram'ska. Belka calmly notched an arrow and took aim. It shot from her bow as the creature erupted into a sudden charge towards her comrade. She'd judged its intent to perfection and the missile ploughed into the Sna'bor's chest, piercing its flimsy armour. The creature staggered and went to one knee. It was struggling to rise when two more arrows joined the first. With a sigh, the creature dropped back to its knees then fell forward and lay still.

Belka signed for her friends to stay hidden. She was puzzled as to why this soldier had been moving alone in the forest, as well as why they'd not yet caught up with Helr'ath's forward screen of scouts. A loud roar, nearby, made her flinch. Answering roars sounded from all around her. Belka leapt to her feet, 'Back!' she called. 'Withdraw.' Her small group began to run. Sna'bor were the least of their worries now.

'Can't we stop for a rest?' pleaded Madeleine. They'd been moving for hours, and the humid air was draining her of energy. 'I need water.'

Muller turned and glared at the young woman. 'If an old man like me can keep going, why can't you?'

'I'm not used to this,' answered Madeleine. I've not eaten for a long time and I'm afraid.' She sat down, her back to a tree. 'Where are we going anyway?'

Muller sighed and walked towards her. 'As far from Helr'ath's fortress as possible. I need to find Sagana, but the demon Lord and his forces are between us. Knowing Sagana, he'll find a way to whittle down the Sna'bor, but in the meantime we have to stay out of Helr'ath's clutches.' As he spoke, the old man played with a smooth stone in his right hand. 'Come on,' he urged.

Hidden high among the thick leaves of a tree and with plenty of interconnecting branches providing escape routes to other trees, Sagana and Wallace waited for any sign of their foes. The Master ran his fingers across a pebble in his left hand, and Wallace noted that he seemed a little distracted.

'Is that a tol'agr'un?' he asked.

Sagana looked at him in surprise. 'You remembered! Yes, it is. I'm trying to locate your friend.'

Wallace frowned. 'She doesn't have one of those and wouldn't know how to use it anyway?'

'No. But Muller does.'

'Muller!' Wallace spat out the name. 'Madeleine is with that evil old man? I swore to kill him next time I set eyes on him. If he touches her ...'

'And with good reason, I know. But right now, he's all that stands between Madeleine and Helr'ath. Think of it as my enemy's enemy is my ally?' He looked down at his hand. 'Let me concentrate.'

46: MR BLACK'S HOUSE

Whiston counted off the seconds in his head whilst keeping an eye on Figulus and Nathan. He tried to appear calm, but his heart was racing. Images of Rose floated before his eyes, alternating with those of the alien spider-like creature which had killed her and tried to do the same to him. He wondered where the thing had gone. Then, realising that he was losing the rhythm of his count, he pushed that particular thought to the back of his mind.

'Right, Michael should be in position. Let's pay a call on Mr Black.' He glanced up and down the street to check it was still clear and then set off for the house Figulus had pointed out earlier. Thrust into his jacket pocket, his right hand was curled around a heavy cosh. The pistol used by the young boy earlier that evening nestled in his inside left pocket. Figulus took the lead, Nathan walking alongside Whiston.

As the policeman wiped sweat from his forehead with the back of his hand, Nathan glanced at him. 'Nervous, Mr Whiston?'

'A little yes. Aren't you?'

'Not really. I'm focusing on what this man did to my little sister. It's about time the likes of him learnt they can't do as they please.' He paused, then continued, 'Why do you want him?'

Whiston licked his lips. 'He killed a woman in London. Maybe more than one.'

Figulus had stopped outside of Black's house. He looked at his two companions, a nervous smile on his face. 'Ready?' He registered two nods then turned to the door. It boasted a large brass knocker, shaped like a medieval shield. Taking hold of it with a firm grip, Figulus hammered on the door. At the same time, Whiston and Nathan had taken up position either side of him.

When there was no response, Figulus knocked again, with the same result. He turned to frown at Whiston. 'Now what do we do?' he whispered.

'Street's clear,' said Nathan.

'Can you pick the lock?' asked Whiston.

Figulus turned to look at the door furniture for a moment then smiled. 'Yes, at least I think I can. It looks simple enough. One of the Yale pin-tumbler type.' He fished some tools out of his pocket. 'You two keep an eye out. It might take a few minutes.'

While Figulus poked and prodded the lock mechanism, muttering to himself from time to time, his two companions watched the street and neighbouring houses for any signs of activity. Whiston let out his breath when Figulus suddenly said 'We're in.' He stepped aside, leaving Nathan to turn the handle, push against the door and start to enter the building. Whiston grabbed his collar, pulling him back. 'What are ...?'

Whiston pointed to a thin dark thread tied to the inside door handle. 'What's that for?' He waved his two companions back, flattened himself against the hinged side of the door frame and used his foot to push the door further open. There was a twanging sound and a bolt shot out of the doorway, landing on the outside path with a clatter.

Figulus had turned pale. 'A crossbow! Sneaky bastard.'

Nathan gave a nervous laugh. 'Good job the copper spotted that thread, or I'd have been gutted like a fish.'

Whiston frowned. 'It seems Black may have been expecting us. We'd better be careful in case there's any more unpleasant surprises.'

Figulus waved a hand towards the still open door. 'After you Mr Whiston.'

Inside the hallway, Nathan stopped to close the door, but not before following the string along its elaborate course all the way to a crossbow attached to a small frame at the foot of the stairs. Whiston had found a small oil lamp on the wall and managed to set it alight. As a dull glow lit up their immediate surroundings he spoke. 'Are there any more bolts?'

Nathan looked round and shook his head. 'No. I expect he thought his unpleasant surprise would catch any intruder off guard.' He gave Whiston a hard look. 'How did you know?'

Whiston shrugged. 'I spotted the string and wondered why it was there. The rest was a mix of instinct and pure luck, I suppose.'

Nathan grunted.

Figulus pointed down the hall. 'Should we let your brother in? He'll be less conspicuous inside the back door.'

'Good idea.' Whiston signalled for Nathan to stay close as Figulus set off down the hall. 'Let's not become separated,' he added as Nathan reached his side.

Halfway down the hall, Figulus stopped and pointed to a door to his right. The three repeated their positioning from outside the front door and Figulus chuckled. 'No lock this time.'

'Doesn't mean it's safe though,' muttered a scowling Nathan.

The three looked at each other, Nathan and Whiston tensing as Figulus pushed the door open, stepping back and to his left as he did so. At the same moment, Nathan pulled a cosh from his coat pocket. For a moment nothing happened and Figulus was about to step back towards the room when there was a vicious snarl from something inside. A dark shape moved towards the trio, emerging into the dim light. All three men froze at the sight of the enormous dog charging towards them. Figulus recovered first, uttering a shriek as he scrabbled backwards. 'It's Black's devil dog. A man-killer.'

In the doorway, the dog paused, as if weighing up its options. Then it launched itself at Nathan, landing with its huge paws on his shoulders as its weight bore him to the ground. It opened its massive jaws, preparing to rend flesh as Figulus ran for the back door while Whiston headed for the dog, a cosh in his hand.

Nathan was struggling to hold the dog's jaws away from his face when Whiston delivered a swinging blow with his cosh, catching the dog along the left side of its head. Spittle and froth flew from its mouth as it turned towards this new enemy. Forgetting Nathan, the dog turned its full attention to Whiston, its powerful jaws snapping shut on thin air as he drew his arm back and started a second swing with the cosh.

Feeling the weight on his chest ease and seeing the dog's head turn away, Nathan let his instincts take over. He brought his knees up under the dog's chest, half dislodging it but also ruining Whiston's intended second blow as the dog was thrown beyond his reach.

Beyond them, Figulus tried to steady his hand as he fumbled with the key sticking out of the back door lock. He glanced back up the hall and cursed as the snarling dog swung its head to look his way. Turning back, he heard a click and started to pull in panic at the door.

As Whiston struggled to keep his balance after over-reaching himself on his second swing, the dog now turned back towards him. At the same time, Nathan found his feet and let out his own snarl. 'Come on then, you damned stupid mutt. Let's sort this out.' Faced with two adversaries, the dog hesitated. Nathan kept his eyes on the beast as he said, 'Use the damn gun!'

Whiston was already reaching for the weapon when a large dark form burst through the now open back door. As he lined up on the dog, it leapt for him. Nathan tried to distract it with a shout and then there was a loud bang. The dog seemed to slump in mid-air just before it hit Whiston and knocked him against the wall. The pistol spun out of his hand and slid along the floor. The pair finished in a heap, the dog on top but with a hole in the back of its neck. It squirmed for a few seconds, still trying to get at the man pinned beneath it, before collapsing with a grunt. The young policeman lay in shock, even as the two brothers pulled the dog away.

Michael offered a hand, which Whiston clasped almost without thought. As he was hauled upright, he snapped back to awareness. 'You shot it!'

His saviour gave a grin, exposing a large gap between his top front teeth. 'You're not the only one with a pistol.'

'But we've lost the element of surprise.'

Nathan gave a snort. If there's anyone else here, they'd have to be deaf not to have heard that racket before my brother saved your life.'

Whiston looked down, feeling sheepish. His hand was wet and sticky, and he absent-mindedly rubbed it on his trousers. 'Fair point, Nathan.' He held his right hand out to Michael. 'I owe you, Mr Dungannon. I won't forget.' This time, the other man's grip was a little weaker.

Michael shrugged. 'I hope you'd have done the same for me.'

Figulus coughed. 'When we've finished congratulating each other, there's still the rest of the house to search.' He held out the pistol, offering it back to Whiston.

The policeman took the weapon then looked at each of his companions in turn. 'It's clear that Black was expecting someone. This place is full of traps.' He paused, searching for the right words. 'I propose we stick together. I'll lead with one pistol and Michael can watch our backs with the other. Agreed?'

Three heads nodded in unison and the little party set off to explore the rest of the house. The remaining downstairs rooms - a kitchen, a store and two small sitting rooms - were all empty, if not welcoming. Razor sharp wires, designed to disable the unwary, had been strung between some of the furniture in the second sitting room. In the kitchen the four men were stunned to find a large constrictor snake. By a stroke of good fortune, it had gone to sleep. Its bulging stomach suggested it had swallowed something the size of a small child. Michael used a meat cleaver, snatched from a rack on a preparation table, to decapitate the serpent. Then he calmly handed round several candles taken from a pile on a nearby shelf.

Upstairs, with nervous caution, the group explored a number of bedrooms. There was nothing to alarm them in the first two. But as soon as Whiston and Nathan entered the third, several men attacked them. These new foes burst from either side of the doorframe and were armed with machetes.

Michael shot the first attacker in the chest. His brother finished the man off by delivering a series of savage blows to the head from his cosh. The other assailant proved more difficult. As he pressed both Whiston and Figulus back towards a window, he was always on the move, making himself a difficult target for Michael. Whiston also struggled to get a shot away, fearful of hitting Figulus by mistake. The fight ended abruptly when Nathan swept a heavy blanket from the bed and threw it over the man. As he struggled to extricate himself, Michael shot once more. Moments later, a second bullet from Whiston caused the man to crumple to the floor.

Michael prodded the cover-draped body with his boot, before stooping to remove the material. As he straightened up, a machete flicked out, catching Michael across his shin, and opening up his leg. With a curse, he stumbled away. The dead man staggered to his feet, prepared to resume his attack, until Nathan battered him from the side. The two went down in tangle of arms and legs. After a brief struggle, Nathan managed to get on top. Using his greater weight, he pinned his opponent to the floor and proceeded to smash his skull with his cosh.

Stick a knife through his eye,' said Figulus.

'What?' said Whiston.

'Why?' asked Nathan.

'He's a near-man. An undead. You have to damage his brain to make him stay dead.'

Even as Figulus spoke, the man underneath Nathan began to stir. Michael fumbled inside his jacket and threw a dagger to his brother. Catching it by the handle, Nathan plunged the dagger through the smaller man's left eye, leaning forward to force it through and into the brain. The body twitched twice, then lay still. Nathan pulled the dagger out and started to wipe blood and other matter on the discarded bed cover.

340

A sudden thought struck Whiston. 'Where's the other one?'

Four pairs of eyes scanned the room, noting the trail of blood leading out through the door. Nathan leapt up with the dagger in his hand and raced for the door. 'Out here. On the landing.' Whiston and Figulus almost collided in the doorway, but both arrived in time to see Nathan standing over the figure trying to crawl away. He bent down and used the dagger to strike the back of the man's neck several times, before kicking him hard in the ribs. His victim rolled over onto his back and glared up with narrowed eyes. 'You'll be like me, one day.'

Nathan bent down, swatting away an arm as he plunged the dagger through the left eye. The man shrieked in agony, but Nathan paid no heed, kneeling on the chest as he struck at the other eye, twisting the point ever deeper. 'I don't think so.'

Behind Whiston, Figulus threw up. Michael moaned softly, cursing his wounded leg. Nathan regained his feet and looked at Figulus. 'What's a near-man?'

Figulus straightened up, clutching at his stomach with his good hand whilst wiping his mouth with the back of the other. 'I don't know for certain. They're dead people. Somehow, brought back to life. Black does it. Then he uses them. Like slaves.'

Nathan's eyes glittered. 'And you worked for this monster?'

Figulus stepped back, into Michael. 'Yes. I'm not proud of it. And I don't work for him now. I might not be a good man, but I'm not that evil.'

'Let him be,' said Michael. 'If he hadn't warned us, things could be a lot worse.'

Nathan looked unconvinced and his facial muscles hinted at his dislike of Figulus. Then he relaxed. 'I guess so.'

Whiston could feel the tension that still lingered. 'Where's his study?'

Figulus pointed up. 'In the attic.'

47: A DEBT IS PAID

Unwin and Farral staggered out of the tavern but didn't get very far before they had a quarrel. This left them face to face and well placed to survey the immediate area. Satisfied that they were not being watched, the pair amicably resolved their dispute. They staggered off, arm in arm, in the direction of a residential crescent familiar to both of them. A local cat observed their miraculous return to sobriety and watched them leave. Then it returned to the task of washing its front paws.

The pair made swift progress towards their target. As much as possible they kept to the shadows, especially when other night-time revellers were heading towards them. When the pair came to a halt, they were four houses away from the property which had interested them earlier that evening. Now. half hidden behind a large juniper tree, the two assassins watched two familiar figures attempting to enter the same house by climbing up a drainpipe.

The first man squeezed through the window. Moments later, he leant out and helped to pull his companion inside. A third man crouched in the garden and at the foot of the drainpipe, acting as a look-out.

'That's annoying,' said Unwin, pointing to the man left outside.

'We'll worry about him after we see what happens next.'

Unwin glanced sideways at his friend. 'What are you expecting to happen?'

'Let's just say I think our three eavesdroppers may soon regret what they heard not so long ago.' Unwin pointed up towards the open window. Someone had produced a light and a shadow crossed the window.

There was the sound of a commotion and raised voices. Moments later, there was a heavy thud and Unwin could just make out the sound of someone who seemed to be pleading for something. He tensed. 'Get ready.'

As he spoke, a body fell out of the window, landing head first on the ground below. The lookout, startled by this unexpected development, moved closer to inspect the body, glancing up at the window every few seconds. He didn't notice the front door easing open or the well-built man who slipped out and started to creep towards him.

'Come on,' muttered Farral. 'Time to even the odds.'

The man creeping out of the house wore a turban and carried a large knife in his right hand. As Unwin and Farral closed on him, he moved to within striking distance of the look-out. He held the knife up high and started to stab down towards the other man's back.

As if warned by some primitive instinct, the look-out began to turn. His eyes widened and he threw up his left arm to try to defend himself. His opponent grinned, displaying a set of perfect white teeth. 'Tonight, I feast!' The knife swept down, opening the other man's arm to the bone.

The look-out squealed in pain and tried to back away, but soon found himself pinned against the house. 'Please ...'

The other man gave a low chuckle. 'I enjoy carving my own meat.' He smiled, exposing metal-capped teeth, as he yanked his weapon free and struck again, with unnatural speed. This time he sliced open the other man's face from eyebrow to jawline. His victim crumpled to his knees, clutching at his lacerated cheek, his hand already covered in the blood pumping out of this latest wound. His attacker now produced a large nail and used his bare fist to hammer it into the skull of the luckless look-out.

He was bent over the other man when a slight sound made him start to turn – too late to avoid Unwin's sword. Skewered through his ribs, he let out a roar and reached for his new opponent, just as Farral, from the other side, rammed a stiletto into his neck. As the man paused, shock in his eyes, Unwin produced another knife and stabbed him in the groin. It was the big man's turn to fold to his knees. He tried to speak but Farral said 'Hush,' putting a finger to his lips before kicking him in the stomach. The dying man fell forward, face down on the lawn.

'The door *is* open. Shall we?'

'It would be rude not to.' Unwin bowed. 'After you.'

Farral glanced at each of the three bodies outside the house before heading for the open door. 'Doesn't it strike you as odd that no-one has seen fit to investigate the recent disturbances?'

Unwin frowned. 'It's more than just odd. I don't like it.'

Farral paused in mid-step. 'Just how powerful is Wallace McNulty?'

'Powerful enough to convince his neighbours to mind their own business?'

The two men looked at each other. Unwin shrugged. 'Let's finish what we came here for.'

Inside the hall, three gas lights provided good illumination. With their back to a closed door, McNulty and three men stood waiting. The smallest was armed with a pistol, which he levelled at Unwin. A second man held a double-headed axe whilst the third was armed with a pair of sabres. McNulty stood with his arms crossed over his chest, a smile curling his lips. He held up a hand and took a step forward.

'It seems I may have underestimated you, Lemuel. And I found it difficult to believe you had managed to survive your last encounter with one of our Blades, Thomas. How's your breathing by the way?' His eyes glittered with malice.

Unwin held his own pistol, levelled at the chest of the man with the sabres. 'Good to meet you, Wallace. Again. Although I'm a little disappointed you feel the need for so much help. Perhaps you no longer trust your own skills?'

A scowl flitted across McNulty's face. Then he sighed. 'A cheap attempt to rile me, Lemuel? Oh dear. Do the unequal odds bother you so much?' He raised an eyebrow.

'It's not the odds,' replied Unwin. 'I just thought you were more of a man than to hide behind your minions. Despite your numerous character failings, I never before though of you as a coward.' His eyes never left McNulty. 'It's always a shame to have to kill the servants, although in this instance my friend and I are happy to make an exception.'

Without warning, he fired at his target and moments later Farral also discharged his own pistol at the man armed with a similar weapon. The swordsman pitched forward, a neat hole between his eyes. Farral's own shot was less accurate, and McNulty's man staggered as the bullet ripped through his shoulder.

'Tut, tut. Not very sporting.' McNulty's hands moved in a blur as he turned and shot the wounded man in the stomach. His companion fell, a stunned look on his face. 'Now the odds are even. Shall we?'

McNulty surged forward, a rapier in his hand as he lunged at Unwin. The priest barely managed to bring up his own sword in time to deflect the incoming blade, and the familiar ring of clashing steel filled the hall as Farral and the other man also closed in combat.

Farral tried a few exploratory thrusts but soon discovered that his opponent was a master of his chosen weapon, blocking with an ease bordering on contempt. Farral withdrew a few paces, drawing the other man away from McNulty and Unwin.

Meanwhile, the lethal blades in the hands of the other two flashed back and forth in an intricate dance. One mistake was almost guaranteed to prove fatal. McNulty tried to turn his superior height to his advantage, but soon found that Unwin had almost supernatural balance coupled with a great swordsman's instinct. Panting, he acknowledged his opponent's skill. 'You're good, Priest. Almost my equal. But you ... can't ... win.'

'God on ... my side.'

Just one? I have ... many'

'Doesn't ... matter. Mine stronger.'

Even as they talked, both men tried a bewildering series of feints and counters, each seeking a momentary opening.

Farral's opponent switched to a two-handed grip on his weapon. The axe sliced through the air, weaving from side to side in a complex and changing pattern. One step at a time, the man was pressing Farral back. Sensing victory, he started to move his weapon ever faster, grinning as Farral began to sweat and suck in mouthfuls of air.'

'Problem ... priest?' The last word was spat out and at the same time the man stepped forward, whirling the axe round in front of his own face as he tried to close the gap between them.

Farral made no response but continued to concentrate on the flashing blade. He'd seen this style of attack once before and thought he knew what was coming. Sure enough, his opponent suddenly changed his attack in favour of reaching forward, planning to bring the axe down in a deadly chopping motion. Anticipating this change of tactic, Farral sprang to his right and planted the end of his sword in the man's chest.

His opponent's own momentum forced him to swing his weapon down into the empty space where Farral had been just a few moments earlier. It also drove the sword deeper. Without comment, Farral pulled the sword free and then ran his opponent through again. The other man was now looking down in surprise at the red patches spreading across his shirt. The axe hung from his right hand. With a growl he tried to lift it for one last attack as Farral stepped back.

'Problem ... fool?' said Farral.

His opponent dropped the axe and put out a hand to steady himself against the wall. 'How ...?' he began. 'How ...?'

Farral wiped sweat from his forehead. 'I've seen ... your style ... before.' He coughed, feeling feint from his exertions. 'You never ... stood ... a chance.'

As his opponents' eyes started to lose their focus, Farral turned his attention to the other end of the hall, where the ferocious battle showed no sign of easing up.

'Done here,' he said.

Unwin never took his eyes from McNulty. 'Stay out of this. ... It's between ... him and me.' Farral sucked in air, watching the fight with both appreciation and a practised eye. 'If I lose ... shoot him.'

346

Farral scoured the floor for his discarded pistol. In all the confusion it had somehow been kicked towards McNulty, who glanced down before using his left foot to scoop it further towards the back of the hall. Farral cursed under his breath.

That glance cost McNulty dear. Although he was distracted for the merest fraction of a second, Unwin took advantage to slice open his opponents' sword hand. McNulty leapt back, uttering his own curse. Unwin allowed himself a brief, little smile. Now the advantage lay with him. Taking a deep breath, he pressed home his attack, noting the blood that oozed from his opponent's hand. Eventually, this would weaken McNulty's grip on his sword. And then ...

The end came sooner than he'd expected. As the two blades clashed together once more, McNulty's sword flew out of his hand. In an instant, Unwin struck, driving his own sword deep between McNulty's ribs. He pulled the weapon free as McNulty used his good hand to clutch at his side. Unwin struck again, this time aiming for the throat. Farral let out a low whistle as McNulty now stood defenceless, clutching at his throat, blood pouring through his fingers. He struggled to speak. 'You ... wi ...' The fatally wounded man made a strange gurgling sound as he slid to the floor, twisting sideways across the man he'd shot himself.

Unwin leant against the wall, breathing heavily, and shaking from his recent exertion. When he looked up, his face was lit with triumph. 'At last, I have my revenge for Brother Artie and for poor George.' He paused for a few more deep breaths. 'I wasn't sure I could beat him, but I'd like to think God gave me this victory. At last, a debt is paid.'

Farral shrugged. 'What do we do now?'

Unwin stood up straight. 'We search the place for clues to what McNulty has been doing.' He pointed to the stairs. 'Let's find out what happened to our friends up there.'

The two men climbed the stairs with extreme caution, fearing another attack. What they found in the front bedroom did nothing to put them at ease. One of the men who'd listened in on the drunken conversation in the tavern lay very still, in a pool of his own sticky blood. The first one through the window had an almost severed left arm and an ugly split through the top of his skull. He also had a large, ragged wound to his throat, suggesting it had been torn out by a wild beast. His mouth was open in a silent scream of horror.

Farral peered out of the window, worried by the lack of activity out in the street. He glanced at Unwin, who was watching him with his arms folded across his chest. 'Why has no-one come to investigate the disturbance?' Even as he asked his question, a shout from outside broke the silence. Spinning round, he saw several figures shuffling, with an odd gait, towards the house. As the nearest entered the pool of light cast by a street-light, he caught the glint of something metal held in its left hand. 'Ah, Thomas. We have a new problem.' He pointed to the street.

Unwin walked over to the window and surveyed the scene outside. 'Near-men?'

'It would explain the lack of interest in our recent activities.' Farral turned pale. 'You don't think McNulty has killed all of his neighbours?

Unwin's eyes narrowed. 'Those abominations didn't come from nowhere.' He glanced outside. 'I count seven at least. I suggest we get out of here.'

'How? I'm not sure we can fight our way free. And we don't know how many of them are out there or what they're armed with.'

'Let's hope there's a back door.'

'That's your plan?'

'Have you got a better one?'

The two men raced down the stairs, pausing only to close and bolt the front door. They next recovered several pistols and the axe, before heading down the hallway towards the rear of the property. Stepping over the bodies of McNulty and his men, they soon found themselves in a rear parlour with a locked external door made of solid oak. More calls and a hammering from outside suggested that the house was already under siege.

As Unwin scoured the room for a means of egress, he noted bars at the windows. 'We're going to have to make a stand here unless we can break down that door.'

'I can't say as I'm very impressed with this plan,' said Farral, a wry grin on his face.

The sound of breaking glass at the front of the house made both men turn back towards the hall.

48: DEATH OF A DEMON

The tra'll hit Helr'ath's force with the cold fury of a mighty storm. One moment the forest was quiet, perhaps too quiet. The next, it erupted into a mass of snarling, axe-wielding shaggy giants, who ploughed into the startled Sna'bor with almost gleeful abandon. Over a dozen of Helr'ath's guards went down under the initial impact, as the tra'll smashed through them, desperate to get to the demon lord.

Helr'ath barked out orders, trying to organise his soldiers into some semblance of a defensive circle. He struggled to make his voice heard above the cries of the tra'll and the din of battle. Gripping his own double-headed axe, he surveyed the growing carnage. After the initial shock of surprise, his remaining warriors had started to rally and the tra'll were now taking casualties of their own. Even so, it was clear that the outcome of this battle was too close to call. He took two steps towards where the fighting was thickest, then frowned.

Shadows were gliding through the trees alongside the fighting. Without warning, a shower of arrows poured into the melee. With uncanny accuracy, they seemed to strike many of his own fighters but not a single one of the tra'll. Helr'ath watched in amazement as a second volley of arrows cut down even more of the Sna'bor.

He had no idea who these shadows were or why they appeared to be allies of the tra'll, but their intervention had sealed the outcome of the fight. The tra'll warriors, sensing

349

victory, began to push his own fighters back towards their master. True to his nature, Helr'ath made an instant decision. Calling his personal bodyguards to him, the demon lord turned and fled back along the way he'd come.

After the second volley, Belka gave the order for her friends to withdraw from the battle. Their intervention had handed victory to the tra'll. Experience told her it would be a mistake to assume they would show any gratitude to their uninvited allies. As she and the others melted away, Darus'ka gave a low whistle and pointed. Belka smiled. Lord Helr'ath was leaving his guards to die and heading straight towards Sagana and the hu'man warrior.

Muller grabbed hold of her wrist and half dragged Madeleine behind him. 'Keep moving,' he ordered. Sagana and your friend Wallace are waiting for us, but we need to circle round Helr'ath and his guards. He stopped suddenly. 'You will remember that it was me who saved you?'

Madeleine smiled, hearing the uncertainty in his voice. 'I promise to tell them. But I can't predict how Wallace will react to seeing you again.'

'It's not Wallace I'm worried about,' muttered the old man. 'Come on.'

Helr'ath didn't waste time on checking to see how many of his guards had heard him. He was focused on escaping the horde of tra'll who had appeared from nowhere and ruined his plans. Anger surged through him even as his mind sought an explanation for this unprecedented challenge to his authority. An image of an old hag floated before his eyes. 'Angele?' he muttered. A scream distracted him, and he risked a backward glance, just in time to see one of the few guards racing after him fall, an arrow protruding from its back.

As he turned back, something flashed past his head, scratching his cheek. Startled, he set off once more, back towards the safety of his fortress. In his head, he was now planning exquisite tortures for those who dared to oppose him. He tightened his grip on his axe and ploughed on, ignoring the cries from behind as more of his guards fell to the deadly arrows. Someone was going to pay for this brazen attack on a demi-God!

Wallace was the first to hear the sounds of pursuit and to realise that the quarry was being herded towards his and Sagana's hiding place. He glanced at his companion, who pointed down towards the path they'd been following earlier. The sounds grew louder as something large crashed through the undergrowth.

Moments later, Wallace spotted the demon lord himself, charging along the path his forces had created earlier. Behind him came two of the Sna'bor, one nursing an arm which still sprouted the end of an arrow shaft. Helr'ath seemed to be in a panic and Wallace wondered what had wrought this change. It was clear that the demon had run into something he'd neither expected nor been able to cope with. 'What now?' he mouthed to Sagana.

Sagana was studying the trees either side of the crude path and he nodded to himself. 'It seems we're in luck. I think the Fram'ska are driving Helr'ath back this way. But how they managed to overcome his guards I have no idea.'

Wallace shrugged. 'Let's attack while he's vulnerable.'

'But we don't know what he ran into.'

'Right now, I don't care! My sole concern is to rescue Madeleine and I think that task will be much easier with Helr'ath out of the way.'

Sagana nodded his head. 'Alright. I've waited a long time for this. Too long.' He started to climb down the branches. 'We'll need to take him from opposite sides. He can't defend against both of us at the same time.'

As the pair landed on the ground, Belka emerged from behind a tree. The Fram'ska was winded, and she sucked in several large gulps of air before speaking to Sagana. He listened intently and then gave a short reply. Turning to Wallace, he said, 'Belka says that Helr'ath's party was attacked by a large group of wild tra'll. She and her comrades used their bows to thin out the Sna'bor. They noticed Helr'ath abandoning his soldiers and decided to follow him, using their arrows to pick off most of his personal guards and steer him this way.'

'So the Fram'ska kept their word?'

'Yes. I've told her to send two of her warriors to find Madeleine and Muller. She and the rest will wait and recover here while we deal with the demon. Then she and her friends are free to attack the fortress as we promised.'

'I still don't see how they're going to get inside.'

'That's what she said. I suggested she steer those tra'll towards it.'

Wallace grinned. 'Which conveniently gets them out of our way as well.'

'You're learning.'

A snarl of rage announced the arrival of Helr'ath. His gaze swept over Wallace and settled on Sagana. 'You! Are you responsible for this outrage? You dare to violate our agreement?'

Sagana said nothing but moved further away from Wallace.

Helr'ath raised a huge fist and pointed a finger at Sagana. 'You will die for this. Very slowly. But first, I'll kill this weakling that stands gawping at me.' Lowering his head, he charged straight at Wallace, his huge axe whirling in his right hand as he narrowed the distance between the two of them.

For a brief moment, Wallace wondered if Sagana had betrayed him, luring him here to meet his death at the hands of this giant fiend. Then, from the corner of his eye, he saw the look on Sagana's face as he raised his own weapon and started to move towards Helr'ath. Wallace considered his options, knowing that he could not match the demon for brute strength. On the other hand, Helr'ath had but one eye

352

and this must give him a limited range of vision. Wallace hoped the enraged monster would be vulnerable to attacks from his side. He shifted his weight, preparing to move to one side so as to place Helr'ath directly between Sagana and himself. If he'd interpreted the Master's look correctly, Sagana would attack the demon's back. If not, well he'd go down fighting and try to take one of them with him.

And then the demon was almost on top of him! Wallace was already leaning away as the axe blade came slicing in towards his head. He raised his sword to parry the blow. The two blades met with a loud clang and the shock of the impact almost wrenched the sword from Wallace's hand. He struggled to maintain hold of his weapon as he moved out of range, relaxing as he let his natural fighting instinct take over from his conscious mind. The power of Helr'ath was appalling and Wallace knew there was a good chance that any mistake would also prove to be his last.

As the demon prepared the next swing of his own weapon, he started to laugh. Then he bellowed in rage. Sagana had leapt close enough to stab him in the back of his right leg before stepping quickly back.

Wallace watched in admiration as the axe whipped round behind Helr'ath's back. It was a move that would have decapitated Sagana if he'd tried for a second cut. In the back of his mind, Wallace calculated that the two had met in combat before. Or else Sagana had seen Helr'ath fight. Wallace was also conscious of the control required to perform such a move without inflicting self-injury. When it came to personal combat, the demon lord was far from being a novice. He tightened his grip on his sword.

Helr'ath seemed to sense that Sagana had stepped back as he now launched a ferocious attack against Wallace. Out of the corner of his eye, the hu'man saw one of the Fram'ska draw a bead on the demon. Before she could let loose her arrow Sagana called out, 'No! This is between Helr'ath, my companion and myself.'

Wallace cursed and leapt to his left. The axe-blade whipped through the air where he'd stood moments before.

He flicked his sword back as he landed, catching Helr'ath on the wrist. The demon grunted but did not slow the ferocity of his attack. His sword arm tiring, Wallace began to give ground as the blows came raining in. He was beginning to see a pattern to Helr'ath's offense but was also starting to wonder if he would last long enough to exploit his new knowledge. Then the world exploded in a blinding green flash.

Madeleine and Muller watched as the tra'll and the Sna'bor battled each other with raw ferocity. Hidden in a thicket of densely leaved bushes, she wasn't sure which side she wanted to win. Victory for the Sna'bor would save her a bloody and gruesome death at the hands of the shaggy monsters but a win for the tra'll would save her from Helr'ath. Of course, there was always the chance, however slight, that Muller really was trying to get her back to Wallace and Sagana. She studied the old man out of the corner of one eye. He appeared to be engrossed in the battle.

Cautiously, she eased back from his side. When this provoked no reaction, she risked a glance behind her, noting the track they'd been following. She recalled the thick stand of trees off to the left. Holding her breath and placing her feet with great care, she eased further back. Then, judging it was now or never, she bolted for the safety of those trees. Her movement alerted Muller to her escape and he spun towards where she'd been crouched at his side. As she had anticipated, he daren't shout for fear of attracting the attention of the tra'll but the look of fury on his face lent an extra burst of speed to her legs.

Blinking to clear his vision, Wallace recalled the fight with the tra'll in the forest and the weapon Sagana had used there. Helr'ath lay face down, a large hole where his neck and shoulders had been. His right hand still gripped the axe, and, to Wallace's astonishment, the demon lord was struggling to lift himself up.

'Disarm him. Literally,' said Sagana.

What?'

Sagana stood alongside Helr'ath and swung his sword down across the fallen creature's right wrist, severing it from the arm. Brownish liquid spurted from the stump and Helr'ath groaned.

'Your turn.'

'Why? He's beaten.'

'Just do it. Then I'll explain.'

Wallace gritted his teeth and took up position alongside Helr'ath's other side.

The demon struggled to speak, 'Hu'man. Kill Sagana and I will grant you anything you desire.'

The blade flashed down and the sound of crunching bone announced that Helr'ath had lost his other hand.

Wallace frowned at his fallen opponent then looked up at Sagana. 'Why is this necessary? He's dying anyway.'

'The only way to permanently kill him is to drain all of the blood from his body. And make sure none of it gets into any of your own wounds.'

Wallace's eyes opened wider. 'You jest!' Seeing the look on Sagana's face he frowned in confusion. 'You're not joking?'

Sagana's eyes glittered. 'No, I'm being serious. We have to cut him into little pieces and make sure every last drop of blood is drained out of him. None of it must enter the body of another sentient creature.'

Wallace's face was a shade of green. 'That's disgusting.' He held up his left hand. 'Why don't you just blow him into pieces with more of your green things?

'That would be simpler. But that was the last of them.' His eyes measured Wallace's reaction. 'That's why I had to be careful not to waste it. I wanted to be sure he was focused on you, not on me.'

'So you used me as bait? Again.'

'I wouldn't put it quite like that. Anyway, we have work to do. Belka and her friends can help once I've explained a few things to them.' He stooped to pick up Helr'ath's axe. 'This should come in useful.' He licked his lips and continued, 'I should warn you, Wallace, what I'm about to reveal is forbidden knowledge. If you agree to become my apprentice, then your education starts in earnest right now. Or you can walk away.'

Wallace hesitated, considering his options, then said, 'Very well. Then we resume our search for the woman.'

Madeleine raced for the place where the trees stood thickest. She had no real plan, other than to escape from Muller. As she crashed through the undergrowth, branches and leaves whipped against her legs, trying to trip her and end her flight. Glancing back, she spotted a red-faced Muller trying to follow her. She took encouragement from the fact that he was already blowing hard. Then she almost fell as her left foot became stuck under a rotting branch.

With a curse, she untangled her foot. At her side, a twig snapped, and she started to turn to her left. just as a bony fist smashed into the side of her face. Pain lanced through her temple and the world turned black.

When she came to it took a few moments for her vision to clear. She was bound hand and foot and being carried along the forest path. As her eyes focused, she let out a gasp. 'You!' The tra'll in front turned to stare at its captive.

49: MOCKERY

To their surprise, there were no more traps or attacks as they climbed the second flight of stairs up into the loft. Michael insisted on coming with them, although his wound continued to seep blood and he was limping heavily by the time they reached the top of the stairs. They entered Black's study with caution but found nothing more than a well-furnished room dominated by a large desk. Several bookcases and shelving held an unusual variety of books and artefacts, many of which meant nothing to any of the four intruders. Whiston lit two oil lamps stood on the desk.

'We need to search for clues as to what this Black is up to or where he might be,' said Whiston. 'But be careful, who knows what nasty tricks he might have left behind.' He strode towards the desk. 'Look on the shelves and inside the books for a letter or notes or something.'

He looked down at the desk and saw an upside-down envelope half hidden under a grotesque statue of some sort of unidentified animal. Pulling it out he turned the envelope over and almost dropped it. 'What have we here?' he said.

As his companions turned towards him, Whiston spotted a letter-opener lying in a small tray on the desk. He picked it up and used it to slit open the envelope. 'Isn't that private?' asked Nathan.

Figulus grunted in obvious amusement. 'After what we've just been through, you're worried about opening someone else's mail?'

Nathan put his hand over his own mouth and coughed. 'Well, I suppose if you put it like that ...' He gave Figulus an odd grin.

'It's addressed to me anyway,' said Whiston as he extracted a single sheet of high-quality paper. He scanned the writing on the page and snarled in frustration. 'Listen to this. It says, Dear Mr Whiston. I've been looking forward to meeting you but find myself otherwise indisposed. If you've found this letter, then I assume you survived my little tests. Never mind. You know where to find me. I'll see you in the great whenever, my irritating friend. PS. I've left you a little something in the cellar. Your servant, Mr Black.'

Figulus was the first to react. 'Great whenever? What does that mean?'

'I'm not certain,' admitted Whiston. He has a house in London, which the local radicals used to call the 'great wen' back in the 1820s.' He turned the sheet over but soon turned it back again. 'When we've finished up here, we need to find the cellar.'

Figulus looked uncertain. 'I'm not sure I'd rush to find this supposed token of goodwill. Black has an evil sense of humour. It's bound to be another trap.'

'I'm of the same opinion,' said Michael.

Whiston stroked his chin. 'Would you describe your former master as a vain man?' The question was directed at Figulus.

'Vain? I suppose so. He likes to dress in a dapper sort of way.'

'I was thinking more of his need for praise or to prove how clever he is,' said Whiston.

'I wouldn't say he went out of his way to elicit praise. He did like to prove he was smarter than everyone else though,' agreed Figulus. 'Why do you ask?'

'Oh nothing really. I'm just trying to build up a picture of what he's like.'

'We're wasting time,' growled Michael.

'Agreed, Let's see what else we can turn up here' said Whiston. 'Then we explore the cellar.'

While his companions feverishly searched through books, behind paintings, under cushions and elsewhere, Whiston studied the unusual items occupying the shelves behind Black's desk. He had no idea what most of them represented or what they might be used. Assuming they served any useful purpose in the first place. He was puzzling over a strange pebble, which seemed to grow warmer the longer he held it, when Nathan asked, 'Did you find any clues in the desk drawers?'

'Eh? What? Sorry, I was trying to work out what this was. I haven't searched them yet.'

Nathan gave him a scornful look. 'And you're a policeman? God help us!' He yanked open the top drawer. Inside was a selection of small bottles. Nathan took them out, one at a time, holding them up at eye level as he tried to read the hand-written label on each bottle. With a shrug, he turned to Whiston. 'Damned if I can make out this peculiar writing. Whatever it is, it's not written in English.'

Whiston picked up one of the bottles and glanced at the thick green goo inside. He considered the odd characters on the label for a few seconds. Shaking his head, he was about to put the bottle down when he let out a gasp. The bottle's content had somehow moved towards the forefinger and thumb gripping its top. Curious, he used his middle finger, placed halfway down the bottle, to adjust his grip and then moved his forefinger away from the top. To his amazement, whatever was inside the bottle now sluggishly rearranged itself in line with his new hold. 'Look at this. Whatever is inside this bottle seems to be alive!'

Michael glanced towards him and snorted in disgust. 'Don't be stupid. It's just a trick of the light.' Nathan smiled at his brother and shook his head. Figulus seemed to be anxious. He came over to the desk and picked up another bottle, holding it well away from his face. After shaking the pale blue crystals inside, he carefully put it down.

'My strong advice would be not to open any of these bottles.'

Nathan laughed. 'Don't tell me you're spooked as well.'

Figulus ignored him and backed away from the desk. 'I once saw one of Black's business rivals open one of these bottles. Black had offered him tea and said the bottle contained sugar. When the man opened it, whatever was inside flew out and covered the man's face. Then it tried to force its way up his nose and down his throat.' Black sat there smiling as the man choked to death.' He sat down on a bench under the single attic window.

Michael glanced at Whiston then gave a nervous laugh. 'But it was just a trick, right?'

Before Whiston could respond, Figulus spoke again. 'I remember it well because of what Black said when the man had ceased to claw at his own face.' He fell silent, a far-away look in his eyes as he relived the experience.

359

'Well?' said Nathan. 'What did he say?'

Figulus looked up. 'Must have been something he swallowed.' Silence greeted this revelation.

Eventually, Whiston broke the mood. 'Forget the desk for now. Let's see what's in the cellar.'

Figulus led the way, chatting nervously about how he'd never been allowed into this particular part of the house. Nathan interrupted him to comment that, given the man's unpredictable and vicious nature, he doubted many people would volunteer to enter Black's cellar.

In the kitchen they stood in front of what appeared to be a large dresser. It held a collection of various cooking utensils, crockery, and glasses - the usual things associated with this type of furniture. Figulus ran his hand over the right-hand side panels and stepped back. A loud click was followed by movement of the entire dresser as it swung outwards to reveal stone steps leading down into the cellar. A pungent odour flowed out through the widening gap. Whiston and Figulus both held their nose, Nathan frowned, and Michael pulled a face.

'What's that awful smell?' said Nathan.

Whiston ignored him and started down the stairs, holding his hand over his mouth. Ahead it was pitch black and he stopped. 'Pass me a candle.'

At the bottom of the steps the little group stopped, holding several candles at head height as they tried to make out the vague shapes looming out of the gloom. The stench had become worse as they descended the steps. 'We need more light,' said Whiston. Figulus turned and almost ran up the steps. He returned a few minutes later, armed with more candles. As he passed them out and lit one for himself, his face was pale. His lips were pressed together.

The sight that greeted their eyes was almost incomprehensible. Two small bodies had been impaled on butchers' hooks and hung up on the back wall as if they were recently slaughtered farm animals. The smaller of the two was a young girl dressed in a filthy blouse and skirt. Her bare legs and feet bore multiple bite marks and her scalp revealed a large bald patch where her hair had been ripped out by the roots. Her mouth was wide open, as if her last conscious act had been to scream. 'Where are her arms?' asked Nathan in a small voice. Behind him, Michael was emptying his stomach. Figulus edged back up the first few steps.

The other body was that of a boy, perhaps two years older than the little girl. His sole item of clothing was a tattered pair of breeches. The hands and feet had been cut off and his ears were also missing. Several deep wounds across the boy's arms suggested he'd been attacked with a bladed weapon. Whiston guessed the child had tried to defend himself. 'The poor boy never stood a chance,' he muttered.

In one corner of the cellar, a metal cage stood with its door open. An unlocked padlock hung from the hasp. There were two small metal bowls in one corner the cage. One held dirty water and the other was encrusted with what looked like dried porridge. A pile of mouldy straw lay in another corner. The floor of the cage was covered with human faeces.

Against the far wall, a bench held a variety of whips, cudgels, and pincers, plus a heavy metal bar. 'Who could do this to children?' asked Nathan, his face twisted into an ugly scowl. Then he turned, raced up two steps, and grabbed Figulus by the throat, pushing him up against the wall. 'Explain this!' he demanded.

'I. I ...' stuttered Figulus.

'You'd better start talking,' said Whiston.

'It wasn't me,' squealed Figulus. 'I already told you, I was never allowed down here.' He started to cry.

Nathan leant in against him, increasing the pressure on his throat. 'But what are you not telling us?' Figulus started to turn red in the face and he clawed at the arm across his throat.

361

'Ease up a little, Nathan,' said Michael. 'You're choking him.'

His brother shot Michael an angry look but eased his body back a little.

Figulus swallowed hard. 'I heard whispers. They said Black snatched orphans off the street and kept them down here. He used them like the boy who tried to shoot you Mr Whiston. And for other things.' He looked at the policeman, his eyes appealing for aid from a face contorted by misery. 'They said there was a creature down here who looked after the children and ...'

'And what?' Whiston's voice carried a hard edge.

'They said he sometimes ate the children.' His eyes brimmed with tears. 'I thought it was just stories. A warning meant to keep us away from whatever Black had hidden down here.'

'Who's this 'they' you keep referring to?' asked Michael. His tone was calm and neutral as he limped closer to Figulus.

Figulus glanced towards Whiston, his eyes pleading for mercy.

'Other men who worked for Black. I swear I had nothing to do with the children. I thought it was all just stories.'

The two brothers exchanged a look and Nathan stepped back, releasing his hold on the other man. There was a flash of light reflected off a metal surface and Figulus slumped down against the wall with a sigh. A knife stuck out of his chest and a growing dark patch welled around its entry point.

Whiston blinked in shock. 'You've killed him! In the name of God, why?'

'Michael locked eyes with Whiston. 'He was lying. If he was not involved in this, how did he know where to find and operate the cellar door.'

Whiston paused, uncertain how he felt or what to do next. 'We'll never find out now. We could have asked him if he was still alive.'

'And if we were still alive.' Michael spat on the floor. 'That little worm was only interested in saving his own neck. For all you know, Black put him up to this tale of his having changed sides.'

Nathan grunted, although Whiston couldn't tell if it was in agreement or in disgust. 'Black is mocking you, policeman. He's showing you what he's capable of. You're going to need a strong stomach to deal with a monster like that.'

Whiston looked at each brother in turn. 'You're right, Nathan. Let's get out of here.'

'What are you going to do?' asked Michael.

'I'm going to collect my colleague and return to London. I suggest you two lie low for a while. As far as I'm concerned, we've never met. Agreed?' He looked at Michael. 'I said I owed you and I won't betray the man who saved my life.'

Nathan smiled. 'As you say, Mr Whiston. We've never met. I'm sure the doctor will hold his tongue.'

'Don't worry. I'll explain everything to him and make him see the sense in keeping quiet. I doubt he'll be any more inclined to talk to the local police than we are. And he ought to treat your leg, Michael.' He paused, staring at the two children. 'I'm not sure we should just leave them like that?'

He walked over to the back wall and reached up for the body of the young girl. As he struggled to lift her off the cruel hook in her back, he dislodged a small glass bottle wedged between her bottom and the wall. As it fell to the ground, he had a mental image of the small bottles up in Black's study. He leapt backwards and twisted round, running for the stairs. 'Back, back' he cried, 'It's a trap!' As the three men raced up the steps, the bottle shattered on the ground.

At the top of the steps, Whiston glanced back and felt an icy chill crawl down his spine. On the floor beneath the girl, a human shape was forming. Blood red eyes snapped open and glared at Whiston. He stepped into the kitchen and helped the two brothers to push the dresser back into place. As they fled the kitchen, the first of a series of dull thuds came from the back of the dresser.

50: A NEW START

'Round his neck!'

Unwin frowned at his friend. 'What? What was round his neck? And whose neck are you talking about?'

Farral grinned, already heading back along the hallway. 'A key on a chain round McNulty's neck. I glimpsed it during the fight.' A shadowy figure appeared at the other end of the hall. 'Cover me,' shouted Farral, quickening his pace. Unwin groaned and checked that the pistol in his hand was loaded.

Halfway down the hall, Farral skidded to a halt and dropped to his knees. He started to fumble around the throat of McNulty, surprised to find that the body was still warm to the touch. A pair of legs appeared in his peripheral vision as he tried to pull the slim chain away from the corpse's neck. There was a loud report and one of the near-men fell just in front of Farral. He glanced at the neat hole drilled between the eyes of a middle-aged man.

'Hurry up,' hissed Unwin. I don't have an unlimited supply of ammunition here!'

Farral leant back on his heels, tugging furiously at the chain. He almost fell over backwards when the links finally parted and the whole chain came away in his hands. To his dismay, the key he was searching for flew up in the air and away from him, further down the hall. It bounced several times before coming to a rest. Farral went after it on his hands and knees. He tried not to think about the enemies, forcing their way in through the shattered windows, or the growing pile of bodies littering the hallway.

As his left hand closed on the key there was another loud bang. This time, the body fell on top of him, and a spiked cudgel glanced off Farral's shoulder. 'Yeuch! Get off.' The bullet had caught the near-man in the chest. Stuffing the key into a pocket, Farral whipped out a knife from its sheath at his waist and plunged the blade through the dead man's right eye. As he straightened, other figures began to shuffle down the hallway in his direction.

He turned and raced back towards Unwin. The priest gave him a brief grin then resumed re-loading the pistol in his hand. 'Is it me, or are they slowing down?'

Farral was busy trying to extract the key from his pocket. He glanced down the hall. 'You might have a point. Perhaps whatever it is that animates them is weakening now McNulty is dead?'

'Maybe.' There was a splintering sound followed by a loud crash as the front door gave way. 'Uh oh. They'll be coming in force now. Hurry up.'

Farral produced the key and inserted it into the lock of the back door. He tried to turn it but met with stiff resistance. 'Hell! It's the wrong key.'

'Tell me you're joking!'

'I wish I were. We're going to have to fight our way out.'

'Wait. What about the axe?' As he spoke, Unwin shot another near-man who was almost within striking distance. 'I'll hold them off and you smash down the door.'

Farral grabbed the axe from its resting place against the door and started to hack at the timber. Splinters were soon flying everywhere as Unwin fired one more shot before drawing his sword. He took several steps towards the oncoming press of bodies, hoping to give Farral space to work. As the near-men close din, Unwin almost laughed at their increasingly stiff and jerky movements.

To the sound of chopping thuds, grunts and cries, Unwin launched a ferocious attack. He drove his opponents back into the more confined space of the doorway between the hall and the kitchen. There he systematically began to whittle down their numbers, using all his formidable skill to avoid taking any serious injuries of his own. He grimaced at the thought that he would have to kill some of them more than once before they finally stayed dead.

'Curse this English oak,' shouted Farral. It's hard work getting through it.

'Try to smash out the lock.'

'What do you think I'm doing?'

'Faster. I can't hold them much longer.'

Moments later, as he dodged a carving knife, Unwin heard a different kind of thud. 'Locks out,' said Farral. 'Time to go.' Unwin skewered the nearest opponent and kicked the one just behind in the groin, then turned and raced for the outside.

As he cleared the room, he noted the flagstone paving down which Farral was already moving. Ahead, in the gloom, he could just make out a large hedge with a small wicker gate. A howling behind him provided all the necessary encouragement he needed to close the gap between his partner and himself.

Farral tried to vault the gate but caught his trailing foot on the top of it and disappeared over the other side. Unwin followed him and landed awkwardly as he tried to avoid his friend, twisting his ankle in the process. Fortunately, Farral had retained enough presence of mind to roll to one side as Unwin landed. As both rose, Unwin grimaced and hopped on his left leg. 'Damn. I think I've sprained my ankle.'

Farral got to his knees and peered over the gate. Three near-men were shuffling, slowly, towards it. He signalled for Unwin to stay down and whispered, 'They're getting slower. Moving as if they were trying to run through treacle. I'll finish them off. Wait here.'

He clambered to his feet, a knife in his left hand and a sword in the other. Catching sight of him, the remaining near-men began to wail and tried to hurry towards him. The first tried to lift the latch on the gate and paid the price for this poor tactical decision. Farral plunged the knife upwards through its throat and on into the brain. As the creature fell, its two companions came within striking distance. Farral laughed as he sliced the jaw of one down to the bone before leaping back to avoid a crudely aimed swing of its companion's axe. The injured near-man was clutching at his jaw as the axe completed its arc and embedded itself in his left shoulder. As he fell, Farral was ramming his sword up the nose of his companion. With both of his opponents down,

Farral pulled yet another knife from his boot, calmly undid the gate latch and then finished off all three of his opponents.

Glancing at the house, he could see no sign of any further activity. Stooping, he retrieved the knife from the body of the one he'd killed first. He wiped all of his weapons clean on this victims' clothing and then returned his weapons to their various hiding places. Unwin watched without a word until he was finished. Then he said, 'Help me up, will you?'

Farral grinned and put a shoulder under Unwin's arm. 'You'll have to hobble unless I can steal us a horse. At least we can use what's left of the front door now. I think all of McNulty's men are finished.'

'No,' said Unwin. I was examining what's out there,' he pointed into the darkness, 'and believe your earlier guess was right. It appears to be some sort of park. We can't afford to risk being seen leaving here. Besides, I heard a horse whinny over there.'

'Fair enough,' agreed Farral. Just don't expect me to carry you all the way home.'

'Remind me again. Where exactly is home?'

Farral chuckled. 'Well Molay isn't using his place anymore.'

'Good point, my friend.'

It took Unwin and Farral the better part of an hour to find the small stable attached to an annexe of the park. To their disappointment, it held just one broken-down old mare. There was no sign of a carriage or even a cart. After resting up for a while, they resumed their uneven progress. Dawn was breaking when they arrived at Molay's house.

Unwin offered to take the first watch. He argued that Farral had expended more energy. 'Besides,' he added, 'I'm unlikely to sleep until the pain in my ankle eases.' Armed with both pistols, he sat on a large chair at the top of the stairs. His injured ankle rested on a cushion atop a stool placed next to him. In the feint morning light, he smiled as Farral's snores took on a regular pattern. Although he felt drowsy, he was confident the pain would keep him awake.

Pondering recent events, Unwin felt little joy at the death of McNulty. He knew that this individual was but one of the dangerous enemies threatening his Church. And he promised himself that from now on he would renew his efforts to bring about the total destruction of his enemies. Starting with the traitor inside the White Shield. He would talk to Farral about it when his friend awoke. His thoughts turned to the mysterious Guide. Could this creature to be trusted? Was it an angel or a devil? Unwin's head lolled forward on his chest.

As the two assassins were swallowed up by the gloom, a slim figure crept out from behind a large bush and entered McNulty's house. Although he appeared to be in his early 30s, this latest arrival moved with an odd irregular motion. His progress resembled that of a very old man who was no longer fully in control of his limbs. Several times he collided with one of the hallway walls, careening off them as if heavily intoxicated. But, at last, he came to the bodies of McNulty and the man half buried underneath him.

The new arrival knelt down in a clumsy fashion before stretching out a leg alongside the pool of drying blood which had seeped from McNulty's wounds. Fumbling inside his coat, he eventually produced a small, curved knife. He used this, in a clumsy manner, to slice his own trouser leg. In the process he also managed to slash open his newly exposed leg in several places. A trickle of blood ran down his foreleg until the first few drops fell to the floor. Over the next few minutes, a little trail of his blood edged ever closer to that of McNulty's body.

The stranger felt very sluggish as his life blood continued to seep away. His thoughts, never that clear for as long as he could remember, became even more hazy. Somewhere, at the back of his mind, he knew he had an important task to complete. Try as he might, he couldn't quite recall what that task had been. His eyes began to flutter, and his head fell forward on his chest. He didn't notice when his own blood merged with that of his master. His last conscious thought was of two small boys looking up at him.

As the two pools joined together, a dim luminescence began to twinkle above the point where they merged. Next, a tiny ripple spread across the surface of the pool of blood. Over the next few minutes, more ripples appeared, each slightly stronger than the preceding one.

At last, the eyes of the young man snapped open. A casual observer would have been surprised to find that they were covered by a white film. Moments later, the eyes closed again. But it was what came next that would have really surprised this casual observer. As the man lifted his head from his chest, eyes still closed, the blood in the pool began to ripple up his leg and towards the largest of its wounds. Defying the laws of gravity, the blood began to flow upwards and gave every impression of entering back through the wound some of it had previously flowed out of.

Over the next few minutes, the pool on the floor shrank appreciably and the man's leg began to twitch. As the pool of blood on the hall-floor continued to shrink, its recipient stood up and stretched his arms above his head.

The eyes suddenly snapped open and were now filled with intelligence. They stared down at the bodies lying on the ground. The figure licked its lips then took an unsteady step. 'Hmm. I need to give it a little more time before I try anything too strenuous,' it said to the empty air. 'But while I wait for the process to complete, I can at least make a new vow.' The hall fell silent for a few minutes before the figure spoke again. 'I vow to make those two fools suffer every agony at my command before I wipe out their puny organisation.'

Wallace McNulty's face took on an evil grin. 'As if those fools could really kill me.' He shook his head. 'Time to tidy up. Then a bonfire to celebrate my rebirth.' Inside his head and already fading away, what was left of a former insurance clerk's dwindling consciousness screamed in silent terror.

To be continued ...

A REQUEST FROM THE AUTHOR

First, let me say a big thank-you for purchasing and reading this novel. If you enjoyed the book and read it on an electronic device, then please take a few minutes to post a review. Reviews help to spread the word and drive more sales!

And whether you enjoyed it or not, (constructive) reader feedback is always welcome. What did you like or not like about the book? Did the plot make sense? Did you like or dislike the characters?

As an author, I can only improve if my readers let me know how I'm doing.

You can contact me by e-mail at:
stevehewitt.writer@hotmail.co.uk

ABOUT THE AUTHOR

Steve Hewitt hails from Chesterfield, Derbyshire, England. Born in the 19950s, he grew up with a love of reading and an interest in science fiction inspired by his paternal grandfather.

After studying economics at Nottingham University and health economics at York University, he embarked on a brief career as an academic, just as the UK Government ended the university tenure system. He next tried his hand at working for the NHS but soon realised that although it wanted to employ a health economist it didn't want to use this skill set.

Tiring of the politician's fondness for endless and pointless tinkering with the health service, he joined the national education department as an analyst, specialising in international comparisons. Out of the frying pan ...

In 2005 he married Anne and, through her, met a friend who turned out to be a budding author. On announcing – as you do – that he'd always fancied having a go at writing a book, Steve was stunned when this new friend responded with 'What's stopping you?' A little later he joined a writing group to begin learning the basic skills of producing a story.

In 2013 Steve grasped an opportunity to take early retirement so that he could concentrate on writing, walking his dog and doing up his house – not necessarily in that order.

He now spends his time writing, walking his dog and entertaining his granddaughters – again, not necessarily in that order.

'Forbidden Knowledge: Volume 1 – Death of a Demon' is the first in a trilogy of books about the White Shield and the Black Blades.

By the same author - 'Forbidden Knowledge: Volume 2 - Rise of the Blades'. 'Forbidden Knowledge: Volume 3 – The Shield of Faith', and 'A Brief Tour Around My Head' (a collection of short stories) are available in paperback from Amazon and on Amazon Kindle.

You might also like to try **'Jigsaw'** by 'Ellipsis Writers ...' This is an anthology of short stories and poetry written by Steve Hewitt and four other writers based in North Derbyshire and South Yorkshire.

GLOSSARY OF CHARACTERS, CREATURES, AND ORGANISATIONS

Albigenses/Albigensians - other names for the Cathars.
Angele - an old woman and sometime ally of Sagana.
Barclay, Mitchell - a Bristol physician and a friend of Lizzie Cobham.
Barrington, Mr - a clerk at The Grand Hotel, Bristol.
Belka - a Fram'ska warrior.
Black Blades, The - secret military wing of the followers of the Elder Gods. Sworn enemies of The White Shield.
Black, Mr - a strange and vicious creature with sadistic tastes and a violent nature.
Blade of Banishment - a legendary weapon and reputed to be able to kill the Elder Gods.
Blood Cult, The - a group said to worship devils and perform blood sacrifice.
Brinvilliers - a blacksmith in a village near to Muret.
Carlos - one of Sagana's mercenaries.
Carpenter, Mrs - housekeeper to Mitchell Barclay.
de Castelnau, Pierre - a 13th century Papal legate.
Cathars - a religious movement which emerged in 11th century Europe. Based on the early Christian church, it rejected the concept of priesthood and the use of religious buildings. Its tenets were declared heretical by the Papacy and a crusade against the Cathar stronghold of Languedoc was launched in the early 13th century.
Chyvol - devil-dogs. Amenable to rudimentary mind control by agents of The Black Blades and used to hunt down hu'mans.
Clermont-le-Fort - a village to the east of Muret.
Cobham, Lizzie - a waitress in a Bristol hostelry.
Cooper, Mrs - Alice Glanville's landlady.
Count of Roaix, Albert - a minor French noble. Childhood friend of Raymond of Toulouse.
Count of Toulouse, Raymond VI - a French Count who refused to persecute Cathars among his own people. Had a stormy relationship with the Catholic Church.
Countess of Roaix, Cateline - wife of Albert, Count of Roaix.

373

Crawford, Agnes -   Lemuel Unwin's landlady in London.

Coxe, Zachary - a dead assassin (a former member of The White Shield).

Darus'ka - a female Fram'ska warrior.

de LeDrede, Madeleine - a young French woman.

Dubois, Florimond - a warrior and trusted companion of Molitor.

Duk'en - an alien species. Similar to a large flightless bird-like creature. Carrion eaters, found in the forest of the tra'lls.

Dungannon, Michael - a large, strong dockworker. Known to Dr Barclay. Brother of Nathan.

Dungannon, Nathan - a small, wiry dockworker. Known to Dr Barclay. Brother of Michael.

Elder Gods, The - ancient gods of the pre-Christian era.

Farral, Thomas - an assassin. (a former a member of The White Shield. Missing and presumed dead).

Figulus, Christian - a young man in Bristol.

Forsyth, Dr - a mysterious doctor who signed the death certificate of Brother Gervaise. Subsequently disappeared without a trace.

Fram'ska - an alien life form. Six-limbed and war-like.

Frederick - an archer and leader of Sagana's mercenaries.

Freddy - a young thief in Bristol.

Fulbright, Arthur - a priest and friend of Lemuel Unwin.

Gervaise, Brother - a deceased clergyman.

Ghast - an alien carnivorous species. Similar to a ghoul but possessed of startling ferocity.

Glanville, Alice - a whore.

Gol'bin - an alien carnivorous species. Small and vicious creatures which hunt in packs. Resemble the minor devils of Christian theology.

Greene, Augustin - a disgraced bookkeeper and resident in Mrs. Crawford's lodging house.

Grey, Angus - a dockworker and resident in Mrs. Crawford's lodging house.

Guide, The - a mysterious entity and servant of the Elder Gods. Acts as an intermediary between them and their servants and followers.

Guiscard - the court fool of the Count of Roaix. Also an assassin, trained by Sagana.

Helr'ath - a demon and lord of the Blood Cult.

High Council, The - ruling body of The White Shield.

Hu'mans - name given to their creations by the Elder Gods.

Hunt, George - an assassin and member of The White Shield.

Imoybil powder - an immobilising powder, made from a poisonous plant. Readily absorbed through soft tissue and usually blown in the face of the intended victim so as to be absorbed through the eyes and mucus membrane. Effective for a period of between 15 minutes and three hours.

Isaac - an elderly clerk. Works as a messenger for Inspector Johnson.

Jack - a youth who works for Mistress Lydia.

James - a young porter, working at a hotel in Bristol.

Jeanne - a pretty young servant girl. Works for the Count of Roaix.

Johnson, Inspector - a senior police officer. Slow witted and pompous.

Keeper, The - mysterious entity and servant of the Elder Gods. Acts as an intermediary between them and their servants and followers.

Koyl - Lord Helr'ath's jailer.

K'liggen - hairy, rat-like creatures. Small but aggressive with poisonous fangs. Hunt in packs.

Kr'omk - a nasty parasitic creature whose reproductive cycle kills its host.

Llandoger Trow - a seedy tavern in the docks area of Bristol.

Lu'Ki'Fer - one of the Elder Gods (Lord of Death).

Lydia, Mistress - owner of a London brothel.

Mason, Jeremiah - a violent thug.

McNulty, Wallace - a wealthy Victorian aristocrat.

Mindelen, Joseph - a police sergeant.

Molay, Jannes - a Dutch spymaster living in 19th century London.

Molitor - the leader of one of the small Papal forces in southern France. Determined to destroy the Cathar 'heresy'.

Muller, Clovis - an old man. Servant of Sagana.

Muret - location of a major battle in 1213 between the forces of the Catholic Church and forces loyal to Raymond, Count of Toulouse.

Nancy - a young maid in the employ of Dr Barclay.

Near-Man - a reanimated hu'man corpse. Used as soldiers and servants by high-ranking members of the Blood Cult.

Oln'ik - a demon and lord of the Blood Cult.

Organ Beetle - an alien lifeform. It lays its eggs in water. Other creatures unwittingly ingest these eggs which then incubate and hatch inside the host body. The young beetle then eats the internal organs, normally emerging just before the host dies.

Peter, King of Aragon - a Spanish ruler and ally of Raymond, Count of Toulouse.

Picart, Gilles   - a friend of the father of Madeleine de LeDrede.

Po'glet - an ancient life-form encountered beyond the Veil. Similar to a boar but with venom injecting tusks.

Portal - a gateway between worlds.

Rent, The - a metaphysical boundary between the worlds (also known as The Veil). Penetrable by the followers of the Elder Gods.

Rose - a whore and the girlfriend of Edward Whiston.

Sagana - a mysterious and powerful adept. Follower of the Elder Gods.

Samson, Dugald - a doctor.

Seeker, A - a person training to become a member of The Blood Cult.

Seven, The - ruling council of The Black Blades.

Syren - an ancient life-form encountered beyond The Veil. Evolved to feed on the life-force of others.

Sig'areth - an alien lifeform, resembling a gelatinous mass. Its natural environment is a fog-shrouded forest where it shares a symbiotic relationship with the trees.

Smith, Mr - a thug.

Sna'bor - a squat reptilian creature. Used as guards by Lord Helr'ath.

Strutt, Simon - a would-be poet and resident in Mrs. Crawford's lodging house.

Symon - one of Sagana's mercenaries.

Tol'agr'un - a special type of pebble used to communicate over long distances and to locate travellers in other realms. Not native to Earth.

Tra'll - an ancient life-form encountered beyond The Veil. Forest dwelling, huge and vicious brutes.

Unwin, Lemuel - a priest and assassin for The White Shield.

Veil, The - a metaphysical boundary between the worlds (also known as The Rent). Penetrable by the followers of the Elder Gods.

Wallace - an enigmatic 13th century warrior.

Whiston, Edward - a young policeman.

White Shield, The - secret military wing of the Catholic Church. Sworn enemies of the Black Blades.

Willem - one of Sagana's mercenaries.

Printed in Great Britain
by Amazon

10197417R00214